# Surviving the Arena

Karen Leslie

A Building Has Integrity

Just Like A Man.

And Just As Seldom.

–Ayn Rand

# Surviving the Arena

## Ambition, Corruption and Murder

## Karen Leslie

LKC Publications

LKC Publications
2340 Brighton Shore Street
Las Vegas, NV 89128


Copyright © Karen Leslie, 2020


ISBN 978-0-9985036-2-2

In loving memory of my mother, Dorothy.
November 18, 1931 - August 31, 2020.
Thank you, Mom, for giving me the gift of life,
and the gift of your unconditional love.

# 1

## Jamaica

Raging winds unleashed unearthly sounds as they swirled around her. Raindrops the size of marbles pelted her skin as she raced down the path to Mill Road, her small frame moving with the urgency of a gazelle being chased by a tiger. As Jamaica dodged the onslaught of thrashing palm fronds and shielded her face from the wind and rain, she thought of her mother and quickened her pace, leaping with youthful skill over the fallen branches and flooding waters that threatened to block her path.

The storm had come up as storms on the island so frequently did. Darkening clouds appeared with devastating speed over the ocean, reaching the island with alarming power and little warning. There was rarely time to seek cover, and yet Jamaica had chosen to leave the safety of her home to find help.

Brilliant lightning flashes illuminated the sky, revealing ominous black clouds. Deafening crashes of thunder followed mere seconds later. Undeterred by the storm, Jamaica continued down the path until she saw the cluster of palm trees marking the entrance to Mill Road. Only a few hundred yards farther, on the opposite side of the road, rested Johanna's house. It was the only neighboring house for miles and her only hope of finding help for her mother.

A dense area of palms rolling in erratic waves temporarily blocked her vision. Her heart sank when the branches parted to reveal Mill Road. Torrents of water rushed down in the direction of Kingstown. An enormous palm struck down by the storm lay directly in front of her, blocking entrance to the road. To continue beyond it without leaving the path was impossible.

She wrapped her arms around a tree trunk to shield herself from the raging wind, as she considered what to do. Her mother was in pain and needed help. She must find a way to reach the neighbors before the storm worsened.

A sudden bolt of lightning struck another large palm on the opposite side of the road. Sound exploded around her. She lost her grip on the tree trunk and fell hard on the ground. Looking up, she saw the palm, split in half by the lightning strike, crashing down toward her.

She shot to her feet and dove out of the path of the falling palm. It landed a split-second later with an earth-shattering thud, missing her by inches. She cried out in terror at the sound, but when she looked up, terror transformed into hope. The fallen tree had created a makeshift bridge to the other side—a bridge she could use to cross the water.

Jamaica clamored up onto the shattered palm. She stretched her arms and fought for balance as she attempted to cross. After only a few steps, the debris of palm fronds and tree branches carried by the rushing water rose over the top of her makeshift bridge. The debris crashed against her, sending her tumbling into the water.

She grasped the trunk of the tree in a frantic struggle against the current. She dragged herself along, battling to pull herself out of the water and back up onto the path. Water continued to rush over the palm, submerging her face. She gasped for air and held on tight, kicking hard with her feet and inching her way along the tree by clawing with her fingers. Sharp branches coated in slimy moss cascaded over the palm and onto her head. Some became entangled in her hair, while others ripped across her face. She thought of her mother and kept kicking. It was only a bit farther to safety.

Her feet finally sank into soft ground.

Soaked, bruised, and covered with mud, she crawled onto the path and struggled to her feet. Tears filled her eyes as she scraped the moss from her hair and wiped tangled strands from her face.

It was no use. She had to turn back.

She began retracing her steps back up the hill, silently praying she'd reach the safety of her home before being struck down again by the wrath of the storm.

Jamaica battled with fierce tenacity against the endless attack of thrashing palms lining the path. Her lungs burned as she gasped for air. A sudden sharp pain in her chest nearly dropped her to her knees, but she ran on, pressing her left hand against her ribcage in an attempt to quiet the pounding of her rapidly beating heart. Horrible thoughts raced with her up the hill. What would her father think? She had failed. Failed to keep the promise she had made only a few hours before.

His directions that morning were clear. "Aunt Emelia won't arrive from Seaford Town until next week, but today I must go into town. Johanna will come to the house tonight to care for Mama. If she needs Johanna for any reason before that, you must run quickly down to her house on the Mill Road and fetch her."

He plopped her onto his knee and gave her nose a playful tap with his finger. Jamaica beamed with joy.

"You're seven now, old enough to look after your mother for me." He hugged her and lifted her off his lap. "I'll try to return by late tonight. Promise me you'll watch over her?"

She looked up at her father with the eyes of an innocent child, beaming with a desire to please, "I promise, Papa. I'll take good care of Mama."

He'd kissed them both and left early that morning for Kingstown to meet with Mr. Coltrane, the man who was going to take them all to New Orleans. According to her father, Jamaica and her family would soon live on a huge plantation in a new land across the sea. He insisted she'd grow to love her new home and, although she cried for days at the thought of leaving her beloved island, she knew her father was trying to make a better life for them.

Now, all she wanted was to return to the safety of the only home she'd ever known.

The wind was relentless, bombarding her with flying branches and sharp palms as she ascended the hill. When her legs buckled under her and she stumbled to the wet ground, her anger and frustration grew. It was if the howling wind was mocking her. She rose to her feet in defiance and scraped the fallen leaves off her bruised knees. "Only a bit farther," she whispered, forcing herself on.

Jamaica finally reached the end of the path. She darted through the swinging gate a few yards from her house as it slammed back and forth, driven by the wind and thrashing palms on each side. Barely able to see through the raindrops pelting her face, she groped for the front door, summoning all her strength to open it against the force of the wind pressing against her.

The door slammed shut behind her as she ran into her parents' bedroom.

Abigail lay on the bed.

Jamaica rushed to her mother's bedside. Her soaked and shivering little body collapsed on the floor. "The road's blocked, Mama! I tried to get through to Johanna, but there was no way to get past the water!" she cried out.

"Oh, my child, it's all right." Abigail bent down to reach for her daughter. "I'm so relieved to have you back. You shouldn't have gone at all."

"But I promised Papa I'd fetch Johanna if you needed her, and I haven't kept my promise." Jamaica's voice quivered with a combination of exhaustion and shame.

Abigail suddenly cried out, stricken by another of the violent contractions that had begun an hour before. The baby was coming.

Jamaica screamed in horror at the sound of her mother's anguished cry. "Mama, what are we going to do?"

Abigail chose her words with care. "I'm afraid the task won't be easy, but together we must bring this baby into the world." The soft tone of Abigail's voice comforted and calmed Jamaica. She rose from the floor.

"I'll do everything you tell me to do."

"Good girl. Now, first, get out of those wet clothes. Then we'll need hot water and clean cloths."

A lightning flash illuminated the room, followed immediately by a deafening crash of thunder.

Jamaica jumped, her eyes wild with fear.

"Now, now, child, it's only a storm," Abigail said, wincing. The contractions were getting closer together. There was no time to spare. "Run now and get the stove going for water. Get yourself dried off, then gather up some towels. You're about to become a big sister."

***

Jamaica's father stared at the contract lying on the desk in front of him. Garlan had spent most of the day with Mr. Coltrane and a few other lawyers in Mr. Coltrane's firm, signing papers and making the final arrangements for his family's passage to New Orleans. Despite all his efforts to farm his property, he'd not been able to make ends meet. Every year was a struggle to earn enough to pay the taxes on the land, and the severe island storms over the past year had ruined much of the crop, making payment impossible. As much as he loved his island home, life was hard and he wanted something better for his growing family.

Garlan looked down at the fancy pen in his hand. It was gold, with a monogram of Mr. Coltrane's firm engraved on the side. Garlan sighed. The pen was grandiose and impersonal. It was a very different gold from the vibrant, natural golden petals of the island's many bougainvillea trees. Lewis Coltrane Sr., Esq., stood beside him, smiling. At long last, the contract was signed.

For over two years, Garlan had repeatedly refused Mr. Coltrane's offers to buy his property. "I appreciate your offer, Mr. Coltrane, but this land is my home, and it's not for sale, not for any price." But in the midst of his growing financial woes, when Abigail became pregnant with their second child, the time came to face reality and consider taking the offer before it disappeared.

Mr. Coltrane refused to give up and sweetened the offer. "I'll guarantee you a job for life and a new home for you and your family in New Orleans." He went further.

"I'm willing to offer you the position of head gardener on my estate." He promised Garlan and his family their own cottage on the plantation grounds, where they would enjoy the many advantages working for the Coltrane family provided.

"Your children will receive an excellent education and you can buy back at least a portion of your land over time, as your financial position improves."

The more Mr. Coltrane talked, the better it sounded. If Garlan would just, as Mr. Coltrane put it, "listen to reason and do the right thing for your loved ones," Garlan would see that Mr. Coltrane's offer was a more than fair exchange for his distressed land.

And so he made the heartbreaking decision to give up the land that had been his family's legacy for over 100 years.

By the time he finished signing the last of the papers, the storm had reached Kingston. It hit hard and fast.

Garlan set the fancy pen down and looked out the window at the storm raging outside. "I have to get home to my wife." He'd hesitated to leave Abigail so late in her pregnancy, but Mr. Coltrane was insistent. "I've flown down from New Orleans especially to secure the purchase of your property. It's now or never."

The building shook against the force of the storm.

It was too late. Garlan had no choice but to wait out the inevitable, and return home when the storm had passed.

***

Jamaica sat on the bed beside her mother. In her arms, wrapped in a white gauze sheet, she held her baby sister. She watched the infant sleep, rocking her gently as tears streamed down her face. They dropped softly on the gauze blanket she had gingerly wrapped around the baby. She was oblivious to the crashing of the storm outside as she sat quietly on the bed.

The delivery was a nightmare. Although Jamaica did everything exactly as her mother directed, something had gone terribly wrong. She succeeded in delivering the child, but by the time the delivery was complete, her mother was lying in blood-soaked sheets.

Jamaica cut the umbilical cord and showed her baby sister to her mother, before washing the infant and wrapping her as directed.

Her mother told her not to worry about the blood. "Fetch more towels from the bedroom closet and wrap them around me." She offered Jamaica a weak nod of encouragement. "Then, come sit beside me and your sister," she said, gently stroking the infant resting on her chest.

Jamaica retrieved the towels as her mother directed, but when she leaned forward to kiss her mother on the forehead, she reared back, alarmed. Her mother's forehead was hot. Hot and wet. "Mama, are you all right?" she asked.

"Yes, child," she whispered. "But you must see to your baby sister for me." Abigail's voice weakened as she looked lovingly upon her two daughters. She squeezed Jamaica's hand. Her grip was weak, but she managed to pull Jamaica closer.

Jamaica leaned in.

Abigail spoke in a whisper, "Your father and I have been blessed with two precious gifts, two daughters."

Jamaica could barely hear her mother's voice over the howling of the storm. A sudden crash against the house sent a huge branch smashing through the bedroom window, breaking the glass windowpane and toppling a vase of lilies on the stand beside them.

Jamaica screamed, and instinctively leaned her body across her mother and baby sister to shield them from the flying glass.

Abigail pulled Jamaica closer, and gazed down at the mess on the floor. Lilies were strewn across the room. She stared vacantly at the fallen flowers. "We'll call her Lily," she whispered, looking down at the infant cradled in her arms. "A flower has bloomed on this day when Nature sings so loudly."

Jamaica leaned closer to better hear her mother.

"Yes, Lily, a fitting name... I think. ... Yes... Lily..." Abigail rambled, growing delirious from the increasing loss of blood. "I must sleep now, just for a while." She strained to lift her hand to touch her daughter's face. "You've been so brave. Your father... will be so proud. Tell him... tell him how much I love him. ..."

Tears swelled in Jamaica's eyes. There was nothing she could do. Her mother was dying, and she was helpless. "Lily is a beautiful name, Mama." Jamaica bent down and kissed Abigail's cheek. Her tears fell like raindrops onto her mother's face.

"Then Lily it shall be." Abigail closed her eyes and trailed off into unconsciousness.

Now Jamaica could do nothing but wait. Wait for the storm to subside and for someone to come.

She looked down at her baby sister and then, turning her head to gaze upon her mother's lifeless face, so peaceful in its stillness, she thought of her father. What would he say to her? Would he ever be able to forgive her for failing him so miserably?

He loved her. Of that, she was sure. She would earn his forgiveness, and she would never again allow a storm to make her feel so helpless.

Jamaica listened to the thunder and the thrashing of the palms. She felt the awesome power of the storm and realized she was no longer afraid.

With her baby sister sheltered in her lap, Jamaica sat calmly on the bed, stroking her mother's hair and waiting for the storm to pass.

***

Hundreds of flowers covered the ground under Jamaica's feet as she laid a simple bouquet of lilies on her mother's coffin. Her eyes were dry and she was sure her own heart had stopped beating at the same moment her mother's had. She could still see her mother's face, smiling up at her before she closed her eyes forever. Jamaica stayed with her on the bed all night, holding her baby sister and listening to the howling wind and rolls of thunder as the storm raged.

She had little recollection of the events that followed. The doctors told her father she'd experienced a traumatic event and that, over time, she would be fine, but she knew something inside her had changed. Something was gone, something she couldn't describe. It was as if some dark spirit had entered her, lurking somewhere deep inside, replacing her innocence with an eerie sense of foreboding.

Many islanders attended the funeral to pay their respects, quietly comforting Jamaica and her father throughout the services. Jamaica watched as women from Abigail's family hovered over her baby sister. They appeared to be guarding the infant from some imagined danger. Tears flowed freely as the monsignor spoke of Abigail, of her faith and abundant love of family. The service ended with the procession of mourners tossing flowers into the open grave. Their voices were raised in unison as they sang a haunting, native-Jamaican psalm.

The cemetery rested on one of the most beautiful hillsides on the island, with stately palms and island flowers growing plentifully throughout the ample grounds. It looked out over a pristine bay that graced the souls buried on the hillside with the gentle sounds of breaking waves. Jamaica hated the idea of leaving the island, but she took some solace in the knowledge that at least her mother would remain at rest in a peaceful place.

As the funeral party began its descent down the hill, her father took her hand in his. Jamaica looked back and whispered a silent goodbye to her mother and her beloved island. What lay ahead in their new home she didn't know, but whatever was to come, she vowed to herself that it would surrender to her some comfort for all she had lost. She would help her father build a good life for them, a life that would be a tribute to her mother and all that was beautiful here in her world.

Although Jamaica doubted that she herself would ever know it again, she would see to it that her father and her sister found happiness there.

She would do what she had to do to make it so.

# 2

## Sam McCormick
### Las Vegas. Seventeen years later.

Sam McCormick worked his way through the crowded casino, weaving through the endless rows of slot machines, past the gaming tables, and on to the baccarat room. He turned left toward the Harem Lounge, carefully avoiding a stunning cocktail waitress with an overloaded tray of drinks as she charged past him into the pit. Considering the size of the crowd gambling there and the hustle of the young lady, odds were she would likely make several hundred dollars in tips by the end of her shift.

It was Friday evening and the pit was alive, buzzing with the shouts of high rollers. A group of wealthy Texas gamblers were whistling, hollering, and drinking, while betting massive amounts of money at the high-stakes poker and crap tables. The young beauty would earn every penny of those tips, distributing cocktails and dealing with the slaps, pinches, and generally lewd behavior of more than one too many inebriated customers.

The pit was appropriately named, less for its physical location than for the frequently unruly activity going on there. The boisterous groups of men crowded around the gambling tables resembled hordes of frenzied football fans, hovering over piles of chips, as if they were highly prized sports memorabilia. It took beauty, experience, and a lot of juice to work the pit at the Sultan's Palace, and although the humor of the name was lost on the cocktail waitresses, no amount of male testosterone could send a girl packing once she landed a shift in the pit.

Sam smiled self-consciously at the girl as she deftly spun out of his way, smiling herself in appreciation of his gallant effort to avoid a potential calamity. Cocktail waitresses working the pit appreciated a gentleman, and Sam was that, and more.

He grew up in East L.A. on Elvira Street, located in a neighborhood accurately dubbed Casualty Row. Being one of the few white kids in the neighborhood, he quickly learned that diplomacy and a fast set of legs were the tools he needed to survive adolescence.

Now, some years later, that skinny kid had grown into a tall handsome young man with a strong and charismatic presence. His sandy-brown hair and pale-blue eyes complemented his lean muscular frame. His voice was warm and engaging.

Born the son of an auto mechanic, Sam learned to work with his hands at an early age. His fondest memories of childhood were of the hours spent in the garage, watching his father turn wrenches. Under his dad's supervision, he rebuilt carburetors and tuned engines, slowly acquiring the skills of a master mechanic.

His dad taught him a second set of skills that served him well when his job progressed from physical labor to an executive career in sales. "Working with your hands is a valuable tool, son, but common sense is the most useful skill of all. Remember that."

Sam had remembered. At twenty-seven, he was already considered one of the best sign salesmen in the country. His fresh All-American-boy appearance and practical hands-on knowledge of the sign business combined to make him a valued asset in the industry.

The two kings of the sign empire were Jon and Lou Navaro, also known simply as "the Brothers," who owned Regal Sign Company and were Sam's employers.

He'd left his home in California and moved to Las Vegas six years before, to work as a sign hanger for Regal. The job was set up for him by his boss and friend, George Oggenblick.

"Las Vegas is the land of opportunity for a sign man, Sam. It's wide open," George said, as Sam prepared to leave for his new job. "Lots of mob money's going into building those gambling halls. Hell, you just use what I've taught you, and you'll become a very successful man."

George's statement proved to be prophetic. Las Vegas continued to grow and Sam was part of it. He built marquees and hung the names of stars on them. The Strip soon sparkled with Eartha Kitt at the El Rancho, Dinah Shore at the Riviera, Harry James at the Desert Inn, Perry Como at the Flamingo, and Sinatra and his boys at the Sands.

As Sam passed the pit, the shrill clanging of bells rang out from a game nearby. Sam stopped in front of the Golden Python. It was the first interior sign he'd pitched for the Sultan's Palace. The giant Wheel of Fortune was covered in scintillating gold lights in the shape of a writhing snake. Sam watched the wheel spin. The python's green eyes flashed as players looked on, cheering in hopeful anticipation of a big win.

That first sales pitch had launched his career, as the game quickly became a favorite at the casino.

"Five hundred dollars," the sexy blonde dealer called out as the wheel came to rest.

The elated middle-aged tourist from Nebraska who'd spun the wheel shouted with delight. He began jumping up and down, hugging a startled stranger standing beside him.

"Who'll be the next big winner?" the attendant called out, as she handed the Nebraskan five hundred-dollar chips. She gyrated playfully in her skintight green and gold snake suit. "Who's next to try their luck with the Golden Python?"

Customers clamored toward her, eager to spin the wheel.

Sam wove past the crowd, his long, gaited stride passing lightly over the ornate Persian Carpet beneath his feet. Since the day he'd first arrived, Las Vegas had been good to Sam McCormick. As he neared his destination, his thoughts drifted back to three years before, when a series of events, and a simple twist of fate, converged to make his life even better.

*** 

The year was 1969 and the sign business in Las Vegas was booming. Construction of the Thunderbird marquee was nearly complete when Jon Navaro called Sam into his office.

Sam entered to find Jon sitting behind his desk, piles of blueprints and sign renderings strewn across the desk in front of him. "Sam, I've got a favor to ask. Benny DeLuca wants to get his kid into the family business, and he wants the kid to start from the ground up."

Jon explained how Benny, a notorious mobster and the owner of the Sultan's Palace Casino, wanted his kid to build some muscle before tackling the challenges of casino management. "He thinks teaching the kid what goes into building casino signs will toughen him up."

Jon paused. He stood up and placed both hands on his desk. He leaned his tall frame forward, toward Sam. His eyebrows lowered and the expression on his face darkened. "Benny's from Chicago, a tough town." He put extra emphasis on "tough." "Anyway, he's asked me to take the kid on."

"What do you need?" Sam asked.

"Take the kid under your wing and show him the ropes. His name's Antony, but everybody calls him Tony. I've met him and I think he's cut out for sign work. He's young and strong. Kind of reminds me of you when you started with us. How long ago was that, anyway?"

"Nearly three years ago, boss. The Mint was the first time you put me in the air."

"Well, teach the kid what you can. If he gives you any trouble, threaten to tell his old man. Son or not, I doubt the kid wants to disappoint a man like DeLuca." Jon chuckled. "Just think of it as getting on the right side of the cub, before he becomes a great big growling lion like his father."

"Whatever you say, Jon. You're the boss."

"Great. I'll have him report to you tomorrow morning. But be careful when you get him in the air. Don't get him killed, for God's sake. I don't want to wind up wearing cement shoes." Jon grinned, and winked.

Sam responded to Jon's joke with a curious nod. The questionable reputations of some of the individuals he'd encountered working for Jon and Lou had alarmed him at first, but he learned to take it in stride. Las Vegas was a new frontier, filled with opportunity and teeming with unusual characters, most of whom conducted business in unorthodox ways.

With a little luck, Sam would figure it all out. At only twenty-four, he had time.

*** 

On the fateful day, Sam and Tony were standing on scaffolding, eighty-five feet above the ground in a howling wind.

Sam looked down at the ground crew below, working the crane to lift a huge section of steel signage into the air. "Here she comes!" he hollered over the wind. "Thank God it's the last piece! It's getting dicey up here!"

The wind had kicked up steadily throughout the day and everyone on the crew understood the risks involved. As conditions worsened, they proceeded with extra caution and watched one another's backs. Once permits were issued and sign segments delivered to the site, signs went up, regardless of the weather.

"This sucker's heavy!" Tony strained to pull the section toward them.

The two men worked in tandem and had nearly finished securing the section onto the pylon when a fierce gust of wind came out of the northwest.

It hit with a vengeance.

They heard the splintering sound of wood slamming against the sign, as the scaffolding whipped around to the right.

Their safety lines snapped taut.

"Grab onto something!" Sam yelled. "We're going over!" Sam managed to catch the side of the scaffolding with his right arm, but the force of the gust threw Tony completely over the side.

The scaffolding jerked back to the left.

"Our lifelines have twisted around each other!" Tony shouted, covering his face to dodge pieces of falling debris. He dangled helplessly below the scaffolding, while the wind tossed him around like a rag doll. "Look at my line, above you!"

Sam looked up to see Tony's line rubbing against the sharp metal edge of one of the sheet-metal sections above.

It was fraying...eighty-five feet above the ground.

Sam took a deep breath. He pulled himself back up onto the floor of the scaffolding and lay prone on his stomach. "I'm going for your line!" he hollered over the side. "Try not to move!" He reached for Tony's lifeline with his left arm and held himself on the swinging structure with his right. Adrenaline rushed through him as he wrapped the line around his arm.

The rope dug deep into his skin with each wrap, cutting off circulation in his forearm.

"Can you see the ground crew?" Tony hollered up.

"Hang on, Tony!" Sam's mind raced. He could see the ground crew scrambling below to move the crane into a rescue position. But Tony was running out of time.

A sudden gust caught the scaffolding, bouncing it violently against the sign.

Sam felt the sudden impact of Tony's full body weight against his arm. Overhead, Tony's rope had cut through.

It fell in a heap on the scaffolding beside him.

Pain shot through Sam's arm as the section of rope still attached to Tony bore deeper into his skin. He strained to secure Tony's rope by wrapping it few more times around his forearm. Sam heard a loud pop and cried out in agony as his shoulder dislocated. "Tony, you're going to have to pull yourself up!"

Tony managed to climb up his rope a short distance before sliding back down. "No good, Sam!" he yelled up as the rope slipped through his fingers. "No grip!"

"Here comes the crane! Try not to move!" Sam shouted. His shoulder was throbbing and the rope wrapped around his arm was causing it to go numb.

The crane operator below steadily lifted Jake Smith, the rescuer in the bosun's chair, up toward the scaffolding.

"I got you, Tony!" Jake connected a line to Tony's safety belt with carabineers. He swung him into the chair. "Sam, I'm cutting Tony's line!" Jake hollered up.

Jake held firm to Tony and clipped the line.

One cut, and the tourniquet of rope instantly loosened around Sam's arm. He felt faint with the surge of returning blood. He groaned and gritted his teeth in an attempt to stay conscious, as he watched the crane lower the basket holding Tony and Jake to the ground.

Suddenly, another violent gust of wind pitched the scaffolding.

Sam flew over the side. He cried out in agony as the safety belt around his waist snapped taut, jolting his entire body. "Get me down from here!" he shouted.

"On my way!" Jake shouted from the ground as the crane began the second lift. "Hang on!"

Sam lost consciousness seconds after Jake secured the rescue line to his belt.

\*\*\*

Below, Channel 8 and Channel 13 news teams were gathered in full force. They swarmed the area around the ambulance holding Tony, mingling with the crowd of onlookers converging on the site.

"Get back!" enforcement officers shouted as they fought to control the chaotic scene and secure a safe perimeter around the rescue area.

"Move!" A booming voice bellowed from behind the reporters. "Get the hell out of my way!" Benny DeLuca roared. His short, rotund frame plowed through the crowd, knocking over cameras and sending reporters and camera crews scrambling for cover. "Where's my son?"

The alarmed crowd parted to clear a path. At the sound of the familiar voice, the media retreated. Everyone in the news industry knew Benny DeLuca. No sane person dared mess with him.

Benny was meeting with some of his Chicago associates on the construction site of his new casino when he received the call informing him of the unfolding crisis.

He reached the ambulance and threw open the back doors. Tears of relief welled up in his eyes. Tony was lying inside, lacerated and bruised.

But he was alive.

"My God, son, what happened?"

Tony winced as he attempted to rise up from the gurney. He answered with a barrage of questions. "Where's Sam? Did they get him down yet? Where is he?"

The paramedic inside the ambulance cautioned Tony to lie still.

Tony lay back down. "I could've died up there, Dad. He saved my life."

"Move aside!" a loud voice commanded. Two arriving rescue workers emerged from the crowd. They lifted the gurney carrying Sam into the ambulance.

Benny squeezed back to make room.

"Sam? Sam?" Tony strained to see the face of his friend, but the restraints of his gurney held him back. He looked over at his dad. "Is he OK?"

Benny looked at Sam, then turned to the paramedic for a response. He got a tentative thumbs up.

"He's unconscious, son, but he'll be fine. You lay back now, so we can get you and your friend to the hospital."

Tony reached out for his father's hand.

Benny felt a wave of relief as he leaned forward. He grasped his son's hand and spoke softly into Tony's ear. "Rest now, son. It's all right now. Both you and your friend are going to be just fine."

Benny's hands remained clasped protectively around his son's. He looked over at the man lying on the gurney beside them. At the man Tony called his friend. At the man Benny had never taken the time to meet.

He watched as the paramedics set Sam's dislocated shoulder. At that moment, he made a decision. Sam McCormick had saved his son and that made him family. He was a DeLuca now and God help anyone who dared cross him.

As the ambulance sped toward Sunrise Hospital, Benjamin DeLuca closed his eyes and, for the first time in many years, said a silent prayer of thanks to his Maker.

*** 

That fateful day marked a crossroad in Sam's life and the timing couldn't have been better for a sign man. Growth in Las Vegas exploded as new casinos lined the Strip, with more being constructed every year.

Sam entered the Harem Lounge. He scanned the room for Tony. Three years had passed since Benny pulled his son away from sign hanging and into the casino business, where, as Benny had put it, "I can keep him safely on the ground."

Sam was busy selling for Regal and Tony worked full time at the casino, handling all the junkets coming into the Palace, but the two men got together every Friday in the Harem Lounge to catch up on the week's events and enjoy their friendship.

Tony spotted Sam and waved his arms in the air. "Over here, Sam!" He turned toward the bar and called out to his favorite cocktail waitress. "Suzie, we need cocktails over here, doll." He flashed a movie star grin so intoxicating it made her nipples perk up.

Sam smiled as he watched Suzie swoon. Tony DeLuca. Just the sight of him made women feel faint. The black silk shirt clinging to his arms and chest showcased his muscular build, and his skintight jeans left little to the imagination. The gold chain around his neck peeked out of the opened top two buttons of his shirt. It rested on deeply tanned skin, revealing just a bit of the ample chest hair that lay beneath.

Tony had it all. Not only was he brutally handsome, he was also charming. Women found him irresistible and Suzie was no exception. He'd dated beautiful dancers and showgirls, as well as most of the cocktail waitresses in the casino. But he was a playboy and none of his conquests held his interest for long.

Sam reached Tony and Suzie standing near the center of the lounge. He greeted Tony with a hearty bear hug and winked at Suzie over Tony's shoulder.

She was blushing.

"Could you get us a couple of drinks, Suzie?" Tony said. "The usual, please."

"Sure, Tony, right away." Suzie's blonde ponytail swished back and forth against her bare back as she headed for the bar.

"She's a looker." Tony admired Suzie's shapely figure waltzing away. "And a sweet girl, too. We went out a few times and had a few laughs. But you know me, not exactly the type to settle down any time soon."

"That's for sure," Sam laughed. "But someday the right woman will come along. God help her."

"You should ask Suzie out. I can put in a good word for you if you like," Tony teased.

"Oh, sure, with my workload? No woman would put up with the hours I keep. Seeing you on Friday's about as social as my life gets."

"Well, then, sit down. Tell me what's new."

The two men settled into plush chairs in the private VIP section of the Harem Lounge.

"There's an amazing structure going up in New Orleans," Sam began. He leaned forward and rested his arms on the table. "It's a sports arena and it's going to be the largest in the world."

Sam's voice sang with enthusiasm. "And it's domed." He sat up straight in his chair. "It's going to house everything from ballgames and concerts to prize fights."

His eyebrows lifted and his eyes grew wide. A huge grin appeared on his face. "And guess who's got a shot at building the main pylon sign?"

"Well, let me think… You?"

"Yep, yours truly. Wait 'til you see the renderings the Regal artists have drawn up. They're stunning. Anyway, I'm flying down Monday night to make the pitch."

"To New Orleans?"

Sam relaxed back in his chair and caught his breath. "Yep. Tuesday, I check out the site. Wednesday, I meet with the Arena committee to pitch the sign. It's big, Tony. It's a once-in-a-lifetime deal."

Suzie arrived with the drinks and placed them on the table.

Tony handed her a generous tip. "Thanks, Suzie."

"Thank you, Tony," she cooed. "Is there anything else I can do for you? Anything at all?"

"Not at the moment, doll." He flashed another killer grin, then focused his attention back on Sam. "Sounds like a great opportunity." He took a sip of his drink. "I can't wait to tell Dad."

"Your dad probably knows more about the project than I do. He probably knows more about it than the Navaros." Sam gave Tony a knowing smile. "You know I'm not kidding."

"He does keep a pretty close eye on you. After all, you're family."

"I feel the same way. Benny's done a lot for me and I appreciate it."

"Come on, Sam. He won't ever be able to do enough for you, and you know it. Me either. I owe you, always will."

"You would've done the same thing in my place."

"Hell yes, at least I damned well would've tried." Tony raised his glass. "I propose a toast. Here's to good friends, pretty women, and Sam's new sign."

Sam and Tony clinked glasses. Sam looked at his friend with affection, grateful things turned out so well on that fateful day three years before, the day that locked in their friendship and changed his life.

# 3

## Eleanor Coltrane

Eleanor Coltrane was a highly regarded member of the New Orleans social elite and a woman who thoroughly enjoyed her position as matriarch of the Coltrane family. Her husband Lewis, a wealthy New Orleans lawyer and land speculator by profession, inherited the huge Coltrane plantation and all the aristocratic advantages that came with it.

Eleanor was active in New Orleans high-society charity events and ran the social and domestic affairs of the Coltrane Estate with enthusiasm and expertise. She took particular pride in the aesthetics of the mansion and had spent many years, and a small fortune, decorating and overseeing the maintenance of both the mansion and the gardens on the plantation grounds.

The interior décor of the estate showcased vintage mahogany furniture purchased in Italy. It was complemented by luxurious leather couches and chairs, designed by Eleanor and manufactured by the finest artisans in New Orleans. Each piece of fine Waterford crystal and delicate German china gracing the Estate's dining room was hand-selected by Eleanor to be used on a daily basis. She added to the collection each year during shopping trips, frequenting the most exclusive and expensive stores in Europe.

In early September, evenings on the Estate were balmy, with light breezes that spread pleasant floral fragrances throughout the gardens and spacious courtyard.

Shortly before 7 p.m. on Saturday, Eleanor stood outside, directing the staff in the placement of floral arrangements in the lounging areas of the main garden. She was walking through a set of French doors to enter the massive kitchen adjacent to the main dining room of the Coltrane mansion when her daughter-on-law Catherine approached. "Have you seen Lily, Eleanor?"

"No, I haven't seen her since this morning, dear. Why?"

"I haven't seen her either. And it's not like her to disappear. I wonder where she could be off to."

"Well, let's ask around."

The two women entered the kitchen. "Has anyone seen Lily?" Eleanor asked of the kitchen staff assembled there.

"She hasn't been around all day, ma'am," Eleanor's head cook, Clarice Broussard, replied.

"It's odd she didn't come to the greenhouse this afternoon to help with the floral arrangements," Catherine said, a puzzled look covering her face.

"Yes, odd, indeed. Perhaps you might check her chambers upstairs, Catherine."

"Good idea." Catherine left the kitchen.

Eleanor paused to peruse the contents of the pots covering the stovetop. "Well, if you see her, Clarice, please send Lily to me."

"Yes, ma'am." Clarice curtseyed to her employer and dipped her chin. Clarice was an excellent cook. She had run Eleanor's kitchen for nearly two decades, and, over the years, Eleanor had grown fond of her. Nevertheless,

Eleanor expected proper decorum. Clarice kept her head down, and curtseyed again. "I'll let the child know."

Eleanor lifted a lid from a pot, and sampled the soup simmering on the kitchen stove. "This is excellent, Clarice. I trust everything is in order for tonight's dinner?"

"Yes, ma'am," Clarice replied.

Eleanor released a mildly self-indulgent sigh and tapped her finger on the face of her wristwatch. "It's impossible not to love the child, but honestly, the girl simply has no sense of time."

"Yes, ma'am."

"Well, I'll be in my chambers, if I'm needed." With a swirl of her hand, she left the staff to final preparations.

Eleanor climbed the right side of the circular marble staircase to the second- floor east-wing of the mansion. She entered the bedroom suite she and Lewis shared and began her nightly ritual of dressing for dinner.

Eleanor swung open the doors to a large closet. It consisted of walls of designer clothes hanging on long racks. Shoes arranged in neatly stacked cubicles lined one wall. A variety of designer shopping bags, empty, yet displayed brimming with colored-paper chiffons, rested on the top shelf, a shrine to her appreciation of haute couture.

A glass countertop on the opposite side of the closet housed jewelry cases containing hundreds of pieces of jewelry. Some were gifts from her husband. Many others were items she purchased during countless shopping sprees in her favorite boutiques in New Orleans, Atlanta, and New York.

She ran her hand across the garments hanging before her, smiling at the rich textures of the fabrics. "Something bright, but elegant," she whispered, as she considered what to wear.

The evening's dinner party was a formal gathering of members of her favorite charity, to plan a series of fundraising events to benefit the less fortunate in their community. Eleanor always planned such parties on the weekends, with the hope that Lewis would make an appearance.

She looked at a portrait of herself and Lewis on the wall. "I hope you'll be home tonight for the party, darling," she spoke to her husband's likeness in the portrait.

As a busy attorney and real estate entrepreneur, Lewis frequently missed dinner parties at the Estate, but Eleanor always dressed in her very finest for him, just in case he and her son, Jimmy, made it home in time to attend. Even though their more- than-40-year marriage had long been relegated to social and financial convenience, Eleanor never failed to keep up appearances.

"It would be lovely to see my Jimmy as well," she mused. She opened one of her jewelry armoires, warmed by thought of her only child. Much to her delight, upon growing to manhood and marrying, Jimmy had chosen to continue residing in the mansion, along with his wife, Catherine. The two women grew close over the years and co-chaired many worthwhile social events, passing time together in the all too frequent absence of their respective spouses.

Eleanor's eyes scanned the jeweled brooches resting in the armoire. She selected a diamond and ruby brooch to accent the red Chanel suit she'd chosen to wear. She attached it to the silk scarf she'd skillfully tied around her neck. She placed several enormous diamond and ruby rings on her fingers, and stepped back to evaluate the ensemble.

"Perfect," she sighed, pleased with what she saw in the vintage Italian mirror before her. She gazed down with affection upon the many sparkling baubles still remaining inside the armoire, then closed it. Eleanor enjoyed the celebrity of being a Coltrane, and she would host a lovely evening, with or without her husband.

And when Lily returned, Eleanor would lovingly scold the child, for making her worry so.

# 4

## Lily

As the Learjet 23 rose to cruising altitude above the New York skyline, Jamaica stared at the untouched glass of water she'd poured from the Evian bottle on the table in front of her. The initial shock over the phone call she'd received earlier in the day had subsided, only to be replaced by a confusing combination of anger and bewilderment.

"Excuse me, Miss Russe, is everything satisfactory?" The deep voice over the intercom was Tom, the Coltranes' pilot. He had flown the Coltranes' private jet into the Teterboro Airport from New Orleans International, to pick Jamaica up for a return flight back to New Orleans. When her limo arrived at the private terminal, she'd boarded the jet with barely more than a nod of acknowledgment for the pilot.

Jamaica pressed a button on the console beside her. "Yes, everything's fine. Thanks, Tom. How long before we reach New Orleans?"

"It shouldn't be more than a few hours, Miss Russe," Tom replied.

"Thanks, Tom, and please, as many times as you've piloted this plane for me, it's Jamaica."

"Yes, Miss Russe. Jamaica." His voice lowered. "I'm sorry about the circumstances."

"I know, Tom, thanks," she replied, her own voice fading to a whisper as her thoughts returned to Jimmy's phone call.

Lily was dead. Her baby sister, her own flesh and blood, was senselessly gone.

"A freak accident," Jimmy had said. "I can barely bring myself to tell you, sugar. The whole family's devastated."

When Jamaica insisted on details, Jimmy continued, "Doc Beauregard thinks she must've slipped on something and struck her head as she fell. The tumble sent her into the water and, well, there's no sense putting you through this over the phone. Daddy's sent the jet for you and I'll be waiting at the airport to pick you up." He paused and sighed into the phone. "Mama's a mess and, well, you just get home safely, sugar." Jimmy's voice cracked. "Things like this just shouldn't happen."

Then he hung up.

Jamaica stood frozen, phone in hand, for several minutes following the call. The Coltranes were powerful men, not easily rattled. The quiver in Jimmy's voice was nearly as jolting as the news about her sister.

Jamaica looked out the window. As the plane cruised in and out of the clouds, she recalled the last time Tom had flown her home in the Coltrane's corporate jet.

She'd visited two months earlier, for the annual Coltrane Fourth of July bash. Having recently completed the bar exam, she was in the process of closing up her New York apartment, in preparation for a permanent return to New Orleans.

She and Lily passed nearly the whole afternoon that Fourth of July, sitting out under the gazebo, drinking virgin mint juleps and catching up on each other's summer.

Lily did most of the talking. "The summer's been glorious," Lily began. "So many parties here at the mansion, picnics in the garden, and barbecues out at the cottages. Really, it's been just glorious."

Lily's voice bubbled as she described the afternoons she spent helping Eleanor and Catherine in the gardens. "There were so many roses this spring, and Eleanor just wouldn't have known what to do without me."

Jamaica indulged her sister, listening patiently as Lily rambled on. "And Uncle Jimmy says the plantation gardens are my fairyland and I'm his fairy princess."

When the fireworks were set off that night, magically lighting the sky and cascading brilliant colors over the plantation grounds, Lily had wrapped her arms around her sister, her voice singing, "See, Jamaica? Fairyland!"

Jamaica closed her eyes and imagined Lily as she appeared that Fourth of July. She'd worn the mint-green silk dress Jamaica purchased for her in the spring for her seventeenth birthday. Lily had insisted on finding the perfect outfit to wear for the upcoming Fourth of July celebration at the Coltrane Estate.

When she found the dress in a small boutique off Bourbon Street, she beamed. "This is perfect," she said, wrapping the soft fabric around her and twirling in front of the fitting room mirror. When she adjusted her breasts, tugging them up to peek out of the top of the bodice, she grinned. "After all," Lily pointed out, "I'm no longer a child."

They continued shopping for hours, looking for matching mint-green sandals, a challenging feat, even in fashion-conscious New Orleans. After a relentless search, scouring every shoe boutique in the Quarter, they found a pair in the perfect shade.

Jamaica relaxed back in her seat with her eyes still closed, savoring the memory. She and Lily had worn the matching necklaces Jamaica had purchased for them in a fine jewelry store in New York City. Each consisted of a delicately carved shell, encrusted with pearls and tiny diamonds, hanging from a fragile gold chain. Both pendants were meticulously cut from a single nautilus shell and mirrored each other perfectly.

Lily squealed in delight when she first saw the matching necklaces and insisted they both wear them for the Fourth of July celebration.

Jamaica absently fingered the chain holding the shell pendant hanging around her neck. It had been a perfect day. It was also the last day they would ever spend together. Jamaica returned to New York almost immediately after the event to finish tying up loose ends. She called her sister at home a few times, but handling Lily's rambling over the phone required patience. With Jamaica's hectic schedule, the calls were infrequent.

Now she sat, torturing herself with thoughts of Lily. How could the girl have been so careless? How many times had Jamaica cautioned her to be careful wandering the plantation grounds? Lily would just laugh and say, "You worry too much. I'm a big girl now."

Jamaica had worried since the day Lily was born. People often criticized her for being overly protective, but she believed she was sheltering Lily from a world much too cold and cruel for someone as sweet and innocent as her baby sister. When Jamaica left for college, Garlan was there to father his youngest daughter. However, after Garlan's death, Jamaica considered leaving school and returning home to remain close to her sister.

The Coltranes would have no part of it.

Lewis was insistent. "You will stay in New York and continue to pursue your law degree. We'll see to Lily's well-being."

Jamaica reluctantly agreed. Once she graduated and passed the bar exam, she would return to New Orleans, join the Firm, and reunite with her sister.

Jamaica felt the veins in her temples begin to throb. She pressed her fingertips to her temples, squeezed her eyes closed, and braced herself. An all-too-familiar dreaded sensation was returning.

The visions began to come in waves.

A surge of heat rushed through her body as a ghostly image of her sister appeared, moving gracefully in a pool of water. Her long hair floated around her head like a cloud, framing her angelic face.

The water around her began to swirl and Lily's eyes suddenly opened wide.

A look of panic distorted her face.

Jamaica began to shake. She felt herself being drawn away from Lily. She watched, horrified and helpless, as Lily cried out in the distance, engulfed in the rapidly swirling water.

Lily's image faded, slowly disappearing into a darkening abyss.

Jamaica sat motionless, staring into blackness.

She felt cold. Suddenly, the vision changed.

Rain and wind swirled around her.

She was somehow back in her parents' bed, but the bed was outside, surrounded by a raging storm. She was once again a young girl.

She was running, then falling into rushing water.

Again. It was happening again. The same vision, repeatedly haunting her.

The storm.

The raging wind and rain.

Running. Falling. Helpless.

"No!" she cried out.

"Miss Russe? Are you all right, Miss Russe?" Tom called out from the cockpit. His voice startled her, snapping her out of her trance.

She pressed the intercom button. "Yes, Tom. I'm just clumsy," she countered. "I nearly spilled my glass of water. I'm fine."

Jamaica settled back into the soft leather cushions of her seat. She fought the anger building inside her. The visions had plagued her all her life, but she had no time for them now. She turned her thoughts to the family, and the necessary events of the next few days.

"There's so much to do. Funeral arrangements, a coffin..." Her voice quivered as the obscene words escaped her lips.

She picked up the glass of Evian and looked down at the water in the glass, gently rolling with the subtle movement of the plane. The ghostly image of Lily reappeared, floating in an ocean of chiffon, the colors of summer flowers. The fabric swirled hypnotically around her slight frame, creating the illusion of a living, breathing Monet painting.

Lily called out to her, her delicate arms reaching out as she floated toward her sister, "Jamaica."

Jamaica stared into the glass, unable to move as her sister's image faded in the water. Once again, she was being drawn back into her dark place, that unhappy place the Cajuns called her "house of dark spirits."

She summoned all the strength she could muster and began softly chanting the mantra taught to her by the Cajun elders to banish the visions when they came. "By the power of the Cajun moon, spirits be gone," Jamaica chanted, rocking back and forth in her seat, her hands crossed in front of her chest. "As I will it, so mote it be."

She continued chanting, refusing to surrender to the tormenting visions that had haunted her since the day her mother died. "As I will it, so mote it be."

Jamaica closed her eyes and imagined Lily as she had last seen her, alive and full of joy. She struggled to hold on to that vision as she fought back her demons. She had lost her mother and her father. Now, Lily was lost to her as well.

# 5

## Arrangements

The LJ23 rolled down the runway at New Orleans International after making a perfect landing. It came to a stop just a few hundred feet from the private terminal and waiting limousine.

The limo driver emerged from the vehicle and turned to open the passenger door for his employer. "Sir," the driver bowed slightly.

Jimmy Coltrane stepped out of the limo.

Jimmy was a robust 6'2". His slightly balding, reddish-blonde hair framed a deeply tanned face. His complexion was ruddy and his eyes were habitually red, the inevitable result of too many daily scotches. He'd arrived as promised, to meet Jamaica.

During the long drive from the Estate, Jimmy had struggled to steady himself for the upcoming conversation with the young woman he'd known for seventeen years. His normal self-assured and relaxed disposition had disappeared, victim of the present circumstances and the inevitable questions about to come from Jamaica.

He was twenty-one when Jamaica and Lily arrived from the island with their father to take up residence in a cottage on his father's property. Jamaica was only nine and Lily just an infant in those days. Although Jimmy spent most of the time away at school, then busy at the Firm, the two girls became a part of life on the plantation and, eventually, part of the family.

Over the years, he watched Jamaica grow from a child into an intensely focused, intelligent young woman. He had no idea what she would ask first, but his father had insisted he handle the situation and as overwhelmed as Jimmy was by this sudden turn of events, that was exactly what he intended to do.

His mother and wife had reacted predictably to the news of Lily's death. Both were hysterical. Jimmy didn't envy his father who, at this moment, was attending to the unpleasant business of contacting the church, discussing funeral services, and dealing with the horde of inescapable press, all while comforting two sobbing females.

In contrast, Jamaica wasn't the type to make a scene. Jimmy watched her emerge from the jet, helped by Tom. He could see him offer his condolences, which she accepted graciously. She carried herself with uncommon reserve, a trait Jimmy never really understood. In fact, he didn't understand her at all. He marveled at how the Cajun folk understood her, repeatedly implying she was as much Cajun as Jamaican. Some said they believed she held the traits of a voodoo priestess, that she had the gift. He had no idea what the hell that meant.

As far as he was concerned, the only thing the two sisters had in common was their physical genealogy. They were the most beautiful women on the plantation and arguably in New Orleans. Their beauty had enabled their transformation from plantation help to members of New Orleans society, via the Coltrane family. The transition was highly unusual, but the two sisters were unusual.

Now one of them was dead, and the other was approaching him, her eyes full of questions that expected answers.

Jamaica's long legs covered the ground like a thoroughbred rounding a racetrack. She stopped in front of Jimmy.

"Jamaica, dear." Jimmy placed his hands on her shoulders. He kissed her chastely on each cheek. "I'm so relieved to see you, sugar. How was your flight?" he began.

She dismissed pleasantries. "How could this happen? Who found her? Was she alone? How long was she in the water?"

"Now, now, slow down, darlin'." He opened the limo door. "Come, get in, and I'll tell you all I know. Eleanor, Catherine, and Daddy are all waiting. They're all just desperate to have you home."

Jimmy and Jamaica settled into the soft leather back seat of the limo. The chauffeur placed the bags he'd retrieved from the jet into the trunk and entered the driver's seat.

Jimmy gently patted Jamaica's knee in a brotherly gesture of comfort. "We should all be together at a time like this. That's what Lily would want, don't you agree, darlin'?"

As the limo pulled out of the airport, turning west into the setting sun, the two passengers sat close.

Jimmy gingerly put his arm around Jamaica.

She melted against him, relaxing into his comforting embrace. As the landscape raced past her, she looked through moist eyes at the brilliance of the sunset. The sky was blazing in an explosion of reds and oranges. She squeezed Jimmy's hand, fighting back tears, recalling the evening only a few months before, when the sky had exploded in so many brilliant colors and she and her sister had shared a perfect day.

\*\*\*

Once back at the Estate, the family gathered around Jamaica on white-leather couches in the mansion's living room. Jamaica sat between Catherine and Eleanor, listening intently as Lewis explained what had elapsed over the course of the last twenty-four hours.

"Eleanor became worried when Lily missed dinner last night and then couldn't be located anywhere in the mansion later in the evening," he began. "Clarice sent Maynard and Nathaniel out to search for her on the grounds. Maynard discovered Lily floating in the pool at the back end of the main garden behind the cottages around eleven p.m."

"But Lily's an excellent swimmer. I don't understand," Jamaica interrupted.

Lewis acknowledged her with a nod and continued, "The decking of the pool was wet, apparently from a leaking hose along the walkway. The police officers concluded that Lily must have slipped on the decking, struck her head and fallen into the pool."

Lewis responded to the look of skepticism on Jamaica's face. He assured her that he, the police, and Doc Beauregard had done everything possible to determine when and how Lily suffered her accident.

Jamaica remained silent, listening.

"Doc Beauregard discovered a large bump on the back of her head, reinforcing the conclusions drawn by the police. An ambulance transported Lily's body to the coroner's office, where these conclusions were confirmed by the coroner. The blow to the head must have rendered her unconscious and she fell into the water." He paused for a moment, took a deep breath, then continued, lowering his voice. "It appears to have been severe enough to kill her, as no water entered her lungs."

Eleanor sat with her face buried in her handkerchief.

Tears rolled down Catherine's cheeks.

Lewis reached across the couch to take Jamaica's hands. "It was a terrible accident. I'm so very sorry." He patted her hands gently.

Jamaica broke the painful silence that had filled the room. "There's much to be done. Let's begin."

The family agreed the tragedy need not turn into any more of a media circus than it was already becoming, so it was decided that a short viewing be held, followed by a funeral service at Saint Mary's on Thursday afternoon. The family would accompany the casket on the flight to Kingstown a few days later, where Lily would be laid to rest beside her father and mother.

Lewis looked at his watch. "I suggest we rise early and go to the funeral parlor. Lily's body was taken there following the coroner's ruling."

They finished discussing plans for the following day, and Lewis left the room to make the necessary calls. He contacted the press with the obituary information, so it would appear in the Monday paper. He had already arranged to have one of the local television channels send out a unit the following day to interview him about the accident and the wishes of the family regarding the services for Lily.

Eleanor insisted a reception for family and friends who wished to show their respects should follow the service at the Coltrane Estate.

"Catherine and I will arrange a lovely gathering here at the Estate in Lily's honor," Eleanor promised through her tears.

"Thank you, Eleanor." Jamaica rose from the couch. "I'm very tired. If you'll all excuse me, I'll say goodnight."

\*\*\*

Jamaica made her way toward the staircase leading to the upstairs suites. She reached the top and turned to enter the west wing of the mansion.

The hallway decor leading down to Jamaica's bedroom suite was distinctly masculine. Remington sculptures rested on mantles inset on both walls lining the hallway. Between the sculptures, Renaissance paintings purchased during Eleanor's European shopping sprees hung against heavy brocade fabric-covered walls. Glass cases mounted between the paintings housed Lewis's collections of Civil War artifacts and memorabilia. One case displayed two crossed swords mounted above a variety of belt buckles and medals. Another contained a collection of military hats, pistols and metal canteens.

Lewis's treasures went unnoticed as Jamaica walked past them down the hallway. She had nearly reached her suite when she stopped. "There's no point waiting," she whispered. She continued down the hall to Lily's suite, opened the door and stepped inside.

The suite resembled a scene from a child's fairy tale. Soft pink-chiffon curtains hung against pale yellow walls. More pink chiffon draped from the canopy above her bed. The fabric created a gossamer tent that encased the dozens of silk pillows resting there. Vases of flowers resting on pedestals on either side of the bed filled the room with the fragrance of the plantation gardens.

Jamaica opened Lily's closet and looked at the garments hanging there. She shuddered at the obscene task of selecting the last pieces of clothing her sister would ever wear, but a set of Lily's clothing had to be chosen to take to the funeral parlor the following day. She felt Lily's presence in everything she touched as she began going through her sister's things.

Jamaica tossed dress after dress onto the bed, unable to decide. She finally chose the mint-green silk dress she'd purchased for Lily on her trip home the previous spring. She found the matching shoes, then selected the prettiest of Lily's delicates from her lingerie drawer to complete the items needed for the following day.

She sat down on the pile of garments covering Lily's bed and surrendered to the flood of tears she had been holding back all day. Finally, exhausted, she returned to her own suite to attempt a few hours of sleep.

*** 

After a quiet breakfast, the family entered the Coltrane limo and endured the long drive to Our Lady of Mercy Funeral Parlor, engaging in forced, trivial conversation.

Upon entering the funeral parlor, Eleanor and Catherine went to wait in one of the sitting rooms, where they were comforted by a few of the nuns from Saint Mary's Cathedral. Meanwhile, Lewis and Jimmy met with the parlor's representatives to discuss the details of the viewing and funeral mass set for Thursday at Saint Mary's.

Jamaica asked for time to spend alone with her sister.

"Of course, Miss Russe. This way." The parlor director gestured for Jamaica to follow him.

When Jamaica entered the room housing her sister's body, her heart skipped a beat. A white sheet partially covered Lily, folded neatly to reveal her head and upper shoulders. She'd already been embalmed and looked so natural lying on the slab, Jamaica could have sworn she was simply sleeping, resting peacefully.

Jamaica stood frozen beside the slab, looking down at her sister. In her arms she held the garments she had chosen for Lily the night before. An empty closet was open at the far end of the room, next to the casket Eleanor had selected for Lily.

Jamaica walked over to the closet to place Lily's things inside. The soft silk fabric of Lily's dress brushed against her skin as she placed it on a waiting hanger. It sparked a recollection of the day Lily had tried it on the first time. The memory of her sister emerging from the dressing room of the boutique, giggling with delight as she swirled in a circle, brought tears to Jamaica's eyes.

She bent down to put Lily's shoes in the closet and felt her shell pendant swinging in front of her chin.

The pendant.

Jamaica hadn't been able to find Lily's matching pendant in her jewelry box the night before when she was selecting Lily's things. She assumed Lily must have been wearing it when she suffered her accident.

Jamaica walked over to the courtesy phone resting on a chest of drawers. The chest was covered with brochures and various books offering choices of floral arrangements, crosses, and memorial poems. They were provided to aid in the difficult decisions that families of the departed were forced to make upon the death of a loved one. She pushed them aside, lifted the receiver and called for an assistant.

A few moments later, an elderly gentleman in a dark suit appeared. "How may I assist you, Miss Russe?"

"Where are my sister's personal effects?" she asked.

The man opened the top drawer of the chest and pulled out a box. He set it carefully on the slab next to Lily's body. "This is the clothing your sister was wearing when she fell."

Jamaica opened the box and examined the contents. Lily's pendant wasn't there. "Where is my sister's necklace?"

"Miss Russe, everything she was wearing is here. The police made a list of all the articles found on your sister at the scene, and all those items accompanied her body to the coroner's office for examination." He spoke in a soft monotone, a voice experienced in the delicate task of dealing with families of the departed.

He looked at Jamaica, shrugging apologetically. "I know nothing of a pendant. It is my understanding that both Mr. Coltrane and your family physician, Doc Beauregard, attended Lily's examination at the coroner's office. Perhaps your sister's pendant was removed then." An awkward pause followed. "If you have any questions, they may be able to help. Shall I inquire for you?"

"Thank you, but that won't be necessary. I'm sure I just missed something when I was preparing her clothing."

The man nodded and left the room, leaving Jamaica once again alone with her sister.

Jamaica looked at Lily's face. "I'll find it, Lily, wherever it is." The small token of her love must be with Lily when she was laid to rest next to her parents on the hillside in Jamaica. Her own pendant would act as a special reminder of her sister—and the bond they had shared since Lily's birth. She would look again in Lily's room.

After a few more moments with her sister, Jamaica rejoined the family. Once everything was arranged to the family's satisfaction, the group reentered the limo and returned to the Estate to meet with Father Kilpatrick.

***

Father Kilpatrick was waiting at the Coltrane Estate when the limo pulled up to the main entryway of the mansion. He was close friend, as well as spiritual advisor, to the Coltrane family, and took both callings seriously. He embraced Garlan and his girls, upon their arrival from Jamaica, and welcomed them into his congregation. Years later, at the Coltrane family's request, Father Kilpatrick flew to Kingstown to conduct Mass at Garlan's funeral. After years observing the special care and guidance the priest showed Lily throughout her childhood, the gesture had further endeared him to Jamaica.

Father Kilpatrick rose, with some difficulty, to greet the family, as they entered the main hall of the mansion. "My dearest Jamaica," he began, "I'm so terribly sorry for your loss." He took her hands with the gentle touch of a loving parent. "Lily was a blessed child, a favorite of all of us at Saint Mary's. I am here as God's servant, to help you through this difficult time."

"Thank you, Father," Jamaica replied. "Lily loved the church. Your presence here is a comfort." She spoke the words, more for Father Kilpatrick's sake than her own. Although she was never able to embrace the calling of the church, her affection for the priest had grown over the years. His frailty only served to make him all the more endearing. "Would you stay for dinner, Father, and pass some time with the family?"

Eleanor jumped at the suggestion, "Oh, yes, Father, please, do join us."

A sly smile covered his face. "Will Clarice be cooking? You know how I love her food."

"Of course, Father." Eleanor's face brightened at his comment. "I'll have our Clarice prepare all your favorites."

"Well, then," Lewis swept his arm around Father Kilpatrick, "Let's all retire to the study, shall we? I'll prepare a toddy for those old bones of yours, and we can chat."

As the rest of the group entered the study, Jamaica excused herself. No one had been able to tell her where her sister's necklace was. When she asked Lewis about it, he assured her that Lily wasn't wearing it when Maynard pulled her out of the pool. He promised a thorough search of the pool area.

"In the meantime," Jamaica said, "I'll look again in Lily's room. Lily may have set it somewhere in her quarters and I failed to notice it. On the other hand, it may have indeed fallen off her neck and will be found at the bottom of the pool."

She fondled her own necklace as she climbed the massive staircase to the bedroom suites. With each step, she imagined Lily by her side.

She fought back tears as she envisioned her beloved sister, reunited with her father and her mother. They would rest together soon, on that beautiful hill on the island.

The thought of it brought her some comfort as she reached the top.

# 6

## New Orleans

In addition to securing local contracts in Las Vegas, Sam's job included extensive travel. He sold and supervised the construction of signs in San Francisco, New York and Los Angeles. Occasionally, the Regal corporate jet was available for his use, but generally he flew commercial airlines. On this, his first trip to New Orleans, he was booked in business class on Western Airlines.

A few hours before the flight departed Las Vegas, Jon Navaro set the ground rules for the pitch. "Clyde Peterson's been in New Orleans for over a week, setting the stage for the meeting. He's a decent salesman, but he lacks the necessary expertise to pitch this sign." Jon poked his fork at the Caesar salad he'd ordered at the airport's Admiral's Club restaurant. "This pitch requires your special touch. I wouldn't trust it to anyone else."

He looked across the table at Sam and continued his pep talk. "Regal can damn well show those Southerners a thing or two about the right way to build a sign." Jon paused and set down his fork.

Sam could practically hear the wheels spinning around in his boss's head.

"But you'll be facing politicians, Sam. Don't be fooled. They're a ruthless lot. And they feed off each other like a wake of hungry vultures."

When the airport intercom announced boarding at Sam's gate, the two men left the restaurant.

Jon gave Sam a fatherly pat on the back as he walked him to the gate. "Just bring back that contract."

*\*\**

Sam set his champagne glass on the fold-down table in front of him and attempted to review the notes he'd prepared for his upcoming meeting with the Arena committee. A sudden jolt of turbulence nearly tipped the glass into the empty seat beside him. He saved it with a quick catch, set it back on the table, and slid his notes back into his briefcase. "This is pointless," he whispered. He turned his head to gaze at the clouds floating outside his window and began rehearsing the speech he had planned for the committee.

"Gentlemen, Regal is the best in the world when it comes to building freestanding signs," he began, speaking to his reflection in the window. "The brilliantly lit marquees lining the Las Vegas Strip glow in testimony to that fact."

He paused, considering the biggest obstacle in front of him. Competitive bidders had more experience building signs for sports arenas, but, he would argue, "This arena sign project is much larger than anything previously built, anywhere. By its very nature, it requires a company like Regal, capable of building a sign big enough to do justice to the project."

Jon had repeatedly warned Sam he was facing an uphill battle, about to make a pitch to people who had no idea what they were, in fact, asking for.

Sam took a sip of his champagne to calm his nerves. I know I can convince Bonner, he thought.

Bobby Bonner was the contractor who had secured the stadium contract. Bonner's business was construction, and, unlike the bureaucrats Sam would be facing, Bonner was the kind of practical man who would understand the enormity of the task that lay ahead for the company that would provide the sign.

Sam's experience with lawyers and politicians was limited, and he avoided them whenever possible. He was content to watch the Brothers handle concerns raised by public officials over sign projects. When the disagreements became serious, it was the "Bennys" of Las Vegas who stepped in to quickly resolve them.

Sam relaxed in his seat. He was a professional, flying toward the biggest sign contract of his career. He'd established a reputation for landing the big jobs, and he thrived on the challenge. He was ready.

***

Sam exited the plane and walked from the gate toward baggage claim.

The New Orleans International Airport was jammed with travelers. An ocean of tourists in colorful T-shirts blended with men in business suits and ties, carrying briefcases. Sam spotted a gift shop along the corridor and popped in to pick up a copy of the *New Orleans Tribune*. In his experience traveling, the local news revealed a lot about a city, and the more he knew, the better equipped he would be to accomplish his goal. He folded the paper under his arm and thanked the attractive young salesgirl delivering his change.

"You're welcome. Ya'll have a nice day, now," she purred, in a slow Southern drawl.

"That's quite an accent you have, Miss," Sam said. "I've never heard anything quite like it."

She responded with a wink.

Sam winked back and headed off to retrieve his luggage.

"Carousel number three, revolving baggage claim servicing Flight 244 from Las Vegas, is temporarily experiencing a problem," a voice over the airport intercom announced. "Arriving passengers from Flight 244 are advised to stand by in the baggage claim area. The problem will be resolved shortly. Thank you for your patience and welcome to New Orleans."

Sam arrived at carousel number three, sat down on a bench by the conveyor and opened the *Tribune*. He stared at the headlines on the page in front of him.

And the roller coaster ride began.

The lead story's headline, crossing the top of the page, directly involved him — "Bids Begin on Arena Sign."

Under it and to the left, another headline read: "Union Leader Joins Arena Committee."

At the bottom of the page, above a headshot of a stunning young woman, a slightly smaller headline read: "Tragic Drowning at Coltrane Estate."

Sam took a deep breath and began reading the first article.

## BIDS BEGIN ON ARENA SIGN
### By Allen Stein

One Arena contract the citizens of New Orleans should soon know something about is the proposed contract for the main computerized exterior pylon sign and four computerized scoreboards inside the Arena itself. Arena committee members, led by Attorney

Lewis Coltrane, will meet Tuesday with a representative of Las Vegas-based Regal Sign Company to entertain a bid on arguably the largest sign contract of its kind to be awarded to date. Although the committee has gone on record, stating that all companies presenting bids are being considered, a less-than-subtle snub of the New Orleans-based sign company, Leonard Signs, Inc., has led to apprehension as to the fairness of the committee's choices.

"We intend to work in the best interest of our fine community," Lewis Coltrane stated in a recent interview. "If doing so steps on the toes of some of our home-based companies, I can only say that the contracts will be awarded solely on the company's ability to offer the best 'bang for the buck.' We intend to build a great structure, without spending more of the taxpayers' money than necessary. If that means contracting out of state, then that is what we must do."

When asked about concerns over the implications that Regal Sign Company lacks experience in building arena signs, Mr. Coltrane responded, "Well, that's what the committee has been appointed to determine."

Time will tell what Mr. Coltrane and his committee will decide, and whether or not they will indeed determine what is truly in the best interest of the city of New Orleans. Meanwhile, this reporter will be watching closely and reporting to you on the progress, or lack thereof, in choosing the companies best suited to contribute to the success of what many have called an impossible undertaking.

Sam scowled at the implications of the article, the reporter who had written it, and how it might affect him. Time would tell if Allen Stein was going to pose a problem or be a potential ally.

He looked up and, to his amusement, observed several maintenance workers scrambling about the baggage-claim area, struggling to repair the jammed conveyor belt. They reminded him of his own gang of workers back in Las Vegas, his "orangutans," as he affectionately called them.

He returned to his paper and moved on to the second article. He noticed it was written by the same reporter.

## UNION BOSS JOINS ARENA COMMITTEE
### By Allen Stein

Bobby Bonner, recently elected head of the Teamsters Union local, has joined the committee formed to oversee the building of the new sports arena project, officially dubbed, "The Arena." As previously reported, Bonner Construction won the contract to build the Arena structure, and last week, Arena committee members, headed by Lewis Coltrane, voted unanimously to add Mr. Bonner to the group.

"We have determined that Mr. Bonner's expertise in numerous aspects of the Arena project will be invaluable during the building process. We further hope that this addition will ensure an ongoing, cooperative association with the union in the acquisition of labor and materials needed for the construction of the massive structure," Lewis Coltrane commented.

In response to Mr. Coltrane's comments, Mr. Bonner stated, "I'm pleased the Arena committee has chosen to include me in their decision-making regarding these matters. It's important that costs are monitored and contracts are awarded to the companies best qualified to provide the services required in each of the many aspects of this formidable project."

While history between these two individuals has proven to be strained, both men stated their desire to work together in the best interest of the New Orleans community.

Sam shook his head, wondering what "strained history" between the two men meant. If he landed the contract, Regal would be dealing with both of them.

A sudden grinding sound, followed by the thuds of dropping luggage, heralded the successful repair of the conveyor belt. After a few moments, Sam spotted his suitcase, circling aimlessly on the revolving baggage claim.

"Hey, Sam!" a voice called out. "Over here!"

Sam looked across the conveyor and saw his fellow Regal salesman, Clyde, waving. "Welcome to New Orleans," Clyde said, as he approached Sam. "Traffic was a bear. I was worried I'd be late picking you up. How was your flight?"

"A little bumpy, but OK." Sam retrieved his luggage and the two men exited the airport, into intense humidity. It hit Sam like a blanket of steam as he walked with Clyde to the rental car. "Sure is different from Las Vegas," Sam commented, breathing in the heavy air.

Clyde opened the front passenger door. He swept his left arm comically across his body and bowed at the waist, inviting Sam to get in. "You can enjoy the local sights along our route, and I'll fill you in."

"Sounds good," Sam laughed at Clyde's light-hearted gesture, and took his seat.

Clyde sounded two quick honks of the horn, to alert pedestrians passing in front of the vehicle.

Once they had cleared airport traffic, Clyde entertained Sam with a nonstop barrage of facts about the many charms of New Orleans, the famous French Quarter in particular.

Clyde noticed Sam's copy of the *Tribune* sandwiched in the front seat between them. "Lots of stuff in there about us," he said, tapping on the paper. "But this one really got my attention." He pointed to the Bonner article Sam had just read.

"Have you met Bonner?" Sam asked.

"Yep. And that man has a tiger by the tail. This Arena project is a monster. You'll see tomorrow."

"Do you like the guy?"

"Yeah, I do. He's the new Teamsters local leader and I've heard plenty about him." His brow lifted, and he spoke as if he was revealing deep a secret. "I hear Bonner's Cajun, with ties to the Cajun mob." His voice lowered to a whisper, as if he were delivering a line from a gangster movie. "This city has a long history with union corruption, Sam. It's dirty business and Bonner's been trying to clean it up, single-handedly. Poor bastard."

The loud honk of a horn blasted as an aggressive driver swerved in front of the vehicle.

Clyde ignored the incident and continued with his story. "The mob's controlled the union labor force down here for years. They're a dangerous group, that bunch. I wouldn't want Bonner's job for all the money in the world."

"So, tell me, do the citizens of New Orleans want this arena?" Sam asked.

"Oh, sure they do. But it's not going to be easy to build something that big here." Clyde tapped again on the paper. "You see this article?" His fingers rested on the headline about the drowning. "This little girl lived on the Coltrane Estate. Coltrane's the chairman of the committee in charge of building the Arena. You'll be meeting him on Wednesday. He's a powerful lawyer, and he's rich. He owns lots of property here in New Orleans. He's an asshole, if you'll pardon my French." Clyde grinned.

"Well, he's a lawyer," Sam replied. "It's to be expected, I guess."

Both men laughed.

The twinkle left Clyde's eyes. "In my opinion, Coltrane and Bonner will never be able to work together." He gave Sam a solemn look. "A few years back, Coltrane and his group of lawyers shut down construction on one of Bonner's jobs. According to one of the locals I met at a club in the Quarter, it was all because Bonner refused to buy supplies for the project from one of Coltrane's clients. A lot of folks suffered on that one. The guy at the club told me he lost his job."

Clyde paused. "But let's move on to more pleasant topics. We're all set for tomorrow. What's gone up so far on this Arena structure is going to blow your mind."

The sun was setting when Clyde turned off the highway. He drove toward the glittering lights of the Quarter and pointed out favorite spots he'd discovered along Bourbon Street during his week of preparations for the meeting. He made a turn onto Conti Street and pulled to a stop in front of the Marie Antoinette Hotel.

As they exited the vehicle, Sam observed the scene surrounding the quaint entrance to the hotel. The street sparkled with lights from nearby restaurants and shops, all open and catering to the throngs of people milling about.

Clyde lifted the bag out of the trunk and handed it to Sam. "You've arrived in the heart of the famous French Quarter, my friend. Your room reservation is all set up. I'm just down the hall from you. Let's get you checked in."

Sam looked up at the wrought-iron balconies framing the second and third stories of the hotel. He was a world away from home. The adventure had begun.

***

The lobby of the Marie Antoinette Hotel appeared as if it had been somehow transported through time from a bygone era. Elegant antique furniture, velvet couches and colorful Persian tapestries lining the walls conveyed an atmosphere that was both romantic and otherworldly.

Sam and Clyde approached the front desk. A handsome young man stood behind it, meticulously polishing a gold saxophone. He saw the two men approaching and set the sax on the counter beside him. He greeted Sam with a broad smile. "You must be Mr. McCormick. Welcome to the Marie Antoinette."

"Thank you," Sam replied. "That's a beautiful instrument you have there. You must be a musician."

"We're all musicians of sorts here in New Orleans," the young man replied with a chuckle. "At least we all like to think we are. Music's in our blood." He opened the guest ledger in front of him. "Mr. Peterson told me you'd be arriving from Las Vegas. I assume, to work on our new arena?"

"Yes. And I look forward to seeing as much of your city as I can during my stay. Do you perform locally? Perhaps I'll have the opportunity to hear you play."

Clyde interrupted. "He sure does. I've heard him play, and he's great."

"I play most nights at a club here in the Quarter," the man offered. "It's called the Bourbon Blues and it's not far from the hotel. Mr. Peterson, Clyde, here, is too kind. But I will say the club has a reputation as one of the liveliest in all of New Orleans." He extended his hand. "My name's Winston. My band's called the Rhythm Kings."

Sam shook hands with Winston. The man's strong grip and athletic appearance piqued his curiosity. Winston was tall and lean, with jet-black hair and deep brown skin. He appeared to be in his late twenties. The crisp white shirt he wore had short sleeves that revealed arms with the chiseled muscle definition common on seasoned sax players, not unlike the ones Sam had heard play in Las Vegas.

"I'll only be staying a few days this trip, but I plan on returning, providing all goes well with this one."

"Let's get you checked in, Mr. McCormick. You're going to fall in love with our city."

"I'm starving," Clyde said. "Do you want to get something to eat?"

Sam declined. "No. It's been a long day. I'll see you tomorrow morning."

"Well, then, let's meet here in the lobby and get some breakfast before we drive out to the site. See you tomorrow."

Sam followed Winston up the stairs to his room on the second floor and noticed a large collection of framed photos of jazz musicians lining the walls. Most shots were black and white, depicting decades of performers who had played in nightclubs throughout the Quarter.

Winston tapped on one photo as he passed by. "That's my uncle there in the front, playing the trumpet. My dad's on drums."

Sam took a close look. The energy emanating from the photo was palpable. "I think you're right, Winston. I'm already beginning to like your town."

Once he was settled in his room, Sam retrieved his paper. He recalled that the third headline he'd read at the airport was also about Coltrane, something about a drowning.

Sam walked through a set of French doors opening out onto a small balcony that overlooked the cobblestone streets of the Quarter. Paper in hand, he sat down on a wrought-iron chair beside a small circular table and resumed reading.

## TRAGIC DROWNING AT COLTRANE ESTATE

A tragic accident Saturday at the Estate of Lewis and Eleanor Coltrane has shocked and saddened the New Orleans community. Lily Russe, the seventeen-year-old daughter of the Coltranes' late gardener, Garlan Russe, was found dead of an apparent accidental drowning. According to Doctor Benjamin Beauregard, the Coltrane's family physician, the girl slipped on decking at a pool located at one of the estate's private bungalows. She fell into the pool, where she was found floating late in the evening by a member of the Coltrane's gardening staff.

After a thorough investigation by police authorities and examination by Doctor Beauregard, the coroner has officially declared the death an accident.

Miss Russe was a popular young woman, well-known in the New Orleans community for her love of flowers, as well as her participation in the many charitable causes led by Mrs. Coltrane and her daughter-in-law, Catherine Coltrane, benefitting the less fortunate members of the New Orleans community.

Miss Russe is survived by her sister, Jamaica Russe, a recently graduated law student, first cousins Aida and Charmagne Russe, aunts and uncles, Emilia and Charles DeVeau, and Louana and Devon Russe. She lived on the Coltrane Estate with her legal guardians, Lewis and Eleanor Coltrane, the Coltrane's son, Attorney James Sherman Coltrane and wife, Catherine.

Funeral services will be held at Saint Mary's Cathedral Thursday morning at 11a.m. A private reception for friends and family members will be held at the Coltrane Estate immediately following the service.

Sam folded the newspaper and rose from his chair. It seemed an odd coincidence that all three news articles related in some way to him.

He took a long look at the vibrant activity stretching out among the restaurants and shops on the street below him, then walked back into his room. As he closed the French doors behind him, a myriad of questions filled his head. What would he learn the following day? As an out-of-state competitor, would he be able to convince the men on the committee to take a chance on his company?

Would he rise to the biggest challenge of his career?

He picked up the phone on the nightstand and called the front desk to request a wake-up call. With plans confirmed for the following day, Sam unpacked, took a shower, and went to bed.

# 7

## The Site

The first item on Sam's list of priorities for the day was a trip out to the Arena site. Clyde met him in the lobby at 8 a.m. and guided him to the Morning Call, a little bakeshop located across the street from the Marie Antoinette.

After Clyde introduced Sam to the Morning Call's famous powdered donuts and Cajun brewed coffee, the two men took Clyde's rented four-wheel-drive Chevy truck down Highway 33 to the site.

"I'm eager to meet Bobby Bonner and see the property," Sam said. "There's a lot of information to gather before the meeting with the committee tomorrow." After reading the headlines the night before and listening to Clyde's opinion of the committee, Sam confided in Clyde that he anticipated an uphill battle.

"I wouldn't take it all too seriously," Clyde replied. "I've found these folks down here tend to exaggerate a bit about most things."

As they approached the site, Sam witnessed for the first time the huge structure being erected on it. "Wow, Clyde, it's huge."

The main steel structure of the domed ceiling stood, only partially erected. The Arena was more massive than he imagined the first time he saw the specs. As they drove up to the area designated for the sign, Sam scrutinized the series of highways, overpasses, and cloverleaves that would have a view of the sign.

Clyde neared a construction truck with the words "Bonner Construction" painted on the side, parked in the middle of the empty lot. He stopped the Chevy beside the truck and waved a greeting to the man seated inside.

Bobby Bonner emerged from the truck and walked toward them. He was a large, burly man, easily 6'5". His gait was casual and light of foot.

Sam exited the Chevy. He felt his feet sink into soft ground.

"You must be McCormick." Bobby extended his arm and shook hands with Sam. The handshake was warm and firm.

"Quite an impressive structure you've got going up here, Mr. Bonner."

"It's Bobby, please. And, yep, she's a beauty. What can I do for you two fellas?"

Sam explained about the photos he and Clyde would be taking and asked if there was anything Bobby needed from him, prior to the following day's meeting.

"No," Bobby chuckled. "There's nothing either one of us can do, but hope for the best. The characters on the committee are a real piece of work."

Sam shrugged. "Well, in that case, I guess Clyde and I should get to work. I do have a question."

"Shoot."

"It's about the ground. It feels awfully soft. Provided all goes well securing our contract, my crew will need road access to this area. We'll have a lot of heavy machinery and materials coming in. I'd appreciate any suggestion on how to avoid what could **become** a big problem."

"No worries. When the time comes, we'll work it all out. Meanwhile, welcome to the project."

"Thanks, but we don't have the job yet," Sam replied.

"You'll be fine. All we have to do is convince the committee to leave us alone to do our jobs. I'll be there tomorrow—and happy as hell to have another construction man on the team. You'd be amazed how hardheaded this bunch can be."

Clyde chimed in, "That's for sure. They're all lawyers and politicians."

Bobby let out a hearty laugh. "Your friend here's right. With the exception of old man Coltrane, not a one of them has a lick of experience building anything." He laughed again and shook his head. It was a quiet, disapproving laugh that revealed an obvious lack of respect for the committee.

"Now, if there's nothing else, I've got an arena to build." Bobby walked back to his truck. "You fellas have a nice day. I'll see you tomorrow in the lions' den."

"Great meeting you," Sam said. "See you tomorrow."

Bobby waved out the window as he drove up toward the site. His tires dug heavily into the soft marshland under the weight of the vehicle.

"I don't like this soft ground, Clyde. It could jeopardize the safety of the sign footings." He made a mental note to discuss the subject with a structural engineer, once he returned to Las Vegas. "Let's get started with the photos. We can start right over there at the base of that overpass."

Clyde walked to the first designated area while Sam got the Polaroid out of the truck. He began snapping pictures, recording a thorough inspection of the ground and outlying areas. There were many factors to be considered in the placement and building of any sign, but due to its proximity to highways and overpasses, the engineers had determined the location of the proposed sign required special attention. There would be issues to resolve: city ordinances, existing structures limiting visibility from the highway, etc. Sam intended to address every one of them. Nothing could be left to chance.

Several hours passed. After Sam completed taking dozens of photos and pages of notes, the two men drove back to the city. Clyde chose a local Cajun restaurant in the Quarter close to the Marie Antoinette for dinner and Sam experienced real New Orleans Cajun cuisine for the first time. Clyde suggested they continue the evening and visit one of the many jazz and blues joints scattered throughout the Quarter, but Sam declined.

"Let's get through the meeting tomorrow first. Hopefully, once that's over, we'll have something to celebrate." Sam saw the look of disappointment on Clyde's face. He gave Clyde a hearty pat on the back. "Let's bring this thing home, Clyde, the two of us together. By the way, you were right about the food down here. Dinner was delicious."

Clyde brightened. "You're going to love this town, Sam. And you're right. First, we have to get the contract."

Sam suggested they meet for breakfast at the Morning Call to go over a few notes prior to their ride to the courthouse. The men shook hands and Sam walked the short distance back to the Marie Antoinette to prepare for the following day's meeting.

\*\*\*

Bobby T. Bonner was a dangerous man. As a New Orleans born and bred Cajun and the new head of the Teamsters Union, he'd acquired some dangerous friends. Some were laborers. Some were union bosses and some were childhood friends from his roots growing up in the

Bayou, an area run by other dangerous men. Bobby kept his ties to the Cajun Mafia quiet, and few knew the details about the depth of those connections or his ongoing involvement with the city's underworld.

His relationship with the Cajun Mafia was not unlike Sam's relationship with Benny, and the New Orleans syndicate was similar in many ways to the Las Vegas syndicate. Both quietly controlled many aspects of labor in their respective cities and both used muscle when necessary to achieve their agendas.

Although Lewis Coltrane was a powerful man, he'd made the mistake of assuming he could buy off union officials for his own benefit. When Bobby laughed in his face the first time Lewis offered him a bribe, Lewis was infuriated by the affront. Hostility between the two men grew and they barely tolerated each other.

Coltrane's political connections were strong, and presented potential problems for the Union, so Bobby decided, with the blessing and backing of the mob, to do his best to coexist with the man, and "make as few pacts with the devil as possible."

Coltrane knew of Bobby's mob ties and accepted the fact that crossing him unnecessarily was unwise, so the two kept each other at arm's length and tried to keep their mutual dislike private.

When Bonner put in his bid with Bonner Construction to build the Arena, his company was easily the biggest and best for the job. That fact, along with a friendly visit Lewis Coltrane received from a group of Bobby's Cajun friends, all but guaranteed his company the contract early on in the negotiations.

Coltrane was smart enough to know better than to take the polite request of a mob boss as anything other than an ultimatum, so he led the committee in its choice of Bonner Construction for the job. It was a fact that there would be times he'd have to work with Bonner on Bonner's terms. He made it abundantly clear that it was a fact he hated.

Bobby had close friends in the Quarter who were involved in the more colorful and generally illegal activities on the street. Occasionally, he'd get a tip about clandestine trips by members of the New Orleans political elite, occurring on his turf. Usually, they were insignificant, involving prostitution or minor bribery deals. But when something directly affected Bobby or his people, his sources brought it to his attention.

Coltrane occasionally employed a two-bit punk named Spencer, a wannabe Mafia player who made himself available for every sleazy job offered him. Bobby's friends on the street kept him apprised of Spencer's activity when it involved Coltrane and, as a result, he'd acquired plenty of useful illicit information on the man. Bobby kept it all on the back burner, as collateral.

# 8

## The Pitch

The morning of the meeting, Clyde took an indirect, scenic route for the drive from the Marie Antoinette to New Orleans City Hall. The two men enjoyed the view and engaged in small talk to calm their nerves, but once they arrived at their destination, the nerves kicked back in.

Clyde parked the car under the shade of a Spanish moss-covered oak tree on Tulane Avenue and the two walked the short distance to City Hall. Clyde led the way past security guards and the reception desk to the elevators, pausing for a moment so Sam could study the model on display in the main lobby.

The scale model of the Arena sat encased in a large protective Plexiglass cover nearly five feet long and a foot tall. A gold plaque at the foot of the model read: The City of New Orleans presents THE ARENA.

Sam stood captivated by the work of art in front of him. The model made the project come to life. He'd seen only renderings up until yesterday when he witnessed the actual steel structure going up. Looking at it in front of him, completed except for the sign, sent a rush of adrenaline coursing through his veins.

Clyde gave Sam's back a hearty slap. "Hey, we've got this. We're just an elevator ride away from immortality."

The two men entered the elevator. Sam took a deep breath and watched the door close in front of him.

***

"*Ca va*, Mr. Coltrane, Gentlemen. *C'est mon plaisir* to introduce you to Sam McCormick," Clyde greeted the committee in his best Louisiana Creole French accent. "He's come all the way from up yonder in Las Vegas to meet with y'all today." Clyde's natural Midwestern accent had somehow magically transformed into a convincing, local Creole drawl. "This man will convince all y'all that Regal is a fine company, the downright perfect choice to build a mighty fine sign for your fine project."

While Clyde made introductions, Sam studied the group before him. From Clyde's description of the committee members, he recognized the man standing in the center of the group as Lewis Coltrane, the lawyer, land developer and chairman of the committee, the same Coltrane mentioned in the newspaper article he'd read two days before, covering the drowning incident at the Coltrane Estate.

Lewis Coltrane extended his right hand to Sam. "Good to meet you, Mr. McCormick. Allow me to introduce our illustrious group." Coltrane waved his arm in a grandiose gesture spanning the conference table. "These are the senior members of the committee, the gentlemen responsible for the lion's share of the decisions being made regarding the Arena." He pointed to a plump, middle-aged man, sporting a gaudy red tie that rested against an egg-shell-blue shirt, sitting to his left. "First, we have Mayor Riley, our vice-chairman and public spokesman for the project."

Mayor Riley nodded in acknowledgment.

Coltrane walked over to two men sitting next to each other at the end of the table. He stood behind them and placed a hand on a shoulder of each man. "My son, Jimmy Coltrane here on my right, is treasurer and legal advisor for the committee, along with Max DiAngelis, here on my left. Both these gentlemen are esteemed lawyers from the Firm of Coltrane, Coltrane and DiAngelis." He stood for a moment, as if posing for a photo ad for his law firm.

Sam nodded a silent hello to the two men.

Coltrane moved on to the man sitting next to DiAngelis. "City Commissioner Bryant is our liaison to the numerous small businesses involved in this project. He also assists in the acquisition of various permits as needed from the building department. Kind of a jack of all trades, so to speak."

Bryant nodded.

"Moving on," Coltrane pointed across the table. "Over there, we have Mr. Allen Stein. What can I say about Mr. Stein?"

Sam noticed an obvious shift in Coltrane's tone.

"Stein here is an esteemed member of the New Orleans press. Although he's not a committee member, we invited him, anyway." Coltrane shrugged. "Stein's job is to keep the public 'properly informed' of the goin's on conducted by this committee on behalf of our fine city during the various stages of the Arena project." He paused, allowing the cavalier tone of his statement to linger.

Stein was a short man with a strong Jewish presence, accentuated by his dark, curly hair, prominent nose and thick, horn-rimmed glasses. He responded with an apathetic shrug, seemingly unwilling to respond to Coltrane's condescending tone.

"It's our *sincere* hope that by including Mr. Stein in some of our meetings, he will *appreciate* our efforts and report to the fine citizens of New Orleans *accordingly.*"

A short, slightly awkward silence filled the room. For whatever reason, it appeared Coltrane considered Mr. Stein an unwelcome guest. Sam raised an eyebrow, intrigued as to why.

"My goodness, I almost forgot Bobby." Coltrane flashed a feigned look of embarrassment across the table at Bonner. "Sitting over there we have Mr. Bobby Bonner, owner of Bonner Construction. I believe you two gentlemen have already met, isn't that so, Bobby?"

Bobby shrugged a half-hearted response. He acknowledged Sam with a smile, but made no attempt to hide his dislike of Coltrane.

Coltrane pointed to a tall man in a navy suit, standing near the door of the meeting room, smoking a cigarette. "And finally, here we have Senator Keetz. The good senator's flown down here from his perch up yonder in Washington, to keep us all honest. Isn't that right, George?" The sarcasm in Coltrane's voice was obvious, as he waved his arm in a gesture motioning everyone to sit down.

Keetz flashed Coltrane an equally obvious look of disapproval and took a seat at the table.

"Well, son, that's our group," Coltrane concluded. "Now, what have you got to show us?"

Sam rose to his feet. He started by directing the group to the notebooks Clyde had distributed on the conference table during the pleasantries. They contained photos of and information on the numerous major projects Regal had built recently. They included several smaller stadium jobs and waterfront work in San Francisco, but focused mainly on the Las Vegas signage.

"Regal has built many of the largest and most complex messenger units and decorative signs in the United States over the last few years," he began. "I believe these projects speak highly of our credentials, and of our ability to comply with your needs in a timely and cost-effective manner." Sam motioned toward the notebooks. "Please direct your attention to your notebooks. First, I will show you what Regal has already accomplished in the industry. Then, I will present what Regal has designed specifically for you, in keeping with the vision you described for your Arena signs."

Sam continued his presentation, flowing effortlessly through the renderings contained in the notebooks. He explained the details of each of the completed signs.

"This is mighty fine work," Coltrane commented, "but what've you prepared for us?"

"Thank you, Mr. Coltrane. Now that you've seen what Regal has already built, let's move on to what we've designed for you," Sam replied. He turned the page of Coltrane's notebook to reveal the Arena sign rendering. "Gentlemen, if you would turn to page ten."

He began walking the committee through all the phases of Regal's proposed sign. "The rendering of the three-sided pylon you see on page ten incorporates the black-and-white electronic messenger boards. The big box structure on the following page houses the lettering identifying the Arena." Sam studied the faces of the committee members as they examined the renderings.

"As you can see, the three sides are necessary in order for the sign to read from all three of the major freeways approaching the Arena, as well as the parking lot. This allows for maximum exposure in all directions." Sam paused, encouraged at the sight of raised eyebrows and nods of growing interest. "I believe ours is the *only* sign proposed to you that is three-sided. In fact, I'm quite sure it is."

A collective murmur arose from the group.

Sam continued, explaining how the messenger board would be controlled from the press booth inside the domed Arena, making it possible for only two people to run the scoreboard, as well as all the sign functions outside, thus creating a significant savings. He described how the twenty-two-foot-tall illuminated letters would flash off and on, and that they would be programmed for numerous other light patterns. "Your sign will be multi-functional, and therefore extremely cost effective."

The comment raised more eyebrows.

"Cost effective, how?" Senator Keetz asked.

Sam continued, "It will recuperate significant revenue through advertising, beginning immediately upon its use. As soon as the sign is complete, advertising can begin."

The statement drew a buzz of enthusiasm from most of the men in the room. The potential for massive profit through advertising registered with everyone.

Forty-five minutes later, Sam finished his presentation. He opened the floor to questions and comments.

The first question came from City Commissioner Bryant. "Very impressive, but it says here that this sign is supposed to stand two hundred foot tall." He tapped his finger on the summation page in his notebook.

Sam answered confidently, "Yes, sir, that is correct."

A collective snicker filled the room.

Sam's heart sank. "Why is that funny?"

"Well, son, that's just not going to happen." Bryant sat back in his chair and crossed his arms. "I don't know what you people are doing up yonder in Las Vegas, but down in these parts, we don't build our signs that big." He looked around the room at his fellow committee members. A smirk appeared on his face. "I guess maybe we just see better, not being blinded down here by all that money you folks have flying out of those casinos up in your parts."

The commissioner's flippant comment drew more laughter.

Sam frowned. He didn't find it at all funny. "With all due respect, commissioner, the sign has to be that tall to adequately complement the size of the Arena structure itself."

"I'm sorry, son," Mayor Riley said. "You don't understand. We have a law down here on the books. It clearly states that no freestanding sign can exceed forty-five feet in total height. I'm afraid you're going to have to cut her down in size a bit." His tone was dismissive.

Sam turned to Bonner, his eyes begging for support. Bobby shrugged and gave him a look that said, "I warned you."

Sam's mind raced. He searched for a way to get through to the group and make them understand how wrong they were. Suddenly, it came to him.

"Gentlemen, I'm aware that this project is a first for New Orleans and that issues such as this one will inevitably arise, but I'm confident I can offer solutions to whatever problems we may encounter." The plan was forming in his head and he needed some time. "May I request a fifteen-minute break? I'd like to visit the men's room, during which time you can discuss any other aspects of my presentation you may wish to address." He looked at Coltrane. "I'd also ask that the model of the Arena displayed downstairs be brought up to this conference room and the cover taken off. I believe it will help me better illustrate the reasons behind the details you've just heard."

Coltrane responded, "Has anyone got a problem with that?"

When no one responded, Bobby stepped up to help out. "Mr. McCormick's come all this way and I think we should hear him out."

"I want to hear more," Allen Stein agreed.

Senator Keetz spoke up. "I do, too, Lewis. If this sign really offers potential advertising revenue, like he claims, it's worth the time."

"Very well, then. We'll break for fifteen minutes. In the meantime, two of the security guards downstairs can cart the model up here for Mr. McCormick. Fifteen minutes, then, gentlemen." Coltrane rose to leave the room.

Clyde gave Sam a look of confused disbelief as the room cleared. "What the hell is going on? We just got shot down."

"Can I borrow this, Clyde?" Sam took a red Pentel pen out of Clyde's shirt pocket.

"Sure, but what are you going to do?"

"I'm going to go to the men's room." He walked past Clyde and headed out the door.

Sam entered the deserted bathroom and looked around. He found the Kleenex in a silver dispenser on the wall and removed the box from the container. He pulled the Kleenex from the box and tossed it in the trash, retaining only the cardboard.

He walked over to the row of sinks and studied his face in the mirror. *Think of the solution, not the problem, Sam.* He had a crazy idea, but it just might work. He walked into a stall and closed the door. He sat down on the toilet seat and reached into his pocket for his pocketknife.

Ten minutes later, he came out of the stall. He slipped the knife, the re-capped pen and his inspired creation into his pocket. He walked down the hall and entered the conference room. As promised, the model sat on the table, lid removed.

Sam pulled out a chair and sat at the table, awaiting the return of the others.

***

Sam studied the faces of the group returning to the conference room. The spectrum of expressions ranged from boredom to impatience.

Once again, Sam stood and faced the group. "Gentlemen, you've all been very patient and I promise I'll take only a few more moments of your time. First, I'd like to address any additional questions or objections you may have, other than the matter of the height of the sign."

Lewis Coltrane responded for the group, "No additional concerns, Mr. McCormick. Now, what do you have to show us?"

Sam took a deep breath. "Very well, then," he began. "Mr. Bonner, correct me if I'm wrong, but I believe the entire Arena structure measures between seven hundred and eight hundred feet across, and will rise to four hundred feet tall? Am I correct?"

Bobby flashed Sam a knowing smile. "The structure is 780 feet wide by 400 feet tall, exactly."

"Thank you." Sam reached into his pocket. He pulled out the small, crude cardboard stop sign he'd created using pieces of the Kleenex box, colored in with Clyde's red Pentel pen. He placed it down onto the model at one of the freeway entrances. It looked pitifully small, dwarfed against the structure of the model. "Would someone like to tell me what that is?"

"It's a stop sign." Mayor Riley shifted impatiently in his chair. "Is this what we waited around for fifteen minutes to see?"

"With respect, Mayor Riley, it is indeed a stop sign. True to the scale size of this model, it is a forty-five-foot-tall stop sign."

"Are you telling us that stop sign is the same height as the sign you propose?" Commissioner Bryant blurted out.

"No, Sir. Again, with respect, that is the size of the sign *your* present regulations *require* we build for you at forty-five-feet tall."

Allen Stein's burst of laughter resonated out over the gasps filling the room.

Sam continued, "If you'll indulge me for just a few more moments, allow me to show you the size, to scale, of what Regal proposes to build for you."

Sam took a six-inch ruler from his briefcase and set it on end onto the exact location of the proposed sign. "This is pretty close to the height of your sign at two hundred feet tall. Would you agree, Mr. Bonner?"

Bobby rocked back in his chair and nodded, stifling a snicker. "Might be a little short, but I'd say it's damned close, Mr. McCormick."

Lewis Coltrane rose from his chair, clapping his hands in the air to exaggerate his approval. "I'll be damned. I guess you showed us, Mr. McCormick. That was some quick thinking, and a damned clever way to make your point. Down here in Louisiana, we're not afraid to admit it when we, on occasion, very rarely, mind you, make a mistake." He looked at Allen Stein.

Stein's eyes were sparkling behind his glasses, and he was smiling. Coltrane frowned, unmasking his anger that Stein was enjoying himself at the committee's expense.

Coltrane seized the chance to show Stein who was boss. "A sign at forty-five feet is preposterous. We've got ourselves a law to modify, gentlemen, if we're going to pull this project off, without giving Mr. Stein here a headline that will make us the laughing stock of New Orleans." He looked across the table at Stein. "Right, Stein? The last thing this committee needs is more bad press."

Stein shrugged, then lifted his hand to his forehead in a mock salute.

Coltrane turned to face Sam. "However, you still haven't convinced us that your company can actually build a sign of this magnitude."

"Mr. Coltrane, I believe I do have a way to convince you. I propose a trip to Las Vegas for your committee, as guests of Regal Sign Company. You can all see our work for yourselves."

The room fell silent. Sam had their attention. "My bosses, Lou and Jon Navaro, would welcome the opportunity to meet you. We can give you all a tour of our Las Vegas factory and show you how we work."

Bonner gave Sam a nod and a subtle thumbs-up.

Sam took a deep breath and continued, "Gentlemen, you can see the signs we've constructed in Las Vegas and draw your own conclusions."

Coltrane shot a look across the room at DiAngelis, and his son, Jimmy. Both men were nodding yes and smiling at Sam.

"I'm confident that once you see what Regal has already accomplished, you'll have no doubt we have what it takes to deliver a sign that will delight you and all of New Orleans."

He sat down. The Las Vegas visit was the carrot on the end of the stick that would close the deal. He'd nailed the presentation.

Coltrane settled into his chair at the head of the table. "I think I can speak for all of us when I say we've enjoyed your presentation. If you and your colleague don't mind excusing yourselves, this committee has much to discuss. I trust we can reach you at your hotel?"

"Absolutely, sir. We look forward to hearing from you," Sam replied. He could feel the adrenaline in the blood pumping through his veins. He winked at Clyde, who was fighting just as hard to maintain his composure.

"And indeed you will, young man, indeed you will," Lewis Coltrane added. "You'll hear from us by the end of the day."

Sam and Clyde left the conference room, barely making it into the elevator before Clyde totally lost his composure. "I'll be a son of a bitch, Sam! I can't believe you did it! I was sure we were dead in the water. That stop-sign thing was brilliant. You're a genius, a goddamned genius."

The elevator door opened into the lobby.

"Let's get out of here and get back to the hotel." Clyde waltzed out of the elevator, smooth-stepping like Fred Astaire. He spun around to face Sam. "Tonight, after we get that call, I'm going to buy you the best meal you've ever had."

"Hold on. We haven't landed the contract yet, Clyde. I don't want to jinx things," Sam cautioned, but in his gut, he could feel that Clyde was right. The pitch had captured the attention of the committee and Regal was well on the way to clinching the contract. The Navaros would happily foot the bill to fly the committee to Las Vegas, and the group would be dazzled by what they saw.

Sam and Clyde returned to the Marie Antoinette and spent a nervous afternoon, alternately playing cards and pacing across the carpet in Sam's room, awaiting the phone call. It came at 4 p.m.

"Mr. McCormick, Lewis Coltrane here. I'm pleased to tell you that the members of the committee were impressed by your presentation. We all agree that a trip to Las Vegas to see your company's work firsthand is an excellent idea. If all you've told us is true, I believe we may have a deal."

"That's excellent news, Mr. Coltrane," Sam replied, gesturing a thumbs-up to Clyde, who had stood up and was hovering over him.

"Give us a call at the Firm after you've spoken to your bosses. Max and Jimmy will make arrangements to clear a few days on the committee's calendar and contact you to work out the details. You have a pleasant night, now."

Sam hung up the phone and threw his arms around Clyde. "We did it, Clyde. Once we get them to Las Vegas, it's a done deal. I'll call Jon and Lou and give them the news. Then you and I are going out to celebrate. Pick the best restaurant in town."

"You bet I will," Clyde replied. He released his grip on Sam's shoulders. "We deserve it."

"We sure do. Then we'll go listen to some of that great jazz you keep telling me about."

The following day Sam and Clyde returned to Las Vegas, happy men.

Happy, and hung over.

# 9
## Allen Stein

Allen Stein rocked back in his swivel chair. His hands were clasped behind his head and the long ash dangling on the end of his cigarette hung precariously close to falling on his shirt. His legs were propped up, right over left on the top of his desk. The office clock had just chimed midnight. The newsroom was nearly deserted, with only the faint tapping sound of a distant typewriter and the infrequent ringing of a phone.

Allen did most of his writing late at night. There was very little to distract him and he liked to write his column without the constant interruption that was unavoidable during normal working hours, when the third floor of the Tower Building resembled Grand Central Station on a very smoky day.

He yawned and lifted his legs off the desk. He pushed his glasses up onto his forehead and wiped his tear ducts with the thumb and middle finger of his hand. His deadline was fast approaching and, although the finished article in the typewriter in front of him had been easy to write, the more he thought about it, the more dissatisfied he felt. He dropped his glasses back onto the bridge of his nose and read his headline:

**REGAL WOOS COMMITTEE WITH VEGAS VISIT**

The article's headline hinted at impropriety. Allen leaned forward to extinguish what was left of his cigarette in the overflowing ashtray in front of him. He pulled the article out of the typewriter, crumbling it, before shooting it effortlessly into the wastepaper basket ten feet from his desk.

Covering the Arena project was proving to be complicated. His recent articles on Arena subcontracts had questioned the credibility of several of the companies bidding on various projects, and in his most recent article, he had specifically mentioned Regal Sign Company. The safe and easy route would be to continue with the opinions he'd aired up to this point. However, after what he'd seen and heard at the committee meeting earlier in the day, his conscience was getting the better of him.

The McCormick kid from Regal did a great job representing his company and his product, and Allen genuinely liked him. Despite all the power-tripping egos in the room, McCormick succeeded in holding his own; not an easy task under the best of conditions. He'd gone in as an underdog and stolen the show, and Allen loved him for it.

Allen reached for a cigarette from the nearly empty pack on his desk. He rummaged through his pocket for his lighter and thought back to the meeting.

The best part of the day came after McCormick and his associate left. The courteous pretense of southern hospitality displayed by the committee during the presentation disappeared and the real fireworks started. When Lewis Coltrane suggested Allen leave, Allen declined.

"I think I'll stay, Lewis. After, all, as you so eloquently stated earlier, we must accurately relay to the public how well the committee works together." The mockery in his voice was deliberately directed at Lewis. "Yes I think I'll stay on, just to observe."

By the end of the meeting, one of Allen's opinions remained unchanged. Bobby Bonner deserved the contract to build the domed structure. In addition to the fact that Bonner Construction was the largest construction company in New Orleans and the most qualified for the job, the selection also rested in his popularity with the New Orleans community. After Bobby promised to vigorously investigate allegations of widespread corruption within the organization, city laborers had overwhelmingly elected him head of the Teamsters Union. Coltrane folded under social pressure, and Bonner joined the committee as an advisor, shortly after his company acquired the contract.

Coltrane's firm had represented companies in competition with Bonner Construction in several lawsuits in the past and it was common knowledge that Bonner and Coltrane disliked each other. When interviewed by Allen, Bonner was extremely vocal regarding his lack of respect for Coltrane's law practices. During the presentation, Allen observed Bobby's interaction with McCormick, and read between the lines. They were the only two committeemen without a law degree, and, in Allen's opinion, the only two with any common sense at all.

Bonner and Coltrane managed to keep their mutual animosity under control during the meeting, but, once the presentation was over, the façade disappeared.

Allen picked up the notes he had taken during the meeting. "It's here somewhere," he muttered. He skimmed the pages to refresh his memory. "Ah, here it is."

Bobby had demanded assurances that Lewis and the committee would take his union concerns seriously. Lewis blew them off as baseless and unimportant.

Bobby retaliated with veiled threats about union repercussions, if they weren't treated fairly.

Allen continued to peruse his notes. Other topics, ranging from existing subcontracts, to bids on new ones met with opposing opinions by various committee members.

The meeting ended with only two unanimous decisions: first, at the next city commission meeting, the committee would present a motion to pass a special decree for the Arena property, lifting the forty-five foot limit for signage to two-hundred-twenty-five feet. Considering the circumstances, the motion would meet with no opposition.

And second, a trip to Las Vegas was a go.

Allen reached into his desk drawer, pulled out another piece of paper and slid it into his typewriter. "The kid and his company deserve a chance to prove themselves," he said to himself. "There's plenty here to write about."

He took a drag of his cigarette, and chuckled to himself over the fireworks he'd witnessed at the meeting. He typed in his headline:

## UNION PROBLEMS IMMINENT ON ARENA PROJECT
### By Allen Stein

Union leader Bobby Bonner told this reporter today he anticipated problems ahead for the upcoming labor negotiations with the Arena committee.

"I hope Lewis Coltrane will see reason and allow the union to do what it must, to assure fair conditions for the workers of our community," Bonner stated earlier this afternoon.

Meanwhile, recently surfacing rumors of attempts at bribery and payoffs to the union and building

**department by companies desiring to secure contracts remain rumors.**

A cigarette ash fell unnoticed into his lap as his fingers flew across the keys. He grinned, imagining the look on Coltrane's face the following morning when he read the article over breakfast. "This won't be good for your heart, old boy." He clenched the cigarette tight between his teeth. "So be it. I'm not afraid of you, or your committee. I'll be watching."

Allen finished the article and proofread the copy. Satisfied, he pulled it out of the typewriter, stood up and proceeded to take it to his editor's office. The article was going to rattle some cages, but that was a reporter's job. Allen had demonstrated through many articles over the course of his career that he took the corruption running rampant in New Orleans seriously. That sometimes meant crossing dangerous and powerful men.

He knew it. It came with the job.

He'd learned to be careful and watch his back. Many reporters had walked the path before, and survived. Maybe being one of the good guys would keep him lucky.

# 10

## The Funeral

The Coltrane chauffeur pulled the limo out of the garage and stopped at the entrance to the mansion. He assisted Lewis, Eleanor, Jimmy, and Catherine into the limo and began the long drive to St. Mary's Cathedral.

Jamaica chose to take the drive with Clarice and several of the other Cajun members of the Coltrane staff in a limo provided by Our Lady of Mercy Funeral Parlor. Clarice and Jamaica sat side by side as the limo traveled the orchard-lined road leading into the city.

Enroute to its destination, the limo approached the Arena site. The structure loomed in the distance, the steel skeleton rising high into the sky. As the limo drew closer, Clarice placed her hand on Jamaica's knee. Her hand was ice cold.

"Clarice? Are you all right?"

"Yes," she replied. "I just hadn't seen it before."

"Seen what?"

"The Arena." Clarice spoke the words as if they were a vile poison escaping her mouth. She lifted her hand from Jamaica's knee and looked at her with stern eyes. "Child, there's a curse on that land." Clarice pointed at the excavation site where the Arena was being constructed.

"Why do you say that?"

Clarice rarely spoke of curses. They were a deadly serious matter, and Clarice had taught Jamaica that such things were better left alone.

But she was speaking of them now.

Her chin dropped to her chest and she sighed. "It was once the Girod Street Cemetery, built long before you or I were born. Many souls were laid to rest there." She looked up. "My ancestors were buried over there." She gestured to a pile of rusted, wrought-iron fencing a few hundred yards away from the road.

Jamaica shuddered when she saw the fencing. It rested alongside broken tombstones, in a heap at the far perimeter of the site. Bulldozers parked nearby had piled the debris to clear the land.

"This land has been desecrated, child. The dirt is haunted by the souls of Cajun folk and aristocrats alike, wrongly awakened from eternal sleep. They rise." She placed her hand on the amulet around her neck and began chanting softly, summoning.

Jamaica felt a chill. As she looked out at the land, she felt a vision manifesting.

She closed her eyes. She could see the cemetery as it once was. Beautiful vaults above the ground rested in long rows amid tree-laden paths. Tall marble tombstones etched with the names of the departed shone in the sun.

The soft moan of Clarice's chanting drew Jamaica deeper into her vision. She felt her house of dark spirits rising into the light. The sky turned black. The cemetery began to change. The trees came alive, swaying violently in the wind. Wild foliage covering the ground began to move. Writhing vines crawled up to engulf the tombstones, creating a labyrinth of living spider webs

The walls of the vaults rumbled, crumbling to dust and revealing rotting caskets covered in wilted flowers. Ghosts rose from the ground beneath the tombstones. Their skeletal forms darted about, frantically swirling among the trees.

"Jamaica!" Clarice shouted, grabbing Jamaica's arms and shaking her.

The movement jolted Jamaica back into lucidity. "Oh, my dear God!" she cried. "I saw them!"

"Yes, child," Clarice whispered. "Best stay away from this place. The spirits are angry. They curse this Arena and those who venture near it."

Jamaica felt the blood draining from her face.

They rode on to the church in silence.

\*\*\*

The Coltrane mansion echoed with the voices of people who had come for the wake after the funeral service. Servers walked through the crowds of people, presenting trays loaded with succulent appetizers and a variety of beverages to the guests.

Although the staff and a few close friends of the family genuinely mourned Lily's death, the rest of the assembled group attended the event, regarding it nothing more than a social obligation. Most were members of the New Orleans aristocracy and, as the social elite, making an appearance to show sympathy for the Coltrane family over their loss was a requirement. In doing so, they hoped to maintain, or to gain favor with, one of the most powerful families in New Orleans.

Several hundred people milled about the mansion, as well as throughout the main garden and surrounding grounds. They conversed with one another and took turns expressing their condolences to the family over the tragic loss of Lily.

Extravagant floral arrangements rested on tables throughout the estate. Eleanor wandered the grounds directing the staff, ensuring not even the smallest detail was overlooked and from time to time checked on Catherine, sequestered in her wing of the mansion, inconsolable. Clarice busied herself in the kitchen, fighting back tears, as she prepared hors d'oeuvres and supervised the servers.

Jimmy sat alone on one of the large couches in the main living room, staring out a huge bay window at the crowd of people gathered in the courtyard. He grabbed the bottle of Chivas on the table next to him and poured himself another double. His mood was glum. The charade unfolding before him was even more unbearable than the torment he'd endured during Lily's service at Saint Mary's. He cowered in his seat, bombarded by the superficial banter surrounding him. Very few of the guests actually gave a damn about Lily. The hypocrisy of it sickened him.

He swirled the scotch in his glass and brought it to his lips, downing it in one gulp. It burned his throat, but he welcomed the inebriation that would follow. Anything to dull the pain.

And the guilt. His heart ached with guilt and remorse as he remembered his last, precious moments with Lily…

She had smiled at him as he fell upon her, full of lust and desire. He'd tasted her full moist lips. He'd squeezed her firm young breasts and fondled her nipples, delirious with the anticipation of having her.

He'd been instantly aroused and even in the wake of her death, his desire for her had not lessened.

He'd managed to mask his feelings at the funeral service. But now, after Saint Mary's, after looking down at her beautiful body, lying so still in the coffin, he could no longer control his emotions. The guilt was unbearable. He was despicable for still wanting her. She was dead—and all he could think about was his desire for her.

He reached again for the bottle.

The unexpected touch of Jamaica's hand on his shoulder startled him. His hand slipped and he would have dropped the bottle of scotch but for her free hand gently releasing it from his grasp.

"Jimmy, it's hard for all of us, but this won't help, not really," she said tenderly. She set the bottle of Chivas back onto the table and sat down next to him. She looked into his bloodshot eyes. "Are you OK?"

"Oh, sure, sugar, I'm fine. It's just so…hard." A sudden surge of nausea overcame him. "Please excuse me, Jamaica. I don't feel well." He set his glass on the table and rose to walk toward the French double doors opening out into the courtyard. "I need to get some air." He fought for balance as he crossed the room and stumbled outside.

***

Jamaica strolled down the steps onto the veranda facing the garden. Fatigue from the many strained conversations she'd suffered since the funeral showed on her face. She found a comfortable loveseat and sat down. She looked out over the hundreds of beautiful flowers in the garden, flowers nurtured first by her father and then by her sister. A small tear formed in the corner of her eye.

"Jamaica."

She turned at the sound of her name, quickly wiping the tear away.

Lewis Coltrane appeared at the foot of the steps at the base of the veranda. His gait was brisk as he ascended the stairs toward her. "Jamaica, dear, if I could have just a moment of your time, there's something important I need to discuss with you." Lewis sat beside her on the loveseat.

"Of course, Lewis. What is it?"

"Well, you know the Firm has taken on a huge responsibility, and a major investment in the city's Arena project. It will be good for the city and good for the Coltrane family as well."

"I understand, but are we really going to discuss business now?" She looked into his eyes, half expecting him to apologize.

"Yes, this can't wait."

His response forced her to surrender to a sad reality. The subject involved money, and money was always of paramount importance to Lewis.

"Jamaica, the Firm is heavily involved in the legalities of the Arena project and it would be of benefit to me if you'd join us at the Firm right away." He placed his hand on Jamaica's knee. "You've pleased me greatly by passing the bar with such ease. It's time for you to take your place with the Firm and continue to make the family proud."

"Of course," she replied flatly, her face clearly showing her incredulity at his lack of respect for the solemn nature of the occasion.

Lewis continued. A group of us has a trip to Las Vegas scheduled within the next few weeks. It involves a complicated contract negotiation."

"Yes, but what does this have to do with me?"

"I need you to go over some of the basic elements of the proposed contract with Jimmy. I also want you to accompany us to Las Vegas."

"Las Vegas? But what about Lily?" Jamaica asked.

Lewis placed both hands on Jamaica's shoulders. His tone softened. "After we bury Lily, of course."

"Next to my mother and father?"

Jamaica could see that Lewis hadn't anticipated such a request. "I'll never have any peace unless Lily rests in peace."

Lewis recovered quickly from his surprise. "Yes, of course, darlin'. But afterwards, I think this other trip could be a welcome distraction for all of us." He dropped his head and lowered his voice to a whisper. "Only time can dull the pain of losing our precious Lily..." He looked back up, directly into Jamaica's eyes, "...but as a family, we must support one another. Don't you agree, darlin'?"

"Honestly, Lewis, I haven't had much of a chance to think about anything but the accident. I just don't understand how Lily could have fallen so carelessly. And for no one to have seen her? None of it makes any sense."

Lewis squeezed Jamaica's shoulders in a comforting, but slightly too-firm gesture. "Yes, dear, I know. It's confusing for all of us. That's why you should get away for a few days... to clear your head." He released his grip on her shoulders. "Please consider my request. The trip will last only a few days. It would mean the world to me, dear, and to Jimmy as well. You think about it."

"I will, Lewis," Jamaica replied. She attempted to change the subject. "You've been very kind. The funeral service was beautiful and I do thank you and Eleanor for that. It means a lot to me."

"You're family, darlin', and so was Lily. We all loved her." He paused. "Now you try not to think so much about what can't be changed, and think about what I've said. A trip would do you good."

Lewis stood up and walked out into the throng of people in the garden. He joined a group of male guests gathered there.

Jamaica gazed out beyond the group to the hundreds of flowers spread out before her. She closed her eyes and conjured an image of Lily, working beside her father in the garden. She could see them, kneeling together among the flowers, laughing. But the image quickly faded and a different vision appeared. It was Lily, alone and frightened, floating in darkness.

Jamaica shuddered, and shook the ungodly image from her mind. "Maybe it would be good to get away," she whispered to herself.

*** 

Jimmy settled into his favorite lounge chair in a secluded area of the veranda, with a view of the main garden courtyard. He immediately summoned a waiter and told him to bring a bottle. He was in the process of pouring himself another Scotch when he saw his father enter the garden and approach the mayor and Commissioner Bryant.

The three men stood huddled together, keenly engaged in conversation.

Jimmy lifted his glass, mockingly toasting the group. He studied their body language and automatically assumed they were talking about the committee meeting held the day before, and the upcoming trip to Las Vegas. His grief turned to anger. The Arena project was huge and the entire group, led by his father, would profit enormously from it. What did the life of an inconsequential girl matter in comparison?

He turned his eyes to the exotic Birds of Paradise lining the pathways of the atrium.

Lily was everywhere he looked. He'd often watched her from the windows of the music room, fantasizing about her as she gathered baskets of flowers in the garden. Sometimes, she would see him watching her. She would gaze adoringly back at him and his heart would race with excitement. In those moments, he was a voyeur, caught in the act, and being discovered always gave him a thrill.

Jimmy took a long drink. Thinking about her was agony. She was an innocent child all wrapped up in a woman's body. He missed her. He wanted her. And he hated himself. "Oh, God, Lily, I'm so sorry."

As the scotch began to numb the pain, he closed his eyes and reflected back on Saturday.

The argument was still a blur. What was burned into his mind was the look in her eyes: disbelief and anger. Her anger had frightened him. It had all been so horrible.

He hadn't wanted to make the call.

He knew his father would be angry.

If he could just go back, back before it all happened...

# 11

## Saturday at the Willows

A warm breeze spread the fragrance of flowers into the air as Lily began another glorious day in the fields of the Coltrane Estate. The bright yellow chiffon fabric she wore draped around her body moved gracefully as she walked, fluttering around her legs in the breeze. Occasionally, the fabric caught enough air to billow up in folds. Swirling in the air, it resembled huge yellow butterfly wings, propelling her across the expansive green grounds of the estate.

She began at the main house and made her way to each of the four gardens that lay between the house and the bungalow, located over a mile away. She carefully selected a variety of flowers from each of the gardens, cutting them quickly, as she did every Saturday. Eleanor and Catherine cut the more traditional flowers, the roses and lilies, for the main salon and dining table. But the flowers she cut on Saturdays created the arrangements for the sunroom and kitchen, and for her living quarters in the west wing of the Coltrane Estate.

She sang to herself as she gathered the flowers. Saturday was a special day for Lily—it was their day, their secret afternoon together. And this day was even more special, because she had wonderful news for Jimmy. She couldn't wait to share it with him.

Lily approached the last of the gardens on her route to the bungalow. She twirled in a circle, laughing in delight as she danced among the rows of exotic island flowers. Her father had planted hundreds of seeds and bulbs, in the hope they would flourish in the moist earth and air of New Orleans. With his expert attention, the garden had become the most beautiful on the estate.

They'd spent hours together, father and daughter, tending to the flowers. He had told her they were like the flowers that grew on the island where she was born, and that they grew in abundance where her mother lay, on a hill overlooking the ocean.

She'd seen the flowers and the hillside for herself when she returned to the island two years before, to see her father buried beside her mother. Strangers embraced her and introduced themselves as cousins, aunts, and uncles. She'd held Jamaica's hand as her sister comforted her, explaining that their father and mother would rest there in peace, side by side.

Lily stood grasping the flowers her father had planted and gazed up into the clear blue sky. She lifted them over her head. "I always choose the most beautiful flowers for my room, Papa," she said. She pulled the bouquet of blossoms to her face and inhaled their exotic fragrance. Each flower held the memory of her father and she missed him, but she was happy living with the Coltranes. And she was in love.

Lily hurried across the last meadow to the long path leading down to the bungalow. The family had dubbed the quaint hideaway the "Willows," because of the many huge weeping willow trees that surrounded it. In years past, the Coltrane men used the bungalow as a place to relax after hours hunting on the grounds of the massive estate. The Willows had been all but abandoned in recent years, as the Coltranes became too busy with the Firm and their other important business ventures. Golf and fishing trips to various islands replaced hunting and the male Coltranes took the trips frequently.

Now, the Willows had become their secret place.

Her excitement grew as she entered a wooded area and neared the bungalow. The grove of weeping willows appeared alive, the massive spreads of arching branches swaying gracefully in the breeze. Lily took care not to damage the flowers as she ran among them.

She reached the bungalow and gently set the flowers down on the porch. She took a key from a planter in front of a hammock hanging near the front door, unlocked and opened the door, and returned the key to the planter. She gathered up the flowers and went inside.

The ritual was always the same: Place the flowers in water in a large sink on the bar and wait for him.

Within a few minutes, she'd tended to the flowers and made her way into the bedroom, adjacent the living area. She took care to leave the bedroom door wide open.

Lily sat down at the vanity table. She opened the drawer of the vanity and unclasped the chain around her neck, carefully placing her necklace in a small silk pouch in the drawer. Her sister had given the necklace to her the year before, on her sixteenth birthday. She treasured it and wore it every day.

Lily pulled her brush out of the drawer, closed it and began brushing her hair. She could see the front door of the bungalow reflected in the vanity mirror as she sat brushing, and waiting.

The rules were simple. He insisted she be sitting with her back to the door when he arrived. She would continue brushing her hair and waiting until he entered the bungalow, no matter how long it took.

Lily had been brushing her hair for nearly an hour, silently rehearsing the news she planned to share, when the bungalow door opened. Her heart began to race. She continued brushing. She watched Jimmy in the mirror as he approached her. He stopped directly behind her and pressed his body against her back.

\*\*\*

He looked at her reflection in the mirror. He placed his hands on her head and felt the silkiness of her hair between his fingers. He slid them to her neck and then onto her shoulders. He bent over and kissed her neck, his tongue sliding up to her ear as he looked upon her reflection.

"You're so beautiful," he whispered. His hands passed down her back to her ribs, then slid forward to reach inside her dress and touch her breasts. He pressed his groin against her back, his desire aroused as he fondled her firm young breasts.

She moved erotically, moaning in pleasured response to his touch. "Oh, Jimmy."

"So incredibly beautiful," he repeated. His hands began untying the yellow knot of chiffon binding her breasts. His fingers quivered in anticipation of freeing them. He couldn't remember a time when sexual arousal had been more intense, not even in his early years, when frequent orgasm was one of the fringe benefits of being who he was. Scores of beautiful debutantes had competed for his attention and were eager to please. They were willing to do anything for him and he had demanded it all. He'd grown to understand the power that came with wealth and position and he both relished and exploited it.

He loosened the fabric. It fell to her waist, revealing the impossibly beautiful, impossibly young body he was aching to enter.

He lifted her up, turning her to face him. He forced his lips against hers and kissed her passionately. His tongue probed her mouth as he walked her backward, toward the bed. She reached out with both her hands wrapped in yellow fabric, and slid them between his legs. She pressed them against his cock, smiling to find it rock hard through his pants.

"Lily," he moaned in agonized desire. He fell upon her on the bed, tearing at the fabric that was keeping him from her.

He unzipped his fly, freed his aching cock and entered her. Seconds later, he exploded inside her. His body shook with the intensity of the orgasm. He would have her at least twice more, as he did every Saturday, both exhilarated and incredulous at how easily she made him come.

"Tell me you love me," she whispered, as he lay on top of her.

His hot, throbbing cock was still rock hard as continued to move inside her.

"Please, Jimmy, tell me how much you love me."

"Of course I love you, princess. You're the most beautiful creature in the world." He slid one hand under her, pulling her body tight against his. He began to ride her with increasing force and urgency.

She responded to him by wrapping her legs around his waist and forcing him deeper inside. "Tell me about how we'll be together." She kissed him passionately on the neck. Her tongue slid up over his chin and plunged into his mouth.

Jimmy's body trembled with lust. He gasped. "Yes, princess, when the time is right." His cock plunged farther into her sex, and he came again. He groaned, collapsing on top of her.

"When? Tell me when!"

"It's complicated," he whispered, fighting to regain his breath.

Lily wrapped her arms tighter around his neck. She looked lovingly into his eyes. "It's not complicated any more, Jimmy. I'm going to give you a baby."

"Of course you are, princess, someday," he answered. He lifted up. His hands squeezed her breasts. His mouth covered hers in an attempt to silence what had become an increasingly frequent and annoying conversation. He danced around the topic with her every week, when all he cared about was possessing every inch of her.

"No, you don't understand. Not someday. *Now.*" Lily turned her head, pushing his mouth away. She turned back and looked into his eyes. "Jimmy, I'm pregnant!" she shouted, unable to hide her excitement. "Now we can tell everybody we're in love. You promised. The time is right now, today."

Jimmy's cock went limp. He sat up on the bed with his legs straddling her hips. His hands were still pressed against her breasts. He stared down at her, visibly shaken by her words. "You can't be serious, princess. You've been on the pill from the start. You promised you'd take them."

"Oh, I have. I have taken them, and I almost never forget. But it's happened, Jimmy. I'm pregnant with our baby!" She placed her hands over his and pushed them seductively down between her legs. "I can't wait to tell Catherine. She will be so happy for us. She talks all the time about how sad she is that she can't make babies." Lily squeezed his hands with her thighs. "This baby is meant to be, Jimmy. It's a miracle."

Jimmy pulled his hands from between her legs. "We can't tell Catherine about this, Lily. Are you crazy?" His mind raced as he struggled to cope with the terrible reality of the situation. "I'll call Doc Beauregard. He can fix this."

"Fix this?" Lily pushed him away. She sat up on the bed and slid out from under him. Her body began to shake. Her eyes grew wild with disbelief. "Fix what? You mean an abortion? Don't you want this baby, Jimmy?"

"Hell, no! I'm married, for Christ's sake."

"I thought you were my prince, Jimmy!" she cried. "But you're not. You're a monster! Only a monster could be so cruel, lying to me all along, and seducing me with empty promises." She hastily wrapped the yellow chiffon fabric around her. "I hate you!" She glared at him, turned and ran out into the living room.

He hesitated for a moment before following her. "Lily, wait, we have to talk about this…" The tone of his voice changed as he rose from the bed. He no longer uttered the sweet whispers of an impassioned lover. "You're acting like a silly child!"

She began crying hysterically, "It was all lies! All lies!" Reaching the bar, she grabbed the flowers lying in the sink in bunches, wildly hurling them at him.

He reached out for her, trying to restrain her.

She turned away to get away from him.

He grabbed her arm and attempted to stop her.

She spun around and kicked him, striking him with her free hand. "Let go of me!" she cried. As she pulled against his grasp, Lily slipped and lost her balance. Her legs shot out in front of her and she fell back awkwardly. Her eyes stared frantically into his.

He lost his grip on her arm and watched helplessly as her head struck the corner edge of the marble bar, making a loud thud.

Her body went limp and melted to the floor. Her eyes, wide open with rage and hysteria only seconds before, were suddenly vacant and emotionless. The yellow chiffon that had fluttered so freely about her limbs in the breeze now lay in a tangled heap beneath her.

Jimmy stood frozen. He looked down at her, lying motionless on the floor, and felt the sour taste of panic rising from his stomach to his throat. He swallowed hard and bent down. He lifted her to his chest. "Lily, Lily," he repeated. He began shaking her, in a frenzied effort to revive her. "Lily, wake up."

Nothing.

Desperate for some sign of life, he pressed his hands against her chest. She wasn't breathing. He placed his mouth over hers and tried to resuscitate her. He continued his attempt, choking back tears between breaths, but it was pointless.

Finally, he stopped. Jimmy lifted her into his arms. He wrapped the chiffon fabric around her lifeless body and sat on the floor, rocking her back and forth while he sobbed, lost in an incoherent daze.

After a while, his sobbing stopped.

He laid Lily's body gently down on the floor and rose, like a zombie, to his feet. With each step, he crushed the fallen flowers covering the floor as he crossed the room to the telephone.

Jimmy stared at the phone for several minutes, then picked it up and dialed.

# 12

## Lewis Cleans Up a Mess

"Goddamn it, this better be important!" Lewis Coltrane bellowed into the receiver. It was Saturday and no one dared disturb Lewis on Saturday.

"Dad, I'm in trouble. I killed her. It was an accident. She's dead and I don't know what to do…" Jimmy's voice trailed off.

"Jimmy? Is that you, son? Who's dead? What accident? Where are you?" The hairs on Lewis's arms stood erect. "What's going on?"

"It's Lily. I've killed her. I swear it was an accident. Oh, God help me."

"Where are you?"

"I'm at the Willows. We're both here."

"Stay put. Hang up the phone and wait for me. I'm on my way." Lewis hung up, then dialed the extension to the garage.

"This is James."

"Bring my Vette around to the front driveway."

"Yes, Mr. Coltrane, right away, sir."

James was waiting beside a red Corvette convertible in the courtyard driveway when Lewis appeared, bounding down the steps of the Estate's main entrance. James opened the driver door for Lewis and stepped back, barely avoiding colliding with his boss as Lewis bolted in front of him. Lewis jumped in and floored the accelerator, peeling rubber as he sped out of the driveway. He drove down the road, raising a cloud of dust behind him, until he reached the estate's main entrance gates at the bottom of the hill.

The security guard opened the gate and waved in recognition at his boss as Lewis raced by. He proceeded down the road, past the gardens and through the plantation fields on either side. He reached the main road turnoff exiting the Estate property onto Highway 942 and passed it, continuing straight, until he reached a small turnoff on his left leading into a heavily wooded area. He took the turnoff. A few hundred yards later, he stopped the car at a chain-link fence. He got out and walked in tall grass to a latched gate. He swung the gate open and returned to the car. After he had passed through, he put the car in park and returned to close the gate.

His shoes dug into the moist ground under his feet. Lewis grimaced, looking down to see his shoes soiled with dirt. "Damn it," he mumbled under his breath, kicking his shoes on the front tire of the car before getting back inside. He drove another hundred yards through the woods until he reached a small clearing. It revealed a narrow dirt road leading down to the back of the Willows. The bungalow was hidden among a grove of willow trees, a short distance farther down.

Lewis pulled up to a grassy area under the willow trees in the back of the bungalow. He parked beside Jimmy's Mercedes. He got out, slammed the door of his Corvette behind him, and hurried around to the front door.

Lewis entered the bungalow and found Jimmy sitting on the couch, staring blankly across the room at Lily's body. Lewis walked across the familiar room, where he himself had enjoyed many adulterous afternoons, and sat down next to his son. It took only a few seconds for Lewis to realize what had been going on. He tried to restrain his anger. He knew Jimmy had a Saturday playmate, but it never crossed his mind it could be Lily.

"Jesus, Jimmy. All the willing pussy in New Orleans and you couldn't drive a few miles into town to get it? Your wife's right up the hill," Lewis fumed. "Hell, son, what were you thinking? How stupid can you be, down here fucking your mother's little rose-garden buddy? That child's practically your sister."

\*\*\*

Jimmy looked away in shame, unable to bear his father's critical glare. "It wasn't like that, Dad. She was in love with me. After the first time, I couldn't stop. She was like a drug I couldn't quit. I had to have her." He sat with his shoulders slumped over, wringing his hands together and shaking his head. "She'd do anything to please me, Dad, anything. I've never had sex like that." He looked at his father. He saw no hint of understanding in his eyes, no glimpse of sympathy. The stern look of disapproval on Lewis' face stung. He tried to explain. "I made sure to get her on the pill, but today she told me she was pregnant. I told her I'd get her an abortion and she went crazy." He looked across the room at Lily, and then back at his father. "It all happened so fast. It was an accident." Jimmy wiped the tears forming once again in his eyes.

"Pregnant? An accident? Don't give me that bullshit!" Lewis slammed his fist on the arm of the couch. "It was no accident you were down here banging her every Saturday for God knows how long. Why didn't you tell me it was Lily? She just turned seventeen, for God's sake. You've been fucking jailbait, son. Good God. For a Coltrane, that's suicide."

Lewis' face was beet red. "Can you imagine what that son of a bitch Stein would do with something like this? Hell, he'd crucify the whole goddamned family."

Jimmy sat silent, with his head lowered and resting in his hands

Lewis stood up and paced in front of the couch. Then he stopped in front of Jimmy. "I'll fix this," he said. "But first, you have to pull yourself together."

"I'm sorry, Dad," Jimmy whimpered.

"Well, what's done is done. You're goddamned lucky I'm here to clean up this mess. I'll make some calls. But Jesus Christ, Jimmy. What were you thinking?"

Jimmy stared at the floor. "I'm sorry, Dad."

Lewis shook his head at his son. "For Christ's sake, stop crying. We don't have time for this, boy. We've got more important problems."

"More important than my killing Lily? I can't imagine anything worse."

Lewis threw his hands up in the air. "Hell, yes. That goddamned Bobby Bonner and his goddamned union are giving me trouble and I need you sharp for the committee meetings next week." Lewis gestured toward the door. "Get on out of here. You were never here, you hear me? Your old man has fixed worse messes than this. I'll make it go away, but for the love of God, stop bawling."

Jimmy rose to his feet. He kept his head down, desperate to avoid seeing the look of disdain covering his father's face. It was far from the first time Jimmy had seen the look. As in numerous times in Jimmy's past, Lewis had done whatever was necessary to distance his only son from trouble.

But some things even his father couldn't undo.

Jimmy choked back tears. "Lily is dead, and I killed her. Nothing can change that."

Lewis smirked. "You'll get over it."

The two men walked out to the back of the Willows to Jimmy's car.

\*\*\*

Lewis watched as his son drove away. After Jimmy's Mercedes disappeared up the road into the woods, he returned to the bungalow. He picked up the phone and dialed.

"Hello," a voice on the other end answered.

"Spencer?"

"Yeah, who's this?"

"It's Lewis Coltrane."

"Oh, Mr. Coltrane. What can I do for you?"

"I need you to drive out to my property."

Lewis reviewed the route he'd followed himself, 30 minutes before. "Park your car in the woods at the gate, just before the clearing. There's a bungalow not far down the dirt road, behind a grove of trees. My Vette's parked in the back. Jump the fence and come down by foot. I'll be waiting."

"Yes, Mr. Coltrane."

"And Spencer," Lewis added, "no one can know you're coming here. No one, understand? Don't let anyone see you."

"Yes, I understand perfectly."

"Come now." Lewis hung up the phone.

With the call, he had set a plan in motion. Jimmy had created a real mess. The solution was to eliminate the problem, with a little help from Spencer.

Eliminate it, and get back to business as usual.

\*\*\*

Spencer never knew what to expect when he got a call from Lewis Coltrane, except that it meant a job and good money. Whatever the job entailed, he welcomed it with open arms.

Of the many ugly services he performed for Coltrane, most involved beating up a union worker in a warehouse somewhere or roughing up some fat cat politician who interfered with Coltrane's interests, getting information Coltrane needed. Sometimes it was just blackmail. Sometimes it got out of hand and somebody had to be silenced, one way or the other. No task was ever too big a problem for Spencer. The messier the problem, the more Coltrane paid.

Spencer grabbed his keys and hopped in his beat-up Buick Riviera. He'd never been summoned out to Coltrane's property before. On the contrary, publicly he'd been ordered to keep a healthy distance from the whole family. He wove his way through the narrow streets of the Quarter to the highway entrance.

As he sped toward the Coltrane Estate, a sadistic smirk covered his face. "I wonder who I'm gonna hurt this time."

Spencer stopped outside the open door before entering the bungalow. He clawed his fingers back through the greasy strands of hair falling on his face and wiped his fingers across his teeth. He straightened his tie and patted down his suit jacket. He pulled back his shoulders and lifted his head, eager to look sharp on the job.

He walked into the bungalow and looked around. Lewis was standing in the center of the room. Beside him on the floor lay the body of a young woman. Underneath the thin fabric partially covering her, she was naked—and obviously dead. Spencer's eyes grew wide with excitement. "Mr. Coltrane, what can I do for you?"

"Make this go away, Spencer," he said, pointing at the body. "It has to look like an accident. Wait until later tonight. Take her somewhere on the grounds where she won't be found right away."

"Any place in particular?"

"I don't care. Somewhere out of sight. Make it look like the poor girl took a fall, hit her head. Maybe fell into one of the pools. I leave it up to you. And clean this place up. Nothing here can be linked to the girl or anyone else."

Spencer nodded he understood.

Lewis kicked at the flowers strewn on the floor. He pointed across the room into the bedroom. "Get rid of those sheets, all these ridiculous flowers and anything else that could place her here."

"Yes, sir. I'll clean it up. Can I expect any visitors?"

"No. This bungalow's far from the main house. The rest of the family stopped using it years ago. There's no reason for anyone to come down here, but there's no point leaving anything to chance. Be thorough, but be discreet. You *can* do that, can't you?"

"Yes, of course, thorough, but discreet," Spencer echoed the orders. He glanced over at the girl's body, titillated at the prospect of the task ahead. He stifled the smirk on his face, as he felt his cock stiffen.

Lewis gestured toward the door. "Once you've got the place cleaned up and the body moved, call me. Payment as usual and, as usual, you never saw me. Just make it go away."

"Yes, sir, Mr. Coltrane, you can count on me." Spencer walked with Lewis to the back of the bungalow, and watched him get in his car and drive away.

The smirk reappeared on Spencer's face. "Yes, sir, Mr. Coltrane," he mumbled under his breath. "I'm just the right man for the job."

He sighed in admiration of Coltrane's red Corvette as it disappeared up the dirt road. "I'll have to get myself a fine car like that one day. One day, real soon."

***

Spencer left the Coltrane property a little before 10 p.m. The bungalow, and the roads leading to it from the estate entrance, were a healthy distance from the mansion, but he drove carefully in the cover of night just the same. He turned onto Highway 942 and accelerated.

No one had seen him. He was sure of that.

The job had been a breeze. The girl was a wisp of a thing, easy to carry, and no one was around the pool area when he got there to stage the accident. He'd meticulously attended to the little details that would make it all look believable. Spencer had a lot of experience undressing women and did a masterful job redressing the girl, thoroughly enjoying himself in the process. Loosening a garden hose to create puddles along the pool deck was the finishing touch.

Spencer hummed to himself as he drove. Not too many people appreciated Spencer's special abilities, but Coltrane did. And he paid well, eventually.

Cleaning up the bungalow was the only time-consuming part of the job. He'd thoroughly checked out every piece of furniture, wiping everything clean and disposing of anything that could possibly connect to the girl or whoever killed her. He even managed to pick up a few souvenirs for himself. Coltrane told him no one used the bungalow anymore. He touched the small treasures lying beside him on the passenger seat. The Coltranes were filthy rich. They wouldn't miss the trinkets. Even if they did, the items would never be traced back to him.

Spencer fancied himself much smarter than other people fathomed and he hated the fact that he rarely got the credit he deserved. Coltrane was a dangerous man, but the more jobs he did for Coltrane, the more dangerous Spencer felt himself becoming.

He frequently daydreamed about blackmailing Coltrane, but figured there was no rush. He loved money and he made it by being Coltrane's "enforcer," the word he used on the street to describe his occupation. According to Spencer, enforcers played an important role in the scheme of things. And being an enforcer made him an important man.

Spencer took the exit leading to his apartment, located in a run-down neighborhood on the outskirts of the French Quarter. It was nearly 11 p.m. on a Saturday night and the action was just getting started. He wove through the crowds of tourists to an area on Bourbon Street housing a series of strip clubs and bars. He slowed the Buick when he approached a narrow gravel alley on his right. An overhead street lamp nearby was broken and the alley was dark. He turned in to the alley and barely missed a prostitute who was standing in front of a large garbage bin located just inside the entrance.

"Watch it, asshole!" she shouted, jumping out of the way of the moving vehicle.

A wicked grin appeared on Spencer's face. He gunned the engine. A spray of rocks flew up from under the tires.

They struck her scantily clad body, drawing blood from her bare legs. She fell back against the bin, fighting for balance. "Bastard!" he heard her yell out as he sped past.

He glanced in his rear-view mirror to see her flashing him the finger. His grin widened. "If she only knew who I am and what I just did," he said. "She'd know better than to shoot the finger at *this* enforcer."

Spencer parked behind a rundown building at the end of the alley and hopped out of the Buick. He followed a narrow pathway littered with trash and overgrown weeds until he reached the entrance to his apartment building. He went inside and climbed the stairs to the second floor. The stairway walls were covered in graffiti, and the steps smelled of urine and beer.

Not far away, the Quarter was alive with music, the streets filled with the unique charm of the Cajun culture. But the streets in Spencer's part of town offered a different view, a dark glimpse of the sleazy underbelly of a city where dangerous games were played in strip clubs and back alleys.

Spencer was a small player in those games. He was a loner, smart enough to stay out of Mafia business. He sometimes rubbed elbows with the Mob, but a few dangerous run-ins in the past had taught him it was safer to shy away from their playing field.

He preferred working for Coltrane, and as long as the calls kept coming in, Spencer was a happy man.

# 13

## Layla

Layla Beauville was a fixture at La Bijoux, a lavish strip club even though it was located in one of the seedier areas of the French Quarter. An exceptionally beautiful Cajun with ebony skin, a shapely body and dark, exotic eyes, she entertained many regular customers and was one of the most popular and expensive prostitutes working out of La Bijoux.

The Cajun Mafia controlled the Quarter's red-light district, and the mainstream New Orleans community knew little of the culture of drugs, prostitution and illegal gambling that existed at La Bijoux. Behind closed doors, payoffs to cops and various licensing agents were common and business as usual was seldom interrupted.

In addition to his enforcer position with Lewis Coltrane, Spencer was a pimp. He'd turned out Layla when she'd made her way from Livonia, a small swamp town on the edge of the Atchafalaya Basin west of Baton Rouge, to the Big Easy. She was young, green, and vulnerable and she accepted Spencer's offer of protection mere minutes after she stepped off the bus at the Greyhound terminal at the dead end of Howard Avenue next to the expressway. Seven years later, Spencer considered Layla his property; he had no problem spending the money she made hooking and he expected her to be available to him at all times. This had occasionally caused problems for unfortunate johns who were in the midst of enjoying carnal pleasure with Layla when Spencer arrived unexpectedly at her flat. Annoyed by the presence of Layla's customers, he engaged in the foreplay of beating the unfortunate men to a pulp before throwing them out, and starting in on his manhandling of her.

On this night, though, Spencer entered La Bijoux in an unusually good mood. Coltrane had met him earlier in the day and paid him for the job at the Willows. It was a tidy sum and Spencer was ready to party.

The club was busy, the booths nearly filled with customers drinking and socializing with the girls. The chairs lined up along the stage were packed with men watching dancers, while others stood beside and behind the filled seats at the bar.

Spencer chatted for a moment with Dempsey and Virgil, the two bouncers on duty at the door. At 6'2" and 6'4", respectively, both men towered over Spencer. Numerous tattoos covered their bare arms and rippling muscles built up over years of pumping iron bulged underneath their T-shirts and jeans. Standing together, they made an intimidating pair.

Virgil was first to greet Spencer. "Spence, long time no see."

"Yeah, well, I've been busy," Spencer replied. "How's it going?"

"It's been slow. Only one fight so far tonight," Virgil grunted. "Some stupid dude accused one of the girls of stealing money off his table. Dempsey and I 'intervened,' if you know what I mean." Virgil punched Spencer playfully in the arm.

Spencer did his best to pretend it didn't hurt like hell. "So, how'd it turn out?" he asked. "Like I don't already know." For a split second, he considered returning the punch, but changed his mind. Virgil was an animal, not the kind of guy anybody with any sense wanted to mess with.

Virgil started shadowboxing in front of Spencer. His closed fists passed just close enough to Spencer's face to be too close. "We convinced him he was mistaken, right, Dempsey?" Virgil grinned and turned to face Dempsey, still shadowboxing, but nowhere near Dempsey's face.

Dempsey slapped Spencer on the back and laughed, revealing two gold front teeth and breath so foul it was a good bet he'd probably never owned a toothbrush. "We didn't hurt him bad, but he won't be back. We can't have our girls accused of stealing now, can we, Spencer, my good man?"

Dempsey and Virgil regularly roughed up customers and when fights broke out, as they did on a frequent basis, the results were always the same. In the end, it always worked out to the benefit of the club.

Neither Dempsey nor Virgil held the door when Spencer walked through it. Smoke from the fog machine floated across the stage, partially engulfing topless dancers grinding against poles. Others knelt in skimpy costumes, accepting tips from customers seated at stage level. The seating arrangement conveniently placed the men's faces inches from the dancers' private parts. Smoke billowed down over the stage to the floor of the club. It conveniently blocked the view, as lecherous fingers holding folded up bills found their way into the girls' G-strings, frequently lingering there.

*** 

When Layla spotted Spencer, she was among the crowd at the bar, entertaining a middle-aged balding customer, sitting near the far end of the long row of stools. She stood with her ample breasts pressed against the man's suit jacket. Her left hand moved slowly down his pants and between his legs. She stroked his stiffening cock while whispering tantalizing details of all the things she could do for him into his ear. Her tongue was busy sliding around his earlobe when she looked behind him and saw Spencer at the door. She pulled away from the man. A coy smile appeared on her face. She gave the man's cock a squeeze through his pants and promised to return after her turn onstage.

Layla walked slowly toward Spencer. She took her time, lingering between tables to stimulate customers. She slid her hands across their shoulders and allowed her breasts to brush against their backs as she passed by. She neared Spencer, her hips continuing to sway gracefully from side to side. The long white fringe skirt hanging from her hips swung loosely around her, providing peeks at her bare legs and buttocks. Her skimpy halter-top consisted of two tiny sequined triangles held on with thin strings tied at the neck and back, exposing all but her nipples, which she grasped through the tiny pieces of fabric, twisting them, as she cast a provocative glance at Spencer.

"Hi, baby. How's my sexy man?" Layla wrapped her long arms around him and kissed him. Her tongue probed inside his mouth.

"Dump that guy at the bar and get an early out. I just scored a bundle for a job and picked up some blow. I'm horny as hell and I want to party." Spencer reached under the hanging fringe and grabbed her firm ass with both hands. He dug his fingernails into her bare flesh and pressed himself against her. She winced, but said nothing. She looked at his dilated pupils and shuddered. He was already high. Spencer liked it rough and she recognized in his eyes the all-too-familiar look of an agitated man, lusting for violence and eager to inflict pain.

"Sure, baby. I'll let Jake know." Layla dared not question Spencer, especially when he was high on cocaine.

Jake was the boss. He didn't allow dancers to leave the club before their shift was over, even for the real business, for which he always got a big cut. He insisted they use the boudoir fantasy suites in the back and keep business with the johns in the club. However, in the case of Spencer and Layla, Jake made exceptions. Spencer performed favors when Jake needed things done, and it wasn't always easy to find someone to do the things Spencer was willing to do.

"He was here at the bar a minute ago," Layla said. "He must've gone to the office. I'll be right back." Layla left Spencer at the bar and headed for the back office located behind the bar and adjacent to the first fantasy suite.

She knocked on the door and entered. Jake was seated behind his desk, counting cash. Layla leaned across the desk, squeezing her breasts together with her forearms inches from his face, in his direct eyesight. "Boss, Spence is here." She leaned in closer. "He wants me to get an early out."

"He does, does he?" Jake replied. He leaned back in his chair. His eyes lingered on the view in front of him. "He wants a little Layla." He let out a lecherous laugh. "Can't blame him."

"You're such a charmer, boss," Layla teased, pursing her lips and blowing him a kiss. "Can I go?"

Jake was a burly black Cajun with a shaved head. Like Dempsey and Virgil, numerous tattoos covered his massive, muscular body. He'd owned La Bijoux since the unexpected death of Bernard, his brother and former owner of the club.

Jake had enjoyed minor success in the pro wrestling circuit, but suffered a bad back injury in a rough bout with Chief Jay Strongbow in Georgia a few years earlier. The injury ended his wrestling career.

After his injury, Jake went to work as a bouncer for his brother at La Bijoux. When he returned from a two-year stint upstate for aggravated assault on a customer, he figured his brother owed him something. He wanted to be a partner in the club. Bernard balked at the idea, so Jake took matters into his own hands.

After a few months of refusing to make his brother a partner in the club, Bernard suffered an unfortunate encounter with some thugs in an alley not far from La Bijoux. The "robbery" left Bernard dead in the alley, his throat slit and his pockets fleeced. The police spent minimal time investigating the murder, as incidents like Bernard's were common in that particular area of the Quarter. It didn't hurt that Jake had thrown Bernard's best girls and a few bucks at the cops investigating the crime. Shortly after, when Jake declared himself the new owner of the club, there was little fanfare and no questions asked.

"Go on, Layla. It's fine," Jake stated flatly. "But tell him, no bruises. I don't like to see bruises on my girls. It's bad for business. And send Gina over to that guy you were with at the bar before. We don't need no unhappy customers."

Layla did as Jake instructed, then slinked across the club and through the silver tinsel curtain behind the stage to the dressing room to change. She emerged a short time later, wearing an indecently low-cut skintight dress of gold stretch satin. It clung like a second skin to her body, revealing every curve and stopping just short of covering the bottom of her buttocks.

Spencer was sitting at the bar, drinking and watching the girls onstage. Layla's five-inch-high gold stiletto heels pushed her hips forward seductively as she walked toward him. All the girls at the club wore the same style shoe. They called them "fuck me pumps," for obvious reasons. Her long hair hung down across her face, partially covering her eyes. She looked out from underneath her silky locks at Spencer. She tossed her hair off her face and rolled her tongue across her lips as she slinked toward the bar.

Spencer pulled the vacant bar stool he'd been holding for Layla against his own. He wrapped his legs on either side.

Layla stopped in front of the stool. "How about a few more drinks before we go, baby?"

Spencer grabbed her by the waist and sat her down on the bar stool between his legs, pressing her tightly against his bulge. When he showed up at the club, looking for Layla, she always made the effort to sweet talk him into having a few more drinks before they left for her flat. Sometimes, if she got him drunk enough, what followed didn't last as long.

"This club's too noisy. I want to go back to your place now and fuck." Spencer tightened his arm around her waist and pulled her closer to him on the stool, rubbing his crotch against her. "I've got something special to give you."

She raised her arms over her head and reached behind him, running her long fingernails through his hair. "I know you do," she teased. She slid one hand down between their bodies and pressed her palm against his crotch. "I love what you've got, baby." Her banter was all part of a futile effort to get him turned on enough to play nice.

"Yeah, that, too, but I mean something else. I've got few gifts for you, baby. And don't think you aren't going to earn them." He started whispering obscenities into her ear. One hand moved lecherously over her breasts while the other lifted the gold stretch satin to expose her buttocks. His fingers slid between her legs. He grabbed the top of her inner thigh and squeezed hard.

It hurt like hell, but she released a small groan and pretended to like it.

He shoved his fist farther between her legs and lifted her off the stool. "Come on. Let's go."

***

Layla sat gingerly on the edge of the bed. Her long hair hung wet and matted around her face. Her body ached from the hours of violent sex she'd endured, as Spencer, too high on too much cocaine, failed repeatedly to come. He'd ravaged every inch of her body, violating her with increasingly fierce thrusts. In his drug-fueled mania, he'd snorted long lines of coke off her stomach and inner thighs, finishing with a few vicious bites that left her bruised, cut and bleeding.

Spencer's idea of foreplay was striking her, and squeezing her breasts until tears formed in her eyes. He insisted she assume his favorite position, kneeling naked on the bed with her knees spread, so he could mount her and enter from the rear. With his fingers digging into her waist, he would continue to ride her, with callous disregard for the pain he was causing, until he either came or opted for another, equally agonizing position.

The cocaine had made him brutally forceful. His fetish for using it to numb his cock prevented him from achieving orgasm, fueling his frustration and making him even more abusive. The encounter dragged on until he was finally satisfied and when the door to her flat closed behind him, Layla didn't have the strength to rise from the bed.

What was left of the cocaine remained laid out on a mirror on her dressing table. Beside it was the brush he'd given her as a gift when they first arrived at her apartment. It was inlaid with Mother of Pearl on the handle. It was gorgeous, and Spencer had bragged that it was expensive.

She could only imagine where it had come from, where he had stolen it. He'd used it repeatedly to spank her and the resulting welts and scratches made it painful to sit.

Layla fingered the pendant she wore around her neck. She'd gasped with delight when he first showed it to her. It was the most delicate and beautiful thing she'd ever seen, but when he directed her to sit down at her dressing table and squeezed his hands around her neck before clasping the necklace, she knew she was in for a bad time.

On the occasions Spencer gave her gifts before sex, there was always a very real possibility she might not live through the night. The more lavish the gift, the worse the abuse. The brush and the necklace were the finest gifts he'd ever given her and she'd paid dearly for them.

Layla often dreamed of running, of getting out of New Orleans and settling down in some small town like the one she'd grown up in, where she could get away from all the filth of La Bijoux and her life there. She knew in her heart that it would never happen. She was in too deep and knew too much. Jake would never let her leave—and even if she did, Spencer would track her down to the ends of the Earth.

Layla struggled to stand and began walking slowly to the dressing table. There was no sway in her hips or seductive swing of fringe between her legs now. She could barely put one foot in front of the other. She sat down at the dressing table and gazed at herself in the mirror. Looking through eyes without hope, her gaze left the bruised and swollen face in front of her and dropped down to the beautiful shell pendant on her neck. She leaned down, picked up a rolled-up hundred-dollar bill resting on the dressing table and snorted up the last lines of cocaine. Her nostrils burned as she welcomed the rush of numbness filling her head.

Layla returned to work a few nights later, after the swelling went down. She covered her face with make-up to cover the bruises. She drank until she felt no pain. She worked the poles and seduced her customers, praying that, with any luck, Spencer wouldn't be back for a while.

Most of her regular clients were harmless. Some of them were even tender. The nice ones were all married and the idea of leaving their proper lives and perfect families for a common prostitute was nothing more than fantasy.

They loved her sex all right, but not her.

No one loved her. For Layla, there was only one way out of La Bijoux. She would have to die, and it would probably be Spencer who would kill her.

# 14

## The Committee Visits Vegas

The top floor of the Sultan's Palace was a world unto itself. One floor below, luxurious penthouse suites housed high rollers, whatever superstar entertainer was appearing in the main showroom that week, various VIPs, political and otherwise, and the occasional visiting royalty.

The top floor was off limits to everyone but Benny and his friends and associates. It consisted of three huge suites. Two were nearly identical, reserved solely for Benny's Chicago partners and a short list of anonymous individuals whose services Benny required from time to time.

The third suite was Benny's. With the exception of the Chicago boys, Tony, and a handful of bodyguards and maids, no one saw the inside. It faced east, out onto the Strip. From the main living-room area, with its enormous floor-to-ceiling picture windows, Benny could see as far north as Silver City in North Vegas. The view south extended all the way to the Hacienda Hotel. The revolving Sultan marquee, Benny's pride and joy, turned directly below, at the entrance to the hotel.

The Sultan's Palace was completed three years before and the sign was the crowning glory of his new hotel-casino. After Sam McCormick saved his kid's life earlier that year, Benny showed his gratitude. Regal Sign Company was awarded the sign contract. From that point on, competitive bids on Palace property signs were a formality.

With Benny's influence and assistance, Sam's career had blossomed. Almost immediately after the accident, Sam received a promotion to salesman, and began closing sign deals.

Benny insisted that Sam oversee the construction of his Sultan. "You'll have total artistic control of the project, Sam," Benny promised. "I want the best artists and engineers in the business. I don't care what it costs."

Regal exceeded Benny's wildest expectations with the creation of the Sultan. Benny sometimes spent hours sitting in his leather chair, smoking his Cuban cigars, watching it turn. It was his favorite place to think, undisturbed by the outside world. With the sign revolving slowly and powerfully, and the Sultan's crossed swords clearly in his view, he'd made many of his most important decisions.

As Sam and Tony made their way to valet, Benny sat in the surveillance room in his suite, focusing his attention on the large TV screen on the wall in front of him. The room was located beyond the master bedroom and spa, nearest to the doors to the helicopter access on the roof. Benny checked one camera after another, until he'd run through the series of eight cameras recently installed in various locations in the penthouse suite below. Each strategically aimed camera served the same purpose in a different location—to give Benny audio and video access to the monitored area.

Once the camera check was complete, Benny slid the control board forward, concealing it within the massive oak desk. He pushed a button on a side panel by his right hand and the TV screen silently revolved 180 degrees into the wall. On the opposite side hung a priceless nineteenth-century Van Gogh Benny had purchased in Italy, strictly for the purpose of concealing the screen.

Under normal circumstances, only a few hidden cameras monitored the penthouse suites, but with the arrival of Sam's group of guests, Benny's instincts kicked in. He questioned Sam. "Just how much do you know about these men?"

"Well, they're mostly politicians and lawyers. They oversee just about every aspect of the Arena project and they'll decide who'll be building the sign."

"I see." Benny raised a skeptical eyebrow, concerned the kid could be in over his head. In order to protect him, Benny set up surveillance to learn about the group.

Information was insurance, and Benny believed in insurance.

***

Regal's private jet arrived at McCarran Airport at 4 p.m.

Charlotte Lennon, the head of public relations for the Sultan's Palace, exited the Sultan's Palace stretch limousine. She routinely met VIPs arriving at the Palace and catered to their needs during their stay the hotel. But Benny had been uncharacteristically present during preparations for the visit, a clear sign to all that he expected nothing less than absolute perfection.

Clyde coordinated the flight plans out of New Orleans and, upon their arrival in Las Vegas, Ms. Lennon greeted the committee at McCarran Airport. She escorted them to the Sultan's Palace stretch limo, where chilled champagne awaited them, along with caviar and other succulent appetizers.

Charlotte entertained her guests during the ride to the Sultan's Palace with a detailed tour up the Strip. The magic of a fully illuminated Strip would follow later in the evening, as planned.

***

Sam and Tony were waiting at valet when the limo pulled up. A group of four parking attendants opened the limo doors and assisted the arriving guests. During the initial phases of the casino's construction, architects designed an ornate marble porte-cochere. The purpose of the grandiose entrance was to delight guests upon their arrival. From the expressions on the faces of the men as they emerged from the limo, Tony knew it succeeded.

As the group gathered under the porte-cochere, Tony spotted a pair of long, shapely legs stretching out of the limo. He rushed over to the limo and extended his hand. "Allow me to assist you, miss."

Jamaica leaned forward and glanced up at him.

The sight of her left him speechless, but the expression on his face said it all. *My God. What a beautiful woman.*

"Thank you," she replied. She took his hand and rose from the limo.

He followed behind her, eyeing her from head to foot, as she joined the rest of the group.

Once everyone was assembled, Sam addressed the group. "Welcome to Las Vegas. I trust you had a pleasant flight from New Orleans."

Tony stood next to Sam. "May I introduce Tony DeLuca? Tony is the son of Benny DeLuca, owner of the Sultan's Palace and one of your hosts during your stay here at the Sultan's Palace."

Sam gave him a subtle tug. "Tony, this is Mr. Coltrane, chairman of the Arena committee."

Tony pulled his gaze away from Jamaica. "It's a pleasure to meet you, Mr. Coltrane, and your group."

Lewis introduced the remaining members of his entourage, identifying Jamaica last. "This is Miss Jamaica Russe, soon to be the newest member of my firm."

Tony stepped forward. "Miss Russe, I'm delighted to welcome you to the Palace."

Jamaica once again extended her hand. "Thank you for your hospitality, Mr. DeLuca. We were all quite impressed with the tour of your Strip."

"That's good news, Miss Russe," Tony replied, though sadness was written all over her face. Something was troubling this girl. "Mr. McCormick has quite a visit planned for you all."

Sam took the cue. "Miss Lennon will direct you to your accommodations in our penthouse suites. We've prepared a separate suite for you, Miss Russe, on the same floor as the gentlemen in your group. I hope you'll find it to your satisfaction." He gestured to Charlotte, who was standing to his left. "Miss Lennon will address any needs you may have during your stay."

"Yes," Tony added. "Please don't hesitate to ask for anything." His eyes remained locked on Jamaica. "I look forward to seeing you all later." Tony bowed in a cordial farewell to the group, and walked back into the Sultan's Palace.

Sam assisted Charlotte in escorting the group to their perspective suites. He informed them of the evening's planned events. "The Navaros have planned a reception in your honor before dinner. Miss Lennon will come up at six p.m. to escort you to the reception. Once again, welcome and see you at six."

*** 

Las Vegas restaurants were internationally recognized as among the most opulent in the world. The Flying Carpet inside the Sultan's Palace ranked among the finest. Following the reception, a full evening of wining, dining and entertainment lay ahead for the group. The hotel's gourmet chefs assured Lou Navaro that no minute detail had been overlooked.

The cocktail reception took place in the one of the penthouse suites facing the Strip. Lou and Jon greeted the guests, introducing themselves as the owners of Regal Sign Company.

The Sultan marquee towered outside the penthouse's massive three-story windows, fully illuminating in all its glory at sunset, shortly after the guests arrived. The sign revolved gracefully, shining down on the Strip, and dwarfing several nearby hotels and casinos. "I've never seen anything remotely like it," Lewis commented. "Having it turn like that. Ingenious."

Lou smiled. "Ingenuity is one of our strong suits, Mr. Coltrane."

A sign presentation set up by Lou and Jon rested extended the length of one wall of the suite. An easel, showcasing a color rendering of the sign Regal had designed for the Arena, sat prominently in the center of the presentation. It was surrounded by other Regal sign renderings and photos.

"May I have your attention, everyone?" Lou clinked a cocktail fork against his champagne glass. "Jon and I are honored to present this rendering of the sign we have designed for your Arena, as a gift to the committee. Please accept it, along with our thanks to you for making the trip all the way to Las Vegas."

Jon stepped forward and lifted the rendering from the easel. He handed it to a smiling Lewis Coltrane.

Cocktail hour resumed. Attractive hostesses attired in elegant evening gowns mingled among the guests, offering glasses of champagne and a variety of exotic appetizers on silver trays. Handsome bartenders in crisp tuxedos served top shelf liquors from behind a massive marble bar. Champagne flowed freely.

Lou watched, amused, as Lewis Coltrane took a glass of champagne from the tray of a passing hostess. After he finished undressing her with his eyes, he turned to Lou. "I've heard rumors that Las Vegas showgirls are the most beautiful women in the world. Is that true?"

Coltrane's question drew a hearty pat on the back from Lou. "The lovely ladies from the Sultan's Palace spectacular show will be joining us for dinner. You can decide for yourself." Lou winked at Lewis. "I'm confident you'll be charmed." He turned to face the rest of the group. "For anyone who wishes to attend the performance this evening after dinner, I've arranged for you to be seated in Mr. DeLuca's personal VIP booth, on King's Row."

Lewis offered a lascivious look of approval.

Lou returned a sly look of his own. "Of course, the Palace has other sources of entertainment at your disposal, as well. You may wish to try your luck at the tables." He raised his arm in a sweeping gesture that encompassed all the services provided in the suite. "This is a night for pleasure, gentlemen. Business can wait until tomorrow. You've flown here to experience all Las Vegas has to offer, and I guarantee you'll not be disappointed."

***

Jamaica stood alone by the penthouse windows, trying—unsuccessfully—not to listen to the conversation. When she saw Sam McCormick approaching her, she steeled herself for small talk.

Sam's voice was low in a mild apology, downplaying the lecherous comments she had overheard. "Please don't judge us too harshly this evening, Miss Russe. Las Vegas is a vibrant city. It provides a wide range of entertainment to suit different tastes." He paused. "But the product my company offers is truly the finest anywhere." He gestured out to the street below. "Evidence of that is abundant here on the Strip."

"I believe you, and I'll try to keep an open mind," Jamaica replied. "I'm by no means naïve, Mr. McCormick. I expect members of my group will take full advantage of this trip, on a variety of levels." She pointed across the room to the collection of sign renderings. "Perhaps you could elaborate on these various projects?"

"That would be my pleasure," Sam replied.

As Sam described the details of each rendering, Jamaica reflected on the purpose of the visit. Dealing with Lily's death had been the most traumatic ordeal of her life, even more than her birth. But Lewis, Catherine, even Clarice had insisted the trip would do her good. After meeting Tony and now listening to Sam extol the virtues of large signs, she began to believe that it made sense. She was about to become a member of the Coltrane Law Firm. The trip was providing her an excellent opportunity to witness the Coltranes' professional prowess firsthand, and to observe the behavior of her group, free from the controlled conduct they employed as public figures in New Orleans.

# 15

## The Fun Begins

Sam had it planned down to the smallest detail. He watched in satisfaction as the Navaros led the entourage from the penthouse reception to The Flying Carpet restaurant on the main casino floor. Sam and his staff had laid out the seating arrangements for the evening's dinner. A handful of casino executives were strategically seated among the New Orleans group. Showgirls from the Sultan's Palace main show were sprinkled among the men. Lewis Coltrane sat between Lou and Jon Navaro at the head of the table and Sam situated Jamaica between himself and Tony.

The festivities began when the music started and a bevy of females in sexy harem costumes appeared. The veiled beauties carried overflowing trays of grapes, which they hand-fed to male guests, while they belly-danced in front of them around the table.

Sam stood nearby as Lewis stretched his neck back and opened his mouth to pluck a grape from the cluster being dangled enticingly over his head. "You were right about Las Vegas women, Lou," he said, watching the young woman swirl away from him.

"Just a taste of what's to come," Lou replied.

As more servers appeared, each new course grew more elaborate than the one before, and wine and conversation continued to flow freely throughout the dinner.

Just prior to the dessert course, heads turned when Benny, surrounded by bodyguards, entered the restaurant and made a flamboyant unannounced visit to the group.

Sam had also scheduled the strategic timing of the visit with Benny and rose to acknowledge him. "Allow me to introduce Benjamin DeLuca, owner of the Sultan's Palace."

The showgirls seated at the table blew kisses and waved at their boss, while the rest of the guests looked on. Benny lifted his hands in feigned embarrassment, but his amused smile, and the protective looks on the faces of his bodyguards, painted a clear picture of a formidable man, comfortable in his element.

"Mr. DeLuca chose Regal to build his magnificent Sultan marquee, and he has graciously offered a tour of the inner workings of the sign. Those of you brave enough for a climb will see firsthand the inside composition of one of Regal's proudest achievements."

Benny nodded.

Sam looked across the table at Bonner. "It's sure to interest you, Bobby, and some of the other gentlemen as well." Sam turned his attention back to Benny. "Thank you, Mr. DeLuca, for your hospitality, and for sharing your beautiful property with us."

Tony raised his glass and gestured to the table to do the same. "I propose a toast to my dad, the Sultan himself." The toast invoked applause from the entire table.

Benny gestured for the group to stop, smiling as he spoke, "You're all welcome guests. My Palace is your palace during your stay and my staff is at your service. I wish you all a pleasant evening."

Sam saw Lewis Coltrane making eye contact with Benny. The two men gave each other a respectful nod. The gesture spoke volumes.

A man like Benny DeLuca always made a strong impression on other powerful men. The good old boys from New Orleans were no exception. Power recognized power and the electricity building during dinner confirmed that the evening had taken on a powerful life of its own.

Benny left the restaurant, flanked by his two bodyguards, and Sam took his seat just as Tony turned to Jamaica. "Would you allow me to escort you to the show this evening? I assure you, it's very entertaining, and quite tasteful."

"That would be lovely, Mr. DeLuca."

"Call me Tony, please, Miss Russe."

"Then, Tony, you must call me Jamaica. And "I'm looking forward to seeing the show."

Dinner was winding down when Bobby Bonner rose from his chair. "I'm ready to see the inside of that marquee."

Any other takers?" Jon Navaro asked.

"I want to see it," Mayor Riley said.

Max DiAngelis confirmed as well.

Sam rose from his chair. "Gentlemen, take your time finishing up with dessert. We'll meet in twenty minutes in the lobby to begin Jon's tour of the marquee."

\*\*\*

Lewis gave Max a surreptitious thumbs-up. Earlier, Lewis asked Max to keep the mayor out of the suite for a few hours after dinner ended. Upon learning why, Max had agreed, telling Lewis, "You owe me one."

Lewis sat with Lou, quietly discussing plans for the rest of the evening. The conversation consisted of only a few whispered comments.

"As I mentioned at the reception, I suggest your evening's activities continue," Lou began, "in a more private setting, where you can *fully* enjoy the many amenities the suite has to offer." Lou assured Lewis he would make the necessary arrangements for an unforgettable evening.

"Remember, Mr. Coltrane, Las Vegas is a twenty-four hour town. There'll be plenty of time to explore the Strip, but only after exploring the more 'intimate' areas. Don't you agree?"

"Absolutely, Mr. Navaro."

"Please, call me Lou." Navaro cast him a wicked grin.

Lewis grinned back.

***

Bonner, Riley and DiAngelis stood under the porte-cochere outside the hotel entrance, looking up at the Sultan turning in front of them, 250 feet away. Light emanated from the huge letters spelling out *Sultan's Palace.* They cast a brilliant glow into the night sky, only to be surpassed by the brilliance of the Sultan himself, as he slowly turned, looking out majestically over the city.

"Ready, gentlemen?" Sam asked.

Jon began leading the group. When they reached the base, the mayor, Bonner, and DiAngelis wrenched their necks upward. They were dwarfed by the massive structure looming overhead.

"By God, Jon, this sign is huge. How do you get into this thing?" Mayor Riley asked, looking up at the sign, as if harboring second thoughts about going farther.

"Sam, show them the door." Jon said. "It's not all that complicated, Mr. Mayor. Not yet, anyway."

Sam walked to the back pylon and pushed on a section of the sign, opening a concealed door and a vertical ladder inside. He gestured to the group, "Be aware, gentlemen, it's a long climb to the top. We'll take it in sections." He pointed up. "That first section above us is the reader board. It's only a thirty-foot climb to the platform, and not too high, I think, for all of us."

The group awaited instruction.

Sam continued, "Jon, will you please lead? Mr. Bonner, if you'd follow Jon, then Mr. DiAngelis and Mayor Riley. Take your time, and watch your footing."

Jon led the group up the ladder while Sam followed in the rear, as a safety precaution. The men in front of Mayor Riley made it up onto the platform inside the reader board, when the mayor lost his footing and missed a rung. Sam was following close behind and steadied the mayor, encouraging him on, up onto the platform.

Once they were all safely inside, Jon spoke. "You're now inside the reader board, gentlemen. It's seventy feet long, forty feet tall and eighteen feet wide. We're now standing at thirty feet up." He pointed up. "The top of this cabinet rests seventy feet in the air."

"It's as bright in here as it is outside," the mayor commented. "And hot, too. And what's making that noise?" he asked.

"What you're hearing are the fans running," Jon explained. "They circulate the air to cool the electrical equipment functioning inside this cabinet. If we stayed in here too long without those fans working, we'd all be burnt to a crisp."

By the look on Riley's face, Sam surmised the mayor had gone as high as he was going to. "Gentlemen, let me caution you. The climb is another fifty feet to the base of the Sultan's Palace lettering, and that's after we climb the forty feet to the top of this board. It's important you understand that this sign is constructed to the highest professional standards, using only the best materials available in the industry. Its physical integrity is without question, but if anyone prefers not to continue, Jon and I certainly understand." He studied the men's faces.

Bonner was grinning.

Sam offered a graceful way out to the others. "Not many people are comfortable this high and in such a confined space. But if anyone's game, the Sultan's lettering is the next section and the inside is something quite remarkable."

"This is as far as I go," the mayor responded.

Max DiAngelis agreed. "Me, too. I can feel this sign moving. Maybe I had too much to drink at dinner."

Jon laughed. "The sign is always moving, Mr. DiAngelis. Fortunately, this evening the winds are calm. We wouldn't be taking this tour if they weren't."

Sam turned to Bobby. "Bobby, what do you think?"

"Let's keep going. I want to see more."

Mayor Riley loosened his tie and opened the top button of his shirt. "Since we've made it this far, I'd like to know more about all these lights. Maybe you can enlighten us, Jon, no pun intended." He laughed at his own joke.

Jon explained the inner mechanics of the reader board. "On the face in front of you, are five rows of neon lamps in sets of six. Each set has its own ballast. Ballasts are transformers that convert voltage to power the lamps. There are one hundred-twenty of them in this section alone. There are seven-hundred lamps illuminating the two faces of the board, three hundred-fifty on each side."

Mayor Riley held on to the wall of the enclosure for balance. "Well, I'm totally confused, Jon. But damned impressed." He looked up. "Bonner may want to climb to the thin air at the top of your sign, but personally I've seen enough." He gestured to Max. "I think Max and I'll be safer back on the ground."

The three men laughed. Jon complimented the two men. "You've been good sports. Let's get you two out of here. Our next stop is the Harem Lounge." He saw looks of relief appear. "You both deserve a couple of drinks…on the house, of course."

Sam said, "Thanks for assisting the mayor and Mr. DiAngelis, Jon, while Bobby and I continue up."

Bobby returned to the ladder and resumed the climb, with Sam following close behind him. When Bonner reached the top of the reader board, he pushed open the door on the roof and looked back at Sam.

"It's only a fifteen-foot climb up to the next door, Bobby," Sam called up. "Are you game?"

Bobby popped his head out of the open door and looked up at the Sultan's Palace letters above him. "Holy shit, man, you're a brave son of a bitch. We're not even half way up this monster. Hell, yes, let's keep going!"

"OK. Same drill when you reach the next door. Open it and go on inside. I'm right behind you."

The two men resumed the climb. Once inside the huge metal structure, Bobby asked about the magenta glow of light surrounding them.

"The blue lights inside the red neon letters create the color effect! The letters spelling out the Sultan's Palace stand twenty-two feet high and span the panels on both sides of the marquee!"

"I can barely hear you!" Bobby shouted over the deafening noise.

"Hear those motors, Bobby? The clacking you hear is the mechanical flashers controlling the lighting sequence on the Sultan's letters!" Sam yelled over the sound.

"How do you communicate up here with all this noise?" Bobby yelled back.

"We use hand signals!" Sam gestured one finger pointing up, then one pointing down. "Do you want to go farther? This one's thirty feet high, then it's fifteen more to the boots of the Sultan!"

Bonner grinned and gave Sam a thumbs-up. Sam grinned back, shaking his finger back and forth, playfully correcting Bobby by pointing up with his finger, and signaling for Bobby to continue.

Bobby and Sam climbed the 30 feet to the top of the sign cabinet and exited the pylon. They stood on the roof of the Sultan's lettering. Bobby held onto a ladder rung as he looked down at the traffic, over 100 feet below. To Sam, it looked like tiny trails of ants, moving up and down the Strip.

Sam stood by while Bobby wrenched his head back to see the boots of the Sultan, 15 feet above, and then farther up, the Sultan himself. He saw the Sultan's neon blades crossed in front of his chest as the massive figure slowly revolved against the night sky.

"That's one hell of a sight, Sam, but I think I'll stop here," Bobby said. "You really are one crazy son of a bitch. I could never work this high, exposed like this."

"You made it up farther than anyone else who's not an experienced sign climber. Very few have stood where you're standing." He pointed up at the Sultan. "You're looking at thirty-five tons revolving up there. At the base of the Sultan's feet, there's a switch that turns the rotator off. We climb through another door to get inside, then we turn him back on, so we can do maintenance and change out brushes."

Bobby nodded his head in understanding. "This climb's just confirmed what I already suspected, Sam. We're cut from the same cloth."

"Yes, we are. Tomorrow when we visit the factory, I'll explain the inside mechanics of the Sultan and how he turns."

Bobby gripped the ladder rung and looked again at the Strip below. "You only made one mistake on his sign, Sam. It's missing one thing."

"What's that, Bobby?" Sam asked.

Bobby grinned. "An elevator!"

# 16

## Surveillance

Benny sat in his big leather chair, milling through files and waiting for the activities to begin. Laid out on the desk in front of him were detailed reports on each member of the New Orleans group.

The reports were a part of the promise he'd made to protect Sam, a promise that now encompassed knowing the players in the proposed Regal sign deal. He'd already sized up the group, prior to receiving the reports. However, the information gathered by his sources that now covered his desk proved his initial assessment to be blatantly insufficient.

The first report was on Bonner. The file revealed that Bonner was a man who'd built things, among them, a healthy disrespect for politicians. Bonner's mob connections came as no big surprise to Benny. It was impossible to be a union man in a place like New Orleans, battling bureaucracy and politics, without being forced to make some tough decisions. Benny, of all people, understood that. In his opinion, from the facts spread out in front of him, Bonner hadn't crossed any serious ethical lines.

Benny picked up another report and sighed. "Certainly not like some of these others."

He stared down at pages of instances of impropriety. With the exception of the girl, the whole group had skeletons, with some of the players worse than others. Coltrane and his partner, DiAngelis, appeared to be the worst. Coltrane's firm made a mockery of the practice of law.

Jimmy, the son, appeared to be the reluctant heir apparent to his old man's legacy of land wealth and dirty political maneuvering. Benny would've felt sorry for the boy, but Benny's mantra, that every man made his own choices, applied to everyone. In Jimmy, he saw a kid who lacked character and was bound to eventually be as bad as his old man.

The reports on the mayor and the city commissioner were more forgiving, although both men were beholden to Coltrane in some way. Pages of newspaper clippings revealed the mayor's relentless obsession with basking in the public spotlight back home in New Orleans. He embellished the truth and exaggerated his accomplishments as a public servant. He boasted to the press about being the best and most honest mayor the city had ever had, but he was, in truth, a braggart, a character flaw Coltrane exploited. He was a small fish in a big pond

Dirt on the city commissioner focused on payoffs received for favors. They came primarily in the form of votes at Commission meetings and preferential treatment in scheduling items on the agenda. The latter was often at the insistence of Coltrane himself. Enough inappropriate and unethical behavior was going on under Coltrane's watchful eye to keep the commissioner firmly under Coltrane's control.

But the report on Coltrane himself was a classic. His actions equaled that of the most ruthless politicians and gangsters in Las Vegas. There were more than a few in town like Coltrane, and Benny had learned to coexist with them.

However, the characters in the rogues' gallery laid out in front of him were from out of town and Benny's job was to gain enough knowledge about them to keep Sam from falling into any of their traps.

The express elevator to the Casbah Suite had begun to rise and Benny turned his attention to the multi-screen monitor on his desk. He gathered up the folders and shoved them into a desk drawer, a grim look on his face. He turned up the volume and focused his attention on the screens monitoring the suite.

When subjected to Benny's watchful eye, secrets rarely remained secrets for long. And he never hesitated to use the many methods available to him to uncover the truth.

If it meant finding out where the bodies were buried, or burying some himself, then so be it.

\*\*\*

Benny took a few casual puffs on his cigar. He watched on the screen as the two Coltranes exited the express elevator and entered the massive Casbah Suite.

The suite had numerous bedrooms, with ample room to accommodate all six of the men in its various wings.

Jimmy and Lewis had adjacent bedrooms, situated across the hall from each other in the left wing on the second floor of the penthouse. The bedrooms shared a common lounge and sitting room area. DiAngelis and City Commissioner Bryant were located on the second floor of the right wing, and Bonner and Mayor Riley were located on the first floor of the left wing. Circular staircases on each side of the main living room area of the penthouse led to the second floor of each of the wings. Double doors provided private access to each of the four wings.

When the elevator door closed, Benny settled back to watch the show.

Lewis and Jimmy entered the suite and proceeded up the stairs to the left wing's common lounge area, located between the bedrooms.

"Let's have a quick drink before the hookers get here, Jimmy. I'm ready to party." Lewis sat down at the bar. "Did you see the tits on that blonde sitting across from the senator? I hope Navaro sends that sweet piece of ass up."

Benny watched closely as Jimmy didn't respond. He was already at the bar, pouring himself a double.

Lewis lit into him. "What the fuck is wrong with you, boy? You were goddamned moody at dinner and now you're really pissing me off. We're about to get the best pussy in Las Vegas and you're still pining over your jailbait back home." He grunted. "At least show your old man some gratitude."

Benny jotted "Jailbait" on a pad on his desk.

Lewis sighed and fell back into an oversized lounge chair beside the bar. "You're damned lucky you didn't get caught, the way you were carrying on. Can you imagine what would've happened if Catherine found out?   He shook his head in disgust. "It's time you pulled yourself together and grew some balls. Now pour me a drink and let's get ready to party."

Jimmy poured his father a drink. He left it on the bar and started for his bedroom.

"Where do you think you're going? You're a Coltrane, goddamn it. Act like one."

Jimmy turned to face his father. "What do you want from me?"

"I want your full attention during this trip. There's a lot of money riding on this contract. We can skim thousands off the top of this project." Lewis pointed to an adjacent chair. "Sit down. We need to talk."

Jimmy sat down. "Fine. Talk."

Lewis leaned forward in his chair. "Listen to me, son. This visit is already paying off. I had a nice, quiet chat with Lou Navaro over dinner and he's game to be *creative* with invoices. We can pad the shit out of material costs and skim a fortune off this sign contract alone. Bryant has the building department in our pocket. We'll throw work to the businesses willing to play ball. The senator won't be a problem. He spends most of his time up in Washington. When he's back home in New Orleans, all you and Max do is show him the right set of books." He paused and looked at Jimmy.

He was staring down at his drink.

"Are you listening?"

"Yeah, go on."

"I can handle the mayor. He's flattered I selected him for the committee, so we just keep him parading around in the public eye. He'll be so busy peacocking for the press, he'll be clueless to what we're doing."

Benny watched closely as Jimmy rose and poured himself a stiff refill. "What about Bonner?"

Lewis frowned. "It's going to be tricky working with Bonner. I sure as hell don't want another visit from those Cajun thugs he calls friends. And we're going to have to be damned smart, dancing around his union."

Lewis downed his drink. He waved the glass at Jimmy. "Get me another one. And there's that son of a bitch, Stein. I'm going to need you to find ways to keep Stein distracted, and Keetz, too, when he's in town. They're a couple of boy scouts, both of them. And it doesn't help that they're good friends, too. Thank God Keetz spends most of his time in Washington."

Jimmy handed the refilled glass to Lewis. He sat down and stared at the floor.

Lewis flicked his hand in the air. "Are you listening? Forget about your girlfriend. You're better off without her."

"Just stop talking about her, Dad!" Jimmy looked up. "You can count on me. Just stop talking about her."

"Relax, son. You just need to get laid. You'll feel better after you get some pussy."

Benny knew that the elevator was about to reach the penthouse, so he wasn't surprised when the conversation was interrupted.

"Is that you two up there?" Commissioner Bryant called up from the bottom of the stairs. "Come on down. The girls should be coming up shortly."

Lewis walked to the top of the stairs and looked over the railing. "We'll be down in a second."

He turned to his son. "Come on, Jimmy. This is Las Vegas and you're a Coltrane. Let's get dirty."

\*\*\*

Benny rummaged through the newspaper articles in the piles of information laid out in front of him. "Where is it?" he mumbled. Somewhere in the articles he'd read something about bribes to the building department that had a connection to Coltrane.

Benny had paid little attention to the details at first, because they hadn't seemed important at the time. But the conversation between the two Coltranes, referring to the mob in New Orleans, changed his mind. He made a mental note to check it out further, once the group returned to New Orleans.

Benny listened with growing interest to the conversation among the three men sitting in the suite's main living room. He checked the tape recorders assigned to the area to ensure they were recording every word. Coltrane was planning to juggle his interests, without stepping on the toes of the New Orleans syndicate, and the devil would be in the details. It was information Benny wanted.

When the call girls arrived at the suite, Benny left the cameras and tapes rolling and started down to the casino. Sex was sex and served as potential blackmail material, but what he had learned so far from the conversations was already proving more valuable.

He left the suite and headed to the pit. Busy nights attracted crossroaders to the tables and slots, players attempting to cheat the casino. Nobody got away with cheating. Not at the Sultan's Palace. And security would give the bum's rush to card counters after surveillance picked them off.

Benny exited the elevator, where he was flanked by his two bodyguards. He entered the casino, smiling to see it packed. The poker tables were occupied with gamblers, and the bars, restaurants and lounges were filled with tourists crowding in to eat, drink and listen to music.

Benny strolled among the crowd, through the rows of players trying their luck at the slot machines. Players at the crap tables cheered or groaned with each toss of the dice. Serious high rollers in the baccarat room sipped on martinis and smoked cigars, while wagering thousands of dollars on each round of cards.

Pit bosses acknowledged Benny as he passed by, confirming with a nod that play was going well in each of their designated areas. The casino in the Sultan's Palace was a well-oiled machine. Behind all the noise, glamour and excitement in the forefront, a complex engine was running the show.

Benny headed for the executive offices, and his private entrance to the eye in the sky, where an army of watchful eyes saw it all.

***

Couples adorned in expensive suits and designer gowns strolled up the staircase to the entrance of the showroom.

In keeping with the strict dress code for attendees of the *Sultan's Palace Spectacular*, all male showroom employees wore tuxes. Shapely cocktail waitresses donned in elaborate harem costumes strolled among the guests.

Tony, decked out in a Christian Dior tuxedo, drew stares from admiring couples, as he guided a radiant Jamaica through the casino and up the stairs to the showroom entrance.

The maître d' was standing at the roped-off VIP guest entrance, to the left of the regular showroom line. "Good evening, Mr. DeLuca. It's a pleasure to see you this evening." He smiled at Jamaica. "Who is this lovely young lady?"

"This is Miss Jamaica Russe. She's here with a special group from New Orleans, visiting Las Vegas for the first time."

Jamaica was a vision in a backless purple silk gown. Her black hair cascaded down over her golden skin and she wore no jewelry, with the exception of her shell pendant and pearl stud earrings. She smiled at Vincent.

He smiled back. "This must be a special occasion, Miss Russe. Mr. DeLuca rarely reserves his father's booth. He generally prefers to watch from the private VIP box upstairs, should he need to leave before the show ends." Vincent bowed slightly. "You must be a very special guest, indeed."

"She certainly is," Tony said, taking Jamaica's arm. "Shall we, Vincent?"

"Yes, of course." Vincent pointed his flashlight onto the stairs leading down into the showroom. "Allow me to escort you to your booth. The performance will begin shortly."

As Vincent led them down to the VIP booth, Jamaica said, "I've never seen such an enormous showroom curtain."

Once they were seated, she continued, "I've been to many shows in New York, from Broadway to the Metropolitan Opera House, but that curtain is unlike anything I've seen before."

"That curtain is a recent addition to our showroom. It consists of hundreds of yards of velvet, with thousands of tiny fibre optic lights sewn into the fabric." He pointed to the curtain. "Do you see how the color patterns are constantly changing?"

"Yes, it's lovely."

"A computer board backstage controls all the colors and the fluctuating patterns of the lights."

A perky cocktail waitress approached the booth with a bucket of champagne and two crystal flutes. Hundreds of tiny coins covering her bust and hip area jingled as she moved. Sheer black chiffon, embellished with tiny crystals, draped over her legs and tied at her ankles. A sheer veil, beginning just below her eyes, masked her face.

"Good evening, Mr. DeLuca, Miss." She set the bucket, napkins and glasses on the table. She pulled the bottle out of the ice and presented it to Tony before opening it.

Tony examined the bottle of Dom Pérignon. "I hope you like Champagne, Miss Russe."

"Tony, it's Jamaica." She smiled back at him, gently touching his shoulder. "And yes, I love Champagne."

*** 

Jamaica lifted the crystal flute to her lips. The bubbles rising from her glass popped playfully against her nose as she sipped her champagne. The lights dimmed and the orchestra began playing. She absently fingered her pendant, and her thoughts drifted to Lily.

Lily's necklace was nowhere to be found among her personal effects at the Estate, and after a thorough search of the Estate grounds, the necklace remained missing. The groundskeepers emptied the pool in the hope of finding it stuck in one of the drains, but it wasn't there.

Jamaica released the pendant and sighed. Lily's missing necklace was a reminder of how easily the things she loved in life seemed to disappear.

The swell of the orchestra filled the room and the house lights faded to black. Thoughts of the necklace faded with them as the curtain rose. The stage came alive in an explosion of light and color. Beautiful women donned in vibrant, feathered costumes moved gracefully across the stage. Jamaica watched, as rows of dancers in elaborate, feathered wings ascended an enormous staircase showered in scintillating lights.

Spellbound by the spectacle on the stage, she felt a strange, yet familiar sensation, a moment of déjà vu. It was if she had been magically transported back to her island home, to watch hundreds of birds taking flight, their wings fluttering as they ascended in a kaleidoscope of color, against a backdrop of sparkling stars.

"Beautiful," she said, looking over at Tony.

He looked into her eyes. "Yes, you are."

\*\*\*

Benny watched via live video feed as the New Orleans group prepared to enter the limo and begin their trip back to New Orleans.

Lewis Coltrane and Max DiAngelis stopped a few yards away from the limo. Lewis turned to address Jon, Lou and Sam. "Gentlemen, I'm pleased to tell you that the committee has chosen Regal for the job." He directed his next comment to Sam. "Cal Sign Company also bid on this project, but the tour of your factory closed the deal."

"I'm happy to hear that," Sam replied.

"Their bid was lower than yours, so it will come as an unpleasant surprise to them that we've chosen you." Lewis paused, and nodded at Max.

"Gentlemen," Max spoke on cue, "as we discussed this morning, prints, structural-safety issues and permit details must be reviewed by the New Orleans building department. The interior signs will have to be approved by a structural engineer certified by the state, as well as Bonner Construction, before any money can be exchanged. Finally, you must carry a construction license from Jefferson Parish in order to obtain permits to build, so you must own or be affiliated with a licensed construction company in the Parish."

Lewis stepped in. "This is normal procedure, and I anticipate no problems." He placed a hand on Max's shoulder. "As discussed, Mr. DiAngelis will be our liaison, in charge of coordinating all legal and financial matters with you as these permits, purchases, etc. develop."

Jon, Lou and Sam shook hands with both men and continued with them to the open limo doors.

As Lewis entered the limo, Benny heard him say, "And Lou, thank you for 'showing us the sights'." A cagy look appeared on his face. "We'll have to return the hospitality when you visit us in New Orleans."

Benny, along with Sam and the Navaros, watched as the limo departed for the Regal jet, and the committee's flight back home.

Jon walked beside Sam, toward the casino. "Bringing them to Las Vegas was a good move. This is a beautiful bear of a project." He turned to his brother. "You know it could make or break the company."

Lou shrugged. "We'll be fine. You worry too much."

"Maybe," Jon said. "But we've got work to do. Sam, I want blueprints and specs drawn up, ASAP. And send Clyde back down to New Orleans to find us a construction company. Tell him to buy one, if he has to."

Benny watched it all unfold on the screens in his surveillance room.

# 17

## Adjustments

Adjustments and refinements on the sign structure design began immediately. The structural engineers started first with the issue of the softness of New Orleans marshland. "Any ideas?" Sam began.

Dave Crane, Regal's head structural engineer spoke up. "In order to ensure the safety of the footings, we have to exceed normal structural requirements. The pylons will still go down a hundred eighty feet, but by my calculations, each pylon will have to be set in a bedrock base. I'd say, fifty feet in diameter and a good thirty feet deep for the sign to rest safely."

"How much concrete are we talking about?"

Dave picked up his calculator. "We're looking at pouring eight hundred yards of concrete. We'll have to use number-four rebar to tie the pylons to the steel to hold the sign."

It wasn't good news. The changes would require extensive labor, as well as additional material. The cost was going to exceed what was originally quoted in the preliminary estimate.

Sam made notes. "I'll get with Ming in accounting to calculate additional cost."

The second issue was sourcing the materials needed. Because the most crucial sign components had to be manufactured in the factory in Las Vegas, purchasing materials anywhere else wasn't cost effective. Other materials, such as rebar, cement and cement pilings would come from New Orleans-based companies.

Clyde complained, "I have my hands full finding suppliers that aren't notorious for pushing substandard crap."

"We'll get help from Bonner acquiring materials. He warned me about ruffling feathers when it comes to hiring out-of-state labor, but we need some of our guys on this job to ensure quality work." Sam looked over at Dave. "I seriously doubt we'll find qualified sign men down there, capable of doing the work our guys do."

"What about permits?" Dave asked.

"Commissioner Bryant's our man for permits." Sam looked at Clyde. "Can you work with him?"

"I'd rather it be you, Sam. Politicians don't like me much."

Everyone laughed, and the mood in the room lightened.

"Finish up these prints and stats and get them to me as soon as you can. I'll fine-tune our cost breakdowns and get them down to Coltrane and his people. We'll set up meetings with the Building Department and start looking for suppliers down there." He looked at Clyde. "Then you and I fly down and start hiring."

\*\*\*

Down in New Orleans, the Arena continued to go up. In addition to local newspaper and television coverage, national television networks began covering the story. Nightly news anchors nationwide featured renderings of the Arena, and sports newscasters and athletcs alike raved about the structure.

"The Arena will dwarf the Astrodome and all other sports stadiums in this country. Athletic teams and sporting fans nationwide will experience the thrill of live sporting events as never before," ESPN sports commentator, Ty Williams, raved.

As the project gained momentum, Allen Stein's articles began to go out over the wires nationwide.

## REGAL TO BUILD ARENA SIGNS

In what some have considered a surprising move, the contract to build the signage for the Arena has been awarded to Las Vegas-based sign company, Regal Signs.

"We, the committee, entertained bids from numerous sign companies, both here at home and out of state, and are confident our choice of Regal Sign Company is the right one," Mayor Riley stated yesterday at the committee's press conference covering the ongoing project.

"This is a great day for New Orleans. This structure is going to be hailed upon completion as a true wonder of the world, and a source of massive revenue for the great State of Louisiana. The spectacular sign designed by Regal will be a fine addition to the Arena," Mayor Riley added.

Sign construction will begin upon approval of final designs, and the acquisition of necessary permits and supplies. Interested citizens can see renderings of the sign on display in the Jefferson County Courthouse lobby, along with the Arena model itself.

\*\*\*

Back in Las Vegas, local television networks proudly heralded the selection of Regal Signs for the Arena project. Reporters, fighting for interviews, crowded around Sam in front of the Regal warehouse, shoving microphones in his face and shouting out questions.

Tony sat next to his dad in Benny's suite, watching Sam being bombarded by reporters on live TV. "Look at him, Dad. The poor guy's famous."

Benny bit down on his cigar. "Son, we need to talk business."

"Sure, Dad. What gives?"

"I'm sending you down to New Orleans to introduce our junkets."

Tony's heart skipped a beat at the thought of seeing Jamaica again.

"I see opportunity, son." He flicked an ash from his cigar into the ashtray beside him. "Our junket program will cultivate new partnerships, not just with businessmen, but with politicians and law-enforcement agencies down there. Not to mention the syndicates—like we've established with Detroit, New York, our friends in Chicago—and now, with New Orleans."

Tony listened. Negotiations with the syndicates had proved to be complicated and he'd learned a lot. But he knew nothing about New Orleans. "I don't know, Dad."

"Listen, son, it's a simple equation. We offer the syndicate down there a piece of the action and they'll take it. We make money and they make money." Benny extinguished the small stub left of his cigar and stared into his son's eyes. "It's a balance. At best, it's lucrative. At the very least, we gain knowledge. And knowledge is..."

"I know, Dad, always a good thing."

Tony's thoughts returned to Jamaica. During their brief encounter in Las Vegas, his sexual attraction to her was undeniable. But his desire for her was combined with anxiety over what she'd think if she really knew him. He'd tried to convince her he was a decent guy, in spite of his family connections. She'd been non-committal and Tony hoped that it had more to do with whatever she was hurting from than with him.

After the committee returned to New Orleans, Sam had teased Tony about the encounter. "Your growing obsession with Miss Russe is easy to explain. You can't believe she didn't fall like an autumn leaf for your Svengali routine. She's a challenge you've never faced before. I guess you could always follow her to New Orleans!"

Tony listened to his father discuss the junket plan, and a plan of his own began forming in his head. "Dad, I'll take the job. I'll set up your junkets in New Orleans." A smile covered his face at the thought of seeing her again. He looked at his dad. "How soon can I leave?"

\*\*\*

The vacant lot on the Strip across the street from the Sultan's Palace was finally up for sale. The property was in a prime location on a corner, with just enough acreage to accommodate Benny's dream, a sister casino to the Palace. It was common knowledge that Benny harbored a desire to build a sister casino to the Palace, and his dream for it rested with the property across the street.

The casino would be called the Scheherazade, an exotic counterpart to Benny's Sultan.

Benny's frustration grew as he looked out the massive window of his penthouse, trying to figure out a way to convince the boys in Chicago that investing $500,000 to buy land for a new Vegas casino was a good investment.

Benny stared at the vacant lot across the street. He closed his eyes and envisioned his new casino, rising in exotic glory to share its place beside the Sultan's Palace. "Maybe, just maybe, it can happen," he said aloud to no one.

Benny DeLuca called the shots in Vegas and the boys back in Chicago trusted him to protect their interests in the west. Risks and gambles built Las Vegas, and risks and gambles had reaped big rewards for Benny DeLuca, and for the family back in Chicago.

This time was no different. Benny decided to sleep on it and make a decision in the morning.

# 18

## The Law Firm

Jamaica entered the lobby of the building housing the law firm of Coltrane, Coltrane and DiAngelis. She was the picture of corporate chic in her black St. John business suit. Her hair was twisted in an elegant French braid, perfectly completing the image of a professional businesswoman.

She stopped for a moment to take a look around at the expensive marble floors and towering walls of the massive lobby. Although she'd visited the building many times over the years, this was her first day as a member of the Firm, a fact that was just beginning to sink in.

Jamaica nodded a hello to the guard at the lobby security desk. She entered the express elevator and pressed the button to the firm's executive offices on the top floor.

As the elevator rose, Jamaica reflected on her recent graduation. It was an accomplishment, though noticeably diminished by the absence of her father. She wished he'd been alive to witness her graduate from Columbia University, then ace the bar exam. Fate had dealt a cruel blow, with both of her parents denied the pleasure of witnessing such an important moment in her life.

Jamaica fondled the pendant resting on her neck. She stared at her shadowed reflection in the shiny steel elevator door. With Lily's passing, she felt truly alone. Via the Coltranes, she had ascended into Louisiana high society, but the Coltranes weren't family.

She softened at thoughts of Clarice, back cooking on the Estate. Many of Jamaica's fondest memories were of the Coltrane staff. They all lived in close proximity to one another in the cottages the Coltrane family had built for the cooks, maids and gardeners. She grew up with the other Jamaicans who had sold their land to Lewis and now worked on the Estate, but it was the Cajuns working and living on the property whose culture she grew to embrace.

As a child, she accompanied the Cajun workers to family functions in the various small towns in the Bayou. The Estate was located far from the neighborhoods where they had grown up, and visits back home were infrequent. Still, those visits had created special bonds.

It was there, guided by Clarice, in the company of the elders of the Cajun community, that she first spoke of the visions she'd experienced since childhood. To her surprise, her revelation was met with acceptance and understanding. The elders assisted her in attempts to reveal the meaning of the recurring visions that haunted her.

"We can't make them stop, child," Clarice had told her during the many voodoo rituals she attended, "but we can teach you how to sense their coming."

Jamaica learned to confront her visions and, through the guidance of the elders, control them. While many feared the spiritual folkways of the Cajun culture, Jamaica embraced the use of chants and voodoo ritual that enabled her to control the fear and confusion her visions created.

When Garlan died, Eleanor and Lewis became legal guardians of Lily. Jamaica had already reached legal age as an adult. When she was home from school, she and Lily attended all the events and social activities that were the normal way of life on the Estate. However, except for the company of her Jamaican and Cajun friends, Jamaica considered herself an outsider, admittedly by her own doing.

As the elevator neared the top floor, Jamaica pondered the potential consequences of her new role in the Coltrane family. Eleanor and Catherine championed many charitable events and she respected both women. The Coltrane men, however, had proved over the years to be egocentric, chauvinistic, and as she'd long suspected and confirmed in Las Vegas, adulterous. Out of respect for her father, she never made her feelings known. It was with some misgiving that she agreed to join the Firm, but considering the education she'd received, funded by the Coltranes, she felt obligated.

She'd kept her emotions in check during gatherings at the cottages, when her father reminisced about working his own land on their island home. However, now, with her father and sister gone, she was free to make her own choices. She tugged on the jacket waist of her suit. Working in the Firm on the Arena project would be an excellent way to test the waters. Time would tell whether or not she would stay.

The elevator bell sounded arrival at the top floor.

Jamaica exited the elevator and walked up to the desk. The reception area was ostentatious and distinctly masculine. A large mahogany desk sat facing the elevator door in the center of the room, backed by picture windows that looked out on the city below. Enormous double doors on the other two walls marked the entrances to the law offices of the Firm's senior partners on one side and the conference rooms and offices of the remaining legal team on the other.

Jamaica's high heels clacked on the deep green Italian marble floor. The rich color contrasted with the subtle gray marble walls and contributed to the overall opulence of the massive reception area.

"Good morning, Gloria." Jamaica greeted the receptionist.

"Jamaica, dear. How nice to see you. Mr. Coltrane is just inside." She gestured to the doors on the right. "He told me you were joining us this morning as a new member of the Firm. How wonderful for you, and for all of us," she said. "They're all waiting for you."

"Yes, of course, Gloria. Thank you."

Gloria was a senior member of the Coltrane Firm's staff. She was a single woman in her mid-fifties, small in stature, with prematurely gray hair cut in a stylish bob. Her deep blue eyes exuded a stately calm, at once warm and professional. Jamaica knew that as Lewis Coltrane's personal secretary, there was little she didn't know about the Firm.

"You'll dazzle them, dear. Just between us girls, I welcome another woman on staff. You can help me keep these men in line," she said with a playful wink. "I'll let them know you're here." She lifted the phone.

Jamaica looked out the huge window looming behind Gloria's desk. The sky was alive with billowing clouds, moving gracefully over the city. "I'll make you proud, Papa. I promise," she whispered.

"They're ready for you." Gloria nodded for her to go ahead.

Jamaica walked to the double doors. She paused for a moment to look at the gold lettering identifying the Firm of Coltrane, Coltrane and DiAngelis. She took a deep breath, pulled on the large gold handle on the right door, and entered.

"Surprise!" Balloons, confetti strips and the sound of party horns surrounded her as she stepped into the hallway connecting the offices. The Coltrane family, business associates and law-firm employees clapped and hollered congratulations. Jimmy Coltrane popped open the magnum of Champagne he was holding and began filling champagne glasses.

Lewis gestured for the crowd to pipe down. "Our bright young star has passed the bar and has graciously agreed to forgo a well-deserved holiday, prior to joining the Firm."

He turned to face Jamaica. "Today, it begins. You're a real Coltrane now."

He turned back to face the group. "I propose a toast to Miss Russe." He raised his glass. "Welcome, Jamaica, to the Firm, and to all the benefits it has to offer. I can assure you, they are many."

# 19

## The Negotiation

Sam was busy preparing for his return to New Orleans when Benny summoned him to the executive offices at the Sultan's Palace.

"Sit down, Sam. We've got business to discuss before you fly back down to New Orleans. I've set up a meeting to negotiate the purchase of the property across the street. I intend to build another casino."

Sam's eyebrows lifted. "Wow," he said, taking a seat.

"I know you have your hands full with this Arena business, and I respect that, but before you go, I want your guarantee. If this deal flies, I want Regal to build the signage for the new property. I'll want to get construction started as quickly as possible."

Benny leaned in and planted his elbows on the desktop. He clasped his hands together, fingers entwined, and rested his chin on them. "I want you onboard from the beginning, and I need your assurance that Regal can handle it." He paused. "Will this be problem, given your present obligations in New Orleans?" Benny looked intently at Sam.

"No, not at all. Regal will make you our top priority. I'll take personal responsibility for that."

"I'm glad to hear it, Sam. I expected no less." Benny unclasped his hands and leaned back in his chair.

Sam's mind raced. "I can get our design team started on concept renderings for the marquee, and for the interior hotel and casino signs, immediately."

Ideas were already spinning in his head. "It would be in your best interest to get the marquee itself built, at least in part, at the onset of building. It would be great advertisement for the new casino, and spark curiosity during the building process."

"It doesn't take much to light a fire under you, kid," Benny said, smiling. "I like that. If this deal flies, I want the best work you can offer. It has to be the best on the Strip."

"You have my personal guarantee. You'll receive the best product, for the best price."

Benny's smile disappeared and Sam could see a cloud darkening his mood. "Listen, Sam. I'm not sure you fully realize the enormity of the project you've already taken on. You've got a tiger by the tail, son." Benny crossed his arms in front of his ample stomach and leaned farther back in his chair. "If you start having any problems with those characters down there, you call me."

Sam nodded. "I will." Clyde's comment only a few months before about Bonner's having a tiger by the tail flashed in his mind. He'd smirked off the comment, disregarding it as unfounded, but the look on Benny's face, followed by the same warning, gave him pause.

"And Sam," Benny added, "I want you to keep an eye on Tony for me. I'd feel better knowing you're around, to help him navigate the waters down there."

"Yes, sir. Tony and I've discussed the junket program. The Arena committee spread glowing details throughout the Parishes about their visit to Las Vegas. They raved about the Sultan's Palace, in particular. There's already a lot of buzz circulating down there about Vegas."

"Very well, then. I'll let you know how my meeting goes, and we'll get together again before you and Tony leave." Benny's eyes twinkled behind the cigar clenched between his teeth. He rose and gave Sam a fatherly bear hug. "I'm proud of my boys, both of you."

***

For a young man playing with the big boys in Las Vegas, Jack Meyers had some big balls. He was a good-looking man, 6'2", Italian, with dark eyes and thick, wavy hair. He entered the executive offices of the Sultan's Palace, full of energy and enthusiasm. He flashed a debonair smile at Benny's secretary, Marjorie, and introduced himself.

Marjorie advised Benny of his arrival and directed him into Benny's office.

Meyers entered the office, hand extended, smiling broadly as he approached. "Mr. DeLuca, Jack Meyers. It's a pleasure to finally meet you." His teeth were snow white against his tanned skin. "I hope that one day, the things I intend to achieve here in Las Vegas will garner the same respect and admiration I have for you."

They shook hands.

"That's very flattering of you to say so, Jack." Benny got right to the heart of it. "I hope you'll keep an open mind when considering my offer on your property. Can I get you a drink? Whiskey?"

"Whiskey will be great, thank you." Jack settled into one of the large leather chairs in Benny's office.

Benny poured two glasses of Macallan Estate Whiskey, his favorite, from a crystal decanter on the bar beside his desk.

"I'm eager to hear your offer, Mr. DeLuca. I sincerely hope we'll be able to make a deal."

Benny reached down to hand the whiskey to Jack.

Jack accepted the glass. "My property is, after all, across the street from yours, and I imagine you must have already considered what you could do with it." He waited for Benny's response.

Benny sat down in the large leather chair behind his desk, stone-faced. He lifted his glass. "Cheers."

Jack nodded, and tipped his glass toward Benny.

Benny remained expressionless. "The gaming industry is a complex creature, and no potential venture should ever be approached lightly." Benny took a sip of his drink. "Here's my offer, Jack." He lowered his drink and held it in front of him. He lowered his voice as well. "I'm willing to offer you five hundred thousand, cash." Benny casually swirled the whiskey in his glass, took another sip and set it down on the desk in front of him.

Jack sat silent, poker-faced.

Benny reached across the desk and opened a box containing Cuban cigars. He gestured to Jack, who politely declined with a subtle shake of his head. Benny selected one and used the cutting tool beside the box to cut the cigar. He pulled out a shiny black-lacquer DuPont lighter from his pants pocket and lit the cigar. "It's a more than generous offer," Benny spoke through the cigar smoke billowing in the air between them.

Jack looked past Benny at the framed tapestry hanging on the wall behind Benny's desk. Two Samurai warriors stood facing off, with swords clenched in hand. It was a powerful and intimidating image.

Jack admired the tapestry, appreciating its strategic placement, and the message it relayed. His respect for Benny was immense, but he had something Benny wanted.

He countered, unintimidated. "With respect, Mr. DeLuca, I think we both know my property is worth twice that."

Benny lifted his glass of whiskey. "And so our negotiations begin. I may be willing to offer a bit more. Say, six hundred. But certainly not a *million.*"

"I would think it wise, Mr. DeLuca, for you to consider this. I haven't arrived at my asking price lightly, and you must realize others have expressed interest in purchasing my land."

"I don't suppose you'd like to tell me who these 'others' are?" Benny puffed on his cigar. "I may know them."

Jack released a quiet chuckle. "Indeed, you do. And they know you. Several are eager to offer competitive bids, should our negotiations prove unsatisfactory. I imagine a bidding war is not something you relish."

Jack noticed a few beads of sweat forming on Benny's brow.

"So, you want to play that way, Meyers? Fine. I'll call your bluff. I don't know a single businessman in this town who is ready to fork over a million bucks for that land."

Jack stood up. "Very well, Mr. DeLuca. I won't waste any more of your time." He turned away from Benny and headed for the door.

"Wait," Benny said. "Let's see if we can't work out some kind of compromise. We both want to make a deal. Sit back down."

Before he turned around, Jack wiped the sly grin from his face. "Fine with me. I'll hear you out." He sat down.

"What's the bottom line? How much do you really expect to get?"

Jack reached down for his briefcase, opened it and pulled out a contract. He stood up, leaned over Benny's desk, and laid the contract out in front of him.

Benny nearly choked on his cigar when he looked down at the figures noted in the contract. "You have some nerve, Meyers!" he bellowed, his face reddening. "What kind of a fool do you think I am? You can't come in here and automatically assume I'm going to agree to pay a million bucks for a block of sand!"

"And why not?" Jack remained calm and took his seat. "It's no secret the Sultan's Palace is owned by your friends in Chicago." He picked up his glass and leaned back in his chair, casually crossing one leg over the other. "We both know you can get the million, no problem."

Benny's eyes, still glued to the contract on his desk, bulged, as if they were about to pop out of his head.

Jack pretended to ignore Benny's growing irritation. A smile appeared on his face, accompanied by a casual shrug of his shoulders. "I can easily sell this property to someone else. Strip property is in high demand. As I've already stated, a number of your competitors have already expressed interest. I'll need your answer today."

The beads of sweat that had formed on Benny's forehead dripped down over the scowl on his face. "There's nothing amusing about this, Meyers." Benny was obviously fighting to contain his anger. "I don't like ultimatums." He pounded his fist on his desk. "You can't hardball me!" He stared into Jack's eyes. His expression was deadly. "Do you want to get yourself killed?"

"On the contrary, Mr. DeLuca," Jack responded. "I just want to sell my property at a fair price."

The office door suddenly opened. "Is everything all right, Mr. DeLuca?" Marjorie gingerly peeked around the partially open door. Her timid body language belied her alarm over the ruckus coming from the office.

"We're fine, Marjorie. Mr. Meyers and I are simply having a disagreement. Go back to your desk."

Marjorie quickly closed the door, leaving the two men to their "disagreement."

An uncomfortable silence filled the room. Benny sat back down. As he stared at Jack, his thoughts flashed back to bygone days in Chicago, back when negotiations would've ended differently, with Meyers ending up as fish food in Lake Michigan.

Jack sat up straight in his chair and leaned toward Benny. He looked directly into Benny's eyes. "Let me be crystal clear." Jack's voice lowered. "Unless you want me to walk out of this office and sell my property to one of your competitors, perhaps we can talk seriously about my purchase price." Jack relaxed back in his chair. "I'm firm at one million dollars."

A cunning smile appeared on his face. "If, however, the decision is not yours alone to make…" Jack paused to let the cavalier comment sink in, "perhaps you'll want to confer with your Chicago associates—"

Benny burst in. "You cocky son of a bitch! I don't need anyone's permission. You're goddamned crazy if you think you can come in here and insult me!" He rose to his feet and stared menacingly down at Jack, who remained seated calmly in his chair. "I'll buy your little piece of dirt, but I warn you, if you dare cross me again, it will be the last thing you do." His glare changed into an expression of disgust and dismissal.

Benny turned his back on Jack, and walked over to the door. He swung it open. "This meeting is over. Get the hell out of my sight."

Jack rose from his chair. "You understand, Mr. DeLuca, this isn't personal. It's just business. I'm delighted we've managed to reach a deal." He paused. "And with it, a better understanding of each other." Jack stopped at the open door. "I'll have the necessary papers drawn up and delivered to you within the next few days."

"You're goddamned lucky I really want that land, Meyers. Now get the hell out of here before I throw you out myself." Benny stood with his hand clenched to the doorknob, then slammed the door shut behind Meyers.

\*\*\*

Benny sat down and resumed smoking his cigar, waiting for his blood pressure to drop. He cringed at the thought of spending a million bucks for a piece of desert, but he desperately wanted the land. It was clear, if he was going to have his Scheherazade, she was going to cost him a million bucks just to start.

Benny emerged from his office 10 minutes after Jack's departure and attempted to calm the nerves of a noticeably frazzled Marjorie, who was sitting behind her desk. "Well, it's going to happen, Marjorie. I got my land. I'm not thrilled with the price, but I have to admit, the kid has balls."

Benny knew that Marjorie, having worked as his private secretary for years, had heard her share of arguments coming from behind closed doors.

"I'm pleased to hear it, Mr. DeLuca."

"I do hope we didn't upset you, my dear."

"Certainly not, Mr. DeLuca, not at all," Marjorie replied.

"Well, you're a rotten liar, but I appreciate the attempt. Now, call Tony and set up dinner plans for this evening in my suite. And call Sam McCormick and tell him to set up a meeting tomorrow over here with his design team." Benny leaned across the desk. He gave Marjorie an affectionate pat on the shoulder, before heading for the door to the casino. "That's my good girl."

He made a mental note to have a nice bouquet of flowers delivered to her desk the following day.

Working for Benny, no one would deny the poor girl certainly deserved at least that.

***

Tony arrived at Benny's penthouse suite at eight. "So you decided to buy it." Tony lifted his glass in a toast. "To the future home of the Scheherazade."

The two men clinked glasses.

"Wait until Sam hears about this."

Benny cut a piece of steak from the huge porterhouse on the plate in front of him. "He already knows. I called him shortly after my meeting with Meyers and told him to get a design group together." Benny popped the steak in his mouth and chewed.

Tony chuckled at the sight of his dad, napkin tucked under his chin, Italian-style, devouring the meat.

"I called Harry Rothman, the architect, and told him to come to see me next week. Meyers promised to have all the paperwork for the sale delivered within a few days." Benny looked up from his steak. "The deal could be finalized by Friday." He stopped to lift his napkin from his chest. "Just in time for the visit from the Chicago boys."

Tony smiled at his father's use of the "Chicago boys." He knew the drill: They generally arrived in groups of four, each carrying large leather briefcases, in addition to their personal luggage. After a few days in town, they departed, always individually and on separate flights, carrying with them their respective briefcases.

The fact that the men never returned to Chicago together seemed insignificant. But that each departing guest wore additional jewelry in the form of handcuffs, securing the briefcase to the carrier's wrist, was not. A bell captain working the Palace who witnessed the comings and goings told his girlfriend, who later told Tony, that they dubbed the visits "taking out the laundry." It was a common practice in Vegas casinos, with huge amounts of casino winnings routinely traveling, unceremoniously east.

Benny wiped his mouth with his napkin. "Meyers stood his ground on price. I have to hand it to him. He knew I wanted the land, and he didn't even bother to pretend to negotiate." He pulled his napkin from his collar, slammed it down on the table and grunted, "He crossed a line, though. He had the nerve to imply I needed to consult with Chicago to buy the property."

"That must've riled you up."

Benny nodded. "Well, I have to admit, I actually considered strangling him myself, or calling someone to do it for me. In the heat of the moment, it would have been a pleasure to watch the arrogant little fuck have his neck snapped."

Tony released a small laugh, but the comment drew his thoughts back to Jamaica Russe. I wonder what she would think of me, if she heard that, he thought.

***

Two days later at 9:30 a.m. on Thursday morning, the intercom in Benny's office buzzed. "Mr. DeLuca, a call on line two. One of your attorneys from Goodman, Lewin and Weiss."

Benny took the call.

"Mr. DeLuca, a courier delivered paperwork for the purchase of the Meyers property late Wednesday morning. We examined the documents and found everything to be in order."

"Excellent. Go on."

"You will purchase the property for the sum of one million dollars, at which time the deed to the property will transfer to your corporation, DeLuca and Associates."

"Good. When will you have the check ready?"

"No check. Mr. Meyers prefers to accept cash. He said something about conducting the deal the family way. He said you'd understand."

Benny let out a belly laugh and shook his head in disbelief. The "family way" was code for an under-the-table cash deal. It eliminated the need to report capital gain to the IRS. "I'll be damned," Benny said. "The kid's a player."

*** 

Tony and Sam sat in the VIP lounge, discussing their upcoming trip.

"So you really want to fly down to all that swampland in Louisiana?" Sam teased. "Granted, the Quarter's pretty great and the women down there *are* beautiful." He paused and grinned. "One, in particular."

"Very funny," Tony replied. "I don't know if I have a chance with that girl. I tried, but I couldn't even score a kiss. Now that Dad's asked me to set up our junket business down there, I intend to get a second chance."

"Well, I'll be meeting with lawyers at the Coltrane Firm to go over the contract." Sam winked at Tony. "Miss Russe works there. You want to string along?"

Tony's eyes lit up. "I don't trust lawyers, but if Jamaica's working there, hell yeah!"

# 20

## Building Begins

"Holy crap!" Sam jolted the vehicle to a quick stop. He got out and felt firm ground beneath his feet. When he looked down, he couldn't believe his eyes. Where there had previously been soft, unstable ground, there now lay a 250-foot roadway, leading from the main road all the way up to the location of the proposed sign. It was 25 feet wide. And it was snow white.

Sam got back in the vehicle and raced up the road. "I have to know out how he did it." He spotted Bonner farther up the road, standing a few yards away from his truck. Bonner was gesturing furiously at a man seated inside a red Corvette. The Corvette suddenly started down the road toward Sam, sending white gravel flying everywhere as it sped past. Sam recognized Lewis Coltrane as the driver.

Once the dust had settled, Sam continued up the road and pulled up next to Bonner's truck. He got out of his rental and knelt down to examine the ground below.

"Is that what you had in mind, Sam?" Bobby called out, as he approached.

"Bobby, this is amazing. How'd you do it so quickly, and what is this stuff?"

"Seashells, Sam, crushed-up seashells. They're hard as rock and plentiful down here. You're in New Orleans, my friend. We use what resources we've got, and we've got plenty of shells."

"It's actually beautiful," Sam said, still staring at the blanket of white beneath his feet.

Bobby chuckled. "Well, to me, it's just a road. But I guarantee there's no machinery heavy enough to sink into this. Put all the weight you want on her. She'll hold."

Bobby gestured up the road toward the structure towering in front of them. "How about I give you a little tour? Like the one you gave me back in Las Vegas of your Sultan sign. I'll take you up onto the scaffolding at the top of the Arena roof and show you what we've accomplished so far. For a layman, it doesn't seem like much to look at yet, but I know you'll appreciate how much it's progressed in the past few months."

They walked up the road, until they neared one of the elevators that rose to the top of the arena structure.

Sam looked up. "Four hundred feet is way up there. That's twice the height of the Sultan sign."

Bobby suddenly stopped walking.

"What is it?" Sam asked.

"See that tall, slim man, standing beside an area of fencing separating the site from the street?"

As they got closer, Bobby started waving his arms in the air. "Get out of here!" he shouted at the top of his lungs.

"What's going on?" Sam lifted his palm to his forehead and shielded his eyes from the sun. At over 100 yards away, he could barely make out a man, his head covered in dreadlocks, attaching something to the fencing.

Bobby dropped his hands to his sides. "Damn Creoles. The last couple of months the perimeter's been vandalized. It happens at night when the site's vacant, mostly just graffiti on the fencing and voodoo dolls strewn over the fence onto the grounds. Seems we've got ourselves a group of Creoles, protesting the Arena's being built on this land. I don't take much stock in most of it, but we've discovered a few incidents of dead chickens, and voodoo symbols drawn in blood at the main entrance when we open up in the morning. Looks like it's starting to happen during the day."

"Have you called the cops?"

"No. Won't do any good. No real harm's being done here on location, but Cajuns working the site are getting spooked by rumors of voodoo rituals being held down in the Bayou, so-called spiritual intermediaries communicating with the dead. They claim there's a curse being laid on us, for desecrating sacred ground."

"That doesn't sound good."

"Yeah, well, no point arguing with superstition. I just tell the men to clean up the mess and keep working. The city probably shouldn't have picked an old cemetery site to build on, but it's too late now."

Bobby looked at the expression on Sam's face and burst out laughing. "I wouldn't worry about it, Sam. Besides, we've got enough real problems to deal with." He paused. "I'm sorry you had to witness that little scene with Coltrane just now. We've been going round and round about some of the supply companies his committee's approved. My men are complaining about the rebar, and some of the cement that's been showing up. I think our illustrious committee is trying to cut corners. Have you had any problems so far?"

"Not yet, Bobby," Sam replied, "but I see some ahead."

"Can I help?"

"Well, yes, maybe you can. My company's at a disadvantage, being from out of state. I expect roadblocks finding local suppliers. I'd sure appreciate advice from a man I can trust." Sam extended his hand to Bobby. "I'll watch your back if you'll watch mine."

Bobby shook Sam's hand. "It's a deal. Besides," he added with a chuckle, "if those rituals down in the Bayou continue, we could end up with voodoo dolls in our beds. We'll need all the help we can get!"

Sam laughed and pointed toward the elevator. "I'm ready for my tour."

They grabbed two hard hats, entered the elevator and took a long, slow ride to the top. They exited the elevator at the top of the domed roof of the Arena. Sam looked around, awed by the sheer massiveness of the structure. The view of the city spanned miles in every direction.

Bobby guided him through the maze of scaffolding and described in detail all the complexities of the project, just as Sam had done with Bobby in Las Vegas. Later, as they walked together toward Bobby's office, they agreed to speak regularly, to compare notes on their progress and keep the actions of the committee in check.

*** 

Jamaica's pale peach sundress swung softly against her legs as she walked down Bourbon Street on her way to her lunch date with Tony. The oversized straw hat shading her face was woven with hundreds of strips of blanched straw, a handmade gift from one of the Cajun elders. Her dark sunglasses masked the anticipation in her eyes, as she approached Pat O'Brien's—the first time she'd felt any excitement since Jimmy's phone call about Lily.

Tony had accompanied Sam to the Firm for the contract signing a few days before, specifically to see her. He charmed her with an enormous bouquet of exotic flowers and asked her to lunch. It was Saturday at noon and the Quarter was bustling with a sea of tourists, as she neared her destination. Through the crowd of people, she spotted Tony, standing in front of the restaurant, looking cool in a pale-blue polo shirt, jeans and sandals.

Upon seeing her, he thrust his arm in the air and waved to catch her attention.

Jamaica blushed under her big sun hat. "He's really quite cute," she whispered to herself, as she walked toward him.

"Hello, gorgeous." Tony took her hand and lifted it to his lips. He looked intently at her and kissed her hand.

She removed her sunglasses with her free hand, and exposed the blush the kiss had returned to her face.

Tony dropped his eyes, pretending not to notice, but kept hold of her hand.

"Hi, Tony. I hope you found the restaurant easily in this throng of tourists."

"Oh, no problem at all," he said. "I've been wandering all around the Quarter this morning, looking for an apartment to buy." He gestured with his free hand at the surrounding area. "This is a lively neighborhood."

"You're going to buy a place in the Quarter? After being here only a few days?" Jamaica asked. "That's quite a spontaneous decision."

"Well, I intend to spend a lot of time in New Orleans. I want to learn all about this city. I'm hoping you might show me around." He squeezed her hand. "Come. Let's have lunch and you and I can get better acquainted."

Tony continued to hold her hand as he led Jamaica into the restaurant. She felt the warmth of his gentle grip and a surprising quickening of her heartbeat.

# 21

## Investments

### INVESTORS FLOCK TO INVEST IN ARENA
### By Allen Stein

Momentum is building as advertisers and football franchises embrace the Arena project, committing large sums of money in return for advertising rights and seasonal playing commitments. The much-needed revenue, required to satisfy the escalating costs of building the Arena, has begun to materialize, exceeding the hopes of even the most optimistic of the committee members.

Mayor Riley recently expressed his satisfaction with the increasing financial support, stating, "The gentlemen of the committee, organized and assembled by city and state officials, continue to prove to be well qualified to carry out this enormous undertaking. Our commitment to the city of New Orleans to accomplish this extraordinary goal is beyond reproach. I am proud to be a member of this fine committee and promise the people of New Orleans, they will not be disappointed."

Not everyone shares Mayor Riley's excitement. Some union members, local suppliers and small businesses have expressed concerns over out-of-state workers and imported building materials. When asked about these concerns, union leader Bobby Bonner, whose construction company won the contract to build the Arena, stated, "These are unfounded concerns. We have hired many local workers for this project and when quality materials are available, we purchase them locally. For the record, we have implemented some outside specialized labor, but it is minimal. The bulk of this huge project is directly benefiting local working residents. As spokesman for the Teamsters Union, you have my word on that. As far as the funding aspects of this project go, those questions are best directed to Lewis Coltrane and the other members of the esteemed committee."

In response to Mr. Bonner's comments, Mr. Coltrane was adamant in his reply. "Mr. Bonner knows full well that the committee is closely monitoring all aspects of construction on the Arena, including the distribution of funds. There is no need to alarm the public over manufactured claims questioning the actions of the committee, regarding this or any other issue. Frankly, I find these innuendos offensive, and will certainly be speaking with Mr. Bonner regarding his remarks. I can assure the public that the Committee continues to work in the best interests of the community. Any implications to the contrary are absurd."

Investors appear to agree with Mr. Coltrane, as funding continues to come in from sources eager to buy in to the projected financial benefits of the completed Arena.

***

"How many VIP booths?" Bobby asked.

"They've added twelve," Sam mumbled his frustration. "And the way they protrude out into the balconies will block the view of hundreds of fans."

"What were they thinking? And building a huge gondola in the center of the Arena to hang from the ceiling is nuts." He was referring to a plan for Regal to build a massive hexagon-shaped structure, housing enormous video screens that would be attached to the roof of the Arena to broadcast the live action on the field, thus enabling fans to see the plays from any area in the Arena stands. "A gondola that size, housing those monster screens, will weigh a ton. And it's going to cost a fortune to build and hang."

"You're right, Bobby, but it's the only way to counter the visibility issues these booths will cause."

"Do you see any another way?"

"No. The engineers all agree, adding a gondola is the most logical solution for the problems caused by the addition of these VIP booths."

"This is bullshit."

"I agree, but if spectators behind those booths are going to see the activity on the field, monitors housed in a gondola are essential," Sam replied. "The design team's already on it."

"Fine, but I still say it's bullshit."

\*\*\*

An angry Jon Navaro took a second heart pill and boarded the Regal jet, bound for New Orleans. After reading Stein's article in the *New Orleans Tribune* and receiving unsettling memos about added signage for the Arena, his heart was racing so fast, he'd wisely pocketed extra pills. When the plane landed, he hailed a taxi and headed directly to the offices of the Coltrane Firm. His heart was still racing.

Jon entered the Firm's conference room, foregoing any pleasantries with the men assembled there. He distributed copies of the recently received memos and newspaper article, irritated to discover that only Lewis, Jimmy and Max were present for the meeting.

"Gentlemen, Regal is in dire need of additional funding to cover costs for this extra signage. This was not included in our original contract. If the committee doesn't approve more money, we will not only have to withdraw from this project, Regal will likely go bankrupt." Jon paused to calm himself. The lack of concern on the faces around him only served to anger him more. "This is serious business and at this point in the project, it's just not possible to continue without a major adjustment in the original bid," Jon stated emphatically.

He grabbed the first memo and waved it in the air.

"The first issue is this new development with the press booth. This memo states that, although the booth originally designed is well equipped for event coverage, it's not nearly large enough for the scores of computers needed to run the scoreboards, or our main pylon."

He grabbed the second memo.

"This memo informs us that an eighteen-hundred-square-foot room will be built within the Arena to house the communication center. In addition to twenty new security cameras, it also states that numerous pieces of signage have now been added, to function throughout the Arena structure. Our budget is skyrocketing with 'add-ons,' and the committee has declined to approve any additional funding. We've had no choice but to submit invoices for additional work for these 'add-ons' that you've approved and insisted upon, but refuse to fund."

Lewis sat in front of Jon, leaning back in his chair, looking bored.

Jon's nostrils flared. "*Now* I'm informed that added VIP booths for advertisers will cut off visibility to the main scoreboards and fans with seats behind these booths won't be able to see the plays." Jon took a deep breath, in an attempt to slow down his accelerating pulse. "This second memo from Sam states that, in order to solve the problem, engineers have had to design a six-sided gondola to be lifted and hung from the center of the domed roof." Jon took another deep breath. "With a scoreboard and backlit TV screen! Plus four smaller scoreboards to be added on the sides of booths, all to be manufactured and hung by Regal! Who's going to pay for this, gentlemen? Are you vaguely aware of the intricate computer network necessary to house such an information center?"

"I think you're overreacting, Jon," Lewis answered, his tone nonchalant.

"Overreacting, my ass! I insist, no, I demand you allocate some of the funding you've received from advertisers to Regal, so we can attempt to accommodate you with all these cursed add-ons. You have the funds, gentlemen. Here it is, right in front of you, front page of your own paper."

Jon picked up his copy of the *Tribune* and slammed it down on the table. "Mr. Stein states clearly in this article that investors have been coming forward and committing major funds to the Arena for advertising rights. If I have to have a meeting with Mr. Stein myself, to give him additional information for his next article, believe me, I will. We have lawyers in Nevada, too, gentlemen, and a reputation for using whatever means necessary to ensure our needs are met."

"Are you threatening us, Jon?" Jimmy responded. His tone was flat, as if he couldn't be more bored.

Jon exploded. "It's no threat, sir! It's a promise! I will not tolerate the unprofessional and, frankly, unethical behavior being shown by this committee. Regal has a contract with you, and your changes warrant an increase in compensation." He turned to Max. "Mr. DiAngelis, you're responsible for the distribution of funds on this project. I expect a big check from you in my hand before I return to Las Vegas tomorrow evening. Good day, *gentlemen.*"

Jon turned abruptly and exited the conference room. Before he left Las Vegas, he had warned his brother that the future of Regal was at stake and that he was determined to protect the company. Lou had argued that Jon was making a big deal out of nothing, but Jon refused to back down. "Lou, I'm going down there to get more money."

Once Jon left the conference room, Lewis addressed Max, "Contact Lou. Make sure he understands he needs to honor our arrangement, and keep his brother under control. We'll continue to stall with payments, just to prove we're showing due diligence in reviewing every request for additional funding."

Lewis rose to leave the room. "And Max, you and Jimmy keep padding Regal's invoices. Once we skim ours off the top, and give Lou his cut, release the funds to Regal."

Lewis stopped at the door. "It's all working out nicely, boys. The advertising funds are pouring in. There's plenty more money to be made on this one."

Max heard Lewis whistling, as Lewis headed for the elevator. "I don't know, Jimmy," Max said, shaking his head. "Maybe we're getting too greedy. I hope we don't get caught."

***

## ARENA CONTROVERSY CONTINUES
### By Allen Stein

As the bidding wars continue for contracts ranging from parking lot construction to steel and concrete sub-contracts, questions continue to arise over the methods of operation used by the Arena committee.

Until recently, the committee enjoyed unrestricted freedom in the distribution of building contracts for the project. However, complaints by numerous local businesses charging favoritism, as well as implications of bribes and kickbacks by parties who prefer to remain anonymous, have triggered still more questions in the already controversial project.

"Accusations of misconduct by any of the members of my committee are preposterous, and I will sue anyone who dares challenge the integrity of our choices in this great project," an angry Lewis Coltrane responded yesterday, when asked to comment.

Bobby Bonner, recently elected Teamsters Union leader, addressed alleged union links to illegal conduct in the acquisition of contracts prior to his election.

"I've made it clear since assuming my position as union leader that such conduct will not be tolerated," Bonner stated. "The integrity of our union workers will not be compromised by any individuals who intend to use union labor to line their own pockets. I was elected on the promise that I would protect the working man and end corruption within our union and it's a promise I intend to keep."

Mr. Bonner is a member of the Arena committee, and reports of heated disagreements behind closed doors between himself and committee chairman, Lewis Coltrane, have been officially denied. Reliable sources, however, maintain that problems among members of the committee warrant concern.

The Arena was half built and the signs well under construction when Allen's article covered what everyone working the project already knew. Things were indeed getting messy.

Sam entered the accounting room at Regal.

Ming Lee, Regal's long-term head accountant, was seated behind his desk, peering down through thick glasses at the paperwork in front of him. He looked up. "Hi, Sam. What can I do for you?"

"I just got out of a meeting with Lou. I've noticed inconsistencies in some of the Arena invoices."

Ming laughed. "No kidding. I've noticed them, too. When I mentioned it to Lou, he told me they weren't my concern. Imagine that. I'm the accountant. How could it not be my concern? What's going on down there, Sam?"

"I don't know. Both Lou and Max DiAngelis told me the same thing. They said to stick with getting the signs built and they'd resolve any issues with invoices or payroll. Could you take another look into it for me, just between us?"

Ming gave Sam a nod. "Sure thing, Sam. Just between us, I have a theory about what may be going on. I'll be in touch when I'm sure."

"Thanks, Ming. I'm on my way back to New Orleans. You know how to reach me."

Sam left the accounting room and headed toward the airport and his flight back to New Orleans.

***

Over several interviews and subsequent quiet dinners together at the Marie Antoinette, Sam's friendship with Allen Stein grew.

He listened to Allen's concerns over complaints about Arena spending and labor practices, and tried to reassure Allen that the Arena was not the sinkhole of cash it appeared to be. One evening during dinner, conversation turned to Allen's concerns over Bobby Bonner's ongoing problems with the union. Sam explained what he knew.

"Bonner's been addressing union complaints over substandard building supplies. Some complaints are legit," Sam admitted. "Both of us are critical of some of the companies approved to supply materials. "He's taken his concerns to the committee, but so far, in order for me to get supply orders approved, I've had to settle for Bryant's promise to look into it. Bonner has more pull with the local companies, but he's facing roadblocks as well."

"Look, Sam," Allen replied. "I don't listen to unsubstantiated gossip, but I'm still skeptical and I'm cautioning you." He looked straight at Sam. "Don't trust any of them—not the mayor, not the city commissioner, certainly not Coltrane or his son. And watch out for DiAngelis. That man's in deep with Coltrane. As hard as I try, I can't seem to nail either of them."

"I can't argue the point," Sam said. "I've had my share of disagreements with both of them."

Allen mentioned that he liked Bonner. "He's a good guy, but regardless of how much he denies it, he's in heavy with the syndicate down here. He has to be facing some coercion behind closed doors."

Allen placed his hands on Sam's shoulders. "There's one more thing you need to know. My sources tell me Senator Keetz is about to open an investigation into the whole Arena project. Because questions have been raised about interstate hiring practices, it's going to be a federal investigation. Keetz will take down anyone he suspects of taking bribes. And he suspects, as do I, members of the Arena committee. Keep your eyes open and follow the money. Some of it is bound to be landing in some unexpected places."

Sam declined to comment, but privately, he feared Allen was right. "I had dinner with Jamaica Russe and my friend, Tony, the other night. I asked Miss Russe if she'd noticed anything irregular with Regal's invoices."

"Really? What did she say?"

"She said all the invoices she'd processed appeared legitimate, but she added that she didn't have access to many of the records."

"Did she say who does?"

"Yes. She said Max DiAngelis and Jimmy Coltrane handle most of them like they're top secret documents. She added that she found it very odd and promised to let me know if she discovered anything alarming. She also told me that the longer she worked for the Coltrane Firm, the less she liked it."

# 22

## Affairs of the Heart

A solemn Catherine Coltrane sat alone at the grand piano in the music room. Her long, delicate fingers trickled along the keys, playing a haunting Beethoven sonata. Numerous crystal candelabras, artfully placed on tables and mantles, cast soft candle light throughout. The glow reflected on the many fine objects gracing the room and created an elegantly subdued atmosphere.

Catherine felt a gentle touch on her shoulder. She hoped it was Jimmy, but when she turned, she wasn't sorry to see it was Jamaica. Catherine smiled and continued to play.

"That was lovely, Catherine," Jamaica said, when the piece ended. "You really are an exquisite pianist. Where is everyone this evening? I haven't seen a soul."

"Eleanor has gone to bed and the staff has retired. We appear to be all alone, Jamaica," Catherine responded. "Would you care to join me in a glass of wine? It's quite a fine Cabernet from southern France." She gestured to a half-full crystal decanter of wine sitting on the top of the piano next to a nearly empty crystal wine goblet.

"Yes, I'd like that. We haven't visited much lately and after a grueling day like today, a glass of wine is just what the doctor ordered."

Jamaica walked over to the massive mahogany cabinet against the wall behind her, opened one of the etched glass doors and retrieved a wine goblet from the crystal collection housed inside. She poured a glass of wine from the decanter on the piano and refilled Catherine's glass. The two women moved to a comfortable couch adjacent to the bay window facing the garden.

As the Cabernet began to take effect, Catherine could see that Jamaica had something on her mind. "What is it, my dear? Is something troubling you?"

"Catherine, I'm finding I have reservations about the man I've been seeing. You've met him, and I wonder what you might think."

"Do you mean Mr. DeLuca?" Catherine set her glass down. "He's always so polite when he visits. What kind of reservations, my dear?"

"Well, he's got a notorious reputation. He's known to be quite a lady's man."

"And this is a problem because?" Catherine giggled. "He is single, is he not?"

"Yes, and at first it was nothing more than superficial fling. But in the light of recent events, I find myself being drawn closer to him, and it unnerves me."

"Why?"

"He tells me he's falling for me, and I'm not sure I believe him."

"And are you falling for him?"

"Yes, I believe I am, Catherine, and that's the problem. I've always been a serious person, as you know. For the first time in my life, my emotions have clouded my judgment. When I'm with him, I feel alive in a way I've never experienced before. It's exhilarating, but how do I know I can trust him?"

"Only time, my dear, will tell you that. His true colors will show eventually." She sighed. "You must judge him by his actions, not his words. Over time, you will know. Take my Jimmy." She sighed again. "I was naïve. I should have paid less attention to his promises and more to his deeds. The years, sadly, have revealed a lot."

"I suppose you're right. Tony and I have only known each other a short while. But I find myself thinking about him more and more and looking forward to seeing him."

"That's a good thing, my dear. Enjoy your young man, but observe the things he does. If you admire his actions, there is little danger in surrendering your heart. I hope that helps."

Jamaica smiled at Catherine. "Yes, it does. Thank you."

Catherine poured them each another glass of wine, emptying the decanter before ending their visit. The two women walked arm in arm from the music room into the Estate's huge grand hall. They hugged at the foot of the two massive staircases leading to the wings on the second floor and climbed up opposite sides, to their respective suites.

*** 

Catherine entered her empty bedroom at 10 p.m. She had offered her usual excuses and apologies for Jimmy's absence at dinner and the conversation with Jamaica had only added strength to her melancholy. Small tears formed in her eyes. Once again, Jimmy's habitual nonappearance had embarrassed and saddened her. She'd long since stopped wondering where he might be.

She disrobed and engaged in her nightly habit of summoning memories from happier times, back when she was a young and beautiful debutante and he was a rich New Orleans aristocrat.

She'd managed to catch his eye one evening at a charity event she and her family attended on the Coltrane

Estate. When Jimmy showed interest in her, Catherine played it cool, resisting the advances of a man who was accustomed to getting whatever woman he wanted. Jimmy, intrigued by the challenge, pursued her relentlessly.

Catherine opened the top drawer of her armoire and pulled out a white chiffon negligee. She pressed it to her face and closed her eyes, imagining the one she had worn on her wedding night. She slipped the negligee over her head and felt the fabric caress her body as it fell. The soft chiffon flowed around her legs as she walked toward the mirror on the wall beside the bed.

Jimmy was a renowned playboy when she met him. When Catherine discovered he had resumed his philandering only weeks after their wedding vows, she confronted him, but stopped short of delivering ultimatums.

He had laughed, reminding her that she'd married into high society, a position she had long coveted. He had cautioned her that, if she wanted to remain a Coltrane, she should surrender to playing her part well and turn a blind eye to his affairs.

Over the years, Catherine and Eleanor bonded in mutual sympathy over their spouses' infidelity. They kept busy with social activities and charitable pursuits, while Jimmy and his father slept with whomever they pleased whenever they pleased.

It was Friday night and the chances were, Jimmy would not return for several days. He and his father frequently spent weekends together at the Ambassador Club, returning to the Estate in just enough time to shower and change before leaving for the office. At least one weekend a month, the two men left for the islands on Saturday evening, to return a few days later, tanned, and insistent that the details of the trip were far too boring for conversation.

It was with a broken heart that Catherine learned of her inability to conceive. To her dismay, Jimmy was unaffected by the news, other than to appear relieved by it. With nothing to gain and everything to lose, she chose not to dwell on what might have been and life went on.

Catherine stood in front of the mirror and gazed at her image. She was still a beautiful woman and with every fiber of her being, she wished that Jimmy still thought so.

She looked down at their wedding photo, prominently displayed in a Waterford-crystal frame on the antique table beside her bed. She stared at the image of herself. She was smiling radiantly in the photo. The two of them stood side by side on the steps of St. Mary's. Her flowing wedding gown appeared frozen in time, captured as a memory, in a photo of two newlyweds descending the steps to a waiting limo, and the beginning of a life together.

Catherine reached out to grasp the frame. She placed it face down on the table, pulled open the champagne silk comforter and satin sheets, and went to bed alone.

# 23

## Complications

### INVESTIGATIVE COMMITTEE FORMED
By Allen Stein

During a brief press conference held this morning, Louisiana's U.S. Senator Keetz announced the formation of a federal investigative team to examine the financial records of money spent thus far on the Arena. "Serious questions have been raised about discrepancies in payments made to construction companies and suppliers working on various aspects of the Arena project," Senator Keetz was quoted as saying.

"It is my responsibility to ensure that funds are being allocated properly, and that there is total transparency in all aspects of this endeavor. As taxpayers, the people of New Orleans deserve to know how their hard-earned money is being spent. I am hopeful we will find that everything is above board, but if there has indeed been misuse of funds, we will uncover it and hold those responsible accountable. Over the course of the next few months, my team will be questioning any individuals we feel may have relevant information, in order to address these concerns."

The senator declined to identify any of the individuals he intends to question.

In the weeks that followed, Senator Keetz and his team began exploring the validity of received complaints. Some individuals came forward voluntarily, while others faced subpoenas and were deposed, in an attempt to determine if there was sufficient evidence indicating criminal activity.

*** 

Clyde's truck barreled down the seashell road and came to a halt a few yards from where Sam was standing. He sprang out of the vehicle. "There's a problem at the Regal warehouse, a big one."

"Great. What's wrong now?" Sam asked.

"The trucks from Las Vegas carrying the last set of sign sections just arrived." Clyde's face was flushed and his eyes were like saucers. Sweat poured from his brow. "We've got a riot going on. The local union workers have converged on the trucks. They're protesting our using non-union labor."

"What? That's ridiculous. That's why we purchased Anderson Construction down here, to comply with union law. Hell, they were all employed at Anderson and we hired them all."

"Well, they saw the trucks come in from out of state and jumped to conclusions. We have to get it straightened out."

Sam jumped in Clyde's truck. When the two of them reached the warehouse entrance, Clyde plowed through the open front gate. As he drove toward the location of the riot, he pointed to a wall covered with ominous, spray-painted symbols. "We can't keep up with all the vandalism, Sam. That voodoo crap is all over the place." He slowed the vehicle and inched through the crowd of protesting workers.

Sam exited the truck and pawed his way to the front of the crowd. "Men, you're all misinformed!" He shouted for the unruly crowd to listen. "With the help of your union leader, Bobby Bonner, Regal purchased union membership for the few, I repeat few, specialized workers from Las Vegas needed for the assembly of the signs. No local skilled labor were qualified to create these sign sections." He pointed to the trucks. "You can check with Bonner."

He answered a barrage of questions and, once the facts came out, the union laborers Regal had hired resumed working.

Still, the problems were far from over. Sam knew that Bobby was battling his own ongoing union unrest, and forged ahead on the Arena, at times commenting to Sam that maybe there really was a curse on the project. Despite the wave of irrational fear among laborers over reports of increasingly bloody voodoo rituals in the marshes of the Bayou and the never-ending appearances of dead chickens on the site, the Arena continued to go up.

***

As progress continued on the Arena, Tony was making progress of his own with the City of New Orleans Chamber of Commerce.

He called his dad to report. "I'm building clientele for our junket program faster than I expected," he began. "It's all going well with the Chamber of Commerce, but I need you to come down here. You remember meeting Bobby Bonner in Vegas. He arranged for me to meet with some of his associates—to discuss our program." Tony paused.

"The men he introduced me to are a lot like our associates from Chicago."

"What happened?"

"Well, I go to meet these men at this Cajun restaurant in the Quarter. When I walk in, they're all sitting around a table eating. So I sit down and, first thing, one of them asks about you."

"I expected that, son. Go on."

Tony reiterated the details the meeting. "I'm sitting there, surrounded by this group of men. This burly Cajun guy, with this badly scarred face, looks at me. 'We'd like your old man to fly down to visit with us,' he says. 'We're interested in this junket program of yours,' he says, 'but we have questions.'"

"And what did you say?" Benny asked.

"Well, at the time, I didn't think I really had a choice. I said I didn't see a problem and that I'd call you."

***

Benny read between the lines. He flew down to meet personally with the group—the potential clients, as Tony called them. The Cajun mob, as Benny put it.

"This will be a lucrative partnership for all concerned," Benny said, as he shook hands with various members of the Louisiana syndicate. He sat at the same table, in the same restaurant where Tony had experienced his first encounter with the Cajun mob. After the deal was done, Tony said, "Dad, I have to hand it to you. You were right. The families benefit most."

Before Benny flew back to Las Vegas, he met with Sam to complain about the ongoing sign situation at the Scheherazade. "Listen, Sam, Regal's having trouble upholding its commitments for signage for my new hotel. It's a problem."

Sam had been actively involved during the initial stages of the Scheherazade project, but he'd been noticeably absent in the past few months. Benny knew his full attention was geared to the problems looming in New Orleans, but he wanted action on his own project. Sam apologized. "I'll fly up and get it straightened out for you."

***

Sam kept his word, but ill winds kept fanning the flames. Ongoing issues forced him to fly up to Las Vegas several times to appease Benny and put out fires, only to fly back to face the ongoing drama in New Orleans.

Just when it seemed things couldn't get much worse, he spotted an envelope on his desk.

It was a subpoena.

"Oh, great," he moaned. "This is just what I need."

***

Jimmy held the glass of scotch limply in his hand. He slumped sullenly in his chair, listening to his father and Max discussing the ongoing hearing.

"Things are unraveling, Lewis. Stein's articles and the senator's subpoenas have raised serious questions about who contracts were issued to and why. Keetz is really digging in, putting a lot of federal resources into this investigation. It's only a matter of time before someone slips up and the truth comes out about all these kickbacks."

"What do they know?" Lewis asked.

199

Max paced nervously around the room. "Bryant was in court last week when LaSalle was questioned about building permits and inspections. Thankfully, he handled it well."

"So what's the problem?" Lewis plopped his feet on the conference table.

"The problem, Lewis, is this," Max's jaw muscles clenched, as he spoke Lewis's name. "LaSalle and Ferguson insist they haven't tampered with permits they've issued to the local mob-backed companies we've hired, but I don't believe them. The little 'arrangement' we have with those Cajun thugs has worked out so far, thank God. But for how long?"

Jimmy looked up from his glass, "We really have no choice, Max, not if we want to protect ourselves."

"Well, why are they leaving Bonner alone?" Max asked. "It can only be because he's one of them."

Lewis yawned.

Max raised his voice, angered by Lewis' apparent lack of concern. "Meanwhile, Lewis, the Teamsters have been raising a big stink about building materials and Bonner's on my ass about it. So far, LaSalle and Ferguson have accepted our bribes and approved the substitutions, but what happens if Keetz's lawyers uncover something? These men are unpredictable, and I don't trust them."

Lewis yawned again. "Calm yourself, Max."

Max tried to calm himself. "Jimmy and I've worked hard to protect the Firm. The official set of books inflates material and labor costs to cover the kickbacks. It all looks good on paper. Jimmy's done a masterful job spreading it around."

"Thanks, Max. Nice of you to say so," Jimmy said, slurring his words. He looked at his dad. "If Keetz compares bids, he won't be able to prove any preferential treatment in the contracts we've issued."

"Yes," Max interrupted, "but if these feds keep digging and someone starts talking, it could all come unraveled. If it does, it'll be impossible to explain."

"Oh, God, Max. You're giving me a headache. We've covered our bases. You worry too much." Lewis rolled his head in a circle, stretching the muscles in his neck, before resting it on the back of his chair.

"Oh, really, Lewis? Well, now McCormick's being questioned. His testimony could bury us. What if the feds uncover Regal's padded invoices? Lou will keep his mouth shut, but what about Jon and Sam? How much do they really know?"

"You can relax, Max," Lewis said. "Jon has no idea his brother's been cooking the books. After that little visit of Jon's down here last month, we released the additional funds Regal needed. Lou got his cut and Jon was none the wiser. McCormick's been bombarded with all the new sign extras and we haven't made ourselves available to him to answer questions."

"Lewis, I want to believe you, but we have to divert suspicion away from the Firm. What if the senator's lawyers grill McCormick about our visit to Las Vegas?"

Jimmy rose to pour himself another drink. "Relax, Max. If that happens, you, Dad, and I will deny any knowledge of any deals that might have been going on behind our backs during that trip. Nobody knows what really happened in Vegas."

"That's right, Max, nobody knows and nobody's going to find out," Lewis responded in an increasingly patronizing tone.

Max ignored the slight and continued to make his case.

"We have to cover our asses. If the senator's investigation gets too close, I guess we can use Bryant as a scapegoat. It would be our word against his. Riley, too. He's got no clue what's going on. Jimmy and I could create a paper trail to the two of them. Then, if the kickbacks are exposed, we have someone to blame…"

"Slow down, Max. No need to panic. Everything's under control. Let the senator's people go forward with their questioning. Nobody's going to talk. They all have too much to lose."

"Well, it's a big mess, Lewis. I hope you know what you're doing. I'm counting on you to protect us and I don't feel very safe right now. I'll be in my office if you need me." He gestured for Jimmy to join him.

Jimmy stumbled to his feet. He paused in front of Lewis, drink in hand. "He has a point, Dad," Jimmy muttered. "It is a big mess." He wandered into Max's office and shut the door behind him.

\*\*\*

Lewis sat alone in his office, stewing over Max's newly acquired inability to handle pressure. Lewis had put Max in charge of overseeing the Arena finances, but it was the Firm itself that was entrusted with handling them. Max's present mental state was setting off alarm bells in Lewis's head. Max could become a threat to the Firm—and to Lewis personally.

"In that case, Max, my old friend," Lewis said to himself, rapping his fingers on his desk, "You'll leave me no choice. To protect the Firm, I'll throw you under the bus."

# 24

## The Hearing

When he received his subpoena to testify at the hearing, Sam refused to take the advice given by Max DiAngelis, to stand on the Fifth Amendment. He insisted on defending himself and his company.

Hordes of reporters and camera crews covered the steps of the Jefferson Parish Courthouse early Thursday morning, taking photos and grabbing interviews with individuals involved in the senator's investigation. Although the hearing thus far had failed to uncover proof of any illegal activity, media coverage was expanding nationwide, as interest in the scandal over potential corruption gained momentum.

Sam arrived at the courthouse and stood among the press gathered on the courthouse steps. When questioned about his role in the investigation, he spoke candidly. "I look forward to answering all the senator's questions honestly and I fully expect my testimony to confirm what I know to be true."

"Can you elaborate on that?" A reporter shoved her microphone forward, stopping it inches from Sam's face. Other microphones pushed forward, creating a fan around the front of his head.

Sam leaned back slightly. "Regal Sign Company has acted in a completely professional manner, and we continue in our efforts to provide an excellent product for the City of New Orleans. I expect all you reporters to do your jobs and share the facts with the citizens of New Orleans, once my company has been exonerated of any wrongdoing."

He pushed past the cluster of reporters, shoving away the microphones and cameras blocking his way as he entered the courthouse.

A row of Ivy League lawyers in tailored suits sat at a long table in the courtroom, shuffling through folders and open briefcases. The sheer size of the group assembled by Senator Keetz was intimidating and the stern looks on their faces indicated they intended to uncover the truth, however long it took.

Judge Charles Palmer entered the courtroom at 9 a.m. to preside over the hearing.

Sam was the first witness scheduled on the roster to testify. He was sworn in and the questioning began.

The lawyer seated on the end of the right side of the table housing the senator's group rose and approached Sam. He was in his early thirties and wore thick-rimmed glasses and a dark suit. He stared out over the top of his glasses, directly at Sam. "Good morning, Mr. McCormick. You've sworn to answer our questions, fully and honestly."

"Yes, I have," Sam replied.

After opening with numerous questions about Sam's background, qualifications and work history, the tone of the questioning changed. Another of the senator's lawyers rose from behind the table. In contrast with the first lawyer, the one now approaching Sam was middle-aged. He carried himself with the confidence of a professional who'd seen many hours in a courtroom. He began questioning Sam about the Arena committee's visit to Las Vegas. "Is it true, Mr. McCormick, that you offered the committee an all-expense paid trip to Las Vegas on Regal Sign Company's nickel, all in an effort to coerce them into awarding the proposed Arena signage contract to Regal?"

"Yes, I did," Sam replied.

A loud, collective gasp filled the courtroom.

"However," Sam continued, "coerce is not the right word. The right word is 'convince.' I was convinced that the only way for the committee to see that Regal was the best and only choice to build the sign was to bring them to Las Vegas." His eyes remained locked on the lawyer. "We took the committee members to our factory, to show them firsthand how Regal operates and how the signs are created."

"So, Mr. McCormick, by spending a significant amount of money, flying the group to Las Vegas, and wining and dining them at a flashy casino, the Sultan's Palace, I believe was the name of the establishment, was it your intent to dazzle them, and give your company an unfair advantage over any other bidders competing for the contract?"

"No. Members of the committee were not simply wined and dined, as you've implied. They were guided on an extensive tour of the numerous marquees Regal has built for casinos in Las Vegas. They saw them during the day, and then again at night, fully illuminated. Only in Las Vegas could they see, with their own eyes, what the company has already achieved." Sam looked over at the table housing the two Regal lawyers who had flown down from Las Vegas to counsel him.

Both men were smiling.

Sam continued, "Some members of the committee actually climbed into the Sultan marquee itself, the largest and most complex sign in existence today. I believe that, if they were dazzled, as you say, it was by the beautiful signs designed and built by my company. Our ability to do the work is what Regal wished to show the committee. Their stay at the Sultan's Palace, and all other activities provided during their visit, were intended for that purpose and that purpose alone."

"So you consider all of your actions in Las Vegas to be perfectly ethical and professional?'

"I do, absolutely. The trip was my idea, and I take full responsibility for suggesting it to the committee, and further, to my employers at Regal."

The lawyer tapped his forehead in frustration and requested a moment to confer with his fellow lawyers. He walked over to the group, from which murmuring ensued.

After a few moments, a third lawyer approached Sam. He pursued a different line of questioning. "Regarding a recent incident of union unrest at your warehouse, one that I believe resulted in a riot among workers, can you explain Regal's hiring of outside labor, specifically workers brought in from Las Vegas?"

Sam had been prepped for tough questioning, including addressing the subject of hiring practices. He sat up in his chair and addressed the lawyer. "Specialized labor with unique skills needed for sign construction has been brought in from Las Vegas, but only when comparable skilled labor could not be acquired locally." He tugged at the collar of his shirt. It was hot and humid in the courtroom and the air was stale. He could feel sweat forming on his brow.

The lawyer bombarded him with questions about Regal's hiring of union labor and the sources of material purchases.

Sam answered them all. "I am continually working with Bobby Bonner to ensure local union labor is being hired in all cases where qualified union workers are available. The Arena committee reviews and approves all hiring prior to beginning work on the project. It is important to note the dangerous nature of working a hundred and fifty-plus feet in the air. The hiring of outside labor, specifically the Regal employees brought in to attach the final sections of the sign, remains crucial to the completion of the project." Sam paused.

"I can't stress enough the years of experience required to pull that off successfully, at those heights, without injury to human or sign. Would you expect Regal to allow an inexperienced worker, local or otherwise, to attempt a job of that nature for the first time on a sign that large and hope for the best? There simply are no other workers qualified to perform that task."

The lawyer fidgeted from foot to foot, appearing anxious as answers to his questions bounced back to bite him.

Sam continued, "Regarding materials, Regal purchases them for the sign itself from local businesses." He paused. "The contracts awarded for all materials purchased for the sign are overseen and approved by the Arena committee. We have been experiencing an ongoing problem with substandard materials arriving on site. It's a problem I have repeatedly presented to the committee that, unfortunately, has not been addressed to Regal's satisfaction, nor to the satisfaction of Bonner Construction, which has also complained of inconsistencies in what is being ordered and what arrives in the factories or on the Arena site."

Sam looked out into the crowd seated in the courtroom. Tony was seated beside Jamaica in the back row. They were both smiling at him.

Still more of the senator's lawyers continued to grill Sam over the course of several hours. Finally, the senator's senior lawyer made a statement. "Thank you, Mr. McCormick." He turned to face Judge Palmer. "We have no further questions for this gentleman, Your Honor."

The judge called the senator's lawyers to the bench for a brief consultation, then addressed the crowd assembled in the courtroom. "It is the opinion of this Court that Mr. McCormick, representing his company in an attempt to acquire a contract to build a sign for the city of New Orleans, has acted in good faith. He represented his company in a slightly unorthodox, but perfectly legal, manner." The judge looked down over his left shoulder at Sam, and then back at the lawyers, spectators and press assembled in the courtroom.

Sam struggled to keep from smiling.

Judge Palmer continued, "Further, the Court has been shown no indication that any improprieties occurred during the Arena committee's trip to Las Vegas. I believe Mr. McCormick and his group achieved their objective in a professional manner, thus allowing the committee members to make an informed decision."

He directed his next comment at the senator's lawyers, and at the senator himself, who was seated behind them. "I see no need to question any other members of the Regal group at this time. Mr. McCormick has succeeded in answering questions to the satisfaction of this court."

Looks of relief covered the faces of the two Regal lawyers. An exuberant Tony planted a spontaneous kiss on Jamaica's cheek, prompting a coy smile.

Judge Palmer picked up his gavel. "In the light of this testimony, Senator Keetz and I will meet in chambers to discuss how to continue further with this investigation. Mr. McCormick, you are released, sir. Thank you for your time. This hearing is adjourned. We will resume tomorrow at nine a.m.”

\*\*\*

The judge entered his chambers, removed his robe and sat down behind his desk. He gestured for the senator to take a seat on the other side.

“George, there’s no need for further investigation in the matter involving Regal. Frankly, your investigation has yet to produce any hard evidence of impropriety anywhere.”

Senator Keetz shook his head in frustration. “I expected McCormick’s testimony would reveal something.”

“My point is this,” Judge Palmer added, “the credibility of your investigation is in jeopardy. I’d consider my next step carefully, if I were you.”

“Charles, I agree with you about Regal, but the fact remains that the problem’s not solved. The press has raised too many questions. You may have exonerated the sign company, but there are still questions about the skyrocketing expense of the whole Arena project. Someone has to be held accountable.”

The senator voiced his exasperation over the fact that his investigation wasn’t going well, heightened by his belief that the man at the heart of the whole mess was Lewis Coltrane. He looked across the desk at the judge. “Trust me, Charles, there’s something going on and I intend to find out what.”

Keetz had begun his career as a prosecutor in New Orleans Parish, eventually winning election to become the city’s District Attorney. During the campaign period, he formed a relationship with Coltrane, who became an avid supporter. Coltrane threw lavish fundraising galas in his mansion and used the plantation's huge grounds for the setting of Keetz's speaking events during the campaign period.

The relationship became strained when, during Keetz's tenure as DA, Coltrane's firm came under scrutiny for potentially unlawful conduct in the handling of cases. Despite Keetz's suspicions and aggressive investigations, no hard evidence of wrongdoing was ever found. As a result, the relationship between the two men, both professional and personal, deteriorated.

Despite their differences, Coltrane wanted something in return for what he had done to help Keetz in the early stages of his political career.

Soon after Keetz's election as governor of Louisiana, the demands started. Coltrane attempted to coerce Keetz into using the Coltrane Firm in the acquisition of contracts, representing the state.

Coltrane demanded payback, but Keetz held his ground. "There is no way I will compromise my position as governor by violating my oath to do the best job I can for this state."

When Keetz refused, Coltrane made veiled threats to ruin him. Keetz dismissed the threats, but when he was elected as a United States senator, his misgivings about Coltrane remained. When Coltrane was appointed Chairman of the Arena Committee, Keetz strongly objected, to no avail.

However, now, if the judge allowed the investigation into the Arena finances to continue, Keetz's team of lawyers would subpoena records controlled by the Coltrane Firm.

"The hell with it," Keetz said under his breath. "Charles, I intend to question several of the Arena committee members. I'm starting tomorrow with Max DiAngelis. As a senior member of the Coltrane Firm, he's been in charge of disbursing funds from the beginning. Then, subject to the testimony of Mr. DiAngelis I want to subpoena financial records on this project. I'd like to question Mayor Riley and City Commissioner Bryant as well, to dispel rumors that kickbacks were involved when building contracts were awarded."

The judge hesitated. "Let me think about it, George. You'd best tread carefully here. The mayor and the commissioner are highly regarded public servants. I expect you to handle any questioning of them with the utmost respect. I agree that we must do something. If you manage to uncover any evidence of misappropriations of funds, it's our responsibility to get to the bottom of it."

"I couldn't agree more."

"All right. You question Mr. DiAngelis tomorrow and we'll see how it goes."

"Thanks, Charles."

Judge Palmer's voice assumed a distinctly formal tone. "That will be all, senator. We'll resume tomorrow. After listening to Mr. DiAngelis' testimony, I'll give you my decision on the subpoena, as well as the issue of questioning our city officials."

The judge leaned back in his chair and plopped his feet on top of the desk. His left shoe barely missed the tiny microphone lodged on the inside panel as it brushed by.

# 25

## The Bug

A few weeks prior to Sam's testimony, Spencer, disguised as a member of the courthouse late-night cleaning crew, quietly tiptoed into the judge's chambers.

Lewis Coltrane had given him the addresses of three offices he wanted bugged. In addition to the judge's chambers, he wanted a phone tap in the office of Max DiAngelis and another in Bobby Bonner's office at the Arena site.

"But Spencer," Lewis had insisted, "the bug in the judge's chambers is the most important. It must clearly pick up conversations. Every word."

Spencer tested the tiny voice-activated microphone and transmitter he'd placed under the judge's desk. He walked around the room, counting steadily as he covered the area. He then left the chamber and returned to the alley behind the courthouse, where he had planted the receiver behind a power pole. The judge's chamber window was located directly above it, only a few feet away. He checked the transmission for volume and clarity. Satisfied the signal was strong, he left the alley. He returned in the early evening every day court was in session to retrieve any conversations recorded in the judge's chambers from the planted receiver.

Earlier, on the same evening, Spencer visited the Arena site. It was around 8 p.m. when he approached a warehouse filled with Arena building supplies. Bobby's office was located in the back corner of the building.

The site was quiet, with only one security guard present in a trailer located twenty feet from the warehouse. As Spencer crept past the trailer, he looked through the security window, cursing under his breath in disgust at the middle-aged guard inside. "Lazy bastard," Spencer hissed.

The guard was nodding off in front of his TV, oblivious to what was going on around him. The man depended entirely on the alarm system. If it went off, he acted. Otherwise, he never left his trailer. He was a union worker, secure in his position, regardless of his age and incompetence.

Spencer edged past long piles of rebar and steel beams lining the outside of the building, until he reached the alarms system's access panel. It was located on the wall, just around the corner from Bobby's office.

Spencer looked around. It was pitch black and dead quiet. It had been awhile since he'd committed a B&E without any visible signs of forced entry. Usually, he just crowbarred the door open, but this time, he had to use the finesse he'd learned long ago.

He'd barely been into his teens when he started hanging around the neighborhood bicycle and lock shop, scrounging used parts to keep his Schwinn rolling, then cleaning the place for spare change, and finally helping rekey cylinders on the locksmith's workbench. Once he learned how keys and the pin-tumbler system interacted, it was a short hop to picking locks and Spencer broke into his first house, without having to break anything, when he was 15 years old. It was the beginning of a long life of criminal acts, from burglary to armed robbery, pimping to extortion, kidnapping to murder.

He pulled a leather kit from his back pocket and retrieved two small thin tools. He inserted the rake and tension wrench into the cheap three-pin cabinet lock securing the breaker panel. Flicking on a penlight, he located the alarm circuit supplying AC power to the console, nicely printed on the label, and flipped it off. Then he disconnected the wires attached to the alarm system's main battery.

With the bell disarmed, he rounded the corner to Bobby's office door and used his picks to unlock the knob and access the office.

Once inside, Spencer used his flashlight to locate Bobby's desk. He placed the bug in the receiver of Bobby's phone and quietly exited the office. He returned to the alarm access panel, reconnected the alarm wires, and flipped the breaker back to on position.

The job was completed in less than fifteen minutes.

Coltrane had given Spencer a set of keys to get into Max's office, along with the codes to the security system. He waited to enter until he was sure the building was empty, and took the escape stairs to the top floor.

Spencer saw the gold nameplates on the office doors and noticed that DiAngelis and Jimmy Coltrane had connecting offices. The nameplates gave him an idea.

He shivered with glee as he placed the bug in Jimmy's phone. His ongoing fantasy about blackmailing the old man had given him many moments of pleasure and, with every new job, it grew stronger. After the adventure a few months back cleaning up Jimmy's mess at the Willows, Spencer had accumulated enough info to take down both Coltranes.

He left the office, grinning. "Give me some dirt, sonny boy," he whispered. "The more, the better."

214

***

A few of the tapes proved invaluable to Lewis Coltrane. When he heard them, he stepped into damage-control mode and alerted Bryant of the problem.

Bryant alerted the various suppliers the committee had approved who were responsible for the substitutions. He called his man, LaSalle, at the building department, as well. "Listen," Bryant warned LaSalle, "it's not just Bonner and the union we have to appease. Senator Keetz wants to question you about these suppliers. Be ready."

Keetz questioned La Salle and the suppliers, but Bryant had coached them all well. They'd managed to keep their stories straight, each denying knowledge of delivery of any substandard supplies. Investigators found no proof to the contrary.

But now Spencer had unearthed something from the bugs that he deemed important enough to roust Lewis in the middle of the night. He wondered how long he could manipulate the whole situation—without implementing more drastic measures.

***

Heavy clouds and steady rain shrouded the light of the moon as Spencer pulled his car to a stop at the designated meeting place. It was shortly before midnight. Coltrane never used the same place twice, but every chosen location was a seedy out-of-the-way dive on the outskirts of the city. This time it was the pothole-infested parking lot of a liquor store outside town.

Spencer sat in the dark in the parking lot, watching the raindrops splash off the windshield. As he waited for Lewis, he hummed to himself, reveling in the events of the past few weeks. He'd been pursuing Coltrane's cloak-and-dagger agenda like a regular James Bond, clandestinely skulking about in the dead of night, but the new info he'd retrieved from the judge's chambers surpassed everything he'd accumulated so far.

He'd already provided Coltrane with recordings from Bonner's office of conversations with disgruntled union reps, upset over faulty cable and steel supplies being delivered to the Arena site.

It was approaching 1 a.m., well past the arranged rendezvous time, and still no Lewis. Coltrane was rarely late, but during recent meetings, Spencer had observed the old man beginning to show signs of strain. One recorded phone call, in particular, delivered only a few days before, had set him off. The conversation was between Max and Jimmy.

"Play that part of the tape again." Coltrane said, balking at Max's hesitation to testify at the ongoing investigation. As the tape rolled, his anger grew.

"Jimmy," Max began, "I'm here at the courthouse, and I don't like the way this investigation's going. What if I get subpoenaed? There's no telling what Keetz and his group know, or what they're going to ask. I'm worried. Lewis keeps telling me there's no reason to be concerned, but he's not the one being called to testify."

"I hope I don't get called," Jimmy replied. "We'll go to jail if they find out what we've been doing."

Lewis listened to the conversation, his blood boiling. "Spencer, you monitor the bugs closely, and alert me if anything seems important, no matter how small, especially if it pertains to Max."

Spencer continued to screen all the tapes. On this day, during Sam's testimony, there had been nothing of any consequence recorded in Bonner's office, or the offices of Jimmy or Max. But when Spencer retrieved the bug from the judge's office, recorded shortly after Sam's hearing ended, he called Lewis. "Boss, you need to hear it."

"I'll meet you at midnight, at Manny's." Lewis hung up.

Spencer's fourth cigarette was nearly out when he saw Coltrane's Corvette pull into the parking lot.

"Finally," Spencer said, under his breath.

Lewis stopped beside Spencer's car and waved him over to the Corvette.

The two men sat in the dark in Coltrane's Corvette, while Lewis listened to the conversation between the judge and the senator. When the recording of the conversation ended, Lewis turned to face Spencer. The look on his face chilled Spencer to the bone.

"This is what I want done." Lewis's tone was as deadly as the look in his eyes. "I want to know the details of how you do it, and I want it clean, with no loose ends."

Spencer sat wide-eyed, not daring to respond with anything more than a nod. He listened silently, and when Lewis was finished, Spencer responded, "Yes, Mr. Coltrane, I understand, but it's going to be expensive."

Lewis barked an intimidating reply. "Of course it's going to be expensive! Can you do it or not?"

Spencer felt a knot forming in the pit of his stomach. "I don't know," he said, fighting panic. "I don't want to touch it. I may know someone who will, but you want it done so fast. I may not be able to find him in time to pull it off."

Lewis gave Spencer a look that made his blood run cold. "You'll make this happen, Spencer, or answer to me. Do you understand? It's simple enough." Lewis reached behind the driver's seat and dropped a canvas bag on Spencer's lap. "Here's twenty-thousand for whoever you get to do the job. There'll be five thousand more for you, once it's done. But if you can't find someone else to do this job, do it yourself."

He reached across Spencer and pushed the car door open. "Now get out of the car. You don't have much time."

\*\*\*

It was 3 a.m. when Spencer parked his beat-up sedan on the street in front of Dixie Antiques in downtown Biloxi. He'd walked into Manny's immediately after Lewis drove away and made a call to the antique store from the phone booth inside. Spencer rightly assumed someone would be there to answer the phone, regardless of the time. The illicit business conducted there warranted twenty-four-hour availability.

When a job was really dangerous, Spencer enlisted the services of the men who ran the antique store. The business was used as a front for illegal activity in Biloxi and neighboring New Orleans. Two Croatian brothers owned the store and were members of the Dixie Mafia. They were only two of many members, mostly recruited from prison, who made up a large network of career criminals working the parishes.

Spencer fancied himself a friend of the group, whose sole interest was making money, by any means necessary.

Robbery was the mildest of methods used in achieving their interests. Contract killing was the most severe.

Spencer walked down a dark, narrow path on the side of the store leading to a back alley. He carefully avoided the piles of trash and puddles of rainwater covering the ground as he rounded the corner. He knocked on a large garage door at the rear of the store and waited in the dark, glancing over his shoulder for any movement in the alley. A moment later, the door lifted.

"Get in here, Spencer, and state your business." A short, wiry man, deeply tanned, with red hair and piercing green eyes, appeared behind the door.

Spencer ducked his head under the half-open door and slipped into the store's back warehouse. The room was packed from floor to ceiling with stolen merchandise. TVs, guns, jewelry, art, anything of value was temporarily stored there, prior to being relocated to other "antique stores" in various other locations. The goods were then transported out of state. Eventually, the items would all be fenced or sold to unsuspecting buyers throughout the Southern states.

Curtis Brown, alias "Red," dropped the door back down behind them and reached for the pack of Marlboros rolled up in his T-shirt sleeve. A tattoo of a voluptuous, naked woman ran up his left arm.

Spencer could see half of her head peeking out of the sleeve, as Red removed the cigarettes.

On the other arm, he sported several crude gang tattoos he'd received during a stint in the state penitentiary for armed robbery. He removed a cigarette and offered one to Spencer.

"Thanks." Spencer accepted the cigarette, his head bobbing up and down in an attempt to appear cool. Curtis made him nervous. Curtis made everybody nervous.

"I haven't seen you around these parts lately. You must need something pretty bad to call on good old Red in the wee hours." Curtis casually flipped open his Zippo lighter. He lit his own cigarette, then leaned in to Spencer to light his. "Sit down and tell me what's on your mind."

Curtis pulled out two of the chairs from a set of oak dining-room furniture sitting in the middle of the warehouse. He sat down and plopped his filthy shoes onto the top of the oak table.

Spencer sat down in the second chair, next to Curtis. "Red, this job I've got requires your particular set of skills," Spencer began, relieved to look up at a smiling Curtis. The dangerous man sitting in front of him was in a receptive mood. "The job pays twenty large. It has to happen tomorrow. Actually, it has to happen in a few hours."

"Well, then, let's hear it," Curtis replied. A lethal smile appeared on his face as he carelessly tapped cigarette ash on the floor beside him.

*** 

The storm the night before had passed and the morning sun was shining down on the crowded steps of the courthouse when Max DiAngelis exited the limo. He crossed the street and headed up the courthouse steps.

Jimmy was trailing several yards back when the shots rang out.

Max lurched forward onto his knees. His body arched back and collapsed onto the steps, as the impact of the bullets riveted his chest. Screams filled the air. The panicked crowd scattered in all directions, running for shelter.

Jimmy dropped to the ground and clutched his hands over his head. He cowered on the steps behind his fallen associate and friend. Less than thirty minutes earlier, he had somehow mustered the courage to get into the limo with Max, knowing exactly what was about to happen.

His father's words were still ringing in his ears, crystal clear. Insane words…

"You'll accompany Max to the courthouse. Once he exits the limo and approaches the steps, fall behind. Leave at least a few yards between yourself and Max."

"How can you do this? I could be killed."

"You'll be perfectly safe, Jimmy," Lewis snapped. "Just stay back a bit. You're upset, I know, but we can't allow Max to jeopardize the Firm. We can't trust him to remain calm under questioning. He could panic. He might even try to make a deal and sell us out to save his own skin."

Jimmy stared at his father in disbelief. "Has it really come to this? Murder? A partner and friend?"

"This is the only way, son. It's unfortunate, but necessary. Just stay back. It has to look like you could've been a target as well," Lewis said. His voice was completely devoid of emotion. "Having you just behind, so close to Max, will only ensure sympathy for you and for the Firm. After all, Max has enemies. The Firm has enemies."

"But Dad, this is cold-blooded homicide in the first degree."

Lewis shrugged. His tone remained ice cold. "Max's murder will be perceived as a hit, a revenge killing by someone the Firm damaged in some prior litigation. And if the financial records on the Arena are subpoenaed, you'll be the one to present them. They'll show no evidence of kickbacks or bribes. We may be grilled by the commission, but all we have to do is deny any wrongdoing. They'll never prove otherwise."

At first, Jimmy argued, stunned that his father would even consider such a thing, let alone go through with it. But once he thought about it honestly, he relented. This was who his father was, a man with no scruples. And who was he to throw stones at his own glass house? How many times had he participated in crimes, purely for the financial benefit of the Firm?

He hated himself.

And he missed Lily.

He was dreadfully unhappy, and things just kept getting uglier.

Now, he was an accomplice to murder. When would it end?

# 26

## Conversations

Sam worked onsite all day Friday, supervising the final assembly of the hexagonal gondola. The gondola lift was scheduled for the following Monday morning. Miles of wiring encased in three large aluminum pipes would run from the gondola, up and over the steel structure of the domed roof, to the computer command room.

One of the three pipes contained high-voltage circuitry. The other two contained low-voltage and telephone-command wire. The crew spent the day connecting the hundreds of wires to the extensive computer equipment in the command room. The computers would run not only the gondola screens and the eight scoreboards located throughout the stadium, but the three-sided main sign outside as well. Everything had to be double-checked to insure proper installation prior to the lift.

Sam and Bobby worked in tandem, supervising the workers lining up the flats of metal and screen, while Sam's crew wired the electronic components together.

"Once this thing goes up, dropping the entire thing down into the center of the playing field is going to be the only way to service it," Sam commented as the two men worked.

Bobby looked at the massive structure spread out on the ground in front of them and sighed. "Well, let's hope it won't need maintenance for a while."

After a long and eventful day, the gondola sat in the center of the Arena floor, ready for the lift. Bobby and Sam dismissed the crew several hours after shift end. They promised bonuses to all the workers who had stayed on to complete the assembly.

Sam heard the shocking news about Max when he returned to the Quarter. He entered the bar at the Marie Antoinette, where a crowd of people were glued to coverage of the shooting on the television.

Lewis Coltrane was on the six o'clock news, answering questions posed by a popular local-television anchor. "We at the Coltrane Firm are shocked and saddened by this tragic event. The police are investigating all leads and it is my hope that they will capture the criminal who perpetrated this vile murder, the sooner the better," Lewis said. "Max was a good friend and I will not rest until justice is served."

Sam shook his head, muttering, "Great. Just what this project needs, more drama."

The bartender heard the comment and gave him a sympathetic smile. Sam finished his drink and headed up to his room. He opened the door to the sound of the phone ringing.

It was Tony. "Sam, Dad called. We've got a problem."

"What is it?"

"I'm not sure, but he wants us in Vegas. Now."

Sam grabbed a quick shower and waited at the lobby entrance of the Marie Antoinette for Tony to pick him up.

Tony pulled his shiny red Ferrari to a stop in front of the hotel. "This is quite the mystery, Sam," he said, as the Ferrari pulled away from the hotel.

"What the hell is going on, Tony? First, there's the riot at the warehouse. Then Max gets shot down in front of the courthouse, and now this? I swear, I'm beginning to think this whole project really is cursed."

Tony drove toward the freeway entrance to the airport. "All I know is that Dad told me to get both of us to Las Vegas right away. He sent his jet down. It's at the airport waiting for us."

Tony made it to the airport and parked in ten minutes. They boarded Benny's jet and spent the flight time discussing their suspicions about the murder. Sam questioned if it could be linked to Max's subpoena to testify.

"I don't know about that, but my old man never gets involved in matters outside his own properties," Tony said. "Whatever this is, it has to be something serious."

Sam shuddered. "What in the world could it be?"

They arrived in Las Vegas a few hours later, arriving at the Palace a little after 9 p.m., Vegas time.

Benny was waiting in his penthouse suite. "Come in, boys. There's something you both need to see."

***

Sam sat with his eyes glued to the television screen, watching videos of the committee's visit to Las Vegas. It was common practice for pit bosses and maître d's to supply high rollers with call girls working for the casino, so it didn't shock him to learn that some of the committee members had taken advantage of the service. But his eyes went wide when the group began discussing the plot to skim thousands off the top off the Arena project. A few comments sent chills running up his spine.

Lewis and Bryant mentioned a fellow named Martin LaSalle several times, identifying him as one of the heads of the building department down in New Orleans. Lewis bragged about how he had bribed LaSalle to expedite permits for renovations on several of his newly acquired properties in New Orleans.

"Do you know this guy, Sam?" Benny asked.

"No. I've met with various members of the building department to secure permits, but I've never dealt directly with LaSalle," Sam replied. "But this could explain the problems with getting permits over the past few months."

Benny sat behind his desk, puffing on his cigar. He gave Sam the tapes and cautioned him, "Be careful who sees these, and think long and hard about how you proceed. These are dangerous men, Sam, and New Orleans is a long way from Las Vegas." His voice lowered. "I probably should have shown you these tapes before, but I waited to see if these jokers were serious or just blowing smoke. The shooting of that lawyer made me realize you could be in danger. I can offer you some protection down there, if you feel you need it. Just say the word."

"I appreciate the offer, Benny, but I know what I have to do."

"Very well, but you boys be careful, and keep me posted." Benny extinguished his cigar and stood up. "Have a safe flight back, and call me if you need anything."

*\*\**

Lewis sat smoking a cigarette in the private VIP lounge of the Ambassador Club. His body was tilted back comfortably in luxurious cushions, with both arms spread across the back of the couch. The ankle of his right leg rested across his left knee and his foot bounced steadily up and down as he listened to the nervous ramblings of the two men sitting with him. He'd arranged the meeting in quiet anticipation of the inevitable panic occurring over Max's death. He invited both Mayor Riley and Commissioner Bryant for drinks and dinner at the club. Both men, predictably unnerved by the day's shooting, agreed to meet with him.

Lewis tried to include Jimmy as well, to serve as reinforcement in assuring the others that everything was under control, but he declined. He claimed he needed to be alone, that he was too upset over the ordeal on the courthouse steps that morning to attend.

Jimmy's excuses angered Lewis. He blasted him. "You're my own son, my own flesh and blood, and you're acting like a whimpering child!" He stormed out of the mansion, assuring Jimmy their talk would resume when he got home.

But first he had to handle Riley and Bryant.

"What happened to Max today is very unfortunate, gentlemen, but in no way connected to work done by the committee," Lewis began. "The police investigating this terrible crime will bring the criminals responsible to justice."

Both men listened intently to Lewis. Commissioner Bryant sipped on his martini, while Mayor Riley popped large handfuls of cocktail peanuts into his mouth.

"Now, regarding the hearing, and the potential questioning of any of the committee members," Lewis continued, "our records of distribution of funds for the Arena are nothing less than perfect."

He paused for a moment, watching, as a nervous Commissioner Bryant repeatedly stabbed a long cocktail toothpick at the olive in his martini. "Despite Max's absence, the Firm will continue to handle payment for the contracts and materials we approve."

Bryant stopped stabbing at his olive.

Lewis gave him a reassuring nod. "Just remain calm. Remember, we're respected leaders in this fine city. There's absolutely no evidence of any kind to the contrary."

Mayor Riley responded, "I don't know, Lewis."

"Look, the senator's investigation is nothing more than a witch-hunt," Coltrane said, "manufactured to further his political career."

The mayor shook his head. "How can you be so sure Max's death is unrelated?"

"Look, threats have been made recently against members of my firm." Lewis sighed. "And although this is a serious matter, you can rest assured neither of you are targets." He leaned back in the couch, took a deep breath and released another wistful sigh. "I wish I could say the same for Jimmy and myself." He gave the men a pensive, almost fatalistic look. "We at the firm are the potential victims, after all. You two can relax."

Lewis lifted his glass and took a long drink. "Judge Palmer has wisely suspended the hearings for the time being and the police are thoroughly investigating today's tragedy. The perpetrator will be found and brought to justice, very soon, I hope."

Both men expressed sympathy for the potential danger Coltrane and his firm faced and their expressions softened.

"Well, you be careful," Mayor Riley said, nodding his head in visible relief not to be personally in harm's way.

Lewis feigned appreciation over their concern for his safety. "You're both too kind." He gestured toward the club's restaurant entrance, adjacent to the lounge. "I suggest we order another round of drinks, have a few steaks, then partake of some evening entertainment." Lewis waved a waiter over to the table. "The night is young, gentlemen."

Bryant and Riley both responded with enthusiastic nods. Evening entertainment meant women.

Lewis ordered another round of drinks. He whispered into the ear of the waiter to summon the Club's concierge. With a discreet word to the concierge, he arranged for the company of three call girls following dinner.

Bryant and Riley scarfed down dinner, oblivious to the power Lewis held over them. Lewis owned Commissioner Bryant for accepting kickbacks and Mayor Riley for being too naive to see the nose in front of his egotistical face. Bryant had more than just his reputation to lose if Bonner and the Teamsters ever got wise to what was going on and Riley could never survive the shame of being accused, rightly or wrongly, of stealing from his city. With Max gone, Lewis still had Riley and Bryant on the back burner to sacrifice as scapegoats.

Dinner ended and the men rose to leave the dining room. Lewis slipped cash from his pocket into the waiting hand of the concierge.

"They're in the lobby, Mr. Coltrane." The concierge pointed to three attractive women standing just outside the entrance to dining room.

As the group exited the club and entered the waiting limo, Lewis slipped his wallet back into his pocket and wrapped his arm around the waist of his blonde twenty-something escort. With the payoff for Max's murder and the tidy sum he was about to spend on sex, the day's events were proving to be expensive.

Lewis slid his hand over the blonde's dress until he felt her warm, firm breasts beneath the soft fabric. She turned toward him and pressed her breasts against his chest. "Let's open the Champagne," she said, pointing at the chilled bottle resting in a silver bucket, next to crystal glasses set among an array of liquor bottles lined up in the limo bar.

The other two women cooed in agreement. "Ooh, we just love Champagne."

Lewis leaned forward. He lifted the champagne bottle. Ladies of the night were a costly indulgence, but it didn't matter. There was still a lot more money to be made.

And Lewis was pulling all the purse strings.

# 27

# Remorse

Jimmy Coltrane arrived at the Willows a little before 2 a.m. on Saturday morning. A few hours earlier, while she was sleeping, he'd slipped a note under Jamaica's bedroom door at the Estate, where she would discover it the following morning—then know what to do. He owed her at least the chance for some justice. He knew she'd never forgive him for the terrible things he'd done, but he wasn't deserving of forgiveness.

Jimmy sat alone on the couch in the living room of the bungalow. Even with his eyes closed, the vision of Max's last moments burned in his memory. He could still see him, falling to the ground. The nearly empty bottle of scotch in front of him had failed to silence the sound of gunfire still ringing in his ears. It couldn't dull the horror of all the blood he could still see covering the courthouse steps.

Max's blood. His friend was gone—and he'd done nothing to stop it. He'd stood by, as his own father deliberately orchestrated his murder. Lewis might as well have pulled the trigger himself.

Jimmy's bloodshot eyes filled with tears and he choked on his own words. "Hell, who am I kidding? I'm just as guilty as the old bastard. I should've at least tried to talk him out of it," Jimmy mumbled. "I should've at least tried."

He reached for the bottle of scotch and felt the agony of knowing he would never again share an evening out, drinking with Max. There would be no more nights together, celebrating the Firm's latest victory. Max was gone.

Jimmy opened his eyes. He looked across the room at the chair resting in front of the dressing table. He imagined Lily sitting there on Saturday afternoon, brushing her hair, waiting for him. He looked beyond to the open bedroom door and the bed where they had shared so many hours of passionate lovemaking. What had started out as just another roll in the hay with an insignificant piece of ass had grown into much more. He loved her. The bungalow, once so alive with the sound of her voice and the soft touch of her lips, was now no more than an empty tomb, harboring memories too painful to endure.

Jimmy poured the remaining scotch from the bottle into his glass and downed it in one gulp. He set the glass on the table and rose from the couch. He stumbled to his feet and looked around one last time, before staggering out the open door of the bungalow. The door creaked as it closed behind him, as if bidding an ominous farewell to an unwelcome guest.

He used one hand to steady himself against the outer wall of the bungalow and made his way to his car. He stopped and looked up, caught in the moment. His car was parked underneath the weeping willows. The irony of it hit him like a fatal blow. He would never feel Lily's warm body against his again.

There was no more joy. No happiness. He knew there never would be. Not for him.

He leaned against the door of the Mercedes, pausing once again to look up into the night sky. Thousands of stars sparkled above him. He felt small. Alone.

Jimmy opened the car door and slumped into the driver's seat. His body melted into the luxurious leather encompassing him. He looked up at his reflection in the rearview mirror, into the glazed eyes of the stranger staring back at him. He leaned over to the glove compartment and opened it. Tears streamed down his face as he reached inside.

"Lily," he whispered, as he raised the pistol to his head and pulled the trigger.

***

Bright sunlight filtered through the window onto the bed in Jamaica's suite, waking her. It was a little before 10 a.m. on Saturday morning.

The previous afternoon, when news of Max's shooting reached the law office, Lewis ordered the entire staff home. "You will all decline interviews by media of any kind during the investigation of the shooting," he advised. "You'll be notified when it's appropriate to return to work."

With the office temporarily closed, she planned on having a leisurely Saturday-morning breakfast. Then, encouraged by her conversation with Catherine the night before, she would call Tony. She showered and got dressed in a white-cotton summer dress he bought for her on a trip together to Las Vegas, shortly after they began dating. As she put the dress on, she caught herself daydreaming about the trip and how romantic it had been.

Jamaica headed down to breakfast. She reached for the doorknob and noticed an envelope lying on the carpet just inside her suite.

She picked it up. Her name was written on the front. She walked over to the loveseat at the entrance to her sitting room and opened the envelope. Inside, she found a note.

Jamaica,

Lewis has a safe located behind his gun collection in his private office at the Firm. The combination is three to the right to 23, two to the left to 21, one to the right to 46, then left until the lock drops. In the back of the safe, hidden behind a Rockwell painting of two fishermen, are three folders. I can never forgive myself for being the coward I am, or for the pain I have caused. It is too much for me to bear. Get the folders. You will know what to do. Forgive me.

Jimmy

Jamaica sat on the love seat, puzzling over the note and its strange message, when the phone rang. She reached for the phone. "Hello."

"Jamaica? It's Sam. Tony and I need to see you right away. It's important. Can you meet us now?"

"Of course. Where are you?"

"We're at the airport. We just got back from Vegas."

"You were in Vegas?"

"We'll explain when we see you. Could you come to my room at the Marie Antoinette? Room three-twenty-four."

"I'm on my way." Jamaica hung up. She slipped Jimmy's note into her purse, descended the massive staircase, headed toward the estate's garage and walked quickly to her car. Jimmy's bizarre note was the first surprise of the morning. She wondered what other surprises were coming.

***

Jamaica listened intently as Sam and Tony explained what they'd learned from Benny. After they played her excerpts from the Vegas tapes, the puzzle pieces began to come together.

"I suspected that the Firm's involved in something shady." Jamaica shook her head in disbelief as she listened to the tapes. "Lewis is the mastermind behind whatever's going on. I'm sure of it. I've seen firsthand how skillfully he manipulates people at the Firm. No one ever challenges Lewis. It's all starting to make sense."

The three agreed that the only way to prove what the Las Vegas tapes revealed was to find physical evidence of the kickbacks. Jimmy's note not only reinforced Jamaica's suspicions, it gave her a direction.

"I have to break into the Firm," Jamaica stated flatly. "If there's evidence in the files, breaking into the offices and searching them is the only way to find out."

Sam and Tony listened, as she explained what she intended to do.

"But Jamaica." Tony balked at the idea. "Think about what you're saying. Do you realize how dangerous breaking into those offices will be? It's a crazy idea. I can't allow you put yourself in danger like that."

Jamaica looked into his eyes. They were filled with genuine distress and concern for her safety. "That's very sweet, Tony," she replied. "But I intend to do this."

Both Tony and Sam tried to talk her out of it. She refused to back down and they refused to let her go through with it without them. "If you're really serious about this, we're going with you," Tony insisted.

"Damned straight, we are," Sam echoed.

Sitting together on Sam's bed, they planned the break-in for the following night.

# 28

## The Break In

Tony and Sam sat at the designated meeting place in a quiet bistro around the corner from the Coltrane offices, waiting for Jamaica to arrive. It was 10 p.m. Sunday night and the streets were dark.

Sam fidgeted with the straw resting in his ice tea. "Both Bobby Bonner and Allen Stein warned me about the Arena committee, Coltrane in particular. I wish I'd taken them more seriously."

Tony shrugged. "I'm not nuts about this plan," he said. "But there's no arguing with the woman."

A figure appeared in the distance, barely visible under the dim streetlights. Jamaica rounded the corner and approached the entrance to the bistro.

Tony spotted her. "Here she comes."

The two men rose as Jamaica entered the bistro. The plan she had laid out was simple. Jamaica would gain access to the main office with her own keys. All the extra work she was given recently, while Max prepared for the senator's hearing, had made late nights at the Firm a normal routine. She was accustomed to disarming the security system when she entered after normal business hours. Once inside, the three of them would search until they found something.

Jamaica gave Sam a hug, then turned to Tony. He wrapped his arms around her and kissed her.

"Are you sure about this?" Tony asked.

With a gentle push of her hands against his chest, she pulled away from him.

"I'm sure. Let's go, guys. Let's do this."

***

When Tony purchased a flat in the French Quarter only a few days after their first date, Jamaica had agreed to help him decorate. She introduced him to stores, clubs and restaurants in the neighborhood and after several months seeing each other, light flirtation advanced into a budding romance. When they first became intimate on their weekend trip to Las Vegas, Tony awakened emotions in her that she both welcomed and feared. He stood before her now, determined to protect her, come what may, and the fears she had shared with Catherine only a few nights before began to fade.

Jamaica unlocked the door to Lewis's office with one of the keys she received from Gloria earlier in the day.

When Jamaica confided in Gloria, revealing her suspicions and her plan, Gloria provided keys to all the filing cabinets in Lewis's, Max's and Jimmy's offices. She offered to go with Jamaica to search Lewis's office, explaining that she knew exactly where all the private files were located and which keys opened what.

"I should've come forward before," she said. Her eyes were filled with regret. "After all that I've seen, I was afraid." She pulled a set of keys from her desk drawer. "But if you really want to do this, I want to help."

Jamaica thanked her, but insisted Gloria stay behind. "Just give me the keys I need. If anything goes wrong tonight, I'll say I took them from your desk." She hugged Gloria. "I'll return them as soon as I can."

Once inside the private offices, the three divided the search. Sam and Tony settled into Jamaica's office. They began going over files Jamaica retrieved from Lewis's filing cabinet, along with files from Jimmy and Max's offices.

"Gloria was very specific about which ones to pull," Jamaica explained, handing them stacks of files.

***

Sam and Tony plopped the three piles of paperwork on the desk. They began piecing together the records from Jimmy and Lewis's files and comparing them to the official Arena files in Max's office. They soon discovered two distinctly different sets and evidence of massive padding and kickbacks.

"Oh my God! Tony, look at this!" Sam cried out.

"Lou's been inflating invoices on all these added material requests and DiAngelis approved them, without even considering competitive bids." Sam pointed to a series of figures on a file in front of him. "It shows here that twenty-five percent has been added to the originals. It has to be to cover kickbacks. There are names of suppliers here that I don't recognize."

Sam studied the files in Jimmy's pile further. "An additional fifteen percent was added here to Regal's funding requests, on top of the twenty-five- percent hike."

The money trail of payments to Regal led to checks made out to Lou as the beneficiary.

Sam moved on to another file folder. He compared the invoices for labor to install pan-and-tilt remote-control security cameras and security betas. The invoices for labor to install the winches to lift the gondola and to build the network of trusses and walkways added by Bonner were there as well. All were padded heavily, in contrast to the amounts recorded in the documents in the DiAngelis files.

Tony compared sets of invoices to actual checks written to pay suppliers. He showed them to Sam. The differences were significant.

"Look at the discrepancies in these labor contracts." Sam ran his finger down a long list of figures in a Regal invoice. "This is all wrong. Regal brought in labor from out of state only when special training was required. Otherwise, we hired local IBSW labor. Regal didn't do any of this work." Sam shuffled through more checks and found payments to teamsters, listed by name. "Who are these people?"

Tony replied without looking up, "A bunch of crooks, Sam. A bunch of crooks."

Sam opened a folder containing copies of checks made out to the building department. "Jeez! What's this? These building permits were issued in clear violation of regulations." A money trail of kickbacks connected to the permits led to building department officials. The corruption was widespread.

*\*\**

Jamaica returned to Lewis's office and went directly for the gun collection on the wall. She used the big brass key Gloria gave her to unlock the cabinet. The hinged frame holding the guns separated from the wall and swung open. It exposed the hidden safe, just as Jimmy's note had said. She slowly turned the dial on the safe, using the combination from Jimmy's note to open it... three rotations right to 23, two left to 21, one right to 45, and finally, left until she heard the lock drop.

Jamaica held her breath and pulled on the safe handle. It swung open. She looked inside. In the back of Lewis's safe, hidden behind the Rockwell painting, she found three thick folders: *L/insurance*, *L/property* and *L/firm*. Jamaica walked over to Lewis's desk, carrying the three folders in her arms. She sat down in Lewis's chair and opened the first folder.

The folder labeled *L/insurance* contained lists of campaign contributions to political figures and judges. Some had notations reading "Video," followed by a number. She returned to the safe and retrieved a stack of cassette and beta tapes. Some were marked with names, others with numbers that matched those on the list. There were also long lists of payments labeled "Favors," with names and dates going back years.

The "Property" folder contained deeds, land-value lists, and lists of purchase and sale prices for properties Lewis had purchased, then sold. The properties were primarily in New Orleans and on islands in the Caribbean. Among the many deeds in the folder, she found the one to her father's property. Jamaica read the attached paper, listing the purchase price and, next to it, the actual market value of the property. The actual value, listed on the date Lewis purchased her father's property, was over three times what her father was paid.

Jamaica's lip began to quiver. What she saw in front of her was a lie, an indescribable betrayal. Her father used most of the money he received from Coltrane to pay for Abigail's funeral and the move to New Orleans. Lewis paid Garlan wages during the years her father was his gardener, but he also charged Garlan rent on the cottage where he, Lily, and she had lived up until his death, nearly three years ago.

Her father spoke often of his dream to purchase back the family property, but he feared he would never be able to save enough to do it. When he died and the Coltranes assumed legal guardianship of Lily, the two girls moved out of the cottage and into the mansion. Garlan's dream died with him.

She stared at the deed, wondering how many other families had suffered the same fate.

The third and last folder contained the unspeakable, page after page of lists of sums skimmed from fees charged by the Firm. There were lists of padded expenses paid by the Firm, presented for tax returns. There were lists of payoffs to judges, cops and other individuals, for unspecified reasons. There were notes throughout, in Lewis's handwriting, with names, dates, times and meeting places. The dates spanned years.

Another group of documents had numbers for bank accounts in Jamaica, Bermuda and Grand Cayman. They cited astronomical balances, along with lists of dates of cash deposits. The dates matched scheduled dates for vacation flights Lewis and Jimmy had taken on the Firm's jet to the islands. The trips were labeled, "Golf" and "Fishing."

In the back of the stack of papers in the L/*firm* folder, she found an envelope with the name "Spencer" written on it. She opened the envelope, and started to read the single piece of paper contained inside.

Her eyes widened and the hairs on her arms stood erect. A sudden flash of heat shot out from the core of her body and coursed through her like an electrical current, igniting every fiber of her being. She fought for breath.

\*\*\*

Sam and Tony were busy making copies of the relevant files when they heard an agonizing scream coming from Lewis's office.

"Jamaica!" Tony cried out. The two men bolted into Lewis's office.

Jamaica was sitting behind the desk, looking down. Her left hand was pressed against her chest. When she heard them enter the room, she looked up. Tears were streaming down her face and her body was shaking uncontrollably. She extended her right hand. It was clutching a piece of paper. She waved the paper weakly in front of her. Her face was as pale as a ghost and from the dazed expression on her face, she looked as if she was about to faint.

Tony rushed toward her.

Sam reached out to remove the sheet of paper from her fisted hand.

She released it, then collapsed to the floor.

Tony dropped to the floor and wrapped his arms around her.

Sam smoothed out the wadded-up document. He started reading it. The paper contained a long hand-written list of dollar figures in a column marked "Payments" to someone named Spencer. Beside each amount were a notation and a date. The dates of the payments spread out over several years and each notation was the name of an individual.

He began to read aloud down the list.

Jamaica looked up. "The names beside the larger amounts are the names of witnesses called to testify against clients represented by the Coltrane Firm." Her voice strengthened with increasing resolve. She explained, with each name, that the individuals listed either suddenly refused to testify or inexplicably changed their testimony. A few had suffered horrific freak accidents, with resulting injuries that made it impossible for them to testify. Two had died.

"This is insane," Tony said, still holding her fast in his arms.

The implications were chilling, but two specific notations next to two particular payment amounts on the list had caused Jamaica's scream. When Sam read them out loud, Jamaica burst into tears. "$25,000-*DiAngelis*, and $5000-*Lily*."

Tony and Sam stood by helplessly.

After a few minutes, Jamaica managed to steady herself from the shock of her discovery. She wiped the tears from her face. "We have to think rationally. These discoveries raise as many questions as they answer." Jamaica pulled away from Tony and rose from the floor. She walked back and forth in the confined area, with the tense and deliberate gait of a panther, pacing in a cage. "It's crucial we choose the right course of action."

Sam looked at Tony. He could tell Tony was as dumbfounded as he was by Jamaica's detached demeanor.

"What's the right course?" Sam asked. "We've uncovered proof of some serious crimes here. Maybe even murder."

"He's right. We expose all this, and we're placing ourselves in real danger."

Jamaica was oblivious to their concerns. "I think someone killed my sister," she said. "And I'm going to find out who." Her voice rang with uncompromising resolve. "That's the right course. The only course."

Tony pleaded with Jamaica to think about what she was saying. "Let's think about the safest way to address all this."

"Tony's right," Sam said. "Look, I have an idea. I think we should take this information to Allen Stein. The Tribune might be able to protect us and I don't know who else to trust."

Tony looked at Jamaica. "I can call Dad. He can find out who this Spencer person is."

Sam nodded in agreement, but Jamaica insisted Tony hold off.

"I have Cajun friends who can find this man. If that fails, you can contact your dad," Jamaica promised. "This is personal. I want to find out myself what this man has to do with Lily. I have to know what really happened to my sister." She looked across at the gun collection mounted on the wall.

Tony winced at the expression on her face.

She stared at the guns, as if she was ready to take one off the wall and use it on Lewis herself. "If Lewis had anything to do with Lily's death, I have to know."

"We need to get out of here, Jamaica," Tony said.

Jamaica ignored him. "Lewis is occupied with the police right now, answering questions about enemies of the Firm and trying to shed some light on who had reason to want Max dead. These offices are closed indefinitely, so that should buy us some time."

"Whatever you think is best," Tony said."

Jamaica turned to Sam. "I agree with you about Allen Stein. If you can, set up a meeting tomorrow and tell him what we found in the files. That's a start. I'll return to the cottages on the estate. I know someone there who may be able to lead us to this Spencer person. If not, I'll go to my friends in the Bayou."

Jamaica began gathering up papers. "We have a lot to do, and not much time. We need to finish copying these files and tidy this place up. By the time Lewis realizes there was a break in, it'll be too late." She handed the files on Lewis's desk to Sam. "Once these files, and the ones you two studied are copied, they should go with you. You understand their content best, and how they were altered."

Jamaica picked up the wrinkled paper Sam had set on the top of Lewis's desk. "This paper goes with me." She folded up the Spencer document and placed it in her bra. "I don't care if Lewis discovers it missing." Her tone was defiant. "He'd never admit to its existence."

Tony placed his hands on her shoulders. "Is all this moving a little too fast?"

"We'll bring it forward, of course, in time. But please, until I get some answers about my sister, let's keep this one thing just among us."

"Jamaica," Sam cautioned, "Tony's right. You could be risking your life to find answers. We all could be. We have to be careful."

The three worked quickly and arranged to meet the following day.

"I'll call you both after I talk to Allen," Sam promised.

"I'm going to see what I can find out about this Spencer," Jamaica added.

"We are," Tony interrupted. "I'm staying by your side. This guy's probably no picnic." Tony reached for her hand.

"Okay, Tony. We'll find him together."

"Yes, we will, but not tonight. We could all use some sleep. Tomorrow's soon enough to pursue all this." He squeezed her hand. "Stay with me tonight."

She managed a tiny smile. "Well, I certainly can't go back to the Estate. If I ran into Lewis, I'm not sure what I would do."

Tony pulled her toward him. He said nothing, but his hug said it all. He would do whatever was necessary to make her feel safe... on this night, and every night, if she would let him.

*** 

Sam returned to the Marie Antoinette. He sat on the bed in his hotel room and attempted to organize the piles of paper strewn out in front of him. The scope of the kickbacks was enormous, but he'd found no evidence that Jon Navaro was involved. Lou was another matter.

"I'll call Ming first thing in the morning." Sam stared at the hundreds of rows of figures. "Maybe he can make sense of all this."

After Sam first raised questions about invoices a few months before, Ming did some digging and made some discoveries. Changes had been made in invoices his department had drawn up for the Arena project. The changes were consistent, increases in the amount listed on initial invoices. Lou Navaro's signature appeared on all the modified invoices.

When Sam asked Lou about the discrepancies, Lou gave him a lame explanation. "Jon's visit to New Orleans last month ruffled some feathers, so I flew down there and met with the Arena committee." As a result, Lou insisted, the pending confusion regarding changes in billing was resolved. He blew off Sam's concerns, rudely ordering him, "Just do your job."

Estimates on the costs of building and labor were the primary part of Sam's job when bidding on a sign contract. Being told to basically stay out of it was in complete contradiction to business as usual. In retrospect, he regretted not pursuing the matter further. Now, with Ming's help, he would.

Finally, after several hours delving through the papers, he set his alarm and fell into an uneasy sleep.

\*\*\*

Tony unlocked and opened the door to his apartment. He stepped aside and allowed Jamaica to enter ahead of him. He closed the door and turned to face her. Their eyes met and she fell into his arms.

"Oh, Tony," she whispered, tears forming in her eyes.

Tony wrapped his arms around her and lifted her gently into the air. She buried her face in his neck. He felt her tears flow freely as they fell against his skin. He carried her down the hallway into the living room. He reached the couch and laid her down among its soft cushions.

The curtains on the French doors leading to the balcony were open, revealing the lights of the Quarter sparkling below.

Jamaica looked into Tony's eyes and pulled him toward her with one hand, as the other combed gently through his hair.

His heart melted at her touch. The chemistry between them was evident the first time they made love, but the emotions at this moment took on a different dimension. The tears running down her face and the look of sadness in her eyes implored him to hold her, to comfort her.

Tony whispered into her ear, "It will all be all right. I promise."

She responded with a whimper.

As the melancholy strains of a saxophone playing on the street below drifted into the apartment, Jamaica and Tony pushed aside the events of the past few days. They lay on the couch, wrapped in each other's arms.

*** 

Jamaica fell into a deep sleep, seeking temporary refuge from the outside world and from the nightmares that had plagued her since her youth.

But in darkness of night, deep in the marshes of the Bayou, the sky had turned red with the light of ritual fire. Flames rose in the air, dancing to the sounds of pounding drums and wailing voodoo chants.

Jamaica was suddenly torn from the peace of dreamless sleep. Her eyes suddenly opened wide. She lay in a trance, frozen in the dark, as the vision manifested before her.

A gathering of Cajun priestesses, scantily clad in skirts of dried moss and chicken feathers, circled around a raging fire. They flailed their bodies from side to side, waving smoking pods of incense in the air, while necklaces made of animal bone and chicken claws rattled against their naked chests. On the ground at the base of the fire, the high priestess sat, surrounded by a group of men kneeling before her. Grotesque tribal masks emulating the heads of wild boars covered their faces. Voodoo symbols painted in blood covered their bare chests. The priestesses amassed around the men, their bodies gyrating against them in a frenzy of seductive ritual eroticism. The roaring flames

248

crackled as the voice of the high priestess rang out. She raised her arms in the air, chanting in foreign tongue to summon the spirits of the dead.

Jamaica watched in horror as the priestess leaned forward. Directly in front of her rested an effigy of the Arena. It was carved from animal bone. In one hand, she held a voodoo doll, in the other a long needle, covered in the dried blood of a sacrificed rooster. The priestess placed the doll on top of the Arena effigy and raised the needle high into the air. She plunged the needle into the doll, passing through it, and lodging the tip of the needle into the effigy below.

Jamaica screamed and sat up in the couch, awakened from the vision.

Tony, lying beside her, woke with a start. "What? What is it?" he said, reaching out for her. "My God, you're soaking wet and cold as ice."

Jamaica turned to him. Her eyes were vacant. "The Arena," she said. "Clarice was right. They've cast a curse on the Arena."

# 29

## Lunch at the Bistro

At 10 a.m. on Monday morning, rays of bright sunshine blanketed Allen's desk. He stared past them in frustration at the incomplete copy looming in front of him in his typewriter. The attempted follow-up to his original coverage of Max DiAngelis's murder lacked any new relevant information.

He picked up a pile of articles lying on his desk. Among them was a copy of a prior article covering the Court's ruling Friday, exonerating Sam and his company of wrongdoing in the acquisition of the Regal sign contract.

"At least that article was a pleasure to write," he muttered. He dropped the articles back onto his desk.

With the senator's hearings temporarily halted in the wake of the DiAngelis murder, Allen's pursuit of leads on the growing Arena scandal was failing miserably. He'd discovered hints of wrongdoing, but nothing tangible he could use that provided proof.

He pulled the partially written article out of the typewriter, wadded it into a heap, and shot it into the air. It landed a few inches away from the wastepaper basket. "Great, my aim's about as rotten as the copy on that paper." He placed another piece of paper into the typewriter tray. "Maybe Bonner will give me something to write about."

Information Allen had received the previous Friday from an anonymous source had prompted a phone call to Bobby Bonner. "I've got questions, Bobby," Allen had begun. "A source inside your union tells me that materials originally ordered by Bonner Construction are being substituted with inferior-quality material."

Bonner's reply was blunt. "It's true. Several companies were given contracts without my knowledge. When the inferior materials arrived, I visited the building department and discovered that someone on the Arena committee had approved the change in supplier. The materials were returned, but waiting for the reissue of the original order threw a monkey wrench into our schedule. I'm mad as hell about it."

The conversation sparked plans to meet for lunch.

Allen looked at his watch. It was Monday and his lunch date was only a few hours away. He decided to wait until he met with Bonner to attempt his article, hoping something concrete might turn up.

Allen reviewed the list of questions he'd prepared for Bonner. What happened behind closed doors at the building department between Bonner and whoever gave him the information? Who was the committee member who approved the substitutions? Who in the building department allowed the change to go through? What companies supplied the material?

Allen was adding questions to his list when the phone rang.

"Allen, it's Sam McCormick. I need to see you. It's important."

"I've got a busy schedule today. How important?"

Sam insisted it was urgent.

"Well, I'm meeting Bobby Bonner for lunch today. I suppose you could join us," Allen suggested.

Sam readily agreed. "I have information about the Arena project that concerns Bobby, so the timing couldn't be better."

"I'll call Bobby to confirm. I'm sure he'll welcome hearing what you have to say."

They agreed to meet at the Cajun Bistro at noon.

Allen hung up the phone and looked at the blank piece of paper resting in his typewriter. "Bobby and Sam both want to talk. Maybe I'm finally going to have something to write about."

\*\*\*

Several hours prior to Bobby's lunch date with Allen, his office phone rang.

"Boss, you'd better come down here. There's been an accident."

"I'm on my way." Bobby grabbed his keys and headed for the Arena structure. When he arrived, he discovered that a worker bending back rebar had slashed his arm when the rebar snapped.

"The men are really spooked by all the weird accidents happening lately," the foreman onsite complained. "It's like we're jinxed or something."

"That's ridiculous. These bullshit building materials are the problem," Bobby fumed. He got the injured worker off to the hospital and attempted to calm down the remaining workers. "I'll personally visit the building department today and find the source of this shipment of rebar." He gave them his word and sent the crowd of jumpy teamsters back to work.

Before heading out for the building department, Bobby returned to his office. He felt a sudden urge to sweep the room, as he periodically did, for bugs.

"Not again," he said, removing the mouthpiece from the phone on his desk. Someone had managed to get past security and plant a bug in his office. This time, it was in his phone. He deliberately left the bug in the phone and screwed the mouthpiece back in place. "I'll get the boys in the Quarter to find out who did this and why."

Surveillance cameras onsite picked up any unusual activity occurring during construction hours and Bobby kept his office securely locked. But as union leader, he took other precautions, as well. He did his best to keep sensitive phone conversations to a minimum and, under normal circumstances, made it a point to discuss important business in his office at union headquarters.

However, for months he'd been working long hours onsite, overseeing the project, and numerous heated phone conversations had occurred in his office onsite. Most were calls from union reps reporting minor labor complaints, but some issues were urgent. In such cases, Bobby was forced to engage in lengthy phone calls in the privacy of his office, in order to appease the individuals or group having the problem. The conversations were frequently sensitive and the idea of their content leaking was unacceptable.

Bobby was about to leave the office when the phone rang.

"Bobby, Allen Stein here. Do you mind if Sam McCormick joins us for lunch today?"

"That works for me, Allen," Bobby replied. "I have some issues to deal with first. I'm heading back down to the building department this morning. I'll meet you at the Bistro at noon."

"Thanks, Bobby. See you then." Allen hung up
.

***

After recovering from the initial shock of learning about the break-in at the Coltrane Firm, Allen listened with equal fascination to Sam and Bobby's candid complaints about the Arena project.

Sam began by stating that he and Bobby were right in many of their concerns. "Look at these invoices." He pulled out several of the documents retrieved from the break-in. "These numbers don't add up."

He showed Bobby invoices on materials ordered for some of their overlapping projects. The numbers were not the same. "I shared my concerns with Lou Navaro months ago and what really bothered me was his reaction. He was defensive and insisted there was no need to look for problems where none existed."

"Well, clearly, they do, from what you've discovered," Allen said.

Sam stared at the barely touched bowl of gumbo on the table in front of him. "I'd hoped we were wrong in our suspicions, but these files prove invoices have been padded from the start and money's been skimmed off the top. The last thing Regal needs is a skimming scandal."

"I'm afraid it goes a lot deeper than Regal," Allen said.

"Yeah, a lot deeper," Bobby echoed.

Sam placed his napkin on the table. "This conversation's killed my appetite." He looked at Allen. "Lou isn't the only person I butted heads with. I had issues with Max DiAngelis from the start. I'd submit invoices for materials and labor on the sign, only to have payment inexplicably held up. He eventually got back to me and the

254

money eventually showed up, but the delay prevented us from moving forward efficiently. Now we know why."

"Same thing's happened to me," Bobby added. "I bet we're going to find problems with my building permits as well. We've had too many delays acquiring the most basic ones. My crew's had to wait around, sometimes for weeks until DiAngelis or Jimmy Coltrane got them approved."

Bobby turned to Allen, "I can't get a decent explanation from the building department or the committee members on how material substitutions got approved. Something really rotten is going on. And then, on top if it all, this morning I discovered my office was bugged."

"What?" Allen said.

"Yeah, this morning, just before you called me. I found a bug in my office phone on the site. I routinely check for them." He shrugged. "It's just something I do. I've implemented a lot of changes within the union and there's some anger out there. I left the bug in the phone and called my people. They're good at finding out who's responsible when this kind of thing happens."

"Say, something just occurred to me. What about Coltrane? He's up to his armpits in all this, I guarantee it. This bug would be just his style. Frankly, nothing would please me more than to take that sneaky son of a bitch down." He paused and his tone grew serious. "Like I said, my people are very good at what they do."

"Sam, you say no one knows about this break-in?" Allen asked.

"Just myself, Tony DeLuca and Miss Russe. And now the two of you."

"Any chance someone from the Firm will notice?"

"No. We made copies of all the relevant files and replaced the originals last night. Coltrane closed up the law offices on Friday afternoon and sent the staff home after Max was killed."

Sam paused for a moment. "There's something else, Allen. Miss Russe told me that Senator Keetz wants to see the firm's files on the Arena when the hearings resume."

"Doesn't this woman work for Coltrane?" Bobby asked.

"Yes, but she's the one member of the Firm I trust. She's the one who planned the break-in last night."

Bobby looked surprised. "Ballsy broad."

Sam continued, "She knows I'm giving you this information, Allen. To be perfectly honest, we're not sure how to proceed. Who knows how deep this goes?"

Allen nodded. "Yeah, you're bound to be treading on some dangerous toes."

"You're right about that. We're in some deep water here."

"The question now is how to move forward. Senator Keetz is the best option. We should meet with him right away. If you think Miss Russe is willing, I can make the call."

"She agreed to share this information with you, so I'm confident she'll welcome your suggestion," Sam said. "As far as Bobby's bug problem goes, let him find out the source. Maybe it's got something to do with all this."

"Yeah," Bobby added. "Let's drive the pests out into the open."

Allen nodded in agreement. "Couldn't have said it better myself. It's time to exterminate." He rose from his chair. "I'll call the senator now."

# 30

## A Dangerous Plan

Tony failed to notice the amused looks on the faces of the two women seated beside him as he devoured the pastries on the plate in his lap. "These are delicious," he said, looking up at Clarice and causing a fit of giggles from Jamaica as she wiped a mustache of powdered sugar off his face with her napkin.

"Clarice always made these for Lily and me when we visited her here at the cottage," Jamaica said, tapping Tony's hand playfully as he reached for another pastry.

Clarice lived in the small cottage on the grounds of the Coltrane Estate with her son, Maynard, who had discovered Lily's body on the night of the accident. Clarice's parents were Louisiana Creole of Acadian descent. She was born and raised on Bayou Lafourche in a stretch bordering the swamp. When her husband died, she left the Cypress trees, Spanish moss and alligators behind for the security of employment on the Coltrane Estate. There, she raised her two children, Gina and Maynard.

Gina and Jamaica grew up together on the plantation grounds. They passed much of their childhood mingling with the West African community of Cajuns working for the Coltranes. Gina, much to her mother's dismay, left home two years before to explore life away from her family.

Tony and Jamaica listened as Clarice spoke of her daughter and the life she had chosen in the Quarter. "She comes to visit sometimes. She always brings us money."

Clarice's eyes were filled with sadness as she talked about her only daughter. "She looks so different now, not at all like the sweet little girl I raised. I worry every day about her and the way she's wasting her life. She won't talk about her job, but she talks a lot about a friend she works with. A woman named Layla."

"In the Quarter?" Jamaica asked.

"Yes. Gina shared an apartment with this woman for a while when she first went to the Quarter to work. She told me that she and this Layla became good friends. But then she had to move out of Layla's place and get her own apartment, after she met Layla's boyfriend. She told me he frightened her."

Jamaica placed her hand on Clarice's knee, urging her to continue.

"You asked if I knew of a man named Spencer. I do. I remember, because Maynard was the one who urged Gina to move out of Layla's place. He visited Gina one day at the apartment and saw her roommate all bruised up. Gina told him the boyfriend had done it and it wasn't the first time. When Maynard learned the guy's name was Spencer, he told Gina he knew about the man. Word on the street was that Spencer was bad news and Maynard warned her to stay away from him. I was glad when he told me he'd convinced her to get her own place. That was some time ago."

Clarice's head dropped. She stared into her lap. "She's never let me come to see her, though." She looked up at Jamaica. "Imagine that. I've lost my baby to the Devil's world. Not a thing I can do."

"Do you know how we can find her?" Tony asked.

Clarice nodded. "Maynard checks in on Gina from time to time. He knows where she lives. He can take you there. He tells me it's better I not go to see her in such a place."

Jamaica leaned forward in her chair and embraced the woman.

Clarice responded with a warm hug of her own.

Jamaica thanked her for the information and promised to try to convince Gina to come home. "I'll talk to Maynard and get Gina's address. Tony and I will visit her, together. No need to drag Maynard into it further."

"I appreciate that," Clarice replied. "My Maynard's a big boy, but you know how rough it can be in the Quarter." She released a short sigh. Cajuns knew all too well the dangers of the dark side of New Orleans.

Jamaica took her hand. "I'll always remember the wonderful meals you cooked for my family when we lived in our cottage." She squeezed Clarice's hand. "I do hope Gina will find her way back to you."

Tony leaned over Clarice and gave her a gentle kiss on the cheek. From what they had learned about Gina's life in the Quarter, it was doubtful Clarice would ever get her daughter back from the world that had engulfed her.

Jamaica and Tony left the cottage, filled with apprehension about entering Gina's world. They couldn't be sure what they would find there, but it wouldn't be anything good.

\*\*\*

"Well, I'll be damned." Gina peeked out over the taut latch chain, through the open slit in her door. "Jamaica Russe. What the hell are you doing here? And how the hell did you find me?"

"Hello, Gina," Jamaica said. "May we come in? I promise we'll only take up a bit of your time."

"Suit yourself," Gina replied. She closed the door, slid off the latch chain and then reopened the door.

Tony and Jamaica entered the tiny apartment.

Once inside, Jamaica looked around. The scene was appalling. The apartment was a hovel. Tattered upholstery covering aging wood furniture rested on filthy carpet, stained with wine and dirt.

Worse even than the apartment was Gina herself. Jamaica barely recognized her. They'd played together, gone to school together. They'd been friends. The change was heartbreaking.

Jamaica sat down on the worn couch in the tiny apartment and looked up at Gina. Her once-beautiful face was tarnished by deep creases on her forehead and dark bags under her eyes. Heavy makeup covering her pale and translucent skin failed to disguise her obvious abuse of alcohol and drugs. She appeared much older than her years

"What is it you want, Jamaica?" Gina's tone was abrupt. Her eyes locked on Tony, as he sat down on the couch next to Jamaica. "I suppose you're here to convince me to come home, to go back to being no better than a servant to those white folk, with all their money and uppity ways."

She spat on the floor in disgust, "I may be a working girl, but at least I'm not beholden to those rich bastards. They work my mama weary to the bone in that hot kitchen. And for what? I got my life here and it's just fine."

"That's not why we're here at all, Gina," Jamaica answered softly. "We're here because I need your help."

"Help? Help you?" Gina exclaimed, rolling her bloodshot eyes in distain. "What could I possibly do that would help you, you with all your money and fine clothes."

Her eyes cased Jamaica's expensive silk dress and designer shoes. Her voice was filled with spite.

"Gina, please, I'm looking for a man. He has information I need. His name is Spencer. It's very important."

"Spencer, huh?" Gina responded. Her eyebrows lifted in suspicion. "What kind of information would Spencer have that you would need? And what's in it for me?"

Jamaica looked at Tony. Her heartbeat quickened. "So you do know a man named Spencer?" Jamaica asked.

"Yeah, I know that piece of shit. He sees a girlfriend of mine. Like I said, what's in it for me?"

"For starters, I have a message from your mother. She loves you and misses you. She asked me to tell you that. Of course, she wants you to come home." Jamaica hesitated. "I have no right to ask that of you. But if you need money or a job, I can help."

"Don't be ridiculous. I should just walk out on this life? It isn't that simple, you know. Of course, you couldn't possibly know what it's like." Gina's laugh was cruel and haughty. "You, with your fine life."

"What *can* I do?" Jamaica reached out for her.

Gina reared back and stood up. "Nothing. I don't want your pity. I don't want your money, either. If you want to find Spencer, ask his girlfriend where he is." Gina spun away. She walked over to Tony and stopped in front him. She slid her tongue slowly across her lips. "You're quite the handsome one, aren't you? Maybe you'd like to try a little Gina?" Her voice was saccharin sweet.

Tony gave her a hard look.

Gina let out a wicked laugh and leaned down over Tony. She put both hands on his knees and blew him a kiss. She laughed again and turned her head to face Jamaica. "Her name's Layla. You can find her most every night at La Bijoux."

Gina stood up and backed away from Tony. "You sure you want to find Spencer?" She shook her finger back and forth at Jamaica. "I stayed at Layla's place for a while, when I first started working at the club. But I got out of there quick once he started coming around." Gina's tone was aloof, but her eyes betrayed her.

Jamaica saw a glimmer of genuine concern in the expression on Gina's face.

"Spencer's bad news, Jamaica, real bad news," Gina cautioned. "You both best stay away from him. I mean it. If you value your life, stay away."

Jamaica rose and walked toward Gina. She placed her hands on Gina's arms. "Come home, Gina. We can protect you, I promise."

Tears welled up in Gina's eyes. The anger in her voice disappeared. It was replaced with a resigned sadness. "It's too late, my sister. You go now. You don't belong here. Go with your fine man and leave this place. It's no good for you. If you must find Spencer, be careful. He's a bad man."

*** 

Spicy jambalaya, chicken gumbo, and steaming crawfish sat on the table in colorful ceramic bowls. The food permeated the air with the exclusive aroma of Cajun cuisine and mingled with the lively sound of Winston's saxophone, wailing jazz from the stage a few yards away.

The warm atmosphere at the Bourbon Blues stood in sharp contrast to the intense conversation taking place at the table. Tucked back in a secluded corner of the club, Jamaica and Tony sat across from Sam, listening to him relay the details of his meeting with Allen and Bobby.

"Allen called Senator Keetz and requested a meeting. When Allen explained that he had information relevant to the senator's investigation, the senator scheduled it for tomorrow morning." Sam leaned in to the table. "Due to the sensitive nature of the information, Allen requested the senator keep the meeting private. It's to be held at the senator's estate on the outskirts of the city."

Jamaica pushed her food aside and listened intently as Sam spoke directly to her. "He also informed the senator that you and I would accompany him to the meeting. When the senator asked why, Allen said he preferred not to discuss it further on the phone. The senator agreed and Allen said he sounded intrigued."

"I hope we're doing the right thing," Jamaica said.

"I think we are," Sam replied. "Allen knows the senator pretty well. He said Keetz is frustrated with all the roadblocks hindering his investigation. Your discoveries could lead to subpoenas and possibly indictments." Sam gave Tony a reassuring look. "We should all be much safer once it's all in the senator's hands."

Tony let out a reluctant sigh. "If you say so."

"Did you two find out anything about the Spencer person?" Sam asked.

Jamaica remained silent and resumed eating her jambalaya.

Tony squeezed Jamaica's free hand under the table and told Sam about their meetings with Clarice and Gina.

Sam sat, wide-eyed, as Tony told him about the visit with Gina and their plan for the evening. "Are you two sure you want to do this?" Sam asked. "It's a crazy plan. Sounds risky to me."

"We have no other option, Sam. If we want to get information from this Layla, we have to go into her world. We have to convince her to help us. If we fail, then I'll call Dad." He felt Jamaica's hand pull away from his.

She turned her gaze to Sam. "First, we do it my way. This is important to me, Sam. Most of the friendships I formed growing up were with Cajun families on the plantation. They're the only family I have left. If I call on them to help me, they will." She paused. The words that followed rang with an unmistakable air of finality. "I have to do this for my sister."

"Well, just be careful, and call me if you need me. Call me anyway. I won't get any rest, worrying about the two of you."

"We'll be fine, Sam. I'm a DeLuca. Nobody messes with a DeLuca," Tony replied. "At least, I hope not!"

With Tony's comment, the mood at the table lightened.

A lot was riding on the events of the next twenty-four hours and anything could go wrong, but the plans had been set in motion. The three friends finished dinner, vowing to face the future together, whatever it may hold.

# 31

## The 'Fantasy Suite'

Gaudy red and yellow neon lights flashed off and on, illuminating the sign identifying the nightclub. It formed the shape of a voluptuous woman, reclining on the words "La Bijoux." Her costume consisted of a tiny yellow-neon G-string and flickering yellow-neon pasties, covering the nipples of the hot- pink neon breasts. Red-neon high heels flashed erratically on the feet of her crossed legs. Yellow-neon formed long, wavy hair on her head.

Jamaica liked neon art and wasn't unappreciative of the details of the sign, as distasteful as she also found them. She and Tony entered the club and took seats at the bar. It was 8 p.m. and the place was quiet. Two dancers moved about on a long stage, working the few customers who were sitting around the stage floor. Most of the booths, and all but one of the seats at the bar, were vacant.

Jamaica noticed a man seated in one of the far back booths. He was staring at a nearly nude dancer, wearing nothing but a G-string and high heels, grinding in front of him.

Her legs were straddling his, her crotch only inches from his lap. Both her hands cradled her breasts as she pressed them into his face. When one of his hands passed between her legs and groped her crotch, Jamaica turned her head in disgust away from the lewd scene and directed her attention to the bar.

The plan was simple. Tony would engage the bartender in conversation and ask him where he and his girlfriend could find a playmate for a little fun.

Gina's warnings were adamant. To attempt to talk to Layla about Spencer, they would have to speak to her in private. She explained that Layla was afraid of Spencer and why. To have any chance of getting information from her, Layla would have to feel safe. If she did agree to talk to them, she would demand assurance that nothing she told them would be traced back to her.

"Buying time with her in one of the private VIP rooms is the best idea," Gina advised. "It's expensive and you'll have to pay off the bartender. You might have to tip the bouncers as well."

Tony kept his hands busy, sliding them around Jamaica's waist, as he ordered drinks.

Jamaica played along, responding to Tony's advances and kissing him fully on the mouth in front of the bartender.

"I've heard this is the best joint in town for a little adult entertainment—and that you're the man to see," Tony began. He slid his palm across the bar toward the bartender, lifting it slightly to reveal a folded hundred-dollar bill.

Jamaica watched as the bartender checked out the gold Rolex resting on Tony's wrist.

"I've also heard there's a girl working here who has, you know, unusual tastes." Tony winked at the bartender and tossed his head in Jamaica's direction. "I was told she's a sexy Cajun chick who digs both sexes—and likes it just a little *rough*." After a pause to let that sink in, he said, "Her name's Linda or Laura or something like that." He flashed the bartender a wicked smile. "So you think you can help us?"

The bartender touched the tip of the bill and slid it across the bar. "You're looking for Layla. And sure, I can help you, but it'll take quite a bit more than this." His eyes studied Tony's as he slipped the bill behind the bar and put it in his pocket.

"Of course it will." Tony rolled his eyes in a gesture that was both sarcastic and nonchalant. "So how much and where can we find this Layla?"

"She doesn't start until ten. I can set it up for you. It'll take three more of these," he gestured to the bill stashed in his pocket, "two for Layla, and one for the house. She'll join you after she does her first set onstage. House rules. You can watch the set if you like or just pay for a VIP Suite in the back and she'll join you when she finishes. Why don't you and your girlfriend …" he slowly ran his eyes up and down Jamaica and she could feel Tony's hand tense around her waist, "stick around for a while, have a few more rounds and wait?"

"No, thanks," Tony replied. "We have a few hours to sparc. I think we'll just take the limo for a long ride and warm up a bit." Tony pulled her closer. "We'll be back at ten."

"I'll be right here behind the bar. Just tell the bouncer you're here to see me. I'm Patrice."

***

Jamaica and Tony entered the waiting limo.

Tony directed the driver to take them back to his apartment. "We'll talk to this woman, and we'll convince her to help us find this man."

"I hope so, Tony," Jamaica replied, leaning back in the seat. "If we can find him, maybe we can find out what really happened to Lily." She lowered her head and closed her eyes. "We just have to."

"We will, I promise."

The limo drove down the street, away from La Bijoux and, for a few hours, away from whatever lay ahead.

\*\*\*

The limo returned to La Bijoux a little after 10 p.m. The club was bustling. The tables were full, with just a few open seats by the stage, where a half a dozen girls were dancing.

Virgil was the lone bouncer at the door when they entered. Tony tipped him heavily, telling him they had business with Patrice. Virgil directed them to two empty stools at the end of the bar. Tony caught Patrice's eye and waved his wallet carelessly in the air as he and Jamaica sat down.

Patrice walked toward them. "You're all set," he said. "I talked to Layla. She's in the dressing room. She'll be dancing shortly. Her set lasts about fifteen minutes. You pay me the house's hundred now and Layla will collect her fee when she meets you in the VIP suite."

Tony laughed at the idea of calling any room in La Bijoux a suite.

"What's so funny?" Patrice asked.

"Nothing. Private joke," Tony replied." We want your finest suite and your best bottle of champagne." He pulled two hundred-dollar bills out of his wallet. "This should cover it—and there'll be plenty more for you later if this Layla is all you say she is." He handed the money to Patrice.

"You and your pretty little girlfriend here won't be disappointed." He looked past Tony and gave Jamaica a lewd wink. "So, do you want to watch her dance, sweetheart, or wait for her in the suite and be surprised?"

"We like surprises," Jamaica replied, playing along. "I think we'll wait for her in your suite."

Patrice retrieved a bottle of champagne and called one of the cocktail waitresses over to the bar. The girl was young, sixteen at the most, with blonde hair, and scantily dressed. Her partially exposed breasts peeked out from underneath a short, cutoff T-shirt. Her sheer mini skirt rose only to well below her pierced belly button and covered very little of her behind.

She flashed Tony a flirtatious smile and waited as Patrice placed the bottle in a bucket of ice on her tray, alongside three champagne glasses.

"Take these two to the Fantasy Suit," he said.

Jamaica and Tony rose to follow the waitress. She guided them around the side of the bar to a hallway, slightly obscured by a curtain made of heavy, beaded fringe. Ornate doors painted red with various themed names engraved on large gold plaques lined both sides of the hallway. When they reached the door marked Fantasy Suite, the cocktail waitress turned the knob with her free hand and stepped aside, gesturing for the two of them to enter.

Red-velvet drapes covered sections of the four walls, falling from ceiling to floor. They were separated by large mirrors, and framed pictures of naked women painted on black velvet. The women in the paintings were all reclining in various, seductive poses. The center of the room contained a circular stage elevated several feet above the floor. A red-velvet chaise lounge sat on the stage next to a dance pole. An enormous pit of red-leather couches surrounded the stage. A few small openings provided entry for seating. Glass side tables were built into the pit group to accommodate drinks.

The room décor was as ornate as it was tasteless. Tony looked around, imagining what his father would say if he saw the place. The Sultan's Palace was ornate as well, but beautifully decorated with only the finest materials. The Fantasy Suite was an insult to interior design.

Jamaica and Tony sat down on one of the couches.

The cocktail waitress placed the champagne bucket and glasses on the table closest to them. "Would you like your champagne opened now?" she asked. "Your private dancer will be here shortly."

"Yes, please, miss." Tony looked at the young woman, shaking his head at the thought of all the indignities she must endure working in such a dismal place. Pathetically, she appeared content. She was so young and already hopelessly damaged. He thought about Gina, then about Clarice at the Estate, worried about her daughter. He curbed his anger.

The waitress opened the champagne and poured two glasses. She left the third on the table by the bucket and asked if they needed anything else. Tony tipped her generously, stating that there was nothing further. The waitress pointed out a phone on one of the tables, explaining it connected to the bar, should he want anything else. "Just ring if you need me." She pursed her lips, blew a kiss to Tony, then left the room, leaving Jamaica and Tony alone.

Jamaica reached for Tony's hand and squeezed it, hard. "What an awful place, Tony."

Tony squeezed back. "It's all right. We'll be out of here as soon as we get what we came for."

The two of them sat together in silence, watching the bubbles pop in the untouched glasses of champagne in front of them. Ten minutes later, the door to the suite opened and Layla walked in. She closed the door behind her.

"I'm Layla," she cooed. "I understand you asked for me special."

Tony rose as she approached. "Yes, Layla, we did. And we're prepared to be very generous, if you can help us out."

"Well, baby, whatever it is you and your girlfriend need, I'm sure I can deliver." She stopped and stood next to the couch, close to them. "Of course, there's the small matter of my entertainment fee. We handle that business up front, so we can get it out of the way and just enjoy ourselves."

"Of course. That's fine," Tony replied. "And I'm prepared to pay you more than your usual fee, if you can provide us with what we need." Tony pulled out his wallet, opening it to reveal a thick stack of bills.

Layla's hips swayed seductively, causing her fringed skirt to swish about and reveal her bare legs beneath it. "And just what is it you and your lovely girlfriend need?"

"We need to talk, Layla. We'll pay you whatever you want. Please, sit down and listen." Tony looked over at Jamaica. "This is Jamaica. After you hear what she has to say, you'll understand." Tony gestured for Layla to sit down on the couch next to Jamaica. He nodded at Jamaica, then turned to the table beside them, to pour Layla a glass of champagne.

Layla sat down in the oversized couch, her eyes sizing up the pair of customers as she waited to hear what they wanted. She crossed her legs, began removing the thick feather boa wrapped around her neck, turned her body toward Jamaica, and leaned forward to reveal her huge breasts—and the piece of jewelry hanging between them.

Jamaica stared at Layla's neck in horror and disbelief. "Where did you get that pendant?" Jamaica whispered.

The tone of her voice caused Tony, who was still pouring champagne, to turn and look.

"It was a gift from an admirer." Layla sat back and frowned, eyes narrowing in suspicion. "Why do you want to know?"

Jamaica's eyes locked with Layla's. She lifted her hands and slowly undid the top two buttons of her dress, opening it to reveal the nearly identical shell pendant hanging there.

"I want to know," Jamaica said forcefully, "because you're wearing my sister's necklace. And whoever gave it to you may have killed her."

Tony abruptly set the glass of champagne on the table. He sat down next to Jamaica. His gaze passed from Jamaica to Layla, and then back to Jamaica.

Layla stared at the pendant hanging from Jamaica's neck, and then looked hesitantly up, into Jamaica's eyes. She remained silent, waiting.

She didn't wait long. "We're looking for a man named Spencer."

*** 

Layla sat motionless on the couch, sickened by the story the two strangers were telling her. When Jamaica asked if she could help them, she replied, "I wish I could tell you that Spencer never gives me details of his activities. I certainly would prefer it that way." She paused. "But he's violent and gets off on frightening me with gory details of the jobs he's pulled and the people he's hurt. He's done so many awful things." She fondled the necklace resting on her neck. "But he didn't tell me where he got this."

Nevertheless, when she connected the timing of the gifts Spencer had given her, with Tony's account of Lily's death, she conceded that Spencer could well have done it.

Tony told her about the paperwork Jamaica had discovered at the law firm, linking Spencer to numerous scams and possibly to murder.

"Listen to me. I'm not surprised by any of it, but you can't possibly imagine what will happen to me if I tell you everything I know about him. If Spencer ever found out I talked to you, he'd kill me for sure. I want to help you, but…"

"But you're afraid," Jamaica said. "We understand. We heard all this from Gina."

"Gina? Gina Broussard?" Layla asked, surprised. "How do you know her?"

"We were childhood friends. She was like my sister growing up. She told us that you helped her when she first started working here, that you were a good person we could trust. Her brother told us how dangerous this Spencer is, and how he treats women. If something happened to Gina I'd never forgive myself. That's why I'm trusting you with this information, hoping that you'll trust us in return."

"Yes," Tony promised. "We will never reveal the source of any information you give us."

Tony explained who he was and who his father was, promising she would be protected. "I'll personally guarantee your safety, Layla. If you help us, we'll help you. Whatever you want, you name it."

Layla's mind raced as she considered the possibility that she might actually be able to escape the prison her life had become. As she listened to Jamaica and Tony and their promise that they could be her way out, she wanted to believe them, but she couldn't. Twice she tried to respond that she could, but she thought about Spencer and the words just wouldn't come out.

Jamaica said, "Layla, you're wearing my sister Lily's necklace. She was just seventeen, by the way. And you befriended my other sister Gina when she needed help. In a way, that almost makes us sisters."

Tony jumped in before Layla could object. "I'm sure this is hard for you to get your head around, us showing up like this out of the blue, but if you tell us where we can find Spencer, that particular problem of yours will go away forever. And once that happens, we can start to help you with whatever other problems might need taking care of."

Layla sucked in a deep breath and as she exhaled, she decided to take a chance, knowing that it might be the only one she'd ever get. "I never know when he's going to want to see me. But when he has money, he gambles here at La Bijoux. There's a poker room in the back. Every Friday night, the regulars play and the girls here get bonuses when they get customers to join the games. There's always a lot of action and the house makes a ton of money."

"Any chance he'll be here this Friday?" Tony asked.

"Probably," Layla replied. "Lately he's been throwing a lot of money around in the club. The last time he was in here he bragged that he'd see me soon. That he was about to land another big score. If that's true, he'll be here for sure, to mix it up at the poker tables and fleece the out-of-towners." She sighed. "Probably after he has his way with me."

Layla removed the necklace from her neck and placed it in Jamaica's quivering hands. Her own hands quivered as she took Jamaica's hands in hers. "I'm so sorry about your sister."

Jamaica's hair fell over her face as she looked down at her sister's pendant. A lock of her hair touched Layla's hands.

Layla suddenly remembered the Mother of Pearl hair brush, the one Spencer had used to savagely beat her. She sat up straight in the couch. "Spencer gave me a hairbrush the same night he gave me this necklace. It may be your sister's, as well. If it is, it belongs to you."

She looked at Tony. "He nearly killed me that night. He's a monster. I hope you make him pay for all the pain he's caused. In fact, I hope you kill him."

Layla explained what had to happen next. "We have to leave this room together and return to the bar for another bottle of champagne before you leave the club. I'll stay with you for one glass, then you two are on your own."

Tony nodded.

"Throw some extra money at Patrice. Tell him you plan on coming back soon for more Layla and that you'll make it worth his while. It'll help if your hands are all over each other. That's the only way you'll get out of here without anyone suspecting anything. Do you understand?"

"Yes," Jamaica replied. "Thank you, Layla, for everything."

The three of them left the Fantasy Suite together and headed back into the club.

\*\*\*

Jamaica and Tony returned to his apartment. "We have to call Sam, but first, I'm calling Dad." Tony explained that a man like Spencer wouldn't willingly surrender the information they needed and that Benny had people who could get answers. "No way we're going back to that club. Ever. This way, the only one who gets hurt will be Spencer."

After what they'd experienced at La Bijoux, Jamaica was quick to agree. "I just want the truth about what happened to Lily."

When Tony related the information about Spencer to his dad, Benny's response was blunt. "You two stay away from that place. Your young lady will get her answers. I'll contact you when it is done."

*** 

Sam paced back and forth in his hotel room, waiting by the phone all night for Tony's call. It finally rang.

"Hey, Sam."

"Tony. Thank God you two are all right. Did you get what you needed?"

"We did, but we're exhausted. Jamaica can tell you all about it on the ride out to the senator's estate tomorrow. She'll pick you up at your hotel at nine a.m. Get some sleep and good luck tomorrow." Tony hung up the phone. He looked over at Jamaica. She was fast asleep on the couch.

He walked into the bedroom and pulled the comforter off the bed. He removed her shoes, covered her with the comforter, and placed a pillow under her head. It was nearly 3 a.m. and her meeting with the senator was only hours away. He walked back into the bedroom and set the alarm.

# 32

## The Senator

Jamaica drove past endless rows of peach orchards ripe with fruit on the road leading to the Keetz Estate. Sam gazed out the window, savoring the tranquil scenic beauty of rural New Orleans in full bloom as he listened to Jamaica relay the events of the night before.

"Not many women could have pulled off what you did last night," he said. "At least you agreed to let Benny handle this Spencer lowlife. That was a smart decision, Jamaica."

"I don't know. He's just a creep," she said, staring at the road in front of her.

"Well, maybe, but I've known Mr. DeLuca for years. He knows how to handle assholes like him."

"With all that's going on, I'm fine with having someone else find him. We've got enough to worry about, presenting these files to the senator. They may just be the tip of the iceberg."

"We're giving him concrete evidence to use in his investigation." Sam looked at the briefcase resting between them. "And it'll be out of our hands. The sooner the better, as far as I'm concerned." He released a deep sigh.

Jamaica looked over at him. "What is it?"

"I'm really worried about Regal. After studying our invoices, it's obvious Lou Navaro's been padding them and skimming off the top. It could take the whole company down. At least, what we've uncovered so far shows only one rogue individual at Regal who's the guilty party in our group," Sam said. "After all that's happened on this project, it makes sense."

"The truth will come out, Sam. We'll make sure it does."

Jamaica's comment reminded Sam of something Bobby had said at lunch the day before. "The senator will want to talk to Mayor Riley. He told Bobby Bonner he suspects someone on the committee is taking bribes."

Jamaica reached a thick grove of flowering oleander trees marking the entrance to the Keetz Estate. She took her right hand off the steering wheel and gave Sam's left knee an encouraging pat. "All this is going to be hard for the senator to hear. Let's hope he doesn't shoot the messengers."

\*\*\*

Jamaica's car rolled to a stop at the security station in front of the mansion's gated entrance. After she and Sam identified themselves, the security officer placed a call to confirm their appointment with the senator. He waved them through the iron gates onto the grounds. Jamaica turned onto a circular driveway and parked the car in front of the mansion as directed.

A butler was waiting on the steps.

"Follow me," the man said. He led them into a large lobby just inside the entrance. "Please wait here. The senator will see you shortly."

Jamaica and Sam looked up at the lobby walls towering around them. Huge, framed portraits of Keetz family members going back generations covered the walls. Stately portraits of Keetz patriarchs, from early plantation slave owners to generations of lawyers and politicians, hung majestically side by side.

Romantic oil paintings commissioned to flatter generations of Keetz matriarchs featured women seated on various pieces of vintage furniture from the particular period. The entire room, resplendent in its ghostly lineage of Louisiana aristocracy, generated a distinctly nostalgic aura.

Sam and Jamaica took a seat. Sam's right foot tapped rapidly on the marble tile under his feet. His nervousness stemmed from his fear that the allegations they were about to make about some pillars of New Orleans society would not sit well with the senator.

The senator's aide appeared. She was an elegant woman in her mid-sixties dressed in a fashionable business suit. Her eyeglasses hung from a pearl chain around her neck over her suit jacket. "Miss Russe, Mr. McCormick. Please come this way."

The sound of her high heels clicking on the marble floor echoed off the walls as she guided them down long hallways, through the mansion's spacious living areas, and finally upstairs to a private office. She opened the door and entered ahead of them, announcing their arrival to the senator, who sat behind a large mahogany desk in the center of the room.

He rose to greet them. "Miss Russe, Mr. McCormick, thank you for coming. Mr. Stein called me early this morning. Evidently, a pressing matter at the newspaper has prevented him from joining us today. However, he insisted I see the two of you. He assured me I would find this meeting worthwhile. Please be seated." He gestured to two ornate antique chairs facing the desk.

"May I offer you some coffee, or tea, perhaps?" he asked as they sat down.

Jamaica and Sam politely declined and waited for the aide to leave the room.

The senator resumed his seat behind his desk.

"Senator Keetz," Jamaica began, "I'll get right to the point. We've discovered disturbing documents that prove a deliberate and ongoing plot to steal funds from the Arena project's budget."

"Well," Senator Keetz said. "That's quite a statement."

"Yes," Jamaica replied. "It is. We have with us copies of two sets of invoices discovered in the Coltrane law offices. They show conflicting amounts issued for a large number of contracts and services. All were approved by members of the Arena committee." She gestured to Sam.

Sam opened the briefcase. He removed a large file folder and handed it to Jamaica. She stood and placed it on the desk in front of the senator, separating the paperwork into two marked piles and placing them side by side.

The senator began reading.

"What we've discovered," Jamaica said, "after briefly comparing these two sets, is a pattern. One version of each invoice has been padded, allowing a percentage to be skimmed off the top. We discovered the padded invoices in the official files of documents recording the project's expenditures. We found the original invoices, presented to the committee for approval, in separate files." Jamaica pointed to the top page on each of the two piles. "You'll see a consistent pattern here. Fortunately, what we've surmised, so far, is that not all of the approved funding has been compromised." She gave Sam a quick glance.

He nodded back, encouraging her to continue.

"In fact, we were relieved to see that, although the amount of money skimmed is significant, we were able to isolate, through these invoices, the areas of the project that are being affected, and by whom."

Jamaica heard the senator curse under his breath. "What we found most disturbing is a pattern in which specific members of the committee appear to be responsible. The pattern drawn in these documents implicates the chairman of the committee, Lewis Coltrane, as the mastermind behind the scheme. As you know, he and his associates at the Firm, Jimmy Coltrane, and the recently murdered Max DiAngelis have been in charge of the Arena funds from the beginning."

Jamaica looked over at Sam. "You'll see here that Lou Navaro of Regal Signs also appears to be involved. We believe he acted alone, without the knowledge of his partner and brother Lou or any of the other members of the company."

Jamaica looked up from the papers she had spread out in front of the senator.

He was staring at her in disbelief. "Where did you say you found all this?"

"In the law offices of Coltrane, Coltrane and DiAngelis," she replied. "As I stated before, these are copies, senator. We returned the originals to their original locations after these copies were made."

"My God." Senator Keetz looked back down at the paperwork.

Jamaica looked directly him. "You can imagine my shock and disappointment at this discovery. As a new member of the Coltrane Firm, I have both a personal and professional interest in exposing the guilty parties—and in exonerating those not involved. Mr. McCormick has the same interest. It's our hope that this information will enable you to do just that."

"Yes, Senator," Sam added. "And there are some other disturbing facts you need to know." Sam proceeded to tell him about Bobby Bonner's objections to the substandard building materials approved by the committee. He went on to reveal Bobby's conversation with the mayor, including the building-department issue. "Mr. Bonner wants to speak with you about his ongoing frustration dealing with Mr. Coltrane. The mayor may be able to shed additional light on the actions of some committee members as well."

The senator cupped his left hand around his mouth, shaking his head.

Jamaica sat down next to Sam.

"Miss Russe," the senator broke the silence. "I want to thank you and Mr. McCormick for coming forward with this. I appreciate the difficult position you've both been placed in by doing so. I promise you those responsible for this criminal abuse of power will be brought to justice."

For the next several hours, Jamaica and Sam assisted as the senator compared each of the padded invoices with the originals, noting other people involved in the transactions.

When Keetz asked if there was anything else, Jamaica closed her eyes, took a deep breath, exhaled, and replied," Yes, there is." She gestured for Sam to hand her a second file containing the three sets of folders found in Coltrane's safe. "Although what's contained in this file doesn't pertain directly to the Arena project, it holds records of illegal activity by Lewis Coltrane to financially benefit his firm and to increase his personal real-estate wealth. The activity spans years, possibly decades."

The senator plopped back in his chair, dumbfounded. "What kind of illegal activity?"

"Blackmail, extortion, and possibly murder, all linked to Lewis Coltrane."

Senator Keetz gasped. "You have proof of this?"

"Not yet, but we're close, with your help."

Keetz opened the folder and began to read. "Oh my God. My God!"

Shortly before 1 p.m., the senator excused himself from the room. He returned ten minutes later. "I've just spoken with Judge Palmer, briefly explaining the content and importance of what you've presented here. The judge has agreed to examine this new evidence. Once he sees it, I'm confident the hearings suspended this past Friday will resume. I'll be leaving shortly to meet with him at his home to review these findings and discuss how to move forward. I expect subpoenas to be issued for the original files. It's likely that additional subpoenas, and possibly warrants, will be served once the validity of this discovery is proven in court."

The senator's voice lost its official tone. "The State of Louisiana owes you both an enormous debt of gratitude. I personally owe you both a great deal. Thank you."

"You're welcome," Jamaica and Sam replied in unison. Looks of relief appeared on their faces. The burden of their discovery had transferred to the senator.

The senator gestured toward the door. "Miss Russe, Mr. McCormick, I'll walk you out, then be on my own way."

"Of course, Senator," Sam said. "But before we leave, I have a favor to ask. I believe in the employees at Regal Signs. Please, isolate the one or two bad apples who are guilty of discrediting their hard work," Sam implored.

"Yes, absolutely, Mr. McCormick," the senator replied. "I certainly owe you that."

# 33

## The Curse

Sam and Jamaica watched from the front steps of the mansion as the senator's limo drove away. As the two of them headed for Jamaica's car, Sam asked a favor. "Would you mind terribly if we stopped off at the Arena site on our way back to the Quarter? I really need to check on the progress of the sign. It won't take too long."

"Not at all," Jamaica replied. "I'd like to see the progress on the whole Arena project myself." As they approached the car, she tossed the keys to Sam. "Will you drive? My nerves are shot."

Sam took the wheel of Jamaica's Firebird and headed to the Arena site. During the drive, Jamaica theorized about what legal moves might be coming in the days ahead.

"The first thing the judge will do is review the files we gave the senator. That should result in subpoenas for all the original documents. Like the senator said, once he and his team connect all the dots, the dominoes will start to fall. Not much we can do but watch and wait."

"Well, it's out of our hands now." Sam pointed to the roadway ahead and the Arena structure, looming in the distance. "Time to get back to work on that."

As Sam approached the fence separating the main road from the Arena, Jamaica felt a sudden chill run up her spine. What she saw lodged in the wire lacing of the fence made her gasp.

"Are you all right?" Looking over at the expression of dismay on her face, he slowed the vehicle to a crawl.

She pointed to the fence. "You see those objects woven into the fencing? Those are all Creole voodoo symbols. They've been placed there by a mambo or a houngan as a curse on this place."

Sam burst out laughing. "A what? A curse?" he said. "Are you serious? And what's a mambo?"

Jamaica's eyes remained locked on the fence. "It's not funny, Sam. A mambo is a voodoo priestess. Houngans are voodoo priests. Both practice what many believe to be black magic." She pointed to several strands of fabric, woven into the fencing. "That one. See the moon-shaped trinket tied to it? That symbol is hung to summon night demons." She turned her head away, and pointed down the property beyond the fencing to the place Clarice had identified as the cemetery.

"That place, over there. Do you know what it's going to be used for?"

Sam looked across the ground to an area along the far left side of the property, storing heavy equipment. "Over there? It's just equipment storage now. I think it will eventually be a big parking lot. Why?"

"Oh, no. That can't be. That ground was once a graveyard. It's now haunted by the ghosts of desecrated graves. I know, you think it's silly, but it's true. No good can come of this ground, if the curses placed on it aren't lifted." Jamaica lowered her head. "Let's go see your sign."

Sam had no response and resumed the drive up the white seashell gravel road. Then he saw the sign, gleaming in the afternoon sun with the pylon standing tall against the horizon. He parked the car beside a Regal crane truck and walked over to the workers gathered at the base of the sign.

Jamaica followed along beside him, silent, still shaken by the voodoo symbols on the fence.

Clyde was standing next to Farrell Johnston, the team's foreman, in the middle of the group. Farrell was an experienced Regal sign hanger, brought down from Las Vegas to assemble the sign. When Farrell saw Sam and Jamaica approaching, he waved both hands over his head to get their attention. "Where ya been, boss? Haven't seen you onsite for days."

"Yeah, I've been kind of tied up." He turned to Jamaica. "You remember Clyde. He's been overseeing the sign work with me." He gestured to the workers. "This is my crew."

Jamaica smiled. "That's an impressive sign," she said, looking up at the sign structure.

"Your timing is good, Miss," Clyde said. We were just getting ready to fire up test patterns on the three messenger boards. Boss, the boys have been working all morning and everything's in place." He hesitated. "But first, I'm afraid I've got some bad news."

Sam groaned. "What's happened now?"

"It's the gondola. Monday we had problems with the lift." Clyde shrugged and began to tell the story. "You aren't going to believe it. Everything started out normal. Then, it got strange..."

***

Monday morning had arrived and, after weeks of preparation, the installation of the gondola was nearing completion. The main structure hung, secured by welded steel beams to the skeleton frame of the Arena's domed roof, 300 feet in the air. It was time to lift the gondola into place and secure it to the main structure.

"Motors in place!" Farrell's voice sounded from his megaphone, echoing off the interior walls of the Arena structure.

Clyde stood beside Farrell, watching, as six men held on to lines secured to each of six gondola boards. Six more stood by, manning each of the lift motors located high above on the main structure.

One at a time, they signaled a thumbs-up to Farrell, who was standing in the center of the Arena next to an enormous crane.

Farrell looked up at Andy, who was seated in the crane cockpit. "Ready?"

"Ready as I'll ever be," Andy said with a chuckle. "Hopefully, I won't be needed, but the way this whole gig has gone so far, who knows?"

"OK, men!" Farrell shouted into the megaphone, "We're starting the lift!"

The massive gondola consisted of six electronic messenger boards, attached together in the shape of a hexagon. It sat on the ground in the center of the Arena structure.

"This is going to be a hairy lift," Andy said. He was standing by in case the crane was needed to assist in the event some unforeseen calamity occurred during the lift.

Clyde looked at Farrell. "We double-checked everything this morning," Farrell said. "All six motors are working perfectly and the boys know what they're doing."

He waved up to Andy, who couldn't wipe the concern off his face. "You know, it's like we're lassoing a sleeping bear. One poke, the bear wakes up and it's goodbye gondola. I hope the crew has those motors tied off evenly."

"Let's do it," Clyde nodded a go-ahead to Farrell.

Farrell swirled his right arm in a circle high above his head to signal the start of the lift. "Start 'em up, nice and easy!" he bellowed into the megaphone.

The sound of power filled the air as all six motors turned on and began lifting the gondola in perfect sync. All was going well, until at about twenty feet into the lift, one motor froze up. The lines securing the gondola to the affected area snapped tight and one corner tipped, lurching the entire gondola off balance.

"Watch out! She's dropping!" one crew member yelled. The men on the ground scattered, as mayhem ensued high above.

The motor shaft broke, dislodging the motor and sending the cable and reel tumbling down. It struck the gondola with brutal force. The sleeping bear had awakened. And he was pissed.

Clyde looked up at a rattled crewmember, swinging helplessly from his safety line. He turned to Farrell. "What the hell happened?"

"Hell if I know," Farrell replied. "Everything worked fine this morning." He lifted his palms into the air in a gesture of exasperation. "I swear there's a jinx on this whole project."

Several other crew members who had run for the cover of safety beside the crane grumbled in agreement. "It's the goddammed chickens," one man whispered, tugging on a fellow crewmember's shirt.

Farrell heard the comment. "Well, chickens or not, this is just another one of way too many accidents happening on this job."

Clyde frowned as he and Farrell walked around the gondola and assessed the damage. Motor parts were strewn all over the ground. Shards of metal had scattered hundreds of feet around the Arena, missing fleeing crew members by inches. Others were not so lucky and grimaced as they pulled sharp pieces of metal from various parts of their bodies.

"It's a goddamned miracle nobody was killed," Farrell said.

He and Clyde checked the fallen structure and found the metal panels lining the back of the boards mangled by the fall. Clyde sighed and pointed up in the air toward the crew member still dangling from his belt at the top of the Arena. "Make sure everyone is OK, Farrell. Somebody rescue that man up there, then get to work on repairs. Jinx or no jinx, this gondola is going up."

*** 

Sam shook his head. "Wonderful," he said. "How bad was it?"

"Only minor damage to the gondola itself," Clyde replied. "But the motor was destroyed. We're waiting for a replacement before we can resume the lift. We did get the gondola repaired already, so that's something." Clyde lowered his voice. "The thing is, there was no reason for that motor to fail. I guess I should've called you."

Sam frowned. "Well, the damage is done. I wonder why Bonner didn't mention it when I saw him yesterday."

Farrell let out a sarcastic laugh. "He wasn't onsite when it happened. Hell, it's not his department. He's had enough to worry about, what with all the crazy-ass accidents happening on his building and all those crazy Cajuns hanging outside the fence."

"What?"

"Yeah, security keeps running 'em off. But the other day, a crane operator said he saw one of those Cajun voodoo guys, the one with the dreadlocks and the dead chickens, loitering around the entrance right about the time the gondola fell. He said the guy was smiling like a fool, watching the whole thing."

Jamaica gave Sam a stern look that said, I told you so.

"Well," Sam said with a sigh, "I could use some good news. Go ahead and start the test on the sign. Let's see what happens."

Farrell reached for his intercom system headset and directed the man at the command center inside the Arena to turn on system one. All the blue lights on the boards illuminated. Even in the bright afternoon sun, it was a stunning sight.

Farrell reached for the intercom. "System one's a go. Now give us system two."

The blue lights vanished, replaced by brilliant green.

System three tested next. With all three messenger units testing clean, Sam turned to Jamaica. "So, what do you think?"

"I've never seen anything like it."

Sam stepped back to admire the nearly completed sign. He winked at Jamaica, then turned to Farrell. "Can we illuminate the pylon?" Sam asked.

Farrell directed the computer operator to turn on the pylon. Sam looked up at the three-sided sign, rising 200 feet in the air. Bright twenty-five-watt lights started cascading down the pylon, creating the effect of thousands of falling stars. Each faceted bulb shot light in multiple directions. The sequence completed to the bottom of the pylon and repeated continuously from the top.

Workers installing metal panels on the domed roof of the Arena, 150 feet away, whistled and hollered their approval to the sign crew.

Sam watched the fireworks of light, exploding in brilliant colors across the three messenger boards of the sign. Jamaica stood with her palm to her forehead, blocking the sun, looking up at the spectacle.

Sam tugged on the sleeve of her dress to get her attention. "People from every direction will see this sign create limitless lighting effects. Fourth of July, Christmas and New Year's Eve, all rolled into one giant light show."

Sam gave Farrell a hearty slap on the back. "Good work, Farrell. See you all back here in the morning."

Sam walked with Jamaica back to the Firebird. The sign was nearly complete, standing majestically next to the huge structure it would soon identify. But Sam's cheerful mood darkened as his thoughts returned to the meeting a few hours before. Pride turned to concern over the future of Regal, and his own future. He looked back at the sign and sighed. "How could I have been so naïve?"

Jamaica took the driver's seat. "My turn, Sam. Try not to worry. All we can do now is trust the senator and hope for the best."

Sam and Jamaica drove off the site, filled with mixed emotions, down the snow-white road of shimmering seashells.

# 34

## Dinner at Bourbon Blues

Jamaica dropped Sam off at the Marie Antoinette. As he was stepping out of the car, she asked, "Sam, will you call Tony and let him know I'm driving out to the Estate to pick up some clothes to bring back to the apartment? I shouldn't be more than an hour or so."

"No problem." Sam leaned back into the car. "Great job today," he said and closed the passenger door.

"You, too!" Jamaica called as he walked toward the hotel.

Sam entered his room to the sound of the phone ringing.

\*\*\*

Allen Stein heard Sam pick up the phone and say, "Hello?"

"Sam? Allen here. I know you said you'd call me when you and Miss Russe finished with the senator, but I couldn't wait. How did it go?"

"It went well, Allen," Sam began. He related all the details of the meeting with Keetz, including the senator heading off straightaway to present all the evidence to the judge.

"That's great news, Sam." Allen rapped his knuckles on his desk, knocking on wood that his suspicions about Coltrane were about to be validated. "Can you meet me for dinner in the Quarter tonight?"

"Sure, what time?"

"Let's say seven p.m., at the Bourbon Blues."

Allen hung up the phone and rocked back in his chair. He plopped his feet up on the desk and clasped his hands behind his neck, quietly savoring the moment. "Finally," he whispered, "it's finally going to happen. And heads are going to roll."

\*\*\*

Sam hung up the phone, then dialed Tony's place. He relayed Jamaica's message and invited them both to dinner. "Can you two join Allen and me at the Bourbon Blues for drinks? I assume Jamaica's staying at your place."

"Yeah, she's playing it cool and avoiding the Coltranes as much as possible. And I feel better keeping her close, where I know she's safe. Dinner sounds good. We'll see you there."

\*\*\*

The mansion was quiet when Jamaica arrived. It was nearly 4 p.m. She went directly to her suite and packed a few bags, taking enough clothes and necessities to ensure she wouldn't have to return for a while. On her way out, she passed Catherine hanging up the phone in the living room.

Catherine saw her and motioned her into the room. She saw Jamaica's packed bags and smiled. "I assume you've decided to spend some time with your young man. I'm pleased to see it."

"Yes," Jamaica replied. "Tony has an apartment in the Quarter and it's so convenient. It's located not far from the office and I don't have to make that long drive every day."

"Well, that's as good an excuse as any, I suppose," Catherine said, sporting a knowing smile. "I'm glad it's working out for you." She paused. "You haven't by any chance seen Jimmy, have you? No one seems to know where he might be."

The question alarmed Jamaica, as Jimmy's note and the subsequent break-in came immediately to mind. She set her bags down and did her best to look calm. "I stayed with Tony these past few days, and, as you know, Lewis sent everyone at the Firm home on Friday. I'm afraid I haven't seen him."

"Lewis hasn't seen him either. At least, he says he hasn't." Catherine looked down at the phone. "You never mind, dear. I'll just keep making calls until I find him. He's probably at that club of his. He may walk through the door at any moment."

"If I see him, I'll be sure to tell him to call you." Jamaica picked up her bags and headed for the hallway.

"Enjoy your young man, dear. He's lucky to have you." Catherine waved at Jamaica, and reached again for the phone.

***

Sam was lounging in the open patio area at the front of the Bourbon Blues club, sipping a beer and listening to Bourbon Blues at 7 p.m. Allen sat down and ordered some Cajun popcorn, a few spicy appetizers and a few more beers. The two men sat together, drinking and sharing notes on the day's events.

"I hope Regal survives all this," Sam said. He sipped his beer. "My gut tells me it's all going to point to Lou."

"Have some faith, Sam. It'll all work out," Allen responded sympathetically.

"It's out of my hands. I guess we'll know soon enough."

Allen wiped his chin with his napkin and rocked back in his chair. "By this time tomorrow, the wheels will be set in motion to blow the roof off the top of this whole circus," Allen chuckled.

"I hope the whole mess gets sorted out quickly," Sam said. "I just want to get my signs built. To be honest, I miss Las Vegas." He saw Tony approaching the table.

"Jamaica's running a little late. Good thing the apartment's so close," Tony said, as he pulled up a chair. He acknowledged Allen with a warm handshake. He grinned at Sam. "She was still putting clothes in drawers when I left the apartment. I guess picking out what she needed at her place took longer than she thought." His grin broadened to a Cheshire cat smile. "She'll be staying with me for a while."

Sam gestured to a nearby waitress to bring a beer for Tony. Fifteen minutes later, Jamaica called out from across the street. Sam waved to her as she neared the club. "Would you look at the spring in her step."

Jamaica sprinted across the street. She reached the men's table, wrapped her arms around Tony, and kissed him firmly. The scene drew smiles from onlookers who'd noticed the stunning young woman entering the patio.

Jamaica collapsed into a chair next to Tony, grabbed the closest beer stein, and took a hearty swig. "Sorry I'm late. I was on my way out the door when the phone rang. I just spoke with the senator. His meeting with Judge Palmer went well. The senator's legal team will begin fully examining the files we gave him. It will take a few days and we've all been advised to stay calm and keep what we know to ourselves, at least until the senator's press conference."

She took another long drink and set the beer stein on the table. Her eyes sparkled. "The senator said the judge wants the team to investigate, not only the committee members, but some of the members of the building department. And the judge is considering a raid on the Coltrane Firm to seize the original documents before they can be destroyed."

Allen started clapping. "This is great."

"Yes. The senator said he's determined to prosecute all those involved."She looked at Allen. "There's more. I gave the senator something else that we discovered that night at the Firm, Allen. Something that wasn't included in the Arena documents."

"What else?" Allen sat up straight in his chair.

"Unrelated offenses I discovered in the folders in Lewis Coltrane's safe." She paused and took a breath. "He plans to pursue a separate investigation into all of Coltrane's business dealings, going way back."

"Holy crap," Allen said.

"Holy crap is right," Jamaica echoed. "The senator will be holding a press conference at some point within the next week to discuss the progress of the investigation. He plans to mention the discovery of new evidence. You're going to have quite an article to write."

"Yes," Allen said, smiling. "You bet I am."

Jamaica turned to Sam. "The senator also asked me to tell you that he told Judge Palmer he believes that only one man at your company is involved in all this. Unless evidence implicating others is uncovered, the rest of your company should be exonerated."

Sam stood up and leaned across Tony. He reached out for Jamaica and planted a kiss firmly on her cheek.

"Hey, watch it, pal. That's my girl," Tony warned. He slapped Sam playfully on his back. "Sit back down. Let's order dinner. I'm starving."

# 35

## Jimmy

The waning sun filtered in through the bay window of the Coltrane living room, spreading beams of light on the living-room couch.

Catherine Coltrane hung up the phone. After numerous calls to everyone she could think of, she still hadn't been able to locate Jimmy. Both Lewis and Jimmy had been characteristically absent over the weekend, and when Catherine questioned the butler and valet staff, everyone assured her that, if the two Coltranes weren't at the Ambassador Club, they were no doubt on a fishing trip in Grand Cayman. Her alarm bells didn't go off until Tuesday arrived and no one could recall seeing her husband.

She called the Coltrane's pilot late that morning. Tom told her he hadn't flown the Coltranes anywhere in weeks. When she called the Ambassador Club, the concierge was his usual evasive self, stating that he was "not at liberty to divulge information on the whereabouts of club members."

A few hours earlier in the day, Catherine had noticed Lewis heading out of the mansion. She confronted him under the porte-cochere on his way to his waiting car. She accused him of knowing where Jimmy was and with whom.

Lewis blew off her concerns with a shrug and scolded her for henpecking her husband. Catherine held her ground. "If you know where he is, you need to tell me."

"I haven't seen him, Catherine. But if you do, you let him know his old man is looking for him, too. Tell him I'll be at the police station." Lewis trotted down the steps and sped off in his Corvette.

It was now past dusk. Catherine's conversation with Jamaica only a few hours earlier had shed no light on Jimmy's possible whereabouts, nor had any of her many phone calls.

"I'm calling the police," she said aloud to herself. She picked up the phone and was about to dial when she heard movement in the grand hallway. She rose from the couch. "If that's not Jimmy, I'm calling the police," she repeated. When she saw Lewis entering the main salon, she stopped him in his tracks. "Lewis, I'm really worried. I've been making calls all day and nobody has seen or heard from Jimmy. I'm asking again. Do you know where he is?"

Lewis brushed by her. "I haven't seen him. Have you checked the club?"

She grabbed his arm. "Of, course," she replied, rolling her eyes. "Like that ever does any good. If you're covering for him, fine. I don't care. But at least tell me he's safe. After what happened to poor Max …"

Lewis jerked his arm away from her grasp. "Look, I haven't got time for this. He'll turn up. If it will make you happy, I'll call the club."

"You do that. But if I don't see him or at least hear from him by tomorrow, I'm filing a missing-persons report."

"Don't be ridiculous. I'll find him and have him call you."

Catherine could see that Lewis was considering the situation and was probably realizing that he hadn't seen

Jimmy for days. At least that's what his pensive expression implied.

Catherine stood before him, her hands planted on her hips. "He's your son, Lewis. And I'm worried."

"Enough!" Lewis threw his hand up in disgust. "Jimmy did tell me he wanted to be alone for a while. I think I know where he might be." He made an about face and headed back to the porte-cochere.

***

Lewis exited the mansion. The Corvette was still parked in the driveway. "You'd better have a good explanation for this disappearing act of yours, Jimmy," he mumbled. He started the car and headed down the road. His destination was the Willows.

The glow of a full moon partially lit the night sky, allowing limited visibility, as Lewis neared the Willows. He took the turnoff, and discovered the gate open. He drove through the open gate and down the path leading to the back of the cottage.

"I knew it," he grumbled, peering out the windshield of the Corvette. In the glow of his headlights, he saw Jimmy's Mercedes in the distance, parked at the bottom of the hill. He slowed the Corvette as he neared the Mercedes and noticed the vehicle's driver's door partially open.

"That's odd," he said, squinting to get a better look at what appeared to be a figure, sitting inside the Mercedes. The Corvette drew closer. Even in the dark, Lewis could see that something wasn't right.

He screeched the Corvette to a stop beside the Mercedes. "Oh my God!" he screamed.

He leapt out of his car and rushed over to Jimmy's. He grabbed the handle of the car door and swung it open wide. The stench coming from the vehicle was overwhelming. Lewis covered his mouth and looked inside, his eyes wide with horror at the sight before him. "Jimmy!" he cried. "No!"

Jimmy's body lay slumped over the driver's seat. His bloodied head rested on the steering wheel. His eyes were wide open.

Lewis felt faint. He grasped for the top frame of the Mercedes for balance. He looked beyond Jimmy's body to the open glove compartment. Below it in the passenger seat, covered in blood, the pistol Jimmy had used to kill himself lay against the plush leather fabric, still clenched in his hand.

When Lewis saw it, he dropped to his knees. He'd given the pistol to Jimmy when he graduated from law school, years before. "Oh, God, Jimmy," Lewis said, shaking his head. "Jimmy, Jimmy, Jimmy, suicide's for cowards. You never did have any balls, did you?"

He rose to his feet, turned away from Jimmy's corpse and walked toward the front door of the Willows. "Not to mention, this is goddamned bad timing, son."

The first call Lewis made was to the police. "This is Lewis Coltrane. I want to speak to the chief. Find him."

Lewis got his buddy the police chief on the line, explained his discovery, and had an ambulance dispatched. During the conversation, he demanded assurances that news of Jimmy's death wouldn't be leaked to the press. "I'll be here, waiting," he said and hung up.

His next call was to Doc Beauregard. "Jimmy's gone and shot himself dead. There's blood everywhere and I can't afford a scandal or another investigation. We'll need to get a story together. Something like the one we pulled with the girl a few months back on my Estate. I'll pay off the coroner again, to keep a lid on the details of Jimmy's suicide."

"I don't know, Lewis. What do you want me to say this time?"

"Goddammit, Beauregard! It's simple. We'll say his alcohol abuse, due to his unhappy marriage, combined with the death of his best friend Max DiAngelis, pushed him over the edge."

Lewis grunted. "I can't believe he could do this to me. The ambulance is on the way. I'll meet you at the morgue. Call the coroner and do whatever you have to do to keep this quiet until we can get our story straight."

Lewis hung up and sat on the couch, waiting for the arrival of the ambulance. He squeezed his eyes shut in a futile attempt to shake off the image of Jimmy's lifeless body, covered in a blanket of blood. Jimmy had ended his life sitting in a $200,000 luxury car Lewis had purchased for him as a birthday gift. And he'd done it with a priceless pearl-handled pistol from his father's private gun collection.

Jimmy was his heir, his own flesh and blood. He was the last of the Coltranes. And he'd thrown it all away. Lewis Coltrane sat, alone in the dark, unable to fathom why.

The sound of sirens filled the air. Lewis lifted his head and saw the oncoming lights of vehicles shining through the windows.

\*\*\*

Friday morning. Ten a.m.

A scattering of rain clouds dropped intermittent showers on the clusters of umbrellas. An occasional ray of morning sunshine broke through, casting light on the wet grassy knolls of Metairie Cemetery. Blades of grass sparkled like diamonds on a bright green carpet, only to dull as rainclouds returned. Streams of water flowed along the paths among the many trees gracing the natural landscape of the cemetery.

Elaborate polished marble sculptures marked the family crypts of the wealthiest members of the New Orleans community. Statues of winged stone angels rose majestically in the air above the crypts, their holy countenance unaffected by the inclement weather.

Lewis stood beside the Monsignor, gazing through the mist at Jimmy's closed casket. It rested, surrounded by flowers, inside the open Coltrane family crypt.

News of Jimmy's passing had spread like wildfire throughout the community.

Lewis succeeded in hiding the gory details of the suicide from the public, causing rumors about the cause of death to run rampant. Shocked friends and business associates called in droves to express their condolences, but to avoid further scrutiny, the quickly organized funeral service was kept private. Only a small gathering huddled in the confined area around the crypt.

Catherine and Eleanor stood side by side sharing a large umbrella, several feet away from Lewis and the Monsignor. Jamaica stood behind them, along with Clarice and Maynard.

"It is not for us to understand God's purpose in taking Jimmy from this world," the Monsignor preached. "That is the mystery of God's will and the test of our faith in Him." He reached out to Lewis and gently touched his shoulder. "We pray for Lewis and Eleanor, two loving parents, and Catherine, Jimmy's devoted wife, in the hope they will find comfort in the Lord during this sad time. Let us pray they find peace in the days ahead."

***

Catherine squeezed Eleanor's hand. She glared through the falling rain at Lewis. Neither woman had spoken a word to him since he informed them of Jimmy's suicide late Tuesday night. The details had sent them both back into the state of deep despair they'd barely recovered from since Lily's death, but the callous and cavalier delivery of the news had both devastated and angered them. Their silence, and refusal to acknowledge Lewis at the funeral, spoke volumes.

Paralyzed by grief, Catherine directed all her anger toward Lewis, dismissing his feeble attempts to use Jimmy's alcoholism and an unhappy marriage to justify his suicide. Eleanor's attempts to comfort Catherine proved fruitless, even as she fought to battle her own confusion over the incomprehensible reality of Jimmy's suicide.

"It makes no sense at all, Eleanor," Catherine had insisted upon learning the awful truth. "Jimmy hated guns. Something else is going on here. And Lewis knows what it is. I can see it in his eyes."

She could also see in Eleanor's eyes that she had the same doubts. But she continued to put on the façade of faithful wife and mother, as she mourned in earnest the loss of her only child.

The service was short and, unlike after Lily's funeral, there was no wake. Rather, most of the group, minus Lewis, returned unceremoniously to the Estate.

Lewis left the cemetery alone and drove to his office at the Firm to organize its reopening for business the following week.

*\*\*\**

While Jimmy was being laid to rest at Metairie Cemetery, Senator Keetz was in the courthouse conference room miles away, brainstorming with his legal team.

"I've scheduled a press conference for tomorrow," he said, looking up from the stacks of documents spread out on the conference table. "I intend to announce the reopening of the investigation."

One of the lawyers raised a palm. "Will you be leading the raid on the Coltrane offices as well?"

Keetz leaned back in his chair. He combed the fingers of one hand through his hair and shook his head. "No. It will take place during the press conference. The Arena committee members and the businesses involved in the project are being required to attend, informally of course. Most of the names you see mentioned in the documents before you will be there." A sly smile appeared on his face. "On the strength of what we already have, Judge Palmer agreed to sign the criminal complaint we drew up against Lewis Coltrane on the skimming charges. The Coltrane Firm is still temporarily closed, pending resolution of the DiAngelis murder, but once the raid is executed, we will act quickly on Coltrane. We'll get the rest of them behind bars once we get the original documents thoroughly examined."

The comment drew murmurs of approval.

One lawyer tapped his finger on a set of documents in front of him. "I'm looking forward to seeing the looks on the faces of these men when they finally get what's coming to them—"

"Yeah," another interrupted. "Hauled in by the police in handcuffs!"

Keetz smiled. "Patience, gentlemen. The documents secured in the raid tomorrow will be delivered directly to this room. Once this team matches the original documents with what you have before you now, we'll present irrefutable proof to the judge. And when it all gets to a grand jury, indictments are sure to follow."

Keetz rose from his chair. "As soon as you've organized all these documents, go home and get some rest. Tomorrow's going to be a long day. Let's catch some bad guys."

# 36

# The Poker Game

On Friday night Spencer entered a packed and smoky Bijoux. The money he'd received from Coltrane on Monday for setting up the hit on DiAngelis was burning a hole in his pocket as he strutted into the club, ready to celebrate his newly acquired fortune with a night of gambling and sex.

He approached Patrice at the bar and asked about the action.

"It's cooking back there, Spence." Patrice poured Spencer a shot of cheap tequila. "Lots of big pots and some new faces. Planning on joining the party?"

"As soon as I have a few more of these." Spencer gulped downed the shot and slammed the glass on the bar, shoving it toward Patrice, and gesturing for a refill. "Where's Layla?"

Gambling, poker in particular, was an addiction for Spencer, and every time he received a payment from Coltrane, he headed straight for the Bijoux. His usual practice was to pass some time with Layla first in one of the club's suites to get himself revved up for an evening of intense gambling. On this particular Friday night, though, the girls at La Bijoux were swamped, servicing weekend tourists, in addition to the club's regular customers.

"You can't have her tonight, Spence. Not until later, anyway." Patrice shot him down. "Layla's busy attending to business in one of the suites. As you can see, it's a busy night."

"That's all right. It can wait." Spencer patted the wad of money in his pocket. "I don't need an appetizer tonight." He downed his third shot. "I can always have Layla later for dessert." He tossed Patrice a crass grin, then headed out for the poker room.

Spencer parted the beaded fringe curtain leading to the back, walked down the hall to the poker room, and knocked on the door. A few seconds later, a loud buzzer went off, unlocking the door. He pushed it open and stepped inside. Dense smoke from cigars and cigarettes permeated the room. Spencer looked around. The place was buzzing. All six poker tables were open and active with play.

The usual characters crowded the club. Regulars mixed in with some naïve tourists, seductively wooed into a "friendly" game of poker by girls working the club.

The girls plied the patsies with cocktails and encouraged them to play, promising carnal rewards after they won their fortune at the table. They mingled throughout the room or lounged on plush couches in the adjacent bar area, posing provocatively within sight of their marks.

Spencer saw shills from the club, strategically placed at the tables among players. Their presence ensured optimum profits for La Bijoux and Spencer knew them all well.

"Hey, Spencer! Over here! There's a spot for you at this table," Jake called out from one of the tables. "We've got some new players and they're looking to win some money."

Jake frequently used Spencer as a shill for the club, particularly because he supplied his own buy in for the games. Spencer rarely had a problem finding a seat at a table where the odds were in his favor. And when Jake turned him on to customers from out of town who were sitting in for the first time, he controlled the game.

All the club's shills excelled at raking in whatever money the amateur poker players brought to the back room. When Jake was present at the tables, it meant there was money to be made.

Spencer strolled up to Jake's table. It was understood that a percentage of whatever shills won would go to the club, but with the bankroll Spencer had to play with, the winnings could be huge, even with a significant cut going to the house.

"I'd like you to meet Mr. Baldini and, to his left, Mr. Ricci." Jake gestured to two men seated at the table. "These gentlemen are visiting from out of town and just happened to find themselves at La Bijoux. They asked Patrice where they could find some action and here they are." Jake slapped Spencer on the back. "Gentlemen, this is Spencer. He's a regular here at the tables. He's a decent player, no offense intended, Spence old boy, so I think you'll all get along just fine."

Jake grinned, exposing the gold caps covering all the front teeth in his mouth. He pulled out a chair at the table for Spencer.

"It's nice to meet you fellas. Where you in from?" Spencer asked as he sat down.

"We're from Albany, New York. We're down here for a shoe convention," Baldini replied. "But we love to play poker and we've got a little money to burn."

"Well then, let's resume playing, shall we?" Jake suggested. "House deals first. Dealer's choice. Five-card stud. Good luck, gentlemen." Jake waved at the crowd and made his way to the door. He flashed a wicked smile at Spencer and left him to do his worst.

The game lasted well into the night, with ample drinks being poured and large sums of money changing hands. Hours later after suffering significant losses, the two men from Albany decided to call it a night.

"Spence, I must say, I've never enjoyed losing money to anyone as much as I've enjoyed losing it to you. I just hate to see the evening end. Let us buy you a drink— with the small amount of money you've left us," Mr. Baldini insisted. He and his friend gathered up the remaining wads of bills from their spots at the table, despite their run of bad luck.

Spencer happily consented and he and his two new friends exited the poker room into the nightclub, still packed with customers.

"It's much too crowded in here, Spence. Angelo and I thought we might find someplace quieter to down a few. Maybe we can talk you into a private game, just the three of us? We'd sure love a chance to win back some of our money, wouldn't we, Franco?"

Spencer was appreciative of the fact that Angelo Baldini and Franco Ricci were now on a friendly, nickname basis with him. And he was now Spence to them.

"How about we go back to our hotel? We can order up some booze and resume this game. What do you say?"

Spencer grinned. The evening had revealed the two men to be rotten poker players and they obviously didn't know when to quit.

"Sounds good to me, Franco. I can always use another drink—that is, if you two are buying."

Spencer stifled a smile. He was in his element, skilled at plowing clueless marks with drinks before fleecing them.

"Drinks are on us, Spence. What do you say we get going? Our rental car's parked just outside." Franco slapped Spencer heartily on the back and they began to inch their way through the crowded club.

Spencer spotted Jake fondling a cocktail waitress at the bar as they passed by. Jake saw Spencer with the two men. Spencer gave him a knowing smile and nodded toward the club exit. He'd already taken Baldini and Ricci for a lot of money and the nod told Jake that Spencer wasn't finished with them yet. Jake smiled back and waved him on.

Angelo and Franco guided Spencer to their rented Lincoln Town Car, parked just around the corner from the club. The three men got in, Angelo in the driver's seat with Spencer seated beside him and Franco in the back. After a few blocks, Angelo turned left, onto one of the many dark roadways in the Quarter.

It was virtually deserted, void of traffic so late at night.

As Angelo made the turn, Franco leaned forward behind Spencer, flipped the garrote of thick rope he had retrieved from the back seat over Spencer's head and wrapped it tightly around his neck.

Spencer grabbed for the garrote. He gasped for air. His legs flailed violently in the air, banging against the glove compartment as Franco lifted him back. The garrote pressed tighter against his throat.

"Don't kill him, Franco," Angelo warned, as he drove toward the highway entrance. "He's got some talking to do."

# 37

## The Manchac Swamp

"It doesn't have to be this hard, Spence, old boy. Just tell us what we want to know and we can end all this unpleasantness." Franco let out a deep sigh and took a long step to avoid the pool of blood covering the dirt floor of the abandoned barn.

Angelo walked over to the chair and looked down at the bloody bludgeoned face of his nearly unrecognizable poker-playing friend. He grabbed a hank of hair and forced Spencer's head back. "Come on, Spence. Spill it. We don't have all night."

Benny's instructions had been clear. "First, extract the information. All of it. And then make the piece of shit disappear."

So far, all Spencer had delivered were screams of agony, as Franco tirelessly tortured him with increasingly brutal blows. "I don't know what you're talking about. I don't know anyone named Coltrane or anything about some broad named Lily."

Franco and Angelo knew that Spencer was playing by the rules on the street and those rules were clear: Never snitch. Never be a stool pigeon. If Spencer answered any of their questions and he got away from them, he knew he was a dead man. So he kept pleading. "Please, stop. I don't know anything," Spencer's swollen, lacerated mouth stung as he cried out. He struggled to look up at Angelo, through badly beaten eyes.

The irony was, whatever he said or didn't say, Spencer was a dead man.

"Well, Spence, old boy, this is going to get uglier and uglier for you until you tell us what we want to know. Franco and I are reasonable men. Tell us what you did for the Coltrane guy and this can all stop," Angelo spoke softly and released his grip on Spencer's hair. He watched Spencer's head drop like a rock and turned to see a smiling Franco approaching with electrical cables.

The smile on Franco's face broadened. He walked slowly toward Spencer, clicking the ends of the cables together. They created a stream of sparks as the electric current surged through them, making loud crackling noises.

Spencer responded to the sounds. He mustered what little strength he had left to look up. Through his barely half-opened eyes, Spencer saw Franco coming and fainted.

***

Extracting the information from Spencer didn't take long after that. Once Franco revived him and started in with the electric shocks, it was pretty much over. Spencer gave it all up quickly, weeping as he confessed all the details of how Coltrane had hired him to cover up the little girl's death after Coltrane's son had accidentally killed her in an argument.

Eventually, Spencer told them all the details of his meetings with Coltrane, the bugs, and the hit Coltrane had ordered on DiAngelis to keep him from testifying in court.

Franco had quickly become bored with the cables and switched tools, opting for his fancy new curved cutters. He picked them up in his right hand. When he showed them to Spencer, casually wiggling the fingers of his left hand in front of Spencer's face, Spencer pleaded for his life and told them everything he could remember about jobs he'd done for Coltrane.

Angelo and Franco perked up when Spencer started spilling his guts about Curtis Brown, the Cajun hit man Spencer contacted, who'd freelanced outside his own group's activities to do the hit on DiAngelis. Their eyebrows lifted when they learned that Coltrane had paid $20,000 for the hit. Angelo and Franco agreed it was an impressive figure and celebrated the fact that most of the $5,000 that went to Spencer for setting it up was now in their possession.

Spencer gave them a good description of Curtis, as well as information about his affiliation with the Dixie Mafia. Angelo and Franco busted out laughing at the name. "Spence, what kind of name is Dixie Mafia, anyway?" Angelo asked. "The boys at home will really get a belly laugh over that one!"

Once they had acquired all the necessary information, Angelo ended the interrogation by pulling out a cheap old Smith & Wesson .45 and shooting Spencer point blank in the head. He and Franco gathered up a few of their tools, placed them and Spencer's body in the trunk of the Lincoln, and drove to the outskirts of the Manchac Swamp.

As the two men drove toward their destination, they talked about the fun they'd had earlier in the day. They had risen early Friday morning to do some shopping, then scout for a quiet spot to conduct their business.

***

They'd secured all the equipment needed for the evening's activity at a local hardware store, including the portable generator for power and some electrical cables, just in case their songbird resisted singing and needed extra persuasion.

"Check out all these tools." Franco eyed rows and rows of garden tools, smiling like a kid in a candy store. The store was well-stocked, and Franco purchased a wide variety of items, just to keep himself entertained.

Then they set out to find what they were looking for.

"I've never seen so much farmland or so many blasted trees in all my life," Franco said, as Angelo drove the Lincoln toward the marshes of the Bayou, his eyes peeled for a back road, leading away from civilization. "It's hot and humid as hell in this godforsaken state. Makes me miss the desert."

"Just find us some deserted spot off the main road where we can work in peace," Angelo replied.

They spent the afternoon driving up and down back roads, searching for a remote location to conduct their interrogation. They found an old abandoned farmhouse with a dilapidated red barn, not too far from town, on the western shore of Lake Pontchartrain.

Angelo pulled the Lincoln to a stop. A blanket of thick ivy vines covered the left wall of the barn, wrapping partially around to the front wall and weaving up onto the roof. What remained of the barn door hung askew, supported by rusty hinges and tangled vines.

The two men got out and looked around. "Not a soul for miles," Angelo said, eyeing the perimeter. "Let's check inside." They entered the barn and found it deserted. A few bales of hay rotted on the dirt floor. Beams of sunlight shone down from scattered holes in the roof. The beams peeked through spider webs of hanging vines, creating lacy patterns of light on the floor. "This place will do," Angelo said. "Let's get set up."

Although he wanted to make a sincere effort to use all of his newly acquired toys during Spencer's interrogation, including his favorite, the new cutter he had added to his collection, experience had taught him that cables always got the best results.

After setting up, they went to explore the Manchac Swamp, on a strange tip from a creepy old man at the hardware store. He told them tales of the Bayou, warning of the dangers of the swamps. One in particular, he'd said, the Manchac Swamp, was haunted.

"Legend has it," the old man began, peering through milky cataracts, his eyes sunken into the deep sockets of his weathered face, "that Manchac Swamp is the home of the Rougarou. That's what the Cajuns around these parts call the werewolves of Manchac. The story goes that, back in 1915, there was an oracle, that's a fancy word for voodoo princess, living in Frenier. Frenier's a little town near the swamp. Now, this oracle predicted that, upon her death, she would take all the townsfolk with her."

The lids covering his cloudy eyes lifted. "On the day of her funeral, a great hurricane wiped out three towns, sending hundreds of bodies into Manchac. To this day, Cajuns say that at night, bodies can be seen floating in the swamp, food for the red-eyed crocodiles and werewolves of Manchac."

The old man raised his mangled tree branch of a hand and shook a spiny finger at the two men. "Don't be going into Manchac Swamp, not unless you want to be bit by the Rougarou or eaten by them red-eyed crocs."

That was enough for Franco and Angelo. It was the perfect place to dump a body.

***

"Something's moving in the water over there. What the hell is that?

"Waddaya mean what the hell is that? It's the Boogaloo, or whatever that ghoul at the hardware store called it. The swamp werewolf," Angelo replied, amused.

"Can we please just dump this body and get the hell out of here? Whatever it is, if that thing over there moves any closer, I swear I'm going to shoot it," Franco complained in a loud whisper.

"Well, if you have to shoot, then shoot. Just don't miss." Angelo chuckled. He and Franco pushed on, deeper into the swamp, dodging the cypress branches covering the dense marshland and carefully avoiding stepping off the path into the murky water.

"SShhh. You don't want to wake it, whatever it is," Angelo answered back, amused by his friend's comments. "But I'll tell you what. There's nothing like this back in Vegas."

Angelo and Franco planned to have a good time back home telling their story to the boys—two enforcers from Las Vegas in Armani suits, lugging a dead body into the swamp to be used as fish food.

They'd done everything Benny sent them to do. All that was left was to dump the body, get out of the swamp, and make it home.

"This should do it, Angelo. We're deep enough. Let's toss him in and get the hell out of here." The two men stopped on the path beside a large marshy area of foliage next to the water.

Angelo looked across the marsh and caught a glimpse of movement off the embankment into the water. "Your friend over there's ready for his meal. Unless, of course, you prefer to shoot him and take him home as a souvenir."

"I should shoot him and have him made into some nice shoes. Mine are ruined from walking through this Godforsaken country," Franco complained, shaking mud from his $500 Versace loafers.

Angelo ignored him. "Come on, let's dump this guy. On three, ready? One … two…three!" The two men swung Spencer out and pitched him as far as they could away from the bank and into the murky water.

An instant after the body splashed into the water, a long partially submerged animal on the opposite bank shot toward it, slicing through the water with lightning speed. The moon cast just enough light on the water's surface to reveal a set of glowing red eyes, an instant before the predator's giant teeth encased Spencer's torso in a death grip. The body thrashed violently about in the water for a few seconds, then disappeared beneath the surface. All that remained in the spot where the body had been was the moon's reflection, rolling in the ripples in the water, as they silently fanned outward in a circle toward the shore.

"So, what do you think it was, Angelo, an alligator? Or maybe it was a red-eyed croc?" Franco said, scanning the water's surface.

Angelo laughed aloud. "Who cares? Whatever it was, it's busy dining on old Spence."

"Yeah, well, my stomach's been growling for hours," Franco said. "Let's go get a pizza or something, before we fly back to Vegas. Killing always makes me hungry."

***

Angelo and Franco made their way out of the swamp, and drove back to their hotel in the city. Benny's jet was waiting to fly them back to Las Vegas, upon successful completion of the job.

Pretending to be such awful poker players had been difficult for the two experienced gamblers, especially with Benny's money. But thanks to Spencer, they were returning with Benny's original stake and more.

They knew from the very beginning that a man like Spencer would try to roll the two of them. They knew plenty of small-time thugs like him. Punks like Spencer regarded themselves as tough guys, at least until they encountered the real thing. Unfortunately for Spencer, in his case, the real thing was Angelo and Franco.

He got his wish to play with the big boys, and it ended badly for poor old Spence.

# 38

## The Walls Come Tumbling Down

Saturday at 2 p.m. sharp, moments after the scheduled start of the senator's press conference, an army of federal agents entered the lobby of the building housing the Coltrane Firm.

JJ, the building's security guard, watched warily as the group converged on the place like a swarm of bees. He rose from behind his desk and approached Jamaica Russe, who was walking among the agents. "The Coltrane offices are still closed up, Miss Russe." JJ gave Jamaica a confused look that begged for an explanation.

Her smile and nod were meant to be reassuring, but her response chilled him to the bone. "It's fine, JJ" she said. "We have a warrant."

Jamaica and the rest of the group entered the elevator and JJ watched as the doors closed in front of them.

JJ returned to his desk. He was born and raised in Jefferson Parish and had worked as the security guard in the lobby at 770 Baronne for ten years. He'd handled unpleasant situations at work from time to time, but seeing a federal raid was a first. "That looks like trouble," JJ mumbled. "Mr. Coltrane ain't going to like this."

As the elevator, filled with a group of stone-faced men and women with badges, made its way to the top floor, JJ shook his head. "No, Mr. Coltrane ain't going to like this at all."

\*\*\*

At the same time Jamaica was assisting the senator's agents in the raid on the Firm, the senator was conducting his press conference at the courthouse. As requested, in addition to the press, the Arena committee and officials from the building department were all in attendance, along with sub-contractors and representatives from local supply companies. Keetz stalled for over forty-five minutes, starting the conference a little before 3 p.m.—a deliberate ploy to give his agents ample time to execute the raid undisturbed.

Sam stood between Clyde and Bobby Bonner near the back of the gathering. As the senator's speech progressed, Sam watched the Arena committee members squirm. They grew increasingly nervous, fidgeting and whispering among themselves.

"Check out Coltrane," Bobby said, chuckling. "He looks like he just got hit with one of those damned voodoo chickens we keep pulling off the fence at the site. It's all starting to come down on him, the son of a bitch."

"This is just the beginning," Sam said. "And they're just beginning to realize it. I wonder how many heads are going to roll."

***

Keetz's announcement of the reopening of the Arena investigation threw Lewis into a frenzy. He raced to his car and sweat poured off his forehead as he sped toward the Coltrane law offices. "Goddamned Keetz," he muttered. He nearly crashed his Corvette into the wall before he slammed the car to a stop in his parking spot in the building's garage. He rushed into the lobby, but stopped dead in his tracks when he saw JJ waving him over to the security guard's station, a worried look on his face.

"Mr. Coltrane, sir," JJ began. "I tried to contact you when all those agents came in with Miss Russe."

"What?" Lewis gasped. "When?"

"Over an hour ago. I called your home to tell you, but nobody there knew where to reach you."

Lewis spun on his heels and headed for the elevator.

"They were in and out quick, Mr. Coltrane. Came back down carrying lots of boxes, too. Must've known what they were looking—."

JJ's words were cut off as the elevator door closed.

***

Senator Keetz yawned, leaned back in his seat, and stretched his arms over his head. "It's all here, just like Jamaica Russe said it would be."

Keetz closed the file folder in front of him and gestured for the other members of his legal team to do the same. "It's ten o'clock. Let's lock all this up, call it a night, and resume tomorrow morning." He congratulated his team. "We've already amassed enough evidence to move forward. I'll speak with the judge about securing a grand jury to review it, then begin issuing indictments. What we've got here, fellas, is a slam dunk."

The group was about to leave the conference room, when the senator's private extension rang.

"Senator, Morrison here. We've been tailing Coltrane since the press conference. You were right. He drove straight to his law office after it ended. He reappeared several minutes later and drove out to his Estate. He was there until about an hour ago. I kept a couple of agents on him, like you directed. We kept our distance and followed him when he left."

"Where is he now?"

"That's why I'm calling you. We're at the airport. He's about to board a private jet. What do you want us to do?"

"Hell, stop him from getting on that plane! Arrest him, then find out from the pilot what the destination was going to be. Take him to the precinct. I'll meet you there."

***

Federal agents arrived at the Jefferson Parish police department a little before midnight, escorting a handcuffed Lewis Coltrane into the precinct. Senator Keetz was waiting with arrest warrant signed by the judge in hand. He couldn't help smiling inwardly at all the raised eyebrows as the agents presented their VIP to police officers to be booked and placed in a holding cell.

Keetz couldn't help wanting to stick around, mostly out of sight, to observe the pandemonium created by the unfolding scene. It wasn't every day a well-known New Orleans lawyer landed on the wrong side of the booking process. The humor of it wasn't lost on the regular group of hookers and drunk-and-disorderly misfits sitting on benches in the station, waiting to be booked for their offenses. Coltrane was a well-known public figure. Witnessing his being dragged into the station like a common criminal brought cheers and whistles from the motley group.

"Pipe down!" one officer cried out in a fruitless attempt to quiet the amused group of petty criminals.

During the booking process, Coltrane surrendered his Rolex, gold money clip, and leather wallet in front of the group, resulting in more laughter and a few lewd comments about how Coltrane was going to be "spending his time."

He was about to be led into an adjacent room for fingerprinting when a buxom blonde woman adorned in an evening gown, heavy makeup, and handcuffs recognized him. "Hey, baby!" she called out. "Remember me from the Ambassador Club?"

Officers restrained the woman, but failed to silence her before she identified Coltrane as one of her regular clients, calling him a "cheap son of a bitch and a lousy lay."

The entire room exploded in laughter.

But Keetz wasn't even smiling. Coltrane was merely the latest in a long line of lawyers, lawmakers, and law-enforcement officers made to pay for transgressions against the law. And he wouldn't be the last.

# 39

# Justice

The Sunday morning *Tribune* featured Allen's press conference coverage at the top of page one, along with a photo of Senator Keetz addressing a crowded conference room.

Much to Allen's dismay, word of Coltrane's arrest had filtered in to the news desk late the night before, an hour too late to make the morning edition.

### ARENA INVESTIGATION RESUMES
### By Allen Stein

Louisiana State Senator George Keetz held a press conference yesterday at 2 p.m. in a conference room at the New Orleans County Courthouse, announcing the reopening of his investigation into the city's Arena project.

"The investigation's temporary hiatus, ordered by Judge Palmer, in response to the shooting of lawyer and Arena committee member Max DiAngelis has been lifted," Senator Keetz announced.

Keetz surprised Arena committee members in attendance by stating he would be recalling some prior witnesses for additional questioning. "A new source has come forward with relevant information that, once studied by my team and verified as true, will expose what we have believed from the start of this investigation to be serious mishandling of Arena project finances. Although I am not at liberty to reveal the source at this time, we intend to pursue an aggressive agenda moving forward and will do so with as much transparency as possible."

The senator opened the floor for questions from the press, but declined to elaborate further on the substance of the aforementioned new information.

Keetz's legal team spent Sunday plowing through documents, while Keetz and Judge Palmer sat outside in the backyard patio of the judge's home, discussing the events of the day before over a leisurely lunch.

"We can hold Coltrane indefinitely," Judge Palmer began. "That was a good move on your part, George, requesting we put a tail on him. He wasted no time proving he was a flight risk."

"Yeah, I figured he might try to fly the coop. If Coltrane had made it to Grand Cayman, it would have been hell extraditing him." Keetz looked out from the patio at the expansive view of the Gulf, spread out beyond the sandy beach framing the back of the judge's property.

"I'll fast track his initial appearance, and set bond. Your prosecutor will ask that Coltrane be detained, and I'll grant it. Once we get to his detention hearing, I'll acknowledge he's a flight risk. We'll keep him locked up, pending trial."

"Thanks, Charles. I'll sleep better knowing he's in custody."

The judge shook his head. "I've got to say one thing about Coltrane, though. The way he manipulated people to move all that money for so long was criminal genius. The guy's a real piece of work."

"Yeah, well," Keetz replied, fingering the mint leaf sticking up from the glass of his Mint Julep. "Not genius enough. By the time this gets to preliminary hearing, my team will have documented plenty of evidence to bind him over to a grand jury."He pointed to the stack of papers lying on the table between them. "Meanwhile, I'll have my men execute these subpoenas and search warrants first thing tomorrow."

The judge slapped his hand on the pile of paperwork. "You'll be plenty busy with all this. Once the grand jury has a chance to review all the evidence and issue indictments, I promise you, arrests will follow close behind."

Senator Keetz took a long swig of his Mint Julep. "All this is going to send out shock waves in the community. We'll have months of trials. And years of appeals and lawsuits."

Judge Palmer nodded in agreement. "This whole damned Arena project has been a drama from the start. I swear, if I were a superstitious man, I might take heed of those Cajun folks and their warnings—and shut the whole thing down."

***

Allen Stein was kept busy all that night and the next day following the explosion of new leads. By Monday morning, the wheels of justice were turning fast. The senator's federal agents, accompanied by local police, had entered the building department with a second search warrant. They seized all records pertaining to the Arena permits and served LaSalle and Ferguson with subpoenas. Mayor Riley and Commissioner Bryant were also located and served— Mayor Riley at his home and Commissioner

Bryant aboard his yacht at the New Orleans Yacht Club Marina.

A few hours later, Allen covered the story as Sheriff Wilcox, accompanied by Senator Keetz, held a short briefing in front of local reporters.

### Lewis Coltrane Accused in Arena Scandal
### By Allen Stein

"Lewis Coltrane, chairman of the Arena Committee overseeing the project's finances, was apprehended Saturday night by federal agents while attempting to board his private plane for a flight to Grand Cayman. He was delivered to the Jefferson Parish police precinct, where he is presently being detained, pending appearance before the court," Sheriff Wilcox stated Monday afternoon, at a press briefing called by Louisiana State Senator George Keetz.

Senator Keetz also addressed the press and provided further information, "As you all know from previous press conferences held over the past months, my investigation into Arena finances was launched to address complaints of potential criminal activity in the distribution of funds for the project."

Senator Keetz revealed that evidence discovered at the Law Firm of Lewis Coltrane and Associates on Saturday afternoon uncovered proof of ongoing misappropriation of funds by Arena committee chairman, Lewis Coltrane, and others.

"I can now reveal that information regarding the existence of these documents was initially brought to my attention by Jamaica Russe, a member of the

Coltrane Firm, and Sam McCormick, lead representative of Regal Signs," the Senator said. "On the strength of that information, Judge Palmer issued a warrant to search the offices of the Coltrane Firm. Upon the successful recovery of said documents, and careful review by Judge Palmer, additional search warrants and subpoenas have been issued and are being executed by Sheriff Wilcox, with the assistance of federal agents."

Senior members of the building department are also in question, accused of approving building permits requested by unlicensed subcontractors. Complaints by local union members of just such activity have been ongoing. The evidence will be further examined, and arrests may be forthcoming.

"I believe the extent of the bribes and kickbacks will exceed hundreds of thousands of dollars," the senator is further quoted as saying. "This is felony theft from the people of New Orleans and the great State of Louisiana."

Senator Keetz promised ongoing updates as further information becomes available. Any citizen who may have knowledge of suspicious activity involving any aspect of the Arena project is encouraged to come forward. Bobby Bonner, one of the remaining committee members, met with the senator earlier in the day, but was not available for comment.

# 40

## The Verdict and the Consequences

One week after the scandal broke, Senator Keetz issued an official statement, via the press, to the citizens of New Orleans. The *Tribune* printed the statement on the front page. And Allen finally got his headline.

**COMMITTEE MEMBERS INDICTED!**
**By Allen Stein**

Louisiana Senator George J. Keetz made a major announcement today that rocked the New Orleans community.

"The federal investigative team assembled to uncover allegations of corruption has found that members of the Arena committee, a politically appointed body, deliberately circumvented state public-bid laws and awarded contracts to favored firms and individuals, most of whom made financial contributions to committee members in the form of kickbacks. Sufficient and irrefutable evidence has surfaced confirming that public officials were bribed with payoffs and that numerous invoices for work on the project were padded with funds skimmed off the top of these amounts.

"The committee has therefore been abolished and replaced with a totally new, non-political professional management team to oversee the Arena project. This ensures that construction will continue during the indictments and prosecution of the parties charged.

"I would like to thank my investigative team for their ongoing efforts, as well as the brave men and women who stepped forward with information exposing this scandal."

Months of litigation followed and Allen had a field day reporting on the aftermath, the theme of which he summed up to himself, with satisfaction, as "how the mighty have fallen."

Mayor Riley, embarrassed and publicly humiliated over being duped by Coltrane and his cohorts, testified against his fellow committee members. He finished his term as mayor, but chose not to seek reelection.

City Commissioner Bryant was convicted of coercion in the distribution of contracts and permits, as well as violation of state ethics codes for public officials.

LaSalle and Ferguson were convicted of accepting bribes, filing false public records, and malfeasance in office. All three men were sentenced to terms in state prison.

Lou Navaro was charged as the sole member of Regal Sign Company with accepting kickbacks and creating false documents, along with interstate-business violations. Upon extradition to New Orleans, he was convicted on all counts and returned to Las Vegas to face additional charges of stealing from his own company. He was sentenced to twenty years at Nevada State Prison.

***

In order to move forward more efficiently in the investigation of Coltrane's criminal misdeeds, Jamaica joined Senator Keetz's investigative team. With her help, materials seized at the law office and documents discovered in Coltrane's study on the Estate provided overwhelming evidence of decades of criminal conduct.

Once she came on board, Jamaica took a leap of faith. During discovery, she showed the Spencer document, with its long list of payoffs, to Senator Keetz. She omitted the details of Spencer's disappearance, explaining, "An extensive search for this man has failed to yield results and it's possible he may never be found."

Jamaica couldn't help finding the whole situation deeply ironic. First, in paying for Jamaica's education, Lewis had empowered her to lead the legal charge that resulted in his own destruction. It was equally ironic that, despite his years of profiting from blatantly illegal activity, it was his callous involvement in the cover-up of Lily's death that motivated her most in her pursuit to expose him.

Still, what she discovered shook her to her core.

"Senator, this payoff had something to do with my sister." Jamaica pointed to the $5,000 written next to Lily's name. "From the beginning, the circumstances surrounding her death seemed suspect to me. I think we should summon Doc Beauregard. He examined her the night of her death and assured me it was an accident, but I think he was holding something back." She paused. "And I want to question him."

Keetz agreed and the doctor was called to testify. Once on the stand when questioned by Jamaica herself, Doc Beauregard, laden with guilt, broke down. "It was an accident, a terrible accident," he said, trembling as he spoke. "We didn't see the need to add to the tragedy with details that we believed were better left unsaid."

"Who is 'we'?" Jamaica asked.

"Well, Lewis Coltrane and myself, and, of course, the coroner."

"And what are the details you believed 'better left unsaid?'" Her tone was stern. She stared at the man with fire in her eyes.

Visibly shaken, he answered. "That the young girl, your sister, was pregnant."

A collective gasp filled the courtroom.

Jamaica stood directly in front of the witness stand, frozen. The room began to spin. She fought to regain her composure, finally managing to ask, "And you know this, because?"

"Well, first we took x-rays to determine if she had suffered any other injuries, in addition to the blow to her head. We found none. But we decided to draw blood to see if there were any foreign substances in her system at the time of her death. We discovered through her blood work that she was pregnant. Apparently, she was several months along."

"And the coroner will corroborate this?"

Doc Beauregard shook his head. Shame was written all over his face. "I just wanted to protect you, dear."

"Answer the question."

"Yes, yes," he replied in a whisper. "I'm so sorry."

The doctor's testimony, along with testimony by the coroner and Lewis Coltrane himself, eventually revealed most of the truth about Lily's death.

At first, Lewis denied knowing anything, but the prosecutors chipped away at his lies until he finally confessed. "I was simply trying to protect my son," he said, confirming that Jimmy was the father and that his son had accidentally killed her in the heat of an argument. Coltrane's tone was unapologetic. "Jimmy was a man, after all. And sometimes these things happen."

Jamaica was startled by a scream from the back of the courtroom. She turned to see Eleanor Coltrane attempting to calm a visibly distressed Catherine. Lewis's testimony had revealed the devastating truth that her husband had fathered a child with someone other than her. And the fact that he had done it by seducing a young girl who was barely more than a child herself was, obviously, too much for Catherine to bear. She placed the back of her hand on her forehead, swooned, and fainted in her seat.

"Oh, my dear lord!" Eleanor reached out to embrace her daughter-in-law. "This can't be!" She glared at Lewis from the back of the courtroom. "You knew! All along, you knew, and you did nothing!"

Then, Lewis smiled at her.

It was a smug smile.

Eleanor leapt from the pew and charged toward the witness stand. "Monster!" she screamed, only to be restrained by the bailiff, a few feet away from her husband. "I hope you rot in jail, you pathetic son of a bitch!"

"Order! Order!" The judge's gavel pounded furiously on the bench as bailiffs clamored to revive a distraught Catherine, while others struggled to remove a screaming, hysterical Eleanor from the courtroom.

In the midst of the chaos, Jamaica rose, approached the witness box, and stood a foot from Lewis Coltrane, glaring hard enough at him to singe the edges of his soul. At first, Lewis tried to maintain the smile as he stared back, but finally, the smile disappeared, he turned away, and he hung his head.

Only Jamaica noticed.

***

As he covered the legal proceedings, sitting day after day in the courtroom, Allen Stein wondered if he derived more satisfaction from his personal distaste for Lewis Coltrane or his professional role of publicizing his fall from grace.

Allen could see with his own two eyes the effect that Coltrane's smug smile, along with many callous statements Lewis delivered on the witness stand, soured the grand jury of any tendency toward mercy. His trial lasted months and amounted to dozens of front-page stories for Allen, ending with convictions on twelve counts, including fraud, money laundering, skimming, bribery, blackmail, conspiracy to commit and accessory to murder. Coltrane received two consecutive life sentences. After the appeals process was exhausted, his convictions held.

Stein also covered a hearing at which Layla Beauville identified Curtis "Red" Brown as the murderer of Max DiAngelis, and Lewis Coltrane as the man who ordered the hit. When she entered the courtroom, wearing a leather mini-skirt and four-inch heels, she turned heads, but she insisted on keeping her promise to Jamaica and Tony. She took the oath and revealed all she knew.

"I distinctly remember Spencer bragging about hiring a man from Biloxi, named 'Red,' to execute a hit on a lawyer named Max," she said. "Spencer said this 'Red' was the one to go to if, in his words, 'you wanted somebody wasted.' He told me it wasn't the first time he'd done jobs like that and occasionally, he showed me newspaper clippings about people that had been killed. He loved to brag that he was the one who made them all happen. Him and Red."

When she was asked if she might remember who the victims in the articles were and what the articles said, her answer brought a wave of laughter to the courtroom. "Sure, I'd remember. I may be a hooker, but that doesn't mean I can't read."

Layla's testimony, in addition to the Spencer document, provided enough circumstantial evidence to expand the search for Red's whereabouts to La Bijoux. When questioned by police and threatened with jail time for obstructing a murder investigation, the two bouncers, Dempsey and Virgil, not only ratted out Spencer, but they also gave officers the location of the Antique store in Biloxi where Red could be found.

With a little digging, Allen learned that only a few days after killing Max, Red was arrested on unrelated charges of moving stolen merchandise out of state. He was awaiting trial in Mississippi, when the additional charge of murder was filed against him.

***

Tony kept his promise to Layla. After a brief communication between Benny and his new Cajun syndicate friends, Jake received a visit from local syndicate members. He accepted Layla's departure from La Bijoux with little resistance.

Tony didn't stop there. Immediately following her testimony, he and Jamaica stood with Layla outside the courtroom. "Layla, how would you feel about moving to Las Vegas?" Tony began.

A look of apprehension appeared on her face. "But what would I do?" she asked. "I don't want to move to a new city and go back to the same old life."

"I could get you started with a job at my dad's hotel. You're beautiful and good with people. You'd fit right in. It would be a new start, if you want it."

Layla's eyes brightened. "I've always wanted to visit Las Vegas. And I'm afraid if I stay here, I'll always be looking over my shoulder, waiting for Jake to drag me back to La Bijoux."

"You no longer have anything to fear from him, Layla," Jamaica said. "But I do think you'd be happy in Las Vegas." She looked at Tony. "Hell, if I can be, anyone can."

Tears filled Layla's eyes. She threw her arms around Jamaica and Tony. "I can't thank you enough. Both of you."

"On the contrary," Jamaica replied. "Both of us owe you more."

\*\*\*

Sam remained temporarily in New Orleans, tying up loose ends and calming the waters for Regal in the wake of Lou's indictments. By now, he knew better than to open his mouth when the Arena subcontractors controlled by the New Orleans syndicate somehow escaped scrutiny. Without solid incriminating evidence against any of the mob's interests, business as usual continued.

But Sam was surprised and gratified when the newly appointed Arena management team, eager to ease tensions and quell any additional controversy, reacted to a petition launched by members of the Cajun community, regarding the desecrated site of the old Girod Cemetery. The area was unanimously approved for rezoning, removing it as a section of the massive Arena parking area. The land was gifted to the church, and restored as a memorial site, with funds allocated from the Arena budget. The move drew praise from the community, and halted further voodoo incantations around blazing fires, or the appearance of more sacrificial chickens on the Arena site fence.

Tony, too, had remained behind to support Jamaica during the trials and to run Benny's junket program. With plenty of free time, he began teasing Sam about his nonexistent love life. He and Jamaica made it their mission to find Sam a date.

Tony started in on Sam one night as the three friends ate dinner at the Bourbon Blues. "You need a girlfriend, pal. Jamaica and I both love you, man, but this third-wheel stuff has to end." He looked at Jamaica and smiled. "We have just the girl for you."

Tony's relentless banter, along with a gentle nudge from Jamaica, wore Sam down and sparked a mild flirtation with Layla.

Once the Arena pylon, internal scoreboards, and gondola were all completed, inspected, and approved, Sam returned to Las Vegas where, much to Benny's delight, he focused his full attention on Regal's commitments for the Scheherazade.

Sam continued to date Layla, who'd relocated permanently to Las Vegas, where she began the job Tony arranged for her, as a Sultan's Palace harem girl. She worked a night schedule and Sam could see that she was embracing the joy of her newfound freedom in a town that welcomed her with open arms, often well into the wee hours of the morning. Meanwhile, Sam's early hours and heavy work schedule kept him onsite at the Scheherazade and he and Layla began seeing less and less of each other. The romance fizzled.

During a trip back home to see his dad, Tony met Sam for drinks in the Casbah lounge. "What happened with Layla?" Tony asked, looking dejected. "I thought you two were an item."

"It's fine, Tony, really. Layla's having the time of her life and the girl deserves to spread her wings. Besides, I have plans. I'm looking forward to the opening of that French revue your dad's importing from Paris for the showroom of his new hotel."

"Why? Dad says it's costing him a fortune."

"That may be, but the showroom is incredible and, from the looks of all the fancy costumes arriving in crates from Paris, it's bound to be spectacular."

"What's that got to do with your love life?"

"Well," Sam replied, "from what I've heard, the showgirls he's flying in from gay Paris are gorgeous. And I'm going to be the lucky man putting their names in lights."

Tony perked up. "Ahh! I see. So you and a French showgirl? Ooh la, la!"

"Why not?" Sam replied, with a sly smile. "Stranger things have happened." He looked at his friend with affection. "After all, if true love can happen for you with a girl like Jamaica, it can certainly happen for me! You never know. I just might find the girl of my dreams!"

# Epilogue

News teams and camera crews from across the nation converged on the city of New Orleans en masse to herald the grand opening of the newly completed, state-of-the-art Arena. Video cameras scanned the crowd, filming the thousands of spectators who had gathered from cities around the world to witness the beginning of a new era in sporting events.

As the sun set, the exterior lighting on its domed ceiling glowed brilliantly against the evening sky. The words, "Arena Opens!" scintillated from the huge screens of the Arena's pylon sign and were visible from buildings and highways as far as a mile away.

Benny lit his long Cuban cigar. His eyes roamed across the television screen on the wall of his new penthouse suite on the top floor of the Scheherazade. When the Channel 8 television cameras changed location and panned across the VIP booths inside the massive structure, Benny leaned forward to get a better look. Tony, Sam, and Jamaica were somewhere in the crowd.

He listened with amusement as boisterous television announcers reported glimpses of famous celebrities, sports figures and other prominent guests arriving on the scene to witness the grand opening of the Arena.

Benny shook his head. Hundreds of movie stars and famous athletes had come and gone at the Sultan's Palace over the years. Only recently, they'd flocked to his newly opened Scheherazade. As always, they created a high-maintenance pain in the ass for the property's executive staff. Benny relaxed in the comfort of his leather chair and chomped down on his cigar. He had watched as Sam, Tony and Jamaica faced a stacked deck. Together, they'd succeeded in beating the odds and for each of them, wishes had come true. He looked out his window and chuckled. The smoke from his cigar rose in the air and swirled in front of him, partially masking the view of his newly erected Scheherazade marquee. "Just like the smoke coming out of a genie's bottle," he mused. He turned up the volume and settled in to watch the game.

A deafening roar filled the stadium as the teams entered the field.

Jamaica sat back in Benny's VIP booth, absently sipping on a Mint Julep, while Tony and Sam looked down on the playing field and cheered with the crowd as the game started.

Almost immediately, Sam yelled, "Touchdown!"

A thunderous roar filled the stadium. Thousands of people rose in succession from their chairs, stomping their feet. Their arms flew up in the air as they executed a human wave that rounded the entire Arena. The movement created a rumbling sound that vibrated throughout the stands and echoed off the Arena walls.

Jamaica found strange solace in the sound and the vibration rumbling around her. Not long ago, it would've triggered an altogether different emotion.

She couldn't recall exactly when the headaches and visions stopped. Her "house of dark spirits" and the torment she'd suffered from the visions lurking there disappeared as mysteriously as they'd begun. The storm inside her had simply passed. Clarice told her the power to cast out the demons had always been within her, but she believed it was Tony's love that exorcized them. She looked down at the engagement ring on her finger, then up at Tony and Sam. They'd *all* weathered a storm together, but now the sun was shining and the future held promise.

And not just for her, Tony, and Sam. Also for her adopted city. After enduring five long years of anticipation, New Orleans residents witnessed the first game on the playing field of their Arena. Once the endless roadblocks that threatened the project were overcome, the city reaped the rewards of the millions of dollars spent to achieve its goal.

*** 

In subsequent years, on the playing field that was Las Vegas, eager young entrepreneurs bombarded Benny DeLuca with questions about how to achieve success in the gaming business. They asked repeatedly if all the stories they'd heard about the mob in Las Vegas were true.

Benny would sit back in his big chair and look out the window at his dazzling Scheherazade marquee. "We're the gladiators of our time, my young friends," he would say, "and these streets are the Arena. Your success in life will be defined by what you build here and how. So be bold."

And then, just for fun and with a twinkle in his eye, he would lean forward and place his hands on his knees, looking like a character from a gangster movie.

"Would you really like to know how to get what you want from the people in this town?" he would whisper, pausing to enjoy the wide-eyed faces hanging on his every word. "You make them an offer they can't refuse."

### THE END

# ACKNOWLEDGEMENTS

Sincere thanks to Deke Castleman, whose keen eye and great sense of humor has once again made the editing process a truly enjoyable learning experience. With each new book you help me become a better writer.

To Kim Richards, thank you for providing invaluable assistance in plot structure and line editing during the initial stages of the book's development.

Thanks to my dear friends Lani McCusker and Suzanne Johnson, for their contributions to the cover design.

And most of all, kudos to my husband, Kent, whose real-life experience erecting the original New Orleans Superdome sign inspired the character Sam McCormick and provided valuable insight into the inner workings of the sign industry.

Thanks, Kent, for encouraging me to write this novel.